DAVID DICKINSON was born in Dublin. He graduated from Cambridge with a first-class honours degree in classics and joined the BBC. After a spell in radio he transferred to television and went on to become editor of *Newsnight* and *Panorama*. In 1995 he was series editor of *Monarchy*, a three-part examination of its current state and future prospects. David lives in London.

Praise for The Lord Francis Powerscourt series

'A cracking yarn, beguilingly real from start to finish . . . you have to pinch yourself to remind you that it is fiction – or is it?'
Peter Snow

'A kind of locked bedroom mystery . . . Dickinson's view of the royals is edgy and shaped by our times.'
The Poisoned Pen

'Fine prose, high society and complex plot recommend this series.'
Library Journal

DEATH OF AN OLD MASTER

DAVID DICKINSON

ROBINSON
London

Constable & Robinson Ltd
3 The Lanchesters
162 Fulham Palace Road
London W6 9ER
www.constablerobinson.com

First published in the UK by Constable, an imprint
of Constable & Robinson Ltd 2005,
this paperback edition published by Robinson, an imprint
of Constable & Robinson Ltd, 2007

A copy of the British Library Cataloguing in
Publication Data is available from the British Library.

UK ISBN: 978-1-84119-604-6 (hbk)
UK ISBN: 978-1-84529-580-6

Printed and bound in the EU

1 3 5 7 9 10 8 6 4 2

For My Parents, Tom and Elizabeth

Prologue

Winter 1896

The old man walked slowly across the fields. A fine rain was falling on his bare head. He let himself into the little church and walked to the position he knew so well after forty-five years as the bell ringer of St Peter's Church. He slipped through the faded red curtain and unhooked the rope from its place on the wall. High above him in the tower the bell still carried the inscription from its maker. 'Thomas Wilson made mee, 1714.' The old man began to pull, his arms rising regularly above his shoulders like the swell on the sea.

The bell tolled for a funeral, the funeral of one who would have been the lord of the manor had he still lived there before his God called him home. Charles Edward Windham Fitzmaurice de Courcy was in the church already, his coffin resting beneath the inscriptions to earlier de Courcys on the walls. It was a quarter past ten in the morning, the service scheduled for eleven o'clock.

Two hundred and fifty yards away through the morning mist that swirled across the fields the great Jacobean mansion of de Courcy Hall continued to resist the elements as it had for the past two hundred and seventy years. Inside in the Great Hall a melancholy party was preparing to set off for the church. Alice de Courcy, wife of the dead man, wondered about her future. Edmund de Courcy, the eldest son, wondered about the size of his inheritance. Julia and Sarah, his younger sisters, wondered if they would be able to go and live in London all the year round. None of them had seen the dead man, husband and father, for the past fourteen years.

'Do you think it's time to go, Edmund?' Mother touched her son softly on the arm. 'We don't want to be late.' It was half-past ten.

'Not yet, Mother, there's still time.'

In 1882 Charles de Courcy had abandoned his fields and his family to live with another woman in the south of France. There, so the family believed, he had fathered another two children. There, the family were convinced, he had squandered most of the family inheritance on his mistress. And she, the mistress, had announced her intention of attending the last rites this melancholy morning, though whether she would bring the children no one knew.

'Did Smithson say that woman would come to the house first or go direct to the church?' Alice de Courcy asked for the hundredth time. Alice shook every time she thought about this meeting if meeting there had to be. Smithson was the family lawyer, based in Fakenham, who had been the unhappy conduit of many messages between the two households over the preceding decade and a half. The family knew there had been great arguments about a will, with lawyers coming up from Norwich and even London to thrash out the rights of an estate owner to dispose of his property as he wished in the dusty offices of a Norfolk town. Every conversation in de Courcy Hall since they heard of the death had revolved round this single point. Would the Frenchwoman come to the Hall or would she go direct to the church?

'You know Smithson didn't say, Mama.' Edmund was

2

as gentle as he knew how. 'But I don't think there is time for her and her party to come here and then go to the church. I think we'd better set off.' It was twenty to eleven.

And so the de Courcy family set off across their fields for the last rites of a man they would never see again. In their different ways they prepared to meet another family they had never seen before, half-brothers, half-sisters perhaps. The girls thought it was rather dramatic and exciting, their cheeks turning red as the wind lashed through the trees. Alice was not sure she could bear it. Edmund, aware of his new responsibilities at the age of twenty-five, was uncharacteristically worried about his mother.

To the north, past the sodden cows that huddled for shelter beneath the twisted trees, the North Sea marked the outer limits of the estate. Generations of de Courcys had planted trees in ever-growing numbers as a protection against the storms that whistled in from the angry coastline. To the south the estate stretched for many miles in the direction of Norwich.

Sometimes the bell was very loud, as if it was right in front of them, sometimes it drifted off to the west with the wind.

A bedraggled vicar greeted them at the door. There were tiny holes in his cassock. His boots were leaking. Payments from the de Courcy family had become increasingly irregular over the years.

'Good morning, Mrs de Courcy, Edmund, Julia, Sarah.' The vicar smiled a feeble smile, his eyes flickering down the long drive that led to de Courcy Hall. It was ten minutes to eleven.

Edmund led his family to their pew at the front of the church, his mother huddling up against the wall as if she didn't want to be seen. The bell was still tolling. The organ was playing a Bach fugue very softly. The women

3

fell to their knees to pray. Servants and neighbours were filling up the pews behind them.

On the floor to Edmund's left, two of his ancestors stared up at the ceiling and the next life from their brass memorial on the floor. 'Richard de Courcy lies here, God have mercy on his soul. Lady Elizabeth who was the wife of Richard de Courcy lies here, to whose soul may God be merciful. This in the year of our Lord 1380.' Grave and inscrutable, serious and humble, the ancient faces slept on. It was five to eleven.

In the pew opposite, Mr Smithson, the lawyer from Fakenham, was kneeling in prayer. Beside him a rather smartly dressed young man was staring at the memorial tablets on the walls. As the bell stopped a slow drip began to fall loudly on to the floor just behind the pulpit. It seemed to have caught the rhythm of the bell, the plops on the stone floor sounding at the same interval as the creation of the bellwright Thomas Wilson far above in its tower. Edmund noticed a small trail of green slime making a determined advance on the wall beside the altar.

Edmund stole a quick glance behind him. All the pews were full now, except for the one opposite his own. The organ began to build towards a crescendo. The vicar was busying himself by the altar, water dripping from his boots and forming little puddles on the floor.

At two minutes to eleven Edmund sensed there were new arrivals. You didn't have to look round. There was a low murmur of excitement from the pews behind. There was a firm click as the door was closed by the newcomers. Julia and Sarah began to turn their heads to look until Edmund nudged them both firmly in the ribs. Alice de Courcy huddled ever closer to the wall and sank to her knees again to pray for deliverance.

A handsome woman of about forty years of age, escorted by a boy of ten and a girl of seven or eight, sat down in the pew opposite. Edmund realized with a shock that the little boy looked remarkably like he had done at the same age. All three stared directly in front of them.

The vicar coughed firmly. Resolutely looking at the back of the church he began the service.

'I am the Resurrection and the life.' The vicar's voice was thick as if he had a heavy cold. 'He that believeth in me, though he were dead, yet shall he live: and whosoever liveth and believeth in me shall never die.'

The Frenchwoman in her pew was having difficulty finding her place in the unfamiliar prayer book of the Anglican Church. The smartly dressed young man sitting beside lawyer Smithson leant forward and gave her his own, opened at the correct page. She smiled slightly in acknowledgement.

Edmund's memories of his father were remote. Sometimes he had to admit that he found it hard to remember what his father looked like and he had to go and stare at the portrait in the Long Gallery of de Courcy Hall where an unbroken line of nine of his male ancestors adorned the walls. He dimly recalled his father teaching him to play cricket in the walled garden at the side of the house. He thought his father had been away a lot, in London or Norwich, always apparently on business. He recalled all too well the shouting matches that often accompanied his return, his mother left weeping softly in a corner of the drawing room. This new half-brother and half-sister must have very different, fresher memories but he had no idea what they were. He wondered if the little boy had been taught to play cricket in some hot French garden, with French servants bringing glasses of lemonade to drink under the trees.

'We brought nothing into this world,' the vicar sounded hoarser now, 'and it is certain we can carry

5

nothing out. The Lord gave and the Lord hath taken away; blessed be the name of the Lord.'

Edmund thought bitterly that his father, contrary to the words of the book of Job, had brought a great deal into this world. But had he left anything behind? Edward gazed sadly at the drip continuing its monotonous journey from ceiling to floor. He thought of the estate steward shaking his head as he pored over the account books. What would be left? How much would be left? How would it be divided?

Roger Bilton, the de Courcys' closest neighbour, had risen to read the second lesson. He was a tall, stooping man, reputed never to have travelled any further from his home than the city of Norwich. He spoke the words in a high querulous tone, as if he didn't believe them.

'Now is Christ risen from the dead, and become the first fruits of them that slept. For since by man came death, by man came also the resurrection of the dead. For as in Adam all die, even so in Christ shall all be made alive.'

Another memorial on the floor echoed the words of St Paul's Epistle to the Corinthians. Thomas de Courcy was portrayed on his brass in full armour, holding a very long sword, as if about to go into battle. Edmund remembered the full description of the armour with its archaic vocabulary of gorgets and vambraces, tassets and epaulieres, jambarts and rerebraces, genouillaires and sabbatons.

Livest Thou Thomas? Yeas. Where? With God on
     Highe.
Art thou not dead? Yeas. And here I lye.
I that with men on earth did live to die
Died to live with Christ eternallie.

The vicar was praying now, the prayers interrupted by

his hacking cough, praying that the dead man's sins might be forgiven so he could be received into God's gracious mercy and protection.

Three of his father's transgressions were sitting but three feet away from him, Edmund thought to himself, casting a quick glance at the alternative family in its pew. The mother was impassive, the boy and girl taking their cue from their mother and staring resolutely straight ahead. Julia and Sarah had managed to stand right at the front of their box pew so they could look sideways without being noticed. Alice, their mother, was still huddled against the wall.

The prayers were punctuated by the regular drip on to the floor, sounding another note of desolation and decay, as if not only the body of the dead man but the very fabric of the buildings on his estate was beginning to rot away.

There was no sermon from the vicar. He found it impossible to know what to say in such circumstances.

At last, at twenty minutes past eleven, it was all over.

'The grace of our Lord Jesus Christ, and the love of God, and the fellowship of the Holy Ghost, be with us all evermore. Amen.'

Scarcely had the word 'Amen' died away when the smartly dressed young man sitting beside lawyer Smithson unlatched his door, opened the door of the pew in front of him and escorted the French party out of the church as fast as decency allowed. Just once Edmund met the eyes of his father's mistress. Julia and Sarah had one quick glimpse of the half-brother and sister they had never seen before. Almost before the congregation realized what was happening the French party had fled the field.

The bell began to toll again. Smithson had a brief word with Edmund and his mother as they stood at the gate of the church, staring out at what had been their fields, but might be their fields no longer.

'They're not going to come to the house,' he said, trying to reassure the widow, 'they're going back to their hotel.'

Smithson paused. He suspected that the ordeal of having to listen to the dead man's will being read out, surrounded by his mistress and the bastard offspring, might prove too much for Alice de Courcy.

'The young man who took them away is called McKenna, Richard McKenna. He works for Finch's Bank. McKenna's going to tell them the details of the will there before they go back to France.'

How long did it take, Edmund wondered, to travel from the south of France to a remote house in Norfolk for a service that had lasted less than half an hour? Perhaps it was the will, an unknown financial future, not family piety that had brought them on their long journey into the rain and the wind that surrounded St Peter's Church. Just visible on the long drive that led to the main road, the French carriage was making good speed as if they wanted to escape as fast as they could.

'I thought,' Smithson went on apologetically, 'that a rest would be a good idea before the reading of the last will and testament. Mr McKenna and I propose to call on you at three o'clock this afternoon. Would the library be suitable, do you think?'

'Of course,' said Edmund and steered his mother back across the fields to de Courcy Hall. The congregation drifted off. The vicar wondered yet again if he could afford another pair of boots. The great bell rang out across the countryside and almost reached the sea. This afternoon, it would be decided. This afternoon, they would know their fate and their future.

'"I, Charles Edward Windham Fitzmaurice de Courcy, formerly of de Courcy Hall in the county of Norfolk, currently resident at the Chateau de Fontcaude, Grasse, Alpes Maritimes, France, do hereby cancel, revoke and annul all previous wills and testaments."'

Mr Smithson, the lawyer from Fakenham, had put on his glasses. The library was on the first floor of de Courcy Hall, great oak bookcases rising almost to the ceiling. Many of the books had been purchased in Rome or Geneva, Naples or Venice, by earlier de Courcys on the Grand Tour, shorter visits to Europe than the dead man who had stayed there fifteen years. There was a large mahogany table in the middle of the room. Mr Smithson and his banker companion sat at the head, with the family below them. Outside the rain was still falling. The wind was battering against the windows. Even with a fire the room was cold.

Julia started at the mention of the word 'Chateau'. She had visions of some enormous palace filled with tapestries and exciting histories of romance and elopement. Edmund was wondering how much a chateau would cost to run, even a little one.

There was a lot more legal preamble. Smithson read this as fast as he could. Then he paused. Richard McKenna was looking at what appeared to be a first edition of Dr Johnson's dictionary, the dust sitting thickly on the top as if nobody had checked the meaning of a word for over a hundred and forty years.

'"I come now to my testimonary dispositions."' Smithson glanced at the dead man's family, Alice looking pale, the girls interested, Edmund apprehensive. '"De Courcy Hall, its contents, furniture, pictures, ornaments and everything else pertaining unto it, I leave to my son Edmund George Windham de Courcy."'

The girls looked relieved. They had never lived anywhere else. They would be safe. Smithson coughed. He looked slightly embarrassed as he read on.

' "My estates, farms, woods, horses, cattle and sheep and all other farm animals" ' – there followed a precise geographical description of all these properties – ' "I leave absolutely to Madame Yvette de Castelnau of Grasse for her sole use and that of her children, François and Marie-Claire." '

Charles de Courcy had done the unthinkable. He had failed to keep one of the oldest rules of the English gentry in disposing of their property. He had broken it up. In his wish to accommodate his two families he had separated the house from the lands which supported it. None of the women seemed to understand what had happened. Perhaps they had been hypnotized by the legal prose, the dead language of lawyers come to impose its will on the living.

Edmund did. He did not know just how terrible the news was, but he knew it meant catastrophe for himself, his mother and his sisters.

' "Signed in the presence of witnesses, Albert Clement, notaire of Grasse and Jean Jacques Rives, banker of Nice, on the twentieth day of October 1895." '

Smithson wiped his brow. He coughed apologetically. The women looked dumb. Edmund was staring at the leather volumes opposite him, wondering how much they were worth.

'I am afraid there is more that you must know,' Smithson said, glancing briefly at his companion. 'Mr McKenna here comes from Finch's Bank which handles the family financial affairs. I fear you should hear from him.'

Great God, thought Alice de Courcy, is there worse to come on this terrible day? That woman and her children coming to the funeral was bad. Breaking up the house and the estate, she suspected, was worse.

Richard McKenna drew some papers from his bag and placed them on the table. He spoke very gently. 'The

10

financial position is not good,' he began. 'Let me deal with the house first. There are two mortgages outstanding on the property in which we sit this afternoon. They are for a total of forty thousand pounds, secured on de Courcy Hall itself. The current interest on those mortgages comes to approximately fifteen hundred pounds a year.' The figures dropped into the room like the drops of rain from the leak in the church at the service that morning, cold, regular, unstoppable.

'The estates are also mortgaged,' McKenna went on. Edmund thought he sounded like a doctor telling his patient that they had an incurable disease. Perhaps they had. Financial cancer had spread to Norfolk, a plague of debt and impossible obligations.

'They are mortgaged to the value of sixty thousand pounds. The interest on those loans from Finch's Bank comes to the total of two thousand, two hundred and fifty pounds a year.'

McKenna paused. Now came the hammer blow. 'The rent rolls from the estates have been falling lately. The properties are not perhaps in such good repair as they once were.' His eyes glanced up at the cracks in the ceiling, the broken window panes, the worn patches in the carpet. 'At present the income amounts to just four thousand pounds a year, barely enough to cover the interest payments.'

He looked around at the remaining members of the de Courcy family. Alice had turned even paler and was staring at the floor. Julia and Sarah were gazing in horror at this messenger of despair. Edmund had his head in his hands. 'I fully appreciate,' McKenna purred on, as if he was performing this melancholy rite for the ninth or the tenth time – which he was – 'that this must have come as rather a shock. A terrible shock. At the bank we have considerable experience of dealing with these problems.

We shall continue to extend our credit for the foreseeable future, but a rescue plan must be devised which can extricate you all from this temporary financial impasse.'

Edmund escorted his mother and sisters to the door. He took McKenna to walk up and down the Long Gallery on the other side of the house from the library. Their footsteps echoed up and down the hundred and forty feet of the great room. Long thin windows looked out over a bedraggled garden, weeds and brambles laying siege to the lawns, the unpruned roses running wild across the flower beds.

'I fear I can be more frank with you here than with your mother and your sisters,' said McKenna. 'Nothing need happen for three months. After that I would suggest you send your mother and your sisters abroad. Life is cheaper there. You would be surprised how many of our fellow countrymen live happy and inexpensive lives in southern France.'

'I do not think,' said Edmund, looking sadly at his companion, 'that my mother will be happy going to the south of France.'

'Forgive me,' said the banker. 'It need not be there. There are many other places round the Mediterranean where they could be happy.'

'But how can they be brought back? How will I find the money?'

'We can improve the management of the estates,' said McKenna. Experience had taught him that hope was the most important commodity in these circumstances. 'We can bring in a new steward, that old one seems to have been incompetent. The rent rolls could be doubled in three or four years.'

'I can't leave them abroad for that long. It will break my mother's heart.' Edmund stopped at one of the windows. The last of the afternoon light was going now, a couple of stray dogs patrolling the lawns that led towards the lake. 'I must make some money. But I have no training. What can I do, Mr McKenna? Please help me.'

McKenna looked at the long line of de Courcys on one section of the walls, painted by Lawrence and Reynolds, Hoppner and Gainsborough. He looked further away where some early Italian paintings were becoming invisible in the gathering gloom.

'Paintings,' he said suddenly. 'I hadn't thought of it before. You could sell some of these paintings. Or you could use them as a way into the art world. We have a valued client in London who might be willing to train you up, and to draw on your knowledge of the works of art in the great houses of England.'

Edmund felt the first faint stirrings of hope. 'But is there any money to be made in dealing in paintings and things?' he asked. 'Surely nobody is going to pay hundreds of pounds for some old works of art?'

Richard McKenna laughed. 'The art market is changing, it's changing every day, every month, every year, young man. Rich Americans, rich beyond imagination, richer than the world has ever seen before, are just beginning to buy European paintings. If the trends continue, just three or four paintings, maybe even some of the ones you have on the walls here, would fetch enough to clear all the debts and all the mortgages of de Courcy Hall.'

Part One

Raphael

1

Autumn 1899

William Alaric Piper walked happily through his art gallery in London's Old Bond Street. Every morning he went on a tour of inspection of the pictures, checking they were all straight, that no dust remained on the floor from the previous day's visitors. Piper was a small, rather tubby man in his early thirties. He was immaculately turned out, as ever, with a fresh flower in his buttonhole and perfectly polished boots. The de Courcy and Piper Gallery, for such was to be the name of the new venture, was the boldest move yet on to the London art market of the firm of de Courcy and Piper, art dealers.

In the main gallery, lit in the most dramatic way that London designers could provide, were Titians and Tintorettos, on the opposite wall Bellinis and Giorgiones. In the smaller room next door the lesser gods of the Venetian pantheon were on display, the Bassanos and Carpaccios, the Bordones and the Vivarinis. Venetian Paintings had been acclaimed as the most dramatic exhibition that year in London. The paintings had come on loan from Paris and the great houses of England to dazzle and bewitch the citizens of London with their colour and their enigmatic beauty. Today, Piper reminded himself, the exhibition had been open for exactly one month.

As he reached his office William Alaric Piper took out a large cigar and opened his correspondence. His office was filled with files, for William Alaric Piper believed that knowledge was the key to success. Quite simply he was determined to discover the location of all the valuable paintings in Britain. Then he would move on to France and Italy. Neatly arranged in alphabetical order were the counties of the kingdom, some thicker than others, detailing the collections of Petworth and Knebworth and Chatsworth, Knole and Kingston Lacy and Kedleston Hall. Sometimes individual entries were marked with a strange system of asterisks. These told the initiated how severe were the financial problems of the owners of the paintings. One asterisk meant major trouble, might be persuaded to sell. Two asterisks meant technically insolvent, desperate to raise money. And three asterisks meant that financial Armageddon was imminent and might only be averted by the judicious sale of some of the family heirlooms. This intelligence system was run by Piper's partner Edmund de Courcy. Since his father's death de Courcy had been employed first as an apprentice and then as a junior partner in the business – his speciality to maintain an accurate index of the fluctuating fortunes of the English rich so the firm of de Courcy and Piper could make an offer at precisely the right time.

There was one incongruous item in this haven of knowledge. On the wall directly opposite Piper's desk was an enormous map of the United States of America with the railroad routes marked in a variety of different colours. Crawling across the continent went the Baltimore and Ohio, the Central Pacific Railroad, the Union Pacific, the Atcheson Topeka and Santa Fe. Casual visitors might have thought that Piper was a great devotee of railway travel, intent one day perhaps on traversing the length and breadth of the American continent. They would have been wrong. Piper disliked trains intensely. His favourite means of transport was the transatlantic liner, sailing in unimaginable luxury across the Atlantic.

For Piper the map symbolized American money, the vast American wealth that had been created by the railroads. Vanderbilt and Morgan, Stanford and Huntington had a daily income from the railroads greater than Piper had earned in his entire life. Piper's ambition was to conquer the American art market. The new millionaires with their vast town houses in New York, their improbable chateaux in Newport, their yachts, their vulgar furnishings, were beginning to buy European pictures, usually of inferior quality. They had, after all, as Piper gleefully reminded himself from time to time, a great deal of wall space to fill. Once they had been tutored in the glories of the Old Masters Piper dreamt of Old Master prices, Old Master profits for himself, and a spurious second-hand immortality for their new owners. Already he had plans to infiltrate the beating heart of American money, New York's Fifth Avenue.

As he opened his letters a smile, a rather wolfish smile, crossed his face. A note from his agent in New York told him that a certain William P. McCracken, master of all the railroads that radiated north, south and west of Boston, was coming to London shortly. He had made reservations at the Piccadilly Hotel. Piper too would visit the Piccadilly Hotel. Perhaps he would take the adjacent suite to this William P. McCracken. A meeting would be engineered with the sole purpose of introducing the millionaire to the joys of European painting. Perhaps he would be able to escort him round the National Gallery. Then he would receive a special invitation to the exhibition. Then, if Piper judged the time was right – he had observed that too many of his rivals rushed their fences and lost valuable business by excessive haste in selling – he would tempt the railroad king until he had to buy. Above all, he reminded himself, he had to make a friend of McCracken. He would become a friend for life. After all, McCracken's money was going to last for life. And McCracken, unlike many of his fellow plutocrats, was still fairly young. What a collection William Alaric Piper could build for him! How much wealth could be quietly removed from the McCracken accounts in the banks of Wall Street into the coffers of William Alaric Piper!

A couple of miles to the west a military inspection was under way in Chelsea.

'Stand at ease!' said the tall Sergeant Major figure with the brown curly hair and the blue eyes.

'Attention!' The troops banged their feet on the floor, eyes staring rigidly ahead, fists pressed tightly to their sides.

'Shoulder arms!' shouted the Sergeant Major. A couple of shortened broom handles made their way slowly up into the correct position.

'By the left, quick march!' The little platoon moved off smartly towards the window.

'Squad, halt!' said the Sergeant Major, nearly tripping over a chair.

'About turn!' The figures shuffled awkwardly round to face the way they had come.

'By the left, quick march! Left, left, left, left right left.' The parade was rapidly approaching the double doors of the drawing room. The Sergeant Major, whose mind had temporarily wandered off somewhere else, recalled himself to his duty.

'Squad, halt!' He was only just in time. One more pace and the heads of the platoon would have crashed into the hard wood of the doors.

'Squad, stand at ease!' One of the figures refused to move.

'You there, at the back, you miserable rapscallion, you! What did I just say? I said stand at ease! If you can't obey orders in this battalion it'll be bread and water for thirty days! Stand at ease!'

A foot banged into the floorboards. Two arms went behind the back. A face looked rather sad at the prospect of bread and water for thirty days.

'Squad, dismiss!'

Two small figures turned round and leapt into their father's arms. Lord Francis Powerscourt held his two children, the six-year-old Thomas and the five-year-old Olivia, very tightly and laughed.

'You were nearly in trouble there,' he said, ruffling Olivia's hair. 'Bread and water for thirty days. Don't think you would have liked that, would you?'

'Would you really have done that, Papa?' asked the little girl, staring up into Powerscourt's eyes.

'You never know,' said her father. 'You never know what the Sergeant Major might have to do.'

Lord Francis Powerscourt had served in the army in India as an intelligence officer of the Crown. Since then he had become one of the foremost investigators in Britain, called in to solve murders and mysteries in England and abroad. A month before he had taken the children to visit his former Sergeant Major, recently installed in scarlet luxury as a Chelsea Pensioner. Sergeant Major Collins had always seemed a most formidable figure on the parade ground to Powerscourt but he had been wonderful with Thomas and Olivia. He had shown them the great hall where the Duke of Wellington's body had lain in state before his funeral in 1852, the pensioners guarding the great warrior twenty-four hours a day. He had shown them his tiny room with the bed that folded into the wall. The children had been enchanted and immediately wanted to know why they didn't have a similar arrangement at home. He had sat them down on the lawns that stretched down to the Thames and told them stories of strange Indian tribesmen with great beards, of campfires in the high mountains, of the terrible cold in the Crimea where he had lost a toe.

'God bless them, sir,' Sergeant Major Collins had said to Powerscourt as they left. 'It makes you feel young just to be around them, so it does. I don't have any grandchildren of my own, you see, so it brightens an old man's week.'

'Think of them as honorary grandchildren of your own, Sergeant Major,' Powerscourt had said. 'Make no mistake, we shall come again.'

'I suppose you'll want to look at the pictures,' James Hammond-Burke said rather sadly to Edmund de Courcy that same afternoon. The Hammond-Burkes lived in a crumbling Elizabethan house called Truscott Park in Warwickshire, blessed with red deer and a river running through the grounds. The interior was not blessed. Decades of lack of money had left it in a sad condition.

Edmund had gained entrance by his usual ploy. He had a standard letter which stated that he was compiling a four-volume compendium on the artistic treasures held in Great Britain, to appear volume by volume over a period of ten years. A number of firms were described as being involved in the venture, foremost among them de Courcy and Piper of Old Bond Street, London. De Courcy explained to the houses he visited that the great advantage of his firm being involved was that any owners who wished to extend their collections could apply to de Courcy and Piper who would know where more Carpaccios or Caravaggios could be found and, possibly, purchased to extend existing collections. In the unlikely event of anybody wanting to sell – and how unlikely that must be, de Courcy would always exclaim with a charming smile at this point – then reluctantly, very reluctantly, the house of de Courcy and Piper would see what service they might offer.

It so happened that most of the houses de Courcy visited were in need of repair. New roofs, fresh plumbing, the urgent need for modern kitchens were all crying out for money that was not there.

Most of the Hammond-Burke pictures were in the Great Hall and the dining room. 'I think it might be easier if you left me for a while,' de Courcy said to his host. 'I need to make notes.' He pointed to a forbidding large black notebook in his left hand. Everywhere he went de Courcy made copious notes of all the paintings and sculpture in the houses. This was the cover story. He knew that he could quite soon produce, if he had to, the first volume of the proposed compendium. The real purpose of his visit was to see what might sell, what might fetch the highest prices.

He sat down at a small writing table and set to work. There were few houses he visited which did not lay claim to Titians and Van Dycks. Sure enough, there they were, on either side of the great fireplace. De Courcy inspected them carefully and shook his head. 'Here we go again,' he said to himself. By this stage of his new career Edmund de Courcy had acquired a very considerable knowledge of the works of the Old Masters. He had once boasted to William Alaric Piper that he could spot a fake Titian at fifty paces. Here were some more. Generations of English tourists on the Grand Tour had been fleeced by their hosts. The devious Venetians, the even more devious Romans had been quick to discover which Old Masters particularly appealed to their visitors. A few days or a few weeks later, copies or forgeries would mysteriously appear to be carried home in triumph to the broad fields of Hampshire and Surrey.

'1,' he wrote: 'Isabella, wife of Emperor Charles V of Spain. 2: Christ on the Cross.' Then he wrote 'titian' without the capital T to remind himself that the paintings were not genuine works by the master. He continued through a whole series devoted to ancestor worship which took him from Number 3 to Number 41 across four pages of his book. A cavalcade of previous Hammond-Burkes, sometimes simply Hammond, at other times simply Burke, stared down at him. There were Thomases and Sarahs, Alices and Williams, Henrys and Constances. Most of them looked pretty pleased with their lot, apart from one old woman, painted by an unknown hand, who was scowling at the painter as if she wished he would go away. The artists were various, a couple of Knellers that looked genuine, a couple of Gainsboroughs that looked doubtful.

But it was a painting to the left of the fireplace in the dining room that took his fancy. It was listed in his black catalogue as Number 75.

The Holy Family with Lamb, the inscription on the frame declared. Rafaello Sanzio, called Raphael. De Courcy peered at it carefully. In the top left-hand corner was one of those imaginary Renaissance cities on the edge of a lake, two small figures trudging towards it along a dusty road. In the bottom left-hand corner was the lamb with the infant Christ sitting astride it. Holding on to the child was a Madonna in deep blue with a red blouse. Above her stood an old man, leaning on a staff, peering with adoration at the sacrificial victims below. The painting was suffused with a pastoral devotion. The Madonna, de Courcy decided, was not one of those Florentine beauties to be found in the Uffizi or the Pitti Palace. This one

24

looked as though she might have tilled the fields or milked the cows herself. But Raphael. Was it a Raphael? De Courcy stepped back to inspect the picture from a distance. He took a small eyeglass and looked closely at the brushwork. He contemplated the composition of *The Holy Family with Lamb*. He looked out of the window at the river rushing past the terrace, the deer grazing peacefully in their pasture.

Two thoughts were uppermost in Edmund de Courcy's mind as he completed his entry in the black book. The first was that Raphael commanded very high prices. For some reason he always had. Murillos might drift in and out of fashion, Lawrences could come and go, but Raphael, along with Leonardo and Michelangelo, always sold for fabulous sums. Less than twenty years ago the Government had purchased Raphael's *Ansidei Madonna* for the National Gallery for seventy-thousand pounds from the Duke of Marlborough. The second thought was that this house merited three stars in his private annotation of relative penury. The Hammond-Burkes were virtually bankrupt, if not worse.

He strolled back through the house to greet his host. Hammond-Burke was seated at a small table in a sitting room just off the Great Hall. Outside de Courcy could see the weeds bursting through the gravel, the untrimmed lawns, the broken windows still unrepaired. He remembered the many damp patches on the walls of the dining room. Hammond-Burke was looking disconsolately at a pile of papers in front of him. Reading one or two of them upside down de Courcy noticed that they were bills, probably unpaid, possibly final demands.

'What a splendid collection of pictures you have here,' he began with a flattering smile. 'Easily one of the best I've seen.'

His host was not encouraged by the news. He continued staring at his bills.

'Is there any chance,' de Courcy went on brightly, 'that you might want to add to your collection? Two Gainsboroughs are always an asset, four Gainsboroughs would be more than twice as good!'

James Hammond-Burke laughed. He went on laughing. The laugh turned hysterical. He picked up a couple of his bills and threw them defiantly in the air. 'Add to the collection, did you say?' His face had turned very red. 'Add to it? That's good. That's very good.' He paused and put his hand to his face. 'That's the best thing I've heard this year, oh yes, easily the best.'

He stopped as if he had said too much. The normal look of melancholy pain returned to his features. De Courcy waited. This was the crucial moment. In the early days he and William Alaric Piper had rehearsed the various ways these interviews about the compendium might develop. Piper had the ability to become an irascible if impoverished duke or a proud and haughty squire who would both be quick to anger if the wrong proposition was put to them. Englishmen after all are always loath to part with their possessions, however trying the circumstances. De Courcy thought that the Marlborough sale must have made it easier for them. If one of the foremost members of the aristocracy could sell the most valuable objects in his collection to pay his debts, then the smaller fish in the pond might feel easier about doing likewise. On more than one occasion in these rehearsals the Piper figure had thrown de Courcy out of the imaginary house for impudence and discourtesy.

Sometimes de Courcy waited before he mentioned the word 'sell'. Then a letter would follow his visit, after a respectable ten days, informing the owners that if there was ever any wish on their part to dispose of any of their possessions the firm of de Courcy and Piper would, reluctantly of course, oblige. On other occasions he struck immediately. If de Courcy felt the lack of funds was quite obvious, that family pride was not in the ascendant, he would strike at once.

'Well,' de Courcy said, thinking that he was not going to be offered a cup of tea, 'there is only one other thing I would say about your excellent collection.' He paused. Hammond-Burke looked up at him with miserable eyes. Somewhere in the distance a clock struck four.

'If – and I'm sure it's highly unlikely – if, as I say, you ever wanted to sell, that Raphael would fetch a good price.' De Courcy smiled a deprecating smile. 'A very good price.'

Hammond-Burke's reaction was the most unusual de Courcy had yet seen. Normally the owners protested that that was very interesting, but that they had no wish to sell. Only after some time had elapsed would a rather sad letter arrive at Old Bond Street inquiring about possible disposals. Even then they rarely mentioned money.

Hammond-Burke looked up at him.

'How much?' he said. De Courcy was taken aback. 'How much is that Raphael worth?'

De Courcy slipped into his most polished mode. 'Difficult to say immediately,' he said. He was thinking rapidly of possible purchasers, trying to remember if any American millionaires were due to visit London shortly. He had heard that a number, including the Olympian figure of J. Pierpoint Morgan, whose appetite for art was almost as voracious as his appetite for money, might be coming over in the next month or so.

'I would need to consult with my colleagues.' Always keep them in the plural, he said to himself, bankers, lawyers, advisers, anything to make it grander than a quick conversation in William Alaric Piper's little office in Old Bond Street. 'However, even at this juncture, without such a consultation, I would say that it might fetch as much as thirty thousand pounds. Possibly more.'

De Courcy's calculation of the selling price started at seventy-five thousand pounds. Prices had gone up since the Marlborough sale, after all.

Hammond-Burke looked slightly less miserable. He bent down to retrieve the fallen bills. 'I'd be obliged if you could find out how much it would fetch. And let me know at once.'

As Edmund de Courcy made his way out down the long drive James Hammond-Burke watched him go. Then he walked slowly into his dining room. He stared at the Raphael on his walls. He remained there, locked in contemplation of his Holy Family, until the light faded some hours later.

2

Lord Francis Powerscourt had just sat down in his favourite armchair by the fire in the family's London home in Markham Square. It was early evening. A black cat was asleep at his feet. Something was rubbing at his back. He turned round and extracted a very small Russian doll from behind the cushions. It was brightly painted in red and blue. Powerscourt looked at it affectionately. It must be one of Olivia's collection, he said to himself, and opened his newspaper.

Footsteps were sounding along the hall outside. Lady Lucy Powerscourt stepped slowly into the room. Even after seven years of marriage the radiance of her presence often gave Powerscourt a sort of warm glow inside. She was reading a letter.

She smiled at her husband. 'It's from one of my cousins,' she said.

Powerscourt felt a moment of exasperation as he contemplated his wife's relations. There were so many of them. He had already met over a hundred and fifty. There were still twenty or thirty to go. He thought that by the law of averages one of these relations must one day become Prime Minister or the Archbishop of Canterbury or, better still, Captain of the England cricket team.

There was a sudden gasp from Lady Lucy. 'Oh no,' she said very quietly, 'how terrible. He's been killed.'

'Who has been killed, Lucy?' Powerscourt felt a quick stab of professional interest. He had often joked with Lucy in the past that one day some member of the tribe would be involved in a terrible crime and he, Powerscourt, would have to investigate. Now it was coming true.

Lady Lucy composed herself and sat down by the fire. 'It's Christopher,' she said. 'Christopher Montague. You know Christopher.'

Powerscourt racked his brains. Sometimes he wished he could have an instantly accessible filing system with all the relations neatly tabulated beside their photographs. It would make life so much easier. Montague, Christopher Montague, had he ever met this Christopher Montague? He couldn't remember.

'Oh, Francis,' Lady Lucy said sadly, 'you are hopeless. You met him at Sarah's wedding.'

Which Sarah, Powerscourt thought desperately. There were at least four if not five of those. Then it came to him like the mist clearing on a spring morning. He saw a slight young man in his early thirties at a wedding reception, glass of champagne in hand. He was quite short and perfectly turned out in a grey morning suit. He had a small moustache. The mental image of the late Christopher Montague was telling his companions about the beauties of the Italian countryside.

'Youngish sort of chap, not very tall?' said Powerscourt hesitantly. Privately he felt that there must be at least ten of Lady Lucy's relations who would fit that description.

'That's him,' said Lady Lucy sadly. 'That was him.'

'How did he die?' asked Powerscourt, relieved that the question of identification had been resolved.

'He was garrotted. I think that's what his sister said.

30

Garrotted means having a rope or something similar pulled tight round your throat until you die, doesn't it?'

Powerscourt felt embarrassed that his wife's knowledge of his macabre profession meant that she knew the meaning of the word. 'That is what garrotted means, Lucy. Where did it happen?'

Lady Lucy wiped her eyes. 'He lived with his sister in Beaufort Street in Chelsea. Christopher wasn't married. But he had a little flat in Brompton Square where he used to work. That's where he was killed.' Lady Lucy looked sadly at her husband. 'You will investigate his death, Francis, won't you? I'm sure the family would want you to.'

'Of course I will, Lucy. But what did Christopher Montague do for a living? Did he have private means?'

'I think he did have a little money of his own,' said Lady Lucy, 'but he did quite well out of his writing.'

'Did he write for the newspapers? Was he a journalist with one of the papers?'

'I think he did write for the *Morning Post* sometimes. But always about exhibitions and that sort of thing. You see, Christopher was just beginning to make a name for himself as an art critic.'

Powerscourt wondered what it might be about an art critic's life that could lead to his violent death. Surely, he thought, their days were spent in galleries and libraries, their eyes fixed on the higher glories of the Quattrocento or the allegorical masterpieces of Poussin. Then he remembered all those heads of John the Baptist presented on a plate to Salome, Judith and Holofernes, the terrible torments of the damned in Hieronymus Bosch. Maybe death and art were not so far away. But it could also have been Christopher Montague's private life that had led to his end.

'Francis, Francis, come back, come back.' Lady Lucy brought him out of his reverie. 'There's something else.' She pulled a key out of the envelope. 'His sister has given me the key to his flat. I thought you might want to go and see for yourself.'

'Surely, Lucy,' said Powerscourt, 'the dead man is not still there?'

'I don't know,' Lady Lucy replied. 'He was only found this morning.'

Powerscourt took the key to Number 29 Brompton Square and set out across the London twilight. He passed crowds of people outside South Kensington underground station. He could see the Brompton Oratory rising in its Catholic splendour at the junction of the Cromwell and Brompton Roads. The square was tucked in behind the main road, a pleasant collection of late Georgian houses with a garden in the centre.

Number 29 was in the far left-hand corner, Montague's flat on the first floor. A policeman was on guard inside the porch. After a quick conversation to establish Powerscourt's credentials, he let him pass inside the house. Inspector Maxwell, the constable informed his visitor, was the officer in charge of the case.

'Good evening to you, sir,' said the Inspector warily. 'May I ask what is the nature of your business here?' The Inspector was in the kitchen, staring at a couple of clean glasses on the draining board. Maxwell was a tall, pencil-slim young man with a mop of curly black hair.

'My name is Powerscourt. I am an investigator. The family have asked me to look into Montague's death. I am a distant relation of his.'

Inspector Maxwell shook him by the hand. 'The Commissioner has often talked about you, sir. Good to have you on board.'

Powerscourt had been involved with the Commissioner of the Metropolitan Police on a number of his previous cases. He had always taken great care to maintain good relations with the police force of London.

'The basic facts are these, my lord,' said Maxwell,

checking in his notebook. 'The body was discovered by Mrs Carey, the lady who comes to clean the flat, at about eleven o'clock this morning. The doctors think he was killed sometime yesterday evening. They think the murder weapon was probably piano wire or picture cord, something very simple the murderer could have carried in his pocket. There's another doctor coming any minute before the body is removed. Perhaps you'd like to have a look, my lord. It's not a pretty sight,' he went on, 'but I'm sure you've seen lots of dead bodies in your time, my lord.'

Powerscourt felt nervous as he opened the door of the main room of Montague's flat. Heaven knows, he had seen enough bodies in his time, some mutilated in war, others desecrated in peace, but the prospect of finding another one in a pleasant London square within walking distance of his home did not appeal.

The room must have been the drawing room when the house was a single unit, before it had been turned into three flats. It had high ceilings and fine windows. Bookshelves lined the walls. Slumped at a desk, his head fallen low on to his chest, there was the figure of a man. Christopher Montague might have been working when his killer struck. Powerscourt looked with distaste at the fatal marks on his neck, great weals of purple and black where the murderer had pulled the cord or the wire tight round his neck. Death must have been pretty quick, he thought. He noticed a mark on the leg of the chair where the killer might have placed his shoe to gain extra purchase on Montague's throat.

But the strangest feature of the drawing room of Number 29 Brompton Square was what had happened to the possessions. A number of books had been removed, gaps in the shelves sticking out like recently extracted teeth. Any papers left on or inside the desk had gone. Gently Powerscourt opened the drawers on either side of the knee-hole desk. They were empty.

Powerscourt crawled along the floor, trying to see if any scraps of paper, any notes, might have fallen into one of the dusty corners. There was nothing. He checked the single bedroom. A fine collection of Montague suits and shirts still hung in the cupboards, but there were no books or documents to be seen. Gingerly Powerscourt checked all the pockets. Somebody had been there before him. They were completely empty. Powerscourt thought it impossible that anybody could have completely empty pockets in their jackets. He was always finding old bills, theatre ticket stubs, currency notes in his own pockets. Here there was nothing.

He went back to the kitchen. 'I presume, Inspector,' he said, 'that you and your men have not removed anything from the drawing room?'

'Certainly not, my lord.' Inspector Maxwell was quick to defend the professionalism of his team. 'We haven't moved a thing. And Mrs Carey, the cleaning woman, left everything exactly as she found it. She hasn't touched a thing. Somebody seems to have removed some of the books, mind you. And the desk is empty too. Mrs Carey says he was always scribbling away there, as she put it. Do you suppose the killer took Montague's writings away?'

'We can only assume that he did,' said Powerscourt. 'But why? The man wrote about art, for God's sake. It's not as if were a spy or a diplomat writing out the clauses of some secret international treaty.'

'I'm worried about these wine glasses,' said Inspector Maxwell. 'Mrs Carey says Montague hardly ever had any visitors here. He lived somewhere else. This was where he worked. But here are two glasses which must have been used since Mrs Carey's visit yesterday. She says her Mr Montague never washed anything up in his life. But here we are. Two clean glasses. Two people having a drink.'

'One of them the killer, perhaps?' said Powerscourt. 'And if that is the case then Montague must have opened the door to let him in. He must have known the person who killed him.'

'My thoughts exactly, my lord. Not that it takes us much further forward, mind you. People usually know their killers after all.'

Powerscourt took another look at the glasses. Had Montague cleaned them before he was murdered? Unlikely, he thought, if Mrs Carey was to be believed. Or had his killer cleaned them up after committing the murder? Surely the killer would have wanted to get away as fast as possible. Or had he a particular reason for cleaning the two glasses?

'May I take a last look in the drawing room?' said Powerscourt. 'And I shall keep you informed about anything I find out from the family.'

Powerscourt sat down in a large rocking chair and thought about the life and death of Christopher Montague, one-time art critic. Why had some of the books been removed? Why had his desk and his pockets been so scrupulously emptied of their contents? And why some of the books? Why not all of them? And what about those glasses?

As he made his way back towards Markham Square, he wondered if Montague's private life held the key to his demise. Perhaps the books had been removed as a means of demeaning the dead, to strip him of his most cherished possessions, to leave him mentally naked before his maker. All he could do, thought Powerscourt, was to find all the people who had known him in his last days, to tease out of his relations whether any private scandal had brought sudden and terrible death to Brompton Square.

William Alaric Piper and Edmund de Courcy were sitting in Piper's little office behind the paintings in their gallery in Old Bond Street.

'I think I've found a Raphael, William,' said de Courcy.

'A Raphael, by God!' William Alaric Piper's eyes lit up. His brain hurtled through the prices paid for Raphaels over the past hundred years. He rubbed his hands together in anticipation. 'Where is it? Is it real? How broke is the owner?'

'It's in a decaying Elizabethan mansion in Warwickshire,' replied de Courcy, smiling as he saw the torrents of greed rushing across his partner's face. It was always like this with anything worth more than ten thousand pounds. 'I had a pretty good look at it,' de Courcy went on. 'For my money I should say it is genuine but I couldn't be sure. There's the usual collection of Old Master fakes and forgeries, a couple of Van Dycks that can't be more than fifty years old, a very doubtful Fragonard, a hopeless attempt at a Caravaggio. As for the owner, his house is almost falling down. And he's the only man I've ever met with a reaction like that.'

'What do you mean?' asked Piper, thumbing through one of the cards on his desk, checking the Raphael valuations.

'Normally, William, when you tell them that you might, just might, be interested in buying a painting, they tell you first of all that it was purchased by great great great great grandfather James in Rome or some other Italian bazaar over two hundred years ago. They tell you how much he paid for it. Then you get all the rubbish about how long it's been in the family, how they couldn't bear to part with it, how it has to be passed on along with the house and the estate and the port to future generations. One man who never sold actually got quite tearful when he thought of the family Titian being taken off his walls. But this Hammond-Burke fellow

36

asked straight away how much it was worth. Rather like he was selling a horse.'

'Not much money in Titians,' said Piper sorrowfully. He had a soft spot for Titian. 'Too many of the damned things. Silly old man lived till he was nearly a hundred, as you know. If only he'd died young like our friend Giorgione in the exhibition, he wouldn't have left so many damned paintings. Then the prices would be better.'

'The point is this, William,' said de Courcy, familiar with Piper's normal reaction of applying the laws of supply and demand to the artistic heritage of the Western world. 'James Hammond-Burke's house is falling down. I should say it needs at least twenty thousand pounds spending on it.' De Courcy's expertise in restoration costs for old houses was based on the annual estimate for restoring his own de Courcy Hall in Norfolk. His agent supplied him with these costs every year from an experienced firm in Norwich. Norfolk alone had enough crumbling piles to keep a number of building companies in profitable employment for decades.

'I checked in the village next to the house as well. The general opinion was that the Hammond-Burkes were virtually bankrupt.'

'So, Edmund, so.' Piper was planning his campaign. 'We write to this Hammond-Burke fellow. Do we ask him to bring the painting up to London so our experts can look at it? Or do we go there?'

William Alaric Piper always wanted to bring his victims to London. He doubted if they were used to the capital. He would show them the paintings currently on display in the de Courcy and Piper Gallery. He would assure them that he could make no final decision until he had consulted his experts. He would sound rather doubtful about the provenance of the Raphael or the

37

Rubens. He would send them back to their damp and their decay with hopes slighter than when they arrived. But he would not cast them into total despair. 'We shall see,' he would say, as he ushered them out of his office. 'So many of these paintings turn out to be merely copies of the original and are worth nothing at all. Or they're forgeries. But we shall have to wait a little while. These experts have to take their time examining the work. I have known them wait a month or so before they give their judgement. Once we know, I shall be in touch at once. A very good day to you, sir.'

'I am sure Hammond-Burke would come to London. Absolutely sure of it,' said de Courcy.

'How long ago did you see him, three days ago, did you say?'

De Courcy nodded. He watched his partner calculating the problems in landing this particular fish, a fish that might be worth over fifty thousand pounds profit to the gallery.

'Let's leave him a little longer, Edmund. Let's leave him for three or four days more. Then Mr Hammond-Burke or Burke-Hammond or whatever he's called, will get a letter from us.'

De Courcy had seen many of these letters. They were masterpieces of manipulation. The gallery regretted that the owner was contemplating selling his Raphael. The gallery firmly believed that Old Masters should be left in their ancestral homes, to bear witness to their past and to be a beacon to future generations. However, it was always the policy of the gallery to be of succour to owners who might wish to dispose of their paintings. The gallery always attempted to ensure that they moved on to reputable owners who would guard and cherish the work as it had been guarded and cherished in the past. If Mr Hammond-Burke could bring his painting with him, the gallery, at its own expense, would ensure that it was examined by the foremost experts in the land. If necessary, other experts would be summoned from Paris or Berlin. The gallery believed that every care should be taken to ensure the correct attribution of the work. Then Piper would suggest a date. The date was always very close to the time of arrival of the letter. Get their hopes up, Piper would say. They can work out the cost of repairs on the train on their way here. Once they're here, they're caught. They're in the net of William Alaric Piper.

Very few of them escaped.

3

Lord Francis Powerscourt was walking along Piccadilly. The traffic on one of London's most fashionable streets was so dense that a pedestrian moved faster than the vehicles but Powerscourt's mind was far away. He had spent most of the past four days in and around Brompton Square. He thought he knew every blade of grass in the little garden by now. He had talked to the neighbours of the late Christopher Montague. None of them had seen anything unusual. Inspector Maxwell and his team had checked with the rubbish disposal men in case a parcel of books had been left for collection. No such pile had been observed. He and the police had knocked on every door in the square, searching for information that was not there. Or that the owners chose not to reveal. The killer seemed to have been an invisible man. The day before Inspector Maxwell revealed that the police had found two people who had seen Montague on the day of his death. An Edmund de Courcy had a brief conversation with him at the corner of Old Bond Street and Grosvenor Street late in the afternoon. A certain Roderick Johnston of the National Gallery had seen him leaving the gallery just before six o'clock in the evening. But there was no news of what Montague was working on at the time of his death.

Powerscourt had inquired of all the reputable papers in the capital if Christopher Montague was writing an article for them. He was not. The papers regretted his death but had no clues to its cause. Originally Powerscourt had high hopes of the sister. Surely she, of all people, would know of any dark secrets in his private life that could have led to his death. She did not. Brothers, she had told Powerscourt sadly, did not usually confide their innermost secrets to their sisters. Powerscourt doubted this at first. Then he had thought of his own sisters and he asked himself if he would have told any of the three of them about his private life. On the very day he became engaged to Lucy, he reminded himself, he had taken great care not to tell his sisters the good news. The only intelligence the sister could provide was that Christopher's closest friend was a history don called Thomas Jenkins at Emmanuel College, Oxford, and that he had been encouraged in his work by the President of the Royal Academy, Sir Frederick Lambert.

Powerscourt had been to an exhibition of Lambert's work the year before. Lambert specialized in vast canvases with historical or religious or mythological subjects. People said that he travelled to the countries where the events were supposed to have taken place to steep himself in the light and the colour. Powerscourt had thought they were quite terrible but resolved to keep his views to himself in his interview with the President.

Lambert's office was on the first floor of Burlington House. A couple of his own works modestly adorned the walls. Sir Frederick was a great bear of a man with a huge moustache and a very red face. Powerscourt remembered Lucy telling him that he took great time and trouble to curry favour with the rich and fashionable, presenting some of his own paintings to the Prince and Princess of Wales. Powerscourt doubted if either of them would have known who Agamemnon or Archimedes, regular subjects in the Lambert oeuvre, actually were. Lambert had painted Archimedes sitting in an enormous bath, designing siege engines for the battle of Syracuse while the warships surrounded the city. This incongruous vista was now hanging on the main staircase of the Waleses' London home at Marlborough House.

'How very kind of you to see me at such short notice, Sir Frederick,' said Powerscourt, feeling rather giddy as he looked at some Lambert incident from the Trojan Wars on the wall above him.

'Better have a glass of champagne, Powerscourt,' Sir Frederick greeted him in expansive mood. 'Lucky we've still got some at reasonable prices.'

Powerscourt asked how the champagne had been in peril.

Sir Frederick laughed. 'It's a very good story. The French Ambassador told it to me at a dinner last night at Lady Grosvenor's. D'you know the Grosvenors, Powerscourt?'

Powerscourt felt relieved as he told the President that the Grosvenors, like so much of London society, were distant relatives of his wife's.

'It's these Americans,' Lambert went on, taking a gulp from his glass. 'The millionaire Americans, the ones who own all the banks and all the railways and all the shipping lines. One of them, fellow by the name of Graubman, was in Paris, buying sculptures and paintings and tapestries to take home to Westchester County or wherever he lives. They say he was thinking of making the French Government an offer for the Louvre. Anyway, one of these French art dealers got him interested in fine champagne. Fellow asked where it came from. Art dealer takes out a map and shows him. "Why," says Graubman, "that's a very tiny area. You could put the whole lot into a small corner of New Hampshire!" The French Ambassador says that Graubman owns rather a large corner of New Hampshire. He thought he could make a new corner. In champagne. Buy up all the land and send up the price. The Ambassador says the millionaire took out a notebook full of figures. He asked the art dealer how many bottles of champagne are sold every year. He asked how much they fetched. "Look here," he says to the art dealer, "in my country, once you control everything, you control all the prices. Once you've got all the steel, you can charge what you like for it. Why can't we do the same with this champagne stuff? I'm sure we could make it for less money once we'd got control. Can't see why they need so many bubbles for a start. I reckon" – he was apparently scribbling furiously at this point – "we could easily make a couple of million a year. Maybe more."'

Powerscourt smiled. 'What stopped him, Sir Frederick?' he asked.

Lambert polished off his glass and poured himself a refill. 'Numbers saved us all, Powerscourt. The American was all set to order a special train to take himself and his party to champagne country when the art dealer told him that there were sixteen thousand separate owners to negotiate with. At first he didn't seem too taken aback. He talked apparently of the number of small steel manufacturers he had swallowed whole in his rise to fame and fortune. Then he shook his head. "Sixteen thousand of these French peasants," he apparently said. "Some of them must only own a single vine, if that. I bought out over three hundred steel makers all over America. But sixteen thousand is too many. And they're French. Mind you, I'm sure it could be done. Probably will be some day. It would just take a great amount of American enterprise and expertise. Integrated management, that's the thing. Control the whole chain, from grape to bottling to distribution to selling point. What a lost opportunity!"'

Sir Frederick laughed heartily at his own story. 'Now then, Powerscourt, to business. You said in your letter that you wished to talk to me about poor Christopher Montague. What a sad end to such a promising career.'

Powerscourt decided that flattery might be the best means of advance. 'Sir Frederick,' he began, 'you stand at the very pinnacle of the London art world. From your lofty vantage point and with your long experience, you must have a better idea of what goes on in that world than any other man in Britain.'

He smiled what he hoped was a flattering smile. 'I have been asked by the Montague family to investigate the murder. At this stage I have absolutely no idea what caused his death. I do not know if it related to his personal or to his professional life. Nobody could inform me better about his professional activities than yourself.'

Sir Frederick looked long at one of his paintings on the walls. Hector was being pulled round the walls of Troy, lashed to the back of a chariot, dust and blood running in brown and red trails behind the wheels.

'I saw young Montague a month or so ago at the preview of that Venetian exhibition at the de Courcy and Piper Gallery. He seemed in robust form then. He asked my advice on the best place to stay in Florence. His book must be coming out quite soon. It's on the Northern Italian Painters, a follow-up to his work on the origins of the Renaissance.'

'Do you know by any chance what he was working on at the time of his death?' asked Powerscourt. 'Even his sister couldn't tell me.'

'I'm afraid I don't know the answer to that,' said Sir Frederick.

'Was his work good? What was your opinion of it?' asked Powerscourt.

Sir Frederick Lambert paused before he replied. 'It is quite unusual in my profession for the old to praise the young, Powerscourt,' he said. 'Most of the time we think they are trying to destroy our reputations, the young steers battling for the leadership of the pack. But Christopher Montague was good. He was very good. I think he could have become the most distinguished scholar of his generation. The world of art is widening. More and more people want to know about it. Montague could write in a way that appealed to the intelligent public as much as it did to scholars.'

'But surely that couldn't have caused his death?' said Powerscourt. 'Surely nobody gets killed because they may become the foremost scholar in the country?'

Sir Frederick Lambert paused again. He looked closely at Powerscourt's face. 'No,' he said finally, 'that's how it would seem. That's how it would appear. Maybe you should think of the world of art in London as being like some masterpiece of the High Renaissance. You stare, entranced by the drama of the scene, the gorgeous colours, the depiction of character, the composition of the work. But few people stop to think about the time the artist has devoted to creating that particular illusion, the months, even years spent in bewitching the eye of the beholder.'

Sir Frederick pulled a small book from the shelves behind him. He riffled through the pages, searching for the passage he wanted.

'This is Dürer writing to a friend called Jacob Heller about one of his own paintings. "And when I come over to you, say in one or two or three years' time, the picture must be taken down to see if it has dried out, and then I will varnish it anew with a special varnish that no one else can make; it will then last another hundred years longer than it would before. But don't let anyone else varnish it. All other varnishes are yellow and the picture would be ruined for you. And if a thing on which I have spent over a year's work were ruined, it would be grief to me."'

Sir Frederick took off his spectacles. 'See the care, the concern, to maintain the illusion. Titian once went all the way back from Venice to Ferrara, quite a journey in those times, to readjust the final varnish on his *Bacchus and Ariadne* now on display in our own National Gallery. The art world, the dealers, the restorers, the curators in their galleries love to present themselves like those paintings, the glossy surface, the impeccable clothes, the illusion of perfection. It's as if they hope some small particles of the glories of the past will rub off on to their own shoulders. But underneath, it is quite different. Beneath the surface, behind the fine paint and the varnish, there lurks a different world. Sometimes long ago, when painters mixed their own paints rather than buying them in the shops, trying no doubt for ever more dramatic results, they would invent a paint that nobody had ever tried before. But the outcome could be disastrous. The air, the dust, the surrounding atmosphere would erode the colours. After thirty or forty years, only the canvas would remain. The image upon it had vanished, like the smile of the Cheshire cat. So to a newcomer to the art world, I would repeat the words of Horace, *caveat emptor*, let the buyer beware. All is not what it seems.'

'Do you think, Sir Frederick,' said Powerscourt, 'that all of that could lead to a man's death?'

Sir Frederick rose from his chair and stood by his window. A thin October sun was falling on the courtyard beneath. 'I am an old man, Powerscourt. I have not been able to paint at all for the past three years. My doctors tell me that I have but a short time left to live. Soon I shall be swept away, just as the rubbish on our River Thames gets swept away by the tides to rest on some riverbank far away. So I can speak freely. I know too much about this art world. I would advise you to think of it as you would an Oriental bazaar, or the trading rooms of an unscrupulous financier in the City of London just up the road from here. I do not feel it appropriate to tell you of any of the dishonest activities that go on. But I make you this promise.'

Lambert had turned round now, and looked down on Powerscourt like a benevolent uncle offering unwanted advice to a feckless nephew. 'I hope very much that the world of art in this city did not lead to Christopher Montague's death. I hope there are other causes. But if, in the course of your investigations, you come across anything in the art world, anything suspicious or dishonest, I suggest that you return to me and I will help you. I will give you all the assistance in my power. I rather liked Christopher Montague.'

4

William Alaric Piper was going to a meeting with Gladstone. He descended from his train at Barnes railway bridge and set off beside the river. He was wearing a large overcoat and a hat pulled well forward over his eyes. He peered about him furtively as if he thought he might be followed.

Gladstone was responsible for the secrecy. Not for the cover name, of course. All of de Courcy and Piper's most important agents in the field had their own sobriquets. You could never be too careful, Piper had said to himself when he started his system. One word of who you had seen, one dropped bit of gossip, could lose business. More important, it could lose money.

Only the authenticators, as Piper liked to call them, were named after former Prime Ministers. Some of these deceased statesmen had travelled further in death than they ever had in life. Liverpool had made it as far as Florence, Disraeli was reliving former diplomatic triumphs in Berlin, Peel had only progressed to Paris. But the word of these men, written rather than oral, could add tens of thousands of pounds to the value of a painting. If they said a Velasquez was a fake, it was worthless. But if they said it was genuine, William Alaric Piper's bankers would be delighted. Most important, there could not be any visible link between expert and art dealer. If it was known that the expert was on the payroll of a dealer, his attribution would be worthless. Impartiality, the respected status of academic detachment, the quest for pure scholarship, these were the golden chips in the gambling saloons of the art world. That was why Piper created his cover names, that was why he checked his movements on his way to the Mortlake house this evening. Gladstone was an expert on the Renaissance.

Gladstone lived in a fine Georgian house in Mortlake High Street with a great drawing room at the back looking over the river. Until a few years before, round about the time he first met Piper, in fact, he had lived in a tiny terraced house in Holloway. Now he had more space. The Gladstone butler, a small man who spoke as few words as possible, showed him into the study. The curtains were tightly pulled. On an easel by the window stood the Hammond-Burke Raphael, carefully lit. Hammond-Burke, even more morose in London than he had been in Warwickshire, had delivered it in person the previous week. It had been delivered to Mortlake in secret by one of Piper's porters a couple of days before.

'Well, Johnston' – for such was Gladstone's real name – 'what is your opinion of this painting?'

Johnston smiled. 'I may tell you in a minute. Or I may not. It depends on the terms.'

'What do you mean, terms?' said Piper wearily, all too aware that another round of bargaining was about to begin. They were all the same, these art experts, he had decided long ago. There was not a single one of them who could not be bought. The only question was the price.

Johnston was the exact opposite of what the public would have thought a librarian or a museum curator would look like. He was six inches taller than Piper and at least a foot broader. Piper often thought Johnston could model for one of those paintings of muscular Christians, staff in one hand, Bible in the other, marching resolutely across landscapes derived from *The Pilgrim's Progress*, which sold well to less discriminating palates. Or Goliath before he met David.

'Let us talk of the terms later,' said Piper, peering steadily at *The Holy Family with Lamb*, the terrible innocence of the Christ child as he gazed up at his mother. 'I presume from your initial remarks that you think it is genuine?'

'I do,' said Johnston, suddenly realizing that he might have weakened his hand. 'It is undoubtedly a Raphael, probably painted during his time in Florence before he went to Rome. It is mentioned in Vasari and one or two other chroniclers. There's nothing like a respectable past to convince the world that a painting is genuine, as you know.'

'What then are the terms you refer to?' asked Piper with a smile. Never fall out with these people had been one of his maxims from his earliest days, never offend them, never have cross words. Disagree by all means but a pleasant manner was worth at least five per cent off any particular transaction.

'Our arrangement,' Johnston spoke quickly, 'was that I should be paid this annual retainer in return for advice on any Italian paintings worth under ten thousand pounds. This one, I'm sure, is worth rather more than that.'

'And the holidays, Johnston, don't forget the holidays,' said Piper, seeking for marginal advantage. De Courcy and Piper picked up the bills for Johnston's regular visits to France and Italy.

'What do you say to twenty per cent of the value of the painting?' said Johnston fiercely. 'And I don't mean twenty per cent of what you pay for it. I mean twenty per cent of what you sell it for.' He had promised his wife that he would begin the bargaining at this level but inwardly he was doubtful of success.

Piper reached for his hat which was lying on the table. He started out rather slowly for the door of the Johnston drawing room. 'That would be quite impossible. I very much regret having to terminate this relationship as a guest in your house. But your request is simply impossible. I shall instruct my bankers to cancel the annual payments in the morning.'

Piper was right by the door now, strangely reluctant to go.

Johnston remembered his lines. 'If you do that,' he said, 'I shall denounce your Raphael as a fake. I am one of the foremost experts on him and his school in the whole of Europe.'

'Were you to denounce this Raphael as a fake, my dear Johnston,' replied Piper, still not quite out of the room, 'your career would be at an end.' William Alaric Piper stared again at the Raphael. 'There are always other experts who would say it was genuine,' he said sadly, hoping that the pristine beauty of the picture would not be sullied by these transactions.

'And,' he went on, his hand on the door knob now, 'I should be forced to write to the trustees of your gallery and inform them that one of their most valued employees had been receiving secret annual retainers from an art dealer in return for authenticating his pictures. I fear your employment would be terminated immediately. Other similar employment might be difficult to obtain.' He opened the door and walked out, very slowly, into the hall, placing his hat carefully on his head. 'A very good evening to you, Johnston. I deeply regret that our mutual association, so sensibly conducted until now, should conclude in these unhappy circumstances.'

'Wait! Wait!' Johnston was beaten now. His wife had

not foreseen that he might lose not only his private retainer but his public position as well. He knew he could never face her with that news. 'Come back, please!'

Reluctantly, Piper returned. He closed the door. He did not take his hat off. 'Well?' he said.

'I'm sure we could come to some other arrangement about the Raphael,' Johnston said defensively, hoping that the Piper goose might still have some golden eggs left in its nest.

Piper realized that he could name his price. He could humiliate Johnston in his own drawing room. However much he might relish the prospect, he knew it would be bad for business. Johnston had to be brought back into the fold as gently as possible. There might be further Raphaels. Piper's private fantasy had always been for a lost Leonardo. Only Johnston could put the official seal of approval on such a wondrous event.

'I fully agree with what you said earlier about your retainer only covering paintings worth less than ten thousand pounds,' Piper said affably, his hat still on his head. He had checked his notes of the earlier conversation with Johnston when the deal was struck. Nothing formal had been put down on paper. There were no Heads of Agreement, no correspondence conducted between lawyers or bankers to make the contract legal. That would have been too dangerous.

'Did you have any figure in mind?' Piper went on, taking off his hat and placing it carefully on a table.

'Perhaps,' Johnston was almost stammering now, 'it would be better if you were to suggest a figure and we could take it from there?'

Piper paused. He walked over to the window and opened the curtains a fraction. Outside there was a stiff breeze. A dark Thames was flowing peacefully towards the sea. Five per cent would be too small. Seven and a half per cent? Maybe that would be too much humiliation for Johnston and the absent Mrs Johnston to take. Ten? Quite a lot of money, possibly ten thousand pounds in Johnston's pocket. Fifteen? He winced as he thought of that enormous sum departing from the accounts of de Courcy and Piper.

'What do you say, Johnston . . .' He paused, staring again at the Raphael. Johnston felt sick, wondering how much punishment he would have to take. 'What do you say to twelve and a half per cent of the selling price? I think that's a pretty fair offer.'

Johnston felt relieved. Only a few minutes earlier professional catastrophe had been staring him in the face. 'That sounds excellent to me,' he said. 'And I shall certainly recommend that the gallery makes a substantial offer for the picture.'

William Alaric Piper clapped him on the back. The two men shook hands.

'Splendid, quite splendid,' said Piper. He knew that he could now conduct a dizzy round of bid and counter bid on the price of the Raphael. He could tell Johnston's gallery that a rich American client was considering an offer of seventy-five thousand pounds or thereabouts. Then he could tell a rich American that the gallery were prepared to offer eighty thousand pounds. The game could go on as long as he dared play it.

Johnston thought he would still be able to afford a substantial property somewhere in the Tuscan hills. That would keep Mrs Johnston at bay.

Piper smiled to himself as he strode back to his railway station, hat still pulled well down over his forehead. Gladstone alias Johnston was senior curator in Italian and Renaissance art at London's National Gallery. And, Piper's smile broadened into a chuckle, he had got his services pretty cheap. He would have gone to twenty-five per cent of the sale value if it had been necessary. And now he had his authentication in his pocket, he could make a final offer to James Hammond-Burke to buy the Raphael. Thirty thousand? Thirty-five? Forty thousand? He settled himself happily into the corner seat of his train and dreamt of lost Leonardos.

'I've been thinking about what you said in your letter, Lord Powerscourt.' Thomas Jenkins of Emmanuel College, Oxford was drinking tea in the Powerscourt drawing room in Markham Square. Powerscourt had offered to meet him in Oxford, but Jenkins had to come to London on business. He was consulting some ancient documents in the British Museum. 'I have to confess that I have no idea exactly what Christopher was working on when he died. His book was finished. That much I do know. I talked to the publishers this morning. I last saw Christopher three or four weeks ago. Look,' he went on, delving into his bag, 'I've brought a photograph of him. I thought investigators might like things like that.'

'Thank you very much,' said Powerscourt. The photograph showed two young men standing in the quad of an Oxford college. The one on the left was Thomas Jenkins. The one on the right was a younger, healthier Montague. He was of slight build and short height, with fair hair and a small neatly trimmed moustache. Looking at the Jenkins in front of him Powerscourt thought there was hardly any difference, the same curly brown hair, the air of diffidence, shyness perhaps in front of the lens. Jenkins looked like what he was, an Oxford history tutor, as slight as his friend. Montague looked as if he belonged in more worldly surroundings than the well-manicured lawn and ivy-covered walls of Emmanuel.

'How long ago was this taken?' asked Powerscourt, placing the photograph on a table beside him.

'I think it was a couple of years ago,' Jenkins replied. 'Christopher had come back to Oxford for a party.'

'Let me run through what I know of the bare facts of Christopher Montague's life,' said Powerscourt. 'Then you can fill in the gaps, put flesh on the bones, if you could. Born in London in 1870. Father, now dead, a successful lawyer, left him a modest private income. Educated at Westminster School and New College, Oxford, where he met you. Took a first class honours degree in history. Taught for a couple of years in Florence where he learnt his fluent Italian. Wrote his first book on the origins of the Renaissance four years ago. Book sold well, now in its second edition. Second book, on Northern Italian art, due to be published shortly. Didn't gamble. Didn't live above his means. Lived with his sister in Beaufort Street. Had a small flat in Brompton Square where he worked. And where he was murdered. Not married. Sounds a pretty blameless life to me. Why should anyone want to kill him?'

Jenkins shook his head. 'I've been asking myself that question every hour of every day since I heard the news, Lord Powerscourt. And I can't answer it any more than you could. I hadn't seen Christopher for nearly three weeks when he was killed. He was going to come to Oxford for a week or so two days from now.'

'What about his private life? Forgive me for asking these questions. It goes with my profession. It may help us find the murderer.'

Again Thomas Jenkins shook his head. 'Christopher Montague was the most normal person I ever met,' he said. 'He had fallen in love a couple of times but he never got married. When he was writing his books he said he had very little time for the affairs of the heart. But I know he did want to marry and have children. He was very fond of children. He liked playing with them. Sometimes he'd spend hours charging around with his young nephews up in Scotland.'

Powerscourt tried to remember if those nephews

might be relatives of his too, part of the national diaspora of Lucy's vast family. He'd have to ask her. 'You said that he'd fallen in love a couple of times. Would either of those affairs have left any scars, any wounds that might have a bearing on his death?'

This time Thomas Jenkins smiled. 'I think the scars would have been with Christopher, not the other way round. Once was with a young American girl he met in Florence. I think she and Christopher grew very fond of each other. Then her parents whisked her off. I think they were looking for a title or a great deal of money, not some relatively poor Englishman who wrote books about dead Italian artists. The second time was three or four years ago. Isobel, she was called. She was very beautiful. I think they met at a dance up in London. She was totally bewitching, mesmerizing, that Isobel. I always thought she cast spells on people, they became so infatuated with her. Then she abandoned Christopher and went off with a very wild young man. Christopher wasn't exciting enough for her. Maybe not dangerous enough. Some girls like the whiff of danger about a man, don't you think, Lord Powerscourt?'

'I'm sure you're right, Mr Jenkins,' said Powerscourt diplomatically. 'The more I know about him, the more innocent his life sounds,' he went on sadly. He had rarely started a murder investigation with so few leads. 'I just wish I could discover what he was doing in the days before his death. His sister said he was working very hard, very fast. But she had no idea what he was writing about. And then some of his books and all his papers were taken away. Did he make any professional enemies with those books? Any academic jealousy? Any reputations ruined?'

'Not at all,' Jenkins replied. 'He was always very careful not to offend people. He might imply that his theory was more plausible than theirs, but he never set out to destroy anybody else's work.'

'Have you any idea what he was working on at the time of his death? A book or an article for the newspapers or magazines?'

Jenkins replied that he had no idea what his friend was working on at the time of his murder.

'I mustn't keep you any longer,' said Powerscourt. 'One last question. Did he belong to any clubs in London? Anywhere he might have gone to relax and chat to his friends?'

'Christopher wasn't a very clubbable sort of man,' Jenkins said. 'I think he belonged to the Athenaeum, but he didn't go there much. He sometimes said that his favourite place in London was the reading room of the London Library in St James's Square.'

As Jenkins left, a puzzled Powerscourt asked if he could consult him again. 'Of course,' had been his reply. 'I could take you to Christopher's favourite place in Oxford. But it won't give you any clues to his death.'

5

The Raphael *Holy Family* was going home. Not to Florence or to Rome, but to the English country house whose walls it had graced for the past two hundred years. Wrapped innumerable times in soft cloth and rolls of thick brown paper, tightly secured with heavy string, it nestled between two men in a first class railway carriage en route from London to Warwick.

To its left, by the window, William Alaric Piper stared moodily at the passing countryside, wishing that the train could go faster. To its right sat Edmund de Courcy, searching for something in a great pile of papers on his lap.

'Here we are, William,' he said at last. 'These two estimates might prove useful.'

Piper saw that one was from a building firm in Stratford, the other from one based in Warwick itself, for repair and restoration work on the Hammond-Burke home.

'How on earth did you get these, Edmund?' asked Piper, his eyes racing down the columns until he reached the Total figure at the bottom of page three of the Stratford firm.

'Well,' said de Courcy, 'it wasn't difficult. I borrowed some of our lawyers' notepaper and said I was representing a distant relative called Jason Hammond, currently residing in Worcester, Massachusetts. This Jason character was now an old man but he had made a great deal of money. The letter said that he wished to leave his cousin enough money to effect the restoration of the ancestral home, but needed to know how much would be required. I gave them the details of the interior work from memory, saying it came from another member of the Hammond-Burke clan who had recently been to visit. And I suggested the builders take a discreet look round the property themselves for the roofs and the upkeep of the stables and so on. For some reason, unknown to the lawyers, Mr Jason wanted to keep his intentions secret.'

'One lot of builders say fifteen thousand pounds, another say twenty thousand pounds,' said Piper. 'Let's just suppose, Edmund, that you had an old mansion in need of restoration.'

'You know perfectly well that I do have such a mansion,' replied de Courcy .

'But would you believe these estimates?' asked Piper quickly.

'No, I would not,' said de Courcy bitterly. 'I checked recently with some families in East Anglia who had raised sufficient funds, as they thought, to restore their properties. On average the final bill was over fifty per cent larger than the original estimate. In one case it was almost twice the original figure.'

'I thought as much,' said Piper happily. 'Now, let us suppose that you are this Mr Hammond-Burke we are due to meet,' Piper checked his watch, 'in less than one hour's time. You want to repair your house. A nice dealer from London offers you, let us say, twenty-five thousand pounds for the Raphael. Would you accept?'

'We don't know if Hammond-Burke has asked other dealers what they would pay him for the painting.' De

Courcy looked down at the brown paper and string beside him.

'Ah, but we do,' said Piper. 'I have paid out quite a lot of money in the last few days to the junior staff of our competitors. Nobody has been asking about the price of a Raphael. Unless he has gone to Paris, which I doubt. Perhaps I should have checked there too.'

'To come back to your original question, William,' said de Courcy, 'I think we can assume that Hammond-Burke has a very good idea how much the restoration would cost.'

'Ah, but he doesn't know that we know, if you follow me.'

'I don't think that matters,' said de Courcy. 'If I were him, I would hesitate before taking twenty-five thousand pounds. He could have spent all that and still not have finished. He could end up with the roof off and no money left to replace it.'

'So what would you offer?'

De Courcy looked out of the window. Rows of terraced houses were replacing the green fields of Warwickshire. 'I would offer him thirty or thirty-five thousand pounds, maybe even more to be certain. If only there was some way we could hold out the prospect of more money from selling more of his paintings, in case he runs short.'

'Are his other paintings worth anything at all?' said Piper.

'No, they're not. Not money on the scale we're talking about.'

Piper looked very thoughtful indeed. 'But what happens, Edmund, if he were to find a painting hidden away somewhere? A painting that might be worth tens of thousands of pounds.'

De Courcy laughed. He patted the genuine Raphael beside him. 'You mean that Hammond-Burke could become, as it were, the fourth asterisk?'

'Precisely so, Edmund. We can only form a judgement when we meet the fellow. We mustn't rush things. But, look, here we are. For God's sake handle that Raphael very carefully indeed. It wouldn't do to drop it now. Not now when we may be in sight of the fourth asterisk!'

Powerscourt and Lady Lucy were walking arm in arm up Pall Mall to a family lunch at his sister's house in St James's Square. Lady Lucy was very excited about a recent piece of Powerscourt family gossip.

'Is it true, Francis, that William and Mary Burke have just bought a villa near Antibes? An enormous villa?' Mary Burke was the second of Powerscourt's three sisters, married to a very successful financier called William Burke.

'I believe it is true, Lucy, though I do not have any accurate information as to the size of the establishment.'

'Oh, Francis, you're not investigating your own family. Will we be able to go and stay, do you think?'

'I'm sure we will be able to. I'm not sure that society down there will be much to my taste. I've got nothing against millionaire grocers and successful stock market speculators, I just don't think it would suit me.'

Lady Lucy laughed as they turned the corner into St James's Square. 'You'll be a frightful snob when you're old, Francis. I shall have to push you along the Promenade des Anglais in your wheelchair, checking to make sure your rug is comfortable, while you complain about the Riviera parvenus and the nouveaux riches of Cannes.'

Powerscourt laughed and squeezed his wife's arm. 'I look forward to that, Lucy, I really do.'

Lady Rosalind Pembridge's house was on the right of St James's Square. They were just a couple of paces away when Powerscourt stopped dead in his tracks.

'Lucy, do you mind going in ahead of me? There's just something I've got to do.'

Lady Lucy gazed at her husband with a mixture of exasperation and affection. 'You're not going to be long, are you?' she said anxiously. She remembered the stories of Francis disappearing through the kitchens at a very grand Foreign Office dinner some years before. She distinctly recalled him vanishing again at a reception given by the Archbishop of Canterbury in Lambeth Palace, leaving her alone making small talk with the Archbishop's wife until he reappeared some hours later when the reception had long ended. Business, he had said cryptically. She looked desperately around St James's Square. Had Francis spotted some old army acquaintance? Was his closest friend Johnny Fitzgerald, recently gone to Spain on holiday, returned to lurk beneath the trees in the central garden?

As her husband strode off to the opposite side of the square, she knew. The answer was over there in the corner. Did Francis have any books to return? He hadn't brought them with him. Then she remembered him telling her of his conversation with Thomas Jenkins, closest friend of the late Christopher Montague. He, Montague, had sometimes said that his favourite place in London was the reading room of the London Library in St James's Square.

Lady Lucy was shown into the grand drawing room on the first floor. Rosalind, Lady Pembridge greeted her effusively. 'Lucy, my dear, how very nice to see you! How are the children?' Lady Lucy had barely started to reply when the other two sisters chimed in, almost in unison.

'Where is Francis?' said Mary Burke and Eleanor, Powerscourt's youngest sister, married to a sea captain in the West Country.

'Francis? He said he'd be here in a moment,' said Lady

Lucy, knowing all too well there was nothing Powerscourt's sisters enjoyed more than complaining about him.

'He's disappeared again. Honestly!' said Rosalind.

'I thought he'd grown out of all that by now,' said Mary, looking at Lady Lucy as if she should have taught him better manners after seven years of marriage.

'How very inconsiderate. Typical Francis, spoiling a nice luncheon party,' said Eleanor.

'He must have a new case,' said William Burke who knew rather better than the three sisters how difficult Powerscourt's job could be. 'Is that so, Lucy?'

'It is,' said Lady Lucy, smiling gratefully at her brother-in-law. 'He does have a new case. And at the moment, he's completely in the dark.'

'Luncheon won't wait,' said Rosalind imperiously. 'The soup might keep but the lamb will not. Will Francis be here for the soup, do you think, Lucy?'

'I'm sure he will,' said Lucy bravely. Privately she rather doubted it.

Her husband had reached the inquiry desk that ran round half the entrance hall of the London Library. Portraits of Carlyle and Dickens, founder members, lined the walls. In the centre of the room a flotilla of index cards, housed in great wooden containers, filed away the secrets of the library's contents. Was the librarian available to speak to him, he inquired? He assured the young man that he, Lord Francis Powerscourt, had been a member for many years. He wished to consult the librarian on a matter of the utmost delicacy. Michael Stock, the librarian, he was told, could speak to him in a few minutes. Powerscourt glanced anxiously at his watch. The first course was only minutes away.

'How can we help you, Lord Powerscourt?' Stock was a slim man of middle years with a worried expression and very strong glasses. He pulled from time to time at the corners of his large moustache.

'I am an investigator, Mr Stock,' he began. 'At present I am looking into the death of a young man called Christopher Montague who was a member here. He was murdered. You may have read about it in the papers. I know he was a regular visitor here. One of his friends told me the reading room upstairs was his favourite place in London.'

'I was truly sorry to hear of his death,' said Stock. 'The library sent a wreath, you know. He was very popular here with all the staff.'

'The reason for my visit is this,' Powerscourt went on, casting a surreptitious look at his watch. Damn! They must be on the first course by now. 'I wonder if it would be a simple matter for you to discover which books he had recently borrowed from the library. Some of his books and all his papers were removed from his rooms when he was murdered. If I knew what he had been working on at the time of his death, then it might advance my cause. At present,' he smiled a deprecating smile, 'I am operating rather in the dark.'

'I do hope', said Stock, rather fiercely, 'that none of our books were among those removed from his quarters. Members are only permitted to keep them for a month.'

Powerscourt wondered if the London Library had a system of fining deceased members for the books they had not returned.

'It is not the normal library practice to disclose what volumes have been borrowed by individual members.' Powerscourt suddenly wondered if there were secret stacks of erotica hidden away in the bowels of the building. 'However,' Stock hurried on, suspecting that his earlier comments might not have been altogether appropriate, 'I am sure we can make an exception in this case. If you can give us a few minutes, I am sure we can help you.'

Stock hurried out into his entrance hall. Powerscourt could hear him giving instructions to his staff.

Across the square the soup plates had been cleared away. 'Lucy,' asked Rosalind Pembridge, 'one course down, only three to go. Any prospect of Francis putting in an appearance, do you suppose?'

'Too bad, too bad,' chorused the other two sisters.

Lady Lucy was not going to join the accusations against her husband. She would stand by him, whatever barbs were thrown. 'I think we should just carry on,' she said. 'As if he wasn't here.'

'That's just the point.' Eleanor was quick off the mark. 'He isn't here. Perhaps he's been abducted by some villains.'

'Don't be absurd,' said William Burke. 'This is St James's Square, not Shoreditch.'

Stock trotted back into his office, a pile of borrowing slips in his hand. 'Now then, Lord Powerscourt. This is what we're looking for. And I think Garson here may be able to help further.' Garson was the young man Powerscourt had first talked to in the entrance hall.

'Life of Giovanni Bellini. German author. Life of Giorgione. Another German author. Both translated. Life of Titian. Italian author. Vasari, *On Technique*. And there were two volumes he asked us to obtain from a good Italian source in London. He collected those shortly before his death.'

'Forgive me for asking for yet more information when you have been so helpful already,' said Powerscourt, 'but do you have dates for these borrowings?'

Powerscourt was taking notes now. He saw that all the volumes had been taken out the day after the preview of the de Courcy and Piper Gallery's exhibition of Italian

Old Masters. He inquired about the Italian books on order from another source. Had they been ordered on the same day?

'Yes, sir,' said Garson the young assistant. 'They were.'

'And what,' said Powerscourt eagerly, 'were their titles?'

'Roughly translated, they were called *How to Make Your Own Old Masters*,' said Garson, 'and *The Art of Forging Paintings*. Both published in Rome in the eighteenth century, believed to be contemporary manuals on how to forge Old Masters for English visitors on the Grand Tour, sir.'

'Were they indeed?' said Powerscourt, feeling pleased that a thin shaft of light had opened up on his investigation. 'And what was the other intelligence you have, Mr Garson? Not that you haven't been very helpful already.' He took another surreptitious look at his watch. Christ! They must be on the pudding by now.

'Only this, my lord,' said Garson nervously. 'Mr Montague talked to me quite a lot when he was here. I used to help him find books and that sort of thing. He told me the morning he took those books out,' Garson shuddered slightly, 'that he was going to be the co-founder of a new magazine. He wanted to know if the library would take out a subscription.'

'Did he tell you who the other founder was, Garson?' Powerscourt was feeling rather hungry now. He wondered if Rosalind would have saved him any lunch.

'He did not, my lord. I'm afraid I have no idea.'

Powerscourt thanked the librarians and hurried across St James's Square. It was almost half-past two.

'How very nice of you to put in an appearance, Francis,' said Lady Rosalind, surveying him severely from the top of the table, 'only two hours late.'

'Such a pity we have to leave in a moment,' said Mary.

'And to think that you used to lecture us when we were

small about being punctual and the importance of good manners,' said Eleanor. 'You were always going on about being on time and good manners.'

Lady Lucy sensed a sudden wrath coming over her husband. Francis very seldom lost his temper, the last occasion about four years ago. She patted him affectionately on the knee. For a fraction of a second Powerscourt wanted to shout at his three sisters. He was trying to find a murderer who might strike again. They were merely concerned with punctuality. Beyond the safety of their front doors and the railings around the square there was a dangerous world where people put pieces of picture cord or piano wire round other people's necks and pulled until their victim could breathe no longer. He didn't think that was very good manners. Somebody had to do the dirty work to keep the world secure for society and its rituals.

But he didn't. He smiled apologetically at the assembled company. 'My apologies for being late,' he said. 'I had very important work to do in the London Library across the Square. I must have the food of the penitent if you have such provision. Bread and cheese perhaps? Humble pie and pickles?'

Edmund de Courcy believed he could compile a selling manual based entirely on the talents of William Alaric Piper. Piper was a maestro in his field. He had different voices, different styles depending on his victim. He could cajole. He could bribe. He could bully. He could inspire. He could flatter. He could rhapsodize about the beauty of paintings he was selling. He could be scornful about the ones he was buying. Often the painting would be the same.

Now de Courcy and Piper were sitting with James Hammond-Burke in the morning room of Truscott Park. De Courcy and Piper were on the sofa to the left of the fireplace, Piper in a dark blue suit and sparkling black boots. Hammond-Burke faced them in an armchair with horse hair falling out of the side. Paintings of previous Hammond-Burkes stood on either side of a vast mirror. There was a large crack running down the left-hand side of the glass. The Raphael, still in its wrapping paper, sat incongruously between de Courcy and Piper.

'Mr Hammond-Burke,' began Piper, purring in his most ingratiating tone, 'let me tell you what a pleasure, nay, more than a pleasure, what an honour it has been to have enjoyed the company of your Raphael for the brief period it has been our privilege to care for it. The curves! The colours! The innocence! The beauty! Truly we are blessed that this masterpiece has survived the ravages of time.'

Hammond-Burke made as if to speak. Piper pressed on. 'We have, of course, brought this beautiful object back to you. Only you can be the final arbiter of its fate. We have consulted the finest experts in London about its provenance. Neither you nor I, of course, would doubt for a second that it is a genuine Raphael, but I do not need to tell you that we live in suspicious times. There is always some charlatan prepared to gainsay, to contradict the evidence of our own eyes and our own hearts, our very souls, in fact, that this *Holy Family* is really the work of Raphael. The experts have only confirmed what we knew – that it is genuine. And that means, demeaning though it is to mention money in the presence of such glory . . .' William Alaric Piper paused to cast a reverential glance of worship at the brown paper and string beside him, '. . . that the painting will be valued at its true worth.'

Piper paused again. Hammond-Burke seized his moment 'How much?' he said. It was, de Courcy remembered, exactly the same phrase Hammond-Burke had employed on his previous visit. This was a perfect moment for connoisseurs of the Piper style. De Courcy doubted if the high-flown rhetoric, the gushing Piper would serve now. Hammond-Burke was not a man to be moved by the rhetorical tricks of a Demosthenes or a Cicero or a William Alaric Piper. But he could scarcely change character in mid flow.

Piper did not hesitate for a second. His reply was as blunt as the question. 'Forty-five thousand pounds,' he said. Then he paused briefly. He fiddled about in his breast pocket and passed over a cheque to his host.

Hammond-Burke looked at it. It was probably the largest cheque he had ever seen in his life. Pay James Hammond-Burke, it said, the sum of forty-five thousand pounds. De Courcy wondered if Piper had a series of cheques in his pocket, made out for smaller, maybe even larger, sums. How did he know he was pulling the right cheque out? It would be, to say the least, unfortunate if the written figures were ten thousand pounds less than the spoken word.

'Thank you,' said William Hammond-Burke, his eyes drawn magnetically to the figures on the cheque. 'But I have a few questions for you, Mr Piper.' He looked as if he might be going to ask for more money. 'Is that your final offer?' he said.

Piper leaned forward confidentially in his sofa. 'Mr Hammond-Burke,' he went on, 'believe me when I tell you this. I have loved paintings all my life. In many ways they are my life, my inspiration.' Get on with the business, thought de Courcy to himself. 'It has always been our policy to offer the possessors of such masterpieces the very highest prices. Only on the train on the way down here Edmund was suggesting a lower figure. A considerably lower figure, Mr Hammond-Burke.'

Piper waited to let the thought of a lower figure take centre stage in Hammond-Burke's mind. Then he leaned back into the sofa once more. 'But I overruled him. That is the figure I propose. Not a penny more, but certainly, undoubtedly, not a penny less.'

De Courcy was watching Hammond-Burke's face very closely. Greed and anxiety, in equal portion, passed across his features.

'What will you sell it for?' he asked.

De Courcy sat back and watched the play unfold. He had the best seats in the house. Which Piper would come forth now?

'I have no idea,' he said. De Courcy knew that was a lie. Piper had at least one American millionaire, William P. McCracken of the Boston railroads, in his sights. Maybe there were more.

'It is impossible to say.' Piper shook his head rather sadly. 'It depends on the market, on who wishes to buy at any given time. Sad and regrettable though you and I would regard it, Mr Hammond-Burke, objects of great beauty like your exquisite Raphael are as subject to the whims, the ups and downs of the market as any other commodity like wheat or potatoes. It might sell for fifty thousand pounds. I should be surprised if it did.'

I'll bet you'd be bloody well surprised, you old fraud, thought Edmund de Courcy, you're already thinking of seventy-five or eighty thousand for the contents of the brown paper and the string.

'Equally it could sell for forty thousand, or thirty-five thousand, even as low as thirty thousand. Sometimes it takes years to find the right buyer. My honest advice to you, Mr Hammond-Burke, would be to take the forty-five thousand now.'

Hammond-Burke stared at the floor. We could lose it all, thought de Courcy, the whole thing could unravel rather like the string on the parcel in the next few seconds.

William Alaric Piper was equal to the task. 'We have a further proposition to put you, Mr Hammond-Burke,' he continued, 'if you decide to sell, that is. We would like to send down one of our experts to make a proper catalogue of your paintings. Maybe there are other masterpieces hidden away. I have often known it to happen. Work by an unknown English artist may turn out to be a Gainsborough, some obscure Venetian may turn out to be a Giorgione after all. Our man would conduct a proper search of the house and examine everything. The results would be bound and presented to you with the family crest on the front. Gainsboroughs and Giorgiones might not fetch as much as a Raphael, but they certainly run into tens of thousands of pounds.'

Piper paused to gauge the effect of a possible second bite of the cherry. Hammond-Burke looked down at the cheque in his hand.

'Very good, gentlemen,' he said. 'You have persuaded me. I accept your offer.'

6

Lord Francis Powerscourt and Johnny Fitzgerald, recently returned from Spain, were playing chess at a small table by the window in Markham Square. Bright shafts of sunlight were falling across the room, casting Lady Lucy's face into deep shadow on the sofa. Powerscourt and Fitzgerald had served together in the army in India. They had the special closeness of men who had saved each other's life in battle.

Nobody could have accused Johnny Fitzgerald of being a cautious chess player. He deployed his pieces with great vigour, forever seeking the advantage. '*L'audace*,' he would mutter to himself from time to time, like some headstrong French cavalry commander, '*toujours l'audace*,' as his forces rolled forward up the board.

Powerscourt was more cautious, more patient. He would trap the Fitzgerald advances in thickets of pawns, where they would be clinically captured by marauding knights. He always took great care to guard his King. When he finally advanced it would often only be after a prolonged siege where the Fitzgerald battalions had hurled themselves in vain against the castle walls.

But on this occasion it looked as if the rash were going to triumph over the cautious. The Fitzgerald squadrons, lubricated by regular canteens of Chateau de Beaucastel, were in the ascendant. Left under his command he had his Queen, two rooks, a knight and a solitary bishop to bless his endeavours. He had a couple of lonely pawns, one on each side of the board. Johnny never bothered much about his pawns, sacrificing them recklessly in his advances. Powerscourt had lost his Queen. He had two castles and one knight, and five foot soldier pawns remaining on the field of battle. He was always very careful about his pawns. Powerscourt's King was under heavy attack on the right-hand side of the field.

'How long is it since I beat you at chess, Francis?' said Fitzgerald, preparing already for the sack of the beleaguered citadel, the feast following the victory.

'I think it was about five years ago, Johnny,' said Powerscourt, staring with great concentration at his knight. 'But I'm not finished yet. I shall fight till the last pawn has been slain.'

'Check,' said Fitzgerald, moving his Queen three ranks down the board. The set had been made in India and the Queen was a particularly terrifying figure, resembling, Powerscourt often said, what Queen Boadicea must have looked like when she rode into battle.

Powerscourt hid his King behind a couple of pawns. The threatened monarch was now half-way up the board on the right-hand side. Fitzgerald began moving his knight forward for the final attack. Lady Lucy came to watch the end of the battle, her hand resting lightly on her husband's shoulder. Powerscourt moved one of his castles two squares to the left.

'You could resign now, Francis,' said Johnny Fitzgerald graciously. 'Save you the trouble of playing on till the bloody end. Save your troops from the massacre.'

'No, thank you,' said Powerscourt with a smile. He moved his knight forward. The knight was protected by the castle.

'Check,' he said. It was completely unexpected. Was this a desperate move to gain time? Or had Powerscourt snatched victory from the jaws of defeat?

The full impact of Powerscourt's knight's move hit Fitzgerald at the very centre of his strength. It was a fork. The King was in check and had to move. Or the piece checking could be removed by one of the Fitzgerald forces. But none of them were in a position to do that. And the Queen, Fitzgerald's gaudy caparisoned Queen, was on the other end of the fork, the audacious knight protected by Powerscourt's castle. Any piece rash enough to take the knight, after the destruction of the Queen, would itself be blown to pieces by Powerscourt's castle.

Johnny Fitzgerald laughed. 'Well, I'll be damned,' he said, 'just when I thought I had you in the bag, you've escaped! Houdini comes to the chessboard!'

He could have fought on. But he knew that very soon Powerscourt would convert one of his pawns into a new Queen. Then it would only be a matter of time. In a single move the balance of advantage had switched.

'I shall spare my men the humiliation of captivity and exile,' said Fitzgerald, striking a pose like Brutus in one of his nobler moments, 'I resign.'

The combatants shook hands. Lady Lucy patted them both in the back. 'An excellent game,' she said. 'I think you should have won, Johnny. But the devious old Francis got you in the end!'

The footman knocked on the door and delivered a letter, addressed in a flowing hand, to Lord Francis Powerscourt, 25 Markham Square, Chelsea.

'From the President of the Royal Academy', it said on the letterhead. Powerscourt read it aloud. '"My dear Powerscourt, I promised to let you know anything I heard about the sad death of Christopher Montague. A piece of gossip reached me earlier today. I cannot vouch for its accuracy, nor would I wish to comment upon the morality of this intelligence. But my conscience would not let me rest if I did not inform you. At the time of his death Christopher Montague was said to be having an affair with a married woman in London. The husband is said not to be compliant. I do not have the name. I trust that the work of an investigator is not normally so sordid. Yours, Frederick Lambert."'

Powerscourt passed the letter over to Johnny Fitzgerald who now knew all that Powerscourt did about the strange death of Christopher Montague.

'This could be very important,' said Powerscourt. 'We are still in the dark about the dead man. We assume, from what they said in the London Library, that he was writing an article about forgery when he died. But we don't know what sort of forgery. He could have been going to say that all the Florentine Old Masters in the National Gallery were fakes, or copies, or some other form of misattribution. He could have been intending to attack the curator of a museum somewhere. They're like historians, these art people, nothing they like more than attacking each other.'

'Killing each other?' suggested Fitzgerald cheerfully. He was licking his wounds from the chess game with further draughts of Chateau de Beaucastel.

'I don't know,' replied Powerscourt. 'Garrotting somebody might be more likely to come from an angry husband than an art historian.'

'I tell you what, Francis,' said Fitzgerald, 'I'm going to enlist my auntie in this investigation. She's got a lot of paintings.'

'Is that the auntie who keeps the back copies of the *Illustrated London News*?' asked Powerscourt with a smile. He remembered a journey to Venice in search of a Lord Edward Gresham without a photo of his suspect. Fitzgerald had found him at the front of the train seconds before it left and pressed a copy of the *Illustrated London News*, complete with Gresham photograph, into his hand. Seven years later Powerscourt could still remember the words. 'She collects all these magazines, my auntie. She's got rooms full of them. She says they'll be valuable in the years to come. She's quite mad. She's potty . . .'

'The same auntie, Auntie Winifred,' said Fitzgerald. He shook his head as he thought of the eccentricities of his relative. 'She keeps all the paintings in the attic,' he said. 'God knows why she doesn't keep them on the walls like any normal human being. She says they'll be safer there, the burglars won't be able to see them.'

Lady Lucy smiled. 'Is she quite old, your aunt, Johnny?'

'I think she's about a hundred and three,' said Fitzgerald. 'well, not quite that. But she is undoubtedly very old.' Fitzgerald finished his glass and peered out into the light fading over Markham Square. 'We've got a bit of a problem here,' he went on. 'We don't know what kind of people they are, these art dealers and art experts. Sir Frederick up at the Royal Academy has offered to help, I know. But if they were army people, or society people or even City people, we'd know what kind of persons we're dealing with. We don't with this lot. Don't you agree, Francis?'

'I do,' said Powerscourt. 'But I'm not sure what good a hundred-and-three-year-old auntie is going to be. She doesn't have telepathic powers, or anything like that, does she?'

Fitzgerald gazed back to the chessboard, his King lying on its side, a magnificent Mughal crown and sceptre lying in the dust of the battlefield. 'What's real? What's fake? What's genuine? What's a forgery? Are these art dealers going to say one is the other? Or the other way round, if you see what I mean? Are they

76

genuine? Or are they fakes too? My auntie has in her collection one genuine twenty-four carat Titian. She has one Leonardo which everybody says is not a Leonardo at all. I think I'll take the fake Leonardo round the art galleries to see what price it would fetch. That might be very interesting indeed.'

'Excellent, Johnny, very good.'

'And what is your next move, Francis?' asked Lady Lucy, looking carefully at her husband.

'I am going to Oxford, Lucy. That young man who came here, Thomas Jenkins, I suspect he has been telling me a lot of lies. I am going to the city of dreaming spires and lost causes to find out the truth about the late Christopher Montague.'

William Alaric Piper was waiting for his new American friend William P. McCracken outside the de Courcy and Piper Gallery in Old Bond Street. He looked again at his watch. Ten minutes to go. But then Americans were known for arriving early sometimes. Piper reviewed his courtship of the Boston railroad king. He had secured an introduction by the simple expedient of sitting next to him at breakfast one morning at the Piccadilly Hotel. This manoeuvre was easier to accomplish once some banknotes had been disbursed to the hotel staff. From there it had been a short step to a weekend in a very grand country house near Leatherhead. The house belonged to Piper's banker, and as the pictures from the de Courcy and Piper Gallery on Lord Anstruther's walls had not yet been paid for, such invitations, an enormous advantage in the seduction of rich American clients, were easy to obtain.

He had taken McCracken to the National Gallery. They had been greeted warmly by senior members of the gallery staff who had offered to close off any particular sections McCracken and Piper might want to see.

'We couldn't possibly let you do that.' Piper had beamed happily at the recipients of his earlier largesse. 'We couldn't keep the ordinary citizens of London from their artistic heritage.'

'Now, Mr McCracken,' Piper had said, leading his new friend up the National Gallery steps, 'I can tell that you are a man of considerable refinement. Your compatriots, as you know, are beginning to buy pictures from Europe in considerable numbers.' He paused before the entrance to the Italian Old Masters. 'They are buying the wrong things, Mr McCracken. They buy mediocre works by the Barbizon school, people like Rosa Bonheur and Constant Troyon, the French peasantry transferred to canvas. Can a group of cows sitting about in a field, literally chewing the cud, compare with the works of Leonardo and Raphael? Can a group of peasant girls, carrying strange French produce in baskets on their heads, be compared with the landscapes of a Rubens or a Gainsborough? Art is meant to uplift, to transcend, to make us raise our eyes towards the glory of man and his achievements, not to contemplate the mud on our own boots.'

William P. McCracken nodded sadly. Only the year before he had paid a lot of money for his Troyon. It reminded him of the fields where the McCracken family farmstead had stood on the plains of Iowa before the railroads took him away. Maybe he would have to sell it. Or hide it away in one of the attics.

Piper led him towards a dark Crucifixion by Tintoretto, a suffering Christ surrounded by the two thieves, weeping women in anguish on the ground.

'Why is it so damned dark?' said McCracken, peering at the picture. 'If this Tintoretto guy wanted us to feel sorry for what was going on there why did he paint it so we can hardly see the damned thing? It all looks pretty upsetting, what you can see of it. Not sure Mrs

McCracken would want anything so sad in her house, Mr Piper, not sure at all.'

McCracken had admired a group of Venetian portraits hung together on a side wall.

'Now these,' he had said to Piper, 'these are really fine. This red guy, Count whatever he's called, looks rather like my banker back home in Concord, Massachusetts. And that one over there, Doge Lorenzo is he called? He looks like he was a mighty fine businessman. What do you say to half a million dollars for the four? Would you get a reduction for the bulk buying?'

McCracken was used to obtaining heavy discounts for rails purchased in great quantities. Maybe the same principle should apply for the four pictures.

Piper had explained that none of the paintings in the National Gallery were for sale. He led McCracken to the National Gallery Raphael, the *Ansidei Madonna*. A grey arch framed the picture. Behind it a flat Italian panorama lay bathed in a gentle sunlight. In the centre, seated on a wooden throne that extended right to the top of the archway, was a Madonna in a red dress with a dark blue cape. Her right hand cradled an infant Christ, her left hand, finger outstretched, pointed to a page of scripture. To her right John the Baptist, better clad, Piper thought, than usual, in a brown tunic and a red wrap, gazed up at the Madonna. On her left the studious figure of St Nicholas of Bari, crook in hand, great cloak fastened with a rich brooch, was consulting the scriptures.

'Look at it,' whispered Piper. 'The colours, the composition, the way the arch frames the whole so perfectly.' McCracken seemed impressed. 'Above all,' Piper whispered on, 'look at the grace, the restrained beauty, the tranquil expression on the Madonna's face.

'And,' Piper went on, 'think of this, Mr McCracken. The *Ansidei Madonna* is one of the most expensive paintings in the world. The National Gallery paid seventy thousand pounds for it less than twenty years ago. Seventy thousand pounds.'

'They wouldn't take a hundred grand for it now? Cash rather than stock options?' McCracken asked without much hope. Piper assured him that the Raphael was not for sale. Sadly he informed the American that not even cash would make the gallery part with it, so popular had it become. But inwardly Piper rejoiced. McCracken, if not completely hooked, had swallowed a fairly hefty section of bait. It only remained to bring the fish ashore.

And there he was now, in a bright check suit and brightly polished brown brogues, advancing towards the front door of de Courcy and Piper.

'Mr McCracken, how very kind of you to call upon us in our humble gallery!' Piper was his normal effusive self.

'Kind of you to invite me,' said McCracken, leaving his coat with a porter in the hall.

Piper said he proposed to take his friend round the Venetian exhibition still on show. He had closed the gallery to the public for the morning. And then, said Piper, taking McCracken by the arm to steer him towards the Italians, then he had something very special to show him in the private viewing area on the top floor. Nothing, Piper assured McCracken, was for sale. All the items on display were marked down elsewhere.

At first everything went well. William P. McCracken was much taken by the portraits. 'Seems to me, Mr Piper,' he said, staring at a *Portrait of a Man* attributed to Titian, 'that human nature doesn't change very much over the years. No, sir. Man over there looks rather like a character I came across in business some years ago. Bastard tried to close down my railroad. Damned near succeeded too.'

Then disaster struck. They had turned a corner and arrived at Piper's favourite painting in the exhibition, described as the *Sleeping Venus* by Giorgione. The background was an idyllic Italian landscape, a plain in the centre with some distant mountains. On the right a small town in brown climbed lazily up a hill. Lying across the centre of the picture on a satin sheet with a dark red pillow was a woman. She was completely naked. Sensuous and sensual, the sleeping Venus looked as though she had dropped down from heaven for a peaceful afternoon nap in the Italian countryside.

Piper was about to launch himself on another of his panegyrics. Afterwards he thanked God he had waited, as he said to himself, for the beauty of the painting to sink in.

William P. McCracken turned rather red. He moved away from the picture and strode back into the other room. 'Mr Piper,' he said, 'I am deeply shocked. I am, I would have you know, the senior elder of the Third Presbyterian Church on Lincoln Street in Concord, Massachusetts. Yes, sir. I cannot tell you what the reaction of my fellow elders would be if they knew I was the possessor of such a painting. The Third Presbyterian would not like it at all. And Mrs McCracken and the Misses McCracken, why sir, they would be shocked to the centre of their being. The Good Lord did not make woman to lie about the countryside without a stitch on.'

Privately William Alaric Piper was appalled at the hypocrisy of these American millionaires. He felt sure that they broke at least three of the Ten Commandments every day of their working lives. Thou shalt not steal. Thou shalt not bear false witness against thy neighbour. Thou shalt not covet thy neighbour's house, nor his ox, nor his ass, nor his railroad lines, nor his steel plant nor his banks, nor any thing that is thy neighbour's. He wanted to tell McCracken that the same artist who painted the *Sleeping Venus* had painted some of the most beautiful Madonnas in the world. But he did not. He knew he had no choice but to abase himself before the false gods of the Third Presbyterian of Lincoln Street in Concord, Massachusetts.

'Forgive me, Mr McCracken, please forgive me. I have no wish, no wish at all, to offend your religious beliefs or those of your family and friends in Concord. Perhaps I should have warned you beforehand that sometimes these Renaissance artists painted people in the nude. Your customs are different from ours. Your view of what is acceptable is different from ours. We must respect that. Please forgive me.'

McCracken smiled. 'No need to apologize, my friend. We shall agree to differ. Maybe times will change and my fellow countrymen will come to adopt the different values of Europe. We shall see. But come, you have something else to show me on the top floor, I believe.'

'Of course.' Piper felt relieved. His eternal optimism returned as he led McCracken up to the private viewing room on the top floor. Piper took a large bunch of keys from his pocket and opened the door. The room was almost completely dark. Deep red velvet curtains were drawn tightly against the morning sun of Old Bond Street. Piper pressed a switch. It was like a shrine. Placed at the far end of the room on a large easel draped with velvet was the Hammond-Burke *Holy Family*. The lights played delicately on the curves and the colours of Raphael's masterpiece, originally meant to hang on the walls of an Italian church, now waiting patiently in the top floor of a London gallery to captivate American tycoons and separate them from their dollars.

'Isn't it beautiful! Isn't it divine!' whispered Piper, praying that the elders of the Third Presbyterian didn't believe in the commandment about not making any graven image, or any likeness of any thing that is in heaven above, or that is in the earth beneath. The Madonna looked down with a practical, maternal love at the child beneath her.The sheep had a contemplative air, looking steadily out of the picture to the world outside. Lamb of God that taketh away the sins of the world, have mercy on us. The waters of the lake behind the Holy Family were calm, the trees around the edge casting long shadows across the surface. The horrors of the Agony in the Garden, the hill of Golgotha, the nails being driven into the Cross were far in the future. Piper waited to see what McCracken would say.

'Mr Piper,' he began, 'you said you had something special up here. Boy, you certainly have. Is this for sale?'

Piper shook his head slowly. He knew he could get a splendid price right here and now. But he needed McCracken to want the painting so much that it hurt. He wanted him to lie in his bed at night aching to own it, to possess it, to take this European glory back across the Atlantic. It couldn't be made easy for him. But once he had felt the lure, almost the disease of collecting, he would come back for more.

'I am bound to offer it to another,' said Piper sadly. 'Believe me, Mr McCracken, if there was any way I could let you have this picture, particularly after the offence I caused you downstairs, I would do so.'

'Eighty thousand pounds, Mr Piper. That's my offer. Eighty thousand pounds. Cash, not stock. You said that Raphael in the National Gallery went for seventy thousand pounds. Let nobody say that William P. McCracken doesn't offer a fair price.'

'All I can do,' said Piper, wringing his hands, ' – how difficult this is, how much I hate to disappoint you – is to speak to the other party and get back to you.'

'Can you do that this afternoon?' Piper shook his head. 'Tomorrow?' Piper still shook his head. 'Two or three days?' Again William Alaric Piper shook his head. The longer William P. McCracken was left to wait, the greater would be his desire to possess the Raphael, the greater the possibility of future sales.

'I shall get back to you as fast as I can. I cannot say when that might be. But I shall make it as quick as I can.'

Piper turned off the lights and led the way downstairs. The lights faded quite slowly. For a long time the Madonna's features glowed out of the frame. Then her face and her halo slowly vanished from sight. Raphael's *Holy Family* waited in the darkness for more pilgrims to pay tribute to their beauty.

7

Thomas Jenkins of Emmanuel College was waiting for Powerscourt at Oxford railway station. 'I hope you're wearing a stout pair of boots, Lord Powerscourt,' he said cheerfully, 'we're going for a walk.'

Powerscourt remembered Jenkins saying he would take him to Christopher Montague's favourite place in Oxford. He wondered if he was in for a full tour of the more ancient quadrangles, or an inspection of some of the spectacular gardens or some old and dusty library.

But Jenkins led him away from the town. They crossed over a railway bridge and there in front of them was a huge open space. Jenkins pointed dramatically to his right towards the buildings of the city.

'Over there, Lord Powerscourt, are the walls of Jericho. Here in front of us is Port Meadow, one of the oldest places in Oxford.'

Powerscourt heard no trumpets. But he saw a vast open space of empty land with wild horses and cows roaming about the rich pasture. Two hundred yards away to his left the river snaked its way beneath the hanging trees.

'This was Christopher's favourite place in Oxford, Lord Powerscourt,' said Jenkins, pointing across Port Meadow. 'We used to walk along here, over the river there and along the towpath to an old inn called the Trout for lunch.'

'Let us do the same,' said Powerscourt. 'But why is it still wild? Why has nobody built on it?' Powerscourt's historical curiosity had temporarily won out over the interests of his investigation. A couple of wild horses drew near to the two men. The horses looked at them carefully and trotted off into the meadow.

'The freemen of Oxford have had the right to graze their animals on this stretch of land since the tenth century,' said Jenkins proudly. 'They've held on to it ever since. The right is recorded in the Domesday Book. Before that they say that Bronze Age people used to bury their dead here.'

Jenkins and Powerscourt were crossing the river on an ancient bridge. Small sailing boats were lined up in neat rows, waiting for their masters.

'In a couple of months,' Jenkins went on, 'when winter really sets in, almost all of the meadow is flooded. It's like a huge marsh or bog.'

'Mr Jenkins,' said Powerscourt, stepping smartly out of the way of an approaching trio of cyclists, 'I do not believe you told me the whole truth when we spoke the other day in London.' He looked at his companion severely. Jenkins blushed slightly and stared down at his feet.

'What do you mean, Lord Powerscourt? In what particular?'

Powerscourt smiled at the precise academic usage of 'in what particular'. They were past the trees now. The late October sun was surprisingly warm. 'It may be, of course, that you simply do not know the answers to my questions. But I think you do. There are two particulars. The first is whether Christopher Montague was going to start a new magazine dealing with the fine arts. The second is whether or not he was having an affair with a married woman in London. I suggest, Mr Jenkins . . .' Powerscourt paused to retie his bootlaces. 'I suggest that you consider your answers. We can discuss them more fully when we reach the Trout.'

With that Powerscourt strode ahead up the towpath, overtaking a leisurely canal boat as he went. Ahead was a ruined abbey, the walls covered in ivy, the fading red of the bricks blending in with the landscape.

'Twelfth-century foundation called Godstow Abbey,' said Jenkins grumpily, 'sort of finishing school for the daughters of the nobility. Henry the Second's mistress was a pupil here and met a mysterious death. Maybe that would be a good subject for one of your investigations.'

Powerscourt laughed. 'It's difficult enough investigating mysterious deaths today without asking questions about the past.' He looked back across Port Meadow. The river swirled its tortuous trail through the weeping willows. Far in the distance the spires of Oxford stood out against the sky. An improbable campanile rose above the walls of Jericho. Powerscourt could see why the place had such an appeal.

The beer tasted fruity. Jenkins and Powerscourt were seated by the water's edge in the garden of the Trout. Powerscourt wondered if Johnny Fitzgerald, not quite such a connoisseur of beer as he was of wine, would approve.

'To business, Mr Jenkins,' said Powerscourt. 'I have given you fair warning. You told me you had no idea what he was working on at the time of his death. I think he was writing an article about forgery. It was for a new magazine he was going to found. Surely you must have known something of that?'

Thomas Jenkins took a large mouthful of his beer. 'Well,' he said, and paused. Powerscourt thought he could tell from the look in Jenkins' brown eyes that he had been concealing something, 'Christopher was always talking about founding new magazines. Nothing ever seemed to come of it.'

'With whom? Was it always the same partner?'

'Well, it was always the same chap, actually,' replied Jenkins, 'a man called Lockhart, Jason Lockhart. He's a junior partner in a firm of art dealers called Clarke. They're great rivals of Capaldi's and that new firm of de Courcy and Piper.'

Powerscourt filed the names away. He would write to the President of the Royal Academy on his return. The garden of the Trout was full now, the tables packed, visitors admiring the swirling waters of the mill pond by the bridge.

'And the article on forgers,' Powerscourt went on. 'Did you know anything about that?'

'He might have mentioned something about it,' said Jenkins, taking another swig of his beer. His glass was almost empty. 'But I didn't think it worth telling you about. It was like the magazine. Christopher always had hundreds of schemes in his head at any one time. I didn't mean to mislead you, Lord Powerscourt. There were so many things Christopher talks about.' He stopped. 'Used to talk about.'

'And what about the married woman?' said Powerscourt, raising his voice above the noise. 'Did you think that might be misleading too?'

Jenkins shrugged his shoulders. 'I thought it better to let sleeping dogs lie.'

'What was her name, man? What was she called?'

Thomas Jenkins stared helplessly at Powerscourt. 'You're not going to believe this, Lord Powerscourt. Please don't be angry with me. I don't know her name.'

Powerscourt wanted to bang his fist on the table. He refrained. 'Do you mean that you don't know her Christian name, or you don't know her surname?'

Jenkins looked distraught. 'I don't know her surname,' he said very quietly. 'I never met her.'

'But you knew her Christian name, didn't you?' said Powerscourt.

'She was called Rosalind,' Jenkins whispered.

'And where did she live?'

'She lived in Chelsea.' Powerscourt had to lean forward to catch the name. Good God, he thought. Somewhere in Chelsea, not far from where he lived. Maybe her home was on the other side of Markham Square.

'Do you know what her husband does? Did she have any children? Was she involved in the world of art at all?'

Thomas Jenkins rose from his seat. 'The answer to all those question is don't know, don't know, don't know. And now, if you will forgive me, I am going back to my college. I've done my best. But I'm not going to answer any more questions.'

The entrance hall of the Beaufort Club in Pall Mall was full of Americans. Edmund de Courcy passed quickly through the differing accents, New York, Boston, Chicago, the Midwest. His business was not in the dining room or the smoking room with its large windows and the even larger cigars of the transatlantic visitors. His business was in the basement.

The Beaufort had realized earlier than their competitors along Pall Mall that there was money to be made from the Americans. They had links with the top clubs in all the major cities in America. Financiers, importers, newspapermen, tourists came to the Beaufort and reported home that it was almost like being back in the States. There was American cooking, American whiskey, Cuban cigars. Most important of all there were other Americans to talk to. There was no need in the Beaufort to catch at the nuances of English irony or eat their terrible food. You wouldn't have to talk about cricket. The Beaufort was a home from home, a slice of apple pie in the alien world of London. Many of the Americans felt homesick even going there.

And the Beaufort had the American newspapers and magazines, the *New York Times*, the *Washington Post*, the *Chicago Sun Times*, *Harpers and Queen*, *Vanity Fair*, *The American*. They kept the back copies of all these publications for a year. Sometimes Americans would arrive in London who had spent months in the even more alien climes of France or Italy, Egypt or St Petersburg, Russia, and would want to catch up on events at home.

Edmund de Courcy sat at a small table in the basement with a great pile of America's most fashionable magazines. Within these pages the advertisements for houses started at enormous prices, and no jewellery was on display that cost less than fifty thousand dollars. Here rich America was on display, their mansions, their yachts, their possessions, their wealth flaunted before a jealous world.

Edmund de Courcy was looking for illustrations of two very rich families. Not the husband, or the husband and wife, but husband, wife and children. One such family was the McCrackens, whose husband was, of course, in London, doing business with Edmund's own firm of de Courcy and Piper. The other was a man due to arrive in England in two weeks' time. The Piper intelligence service in New York had given warning that a Lewis B. Black, based in Philadelphia, was on his way. Mr Black may have dwelt in the city of brotherly love but he was said to be the most ruthless steel magnate in all America. His personal fortune – the Piper intelligence service had checked the figures with three different sources – was in excess of one hundred million dollars. And, even more enticing, Mr Black was interested in art.

Nobody knew what kind of art, but a man with that kind of fortune has to collect something.

De Courcy read about society balls in New York. He read of charity dinners in Boston. He read of Lucullan birthday parties in Chicago, and glittering evenings at the Metropolitan Opera. He saw illustrations of the American plutocracy on their yachts, at the weddings of their children and the Commemorative Masses for their dead.

He had gone through four whole months of *The American* before he struck gold. There, in the drawing room of a very grand house, he found an illustration of Mr and Mrs William P. McCracken of Concord, Massachusetts, and their two daughters, aged about eight and ten, a small dog standing alertly beside them. De Courcy tiptoed carefully over to the door to make sure no one was coming. Then he took a small pair of scissors from his pocket and cut the page out of the magazine. He put it inside a large red notebook he had brought with him. The book had slightly larger pages than the magazine. De Courcy didn't want to have to fold it.

Two hours later he was on the verge of giving up. Various Americans had come down to the basement to look up old financial results in the *New York Times* or the football scores in the *Boston Globe*. They had greeted him cheerfully, wishing him a good day as he ploughed through the pile in front of him. But when he found it he was overjoyed. A large photograph showed Mr and Mrs Lewis B. Black, with their twin daughters, outside their new town house on Fifth Avenue. The girls looked about six years old. Mrs Black was wearing a hat composed largely of exotic feathers. Feathers, thought Edmund de Courcy. Hats made of fancy feathers in English portrait paintings. How many of the English Masters had painted such hats in their time? Lawrence, Hoppner,

Romney. Gainsborough, Reynolds. What a treat! Out came the scissors. Mr Lewis B. Black and family joined Mr William P. McCracken and family in Edmund de Courcy's special album.

Powerscourt was scribbling furiously at his writing desk. Jackson, the family footman who had served with his master in India, was waiting discreetly behind the chair. Powerscourt had decided not to call upon Jason Lockhart of Clarke's the art dealers in person. He felt Lockhart might feel constrained in his working surroundings and, for some reason he couldn't pin down, Powerscourt didn't want to show himself yet in the rarefied air of Old Bond Street.

'I am investigating the death of the late Christopher Montague,' he wrote, 'and I feel that you may be able to assist me.' He said nothing of new magazines, of fakes and forgers, of mistresses in the heart of Chelsea. 'If you could fix a time with my man here I should be delighted to see you in 25 Markham Square at your earliest convenience.'

Jackson promised to wait for the reply. Powerscourt found Lady Lucy inspecting the dining room with a worried air. 'Francis,' she said, 'these dining chairs. We've had them for ever so long. But they're beginning to look a bit shabby, don't you think?' Lady Lucy pushed hard at one of the seats. There was a slight wobble, implying that a very heavy person might find themselves sitting unexpectedly on the floor.

Powerscourt was used to these continuous campaigns of domestic improvement. Sometimes he would return home and find that all the furniture in the drawing room had been rearranged. Or that a pair of curtains, previously deemed perfectly satisfactory, had been transferred from his study to a spare bedroom. Once he found that his entire wardrobe had been removed from the bedroom and placed in a closet some yards away down the corridor.

'I just didn't like that wardrobe, Francis,' Lady Lucy had said on that occasion, 'it was so ugly.' Privately Powerscourt wondered if he himself might not be the subject of one of these periodic fits of rearrangement, transferred for ever to the coal hole or the top floor of the stables, thereby guaranteeing the aesthetic perfection of the rest of the house. Sometimes he replied with flippancy, suggesting that the kitchens would work much better if they were transferred into the attics, and that the children should all sleep in the front hall. It would mean that they could get to school quicker. He was reproved for being a domestic Philistine, a non-believer in the search for domestic harmony. In vain did Powerscourt try to tell his wife that perfection was an ideal, like one of Plato's Forms, something to aspire to, a beacon on a distant hill, a vision that could never be achieved, and that all her efforts were doomed to failure.

'You're being absurd, Francis,' Lady Lucy would laugh at him. 'All I'm trying to do is to make our home as nice as possible. You wouldn't want the children growing up surrounded by ugliness, would you?'

Powerscourt decided that instant capitulation was the only solution to the case of the dining-room chairs. 'That looks a bit dangerous, Lucy. I think you'd better replace them straight away.'

Lady Lucy was not accustomed to such rapid victories. Often there would be protests about furniture being able to last a few years longer, sometimes dire and apocalyptic male mutterings about money. She stared hard at her husband's face. Perhaps, as so often, he was teasing her.

'Are you serious?' she said incredulously.

'Yes, I am,' replied her husband. Lady Lucy resolved

to try to find the cause of this immediate acquiescence. If she could identify the reason, then she could time future campaigns to coincide.

'Are you all right, Francis?' said Lady Lucy, worried suddenly that her husband might be ill.

'I'm perfectly all right, my love,' said Powerscourt, giving his wife a quick kiss. 'I'm just in rather a hurry. I've got to get to the Royal Academy. And I want to ask your advice.'

Lady Lucy sat down on one of her dubious dining-room chairs. Powerscourt observed that there hadn't been a moment's hesitation. Were they all in perfectly good condition after all, he wondered? Did just one of them need repair? This was not a battle he was prepared to enter. He banished all thoughts of domesticity from his mind.

'We've got to find somebody in Chelsea, Lucy,' he began. Lady Lucy felt a quick thrill at the use of the word 'we'. Not I. But plural. We.

'Who is this person, Francis?' Lady Lucy smiled.

'All we have,' said Powerscourt, 'is a Christian name. Rosalind. She was having an affair with the late Christopher Montague. Her husband was apparently not compliant. And she lives in Chelsea, this Rosalind. That's it.'

'I could ask Montague's sister,' said Lady Lucy, relieved that the vast tribe of her relations, as Francis referred to them, might come in useful at last.

'You could,' said Powerscourt doubtfully, 'but I have asked the sister already in general terms. She said she didn't know anything about his private life.'

'I see,' said Lady Lucy. 'It's quite tricky, isn't it? You can't very well pin up a notice on Chelsea Town Hall asking for the Rosalind who was having an affair with Christopher Montague to pop round to Markham Square for afternoon tea.'

Powerscourt laughed. 'I wonder about the post,' he said. 'People in those circumstances sometimes spend a lot of time writing to each other, arranging the next meeting, saying how much they miss the other one, that sort of thing. Liable to cause trouble if you leave any of the correspondence lying around, of course.'

Lady Lucy looked suspiciously at her husband. 'Are you an expert in these matters, Francis?'

'Certainly not. I promise you.' Powerscourt laughed. 'But I have been involved in a number of cases where this sort of thing goes on. One chap I heard of even had his messages delivered by carrier pigeon. Of ingenuity in affairs of the heart there is no end.'

'Thomas is a great friend of our postman here,' said Lady Lucy. 'He takes Thomas on his rounds of the square sometimes on Saturday mornings. I've watched Thomas post the mail through the letterboxes. He thinks it's tremendous.'

'Well, the postman might be able to help. But we need Montague's hand on a letter. Those murderers took every scrap of paper out of his flat. We don't know what his handwriting looked like.'

Powerscourt looked at his watch. 'Heavens, Lucy, I'm going to be late. Will you have those new chairs in position when I come back, do you think?'

Lady Lucy laughed. 'Be off with you, furniture Philistine!' she said. But she kissed him warmly as he left.

The gallery of de Courcy and Piper in Old Bond Street was temporarily closed to the public that morning. Opening at eleven o'clock, said the sign outside. All the doors were locked. Edmund de Courcy and William Alaric Piper were in the basement. That door was also locked.

'Only two more to go,' said Piper, panting slightly. He placed a small piece of cloth over a nail on the bottom of a picture frame. He pulled very slightly. The nail did not move. He tried again, pulling fractionally harder. Again the nail did not move.

'Damn these nails!' said Piper. He was reluctant to pull too hard in case damage was done to the painting or the frame. And, as both he and de Courcy knew only too well, one day soon they would have to perform the operation in reverse.

He tried again. Very slowly the nail agreed to part from the frame. De Courcy had a piece of paper ready for it. Bottom row, first from right-hand corner, said the piece of paper. De Courcy placed the nail reverently into its new home. Then he put it into a box. The nails were ordered in the box in the same way they had been in the frame.

'There!' said Piper. The last nail had come out. De Courcy pulled the painting very carefully from its frame. He rolled it into a cylindrical shape and wrapped it in two sheets of linen, specially cut for the purpose. It joined another cylinder on the floor. These two paintings had been part of the de Courcy and Piper Venetian exhibition upstairs. Both had been sold and removed from the show.

'How long has he got?' asked de Courcy.

'I should say up to three weeks. But he works very fast so it may be less,' said Piper, wiping his hands and sliding the box with the nails into a shelf in a safe on the wall. 'I told the new owners they were going off to be cleaned, but that it could take some time. Can he do it in three weeks?'

'Well,' said de Courcy, 'he's going to be pretty busy. I'm sending these two illustrations up there as well.' He showed his partner the two pages he had stolen from the basement of the Beaufort Club.

'The family of William P. McCracken.' Piper peered closely at the page to make sure William P. McCracken and family had not been represented outside the main entrance of the Third Presbyterian Church, Lincoln Street, Concord, Massachusetts. They had not. He breathed again.

'And so this is Mr Lewis B. Black, the king of steel,' said Piper, eyeing up his other prey. 'And Mrs Black! And the Miss Blacks! I can see, Edmund, why you were so excited about the feathers. It's going to be magnificent!'

De Courcy wrapped the two illustrations up. The package would leave London that afternoon, bound for a secret destination known only to de Courcy and Piper. The Black and McCracken families would be accompanied on their journey by the *Portrait of a Man* by Titian and the *Portrait of a Venetian Gentleman* by Zorzi da Castelfranco, better known as Giorgione.

8

Lord Francis Powerscourt stared in disbelief at the paintings on the walls of Sir Frederick Lambert's office. They had been changed around since his last visit. Powerscourt found himself wondering if Lady Lucy had a secret contract to rearrange the furniture here too, popping over from Markham Square to switch round the paintings in the President's office. Hector being dragged round the walls of Troy had disappeared. It had been replaced by an even vaster canvas. In the courtyard of a huge palace servants were rushing towards the centre and placing household objects on a pyre. A magnificent bed was being brought out of a courtyard towards it. Hiding behind a pillar upstairs a distraught Queen stared down below. A courtier was whispering in her ear. In the bottom left a huge man, clad only in a loincloth, his dark skin glistening with oil, was carrying a flaming torch towards the pyre. Dido, one-time lover of Aeneas, reigning Queen of Carthage, was preparing her own immolation.

'Happens every month, Powerscourt.' Sir Frederick had observed Powerscourt looking at the walls with amused interest. 'We change the paintings round. Get fed up with looking at the same thing, even if you've painted it yourself. Maybe especially if you've painted it yourself.'

'A very dramatic work, Sir Frederick,' said Powerscourt politely.

Sir Frederick looked rather ill. His huge frame seemed to be collapsing inwards. The suit was now several sizes too large. The great moustache was still perfectly trimmed but it was drooping. He looked at Powerscourt's letter on his desk.

'Let me begin with these art dealers you asked about, Lord Powerscourt.' He paused and looked up at the pyre on the opposite wall, wondering perhaps about his own more peaceful obsequies. 'What you must realize about these art dealers is that they are in a permanent state of conflict and competition with each other. Clarke's and Capaldi's have been around a long time, of course. De Courcy and Piper are new. I believe de Courcy spends most of his time wandering round the great country houses looking for people who are almost bankrupt but could be saved by selling some of the Old Masters on their walls.' Sir Frederick shook his head sadly. 'Capaldi's have a member of staff whose main job is to read the obituaries in all the major newspapers looking for families who may have to sell up.'

'What about the people who work in these places?' asked Powerscourt. 'What manner of people are they?'

'I wish I could say that they were all devoted lovers of art, Powerscourt. Some of the people at the top are very knowledgeable, of course. For the rest they are just salesmen, but salesmen disguised beneath the finest suits and shirts of Jermyn Street. Younger sons who failed the army examinations – can you imagine? – are quite prevalent. They sound convincing. They look good. They learn the patter and the patois. One of Capaldi's most successful operatives used to sell central heating systems to the aristocracy. But often, the porters who carry the pictures in and out of the building know more than the salesmen.'

'What about the Americans?' asked Powerscourt, surprised at the cynicism of such a leading artistic figure as the President of the Royal Academy. He supposed it came with experience.

'The Americans, my dear Powerscourt, may be starting the biggest change in the art market in living memory.' Sir Frederick paused as he was racked by a terrible coughing fit. His face turned red. He was obviously in considerable discomfort. Powerscourt wondered how long he had left to live. Lambert waved away his sympathy.

'Sorry, Powerscourt. It's part of my illness. Now then, these Americans. They bring enormous amounts of money. I suspect we may be at the very beginning of the biggest buying spree in history. The New World is returning to carry off the artistic heritage of the Old. For the dealers, the opportunities are huge.'

Sir Frederick's face had faded now. The red had turned into a chalky white, the eyes sinking into his head.

'Two last things, Sir Frederick, before I take my leave,' said Powerscourt. 'This magazine that Christopher Montague was going to found with Jason Lockhart of Clarke's. What would the purpose be?'

Sir Frederick laughed. It sounded as if another coughing fit might overcome him. 'War, in Clausewitz' words, is merely the continuation of politics by other means. The magazine would be the same sort of thing, a vehicle for Clarke's to rubbish their opponents, the genuineness of their paintings, the reliability of their attributions. No doubt the other two dealers would shortly have to start magazines of their own. Very good for the printers, no doubt, but unlikely to advance the cause of art.'

'My last question concerns the private affairs of Christopher Montague, Sir Frederick,' said Powerscourt. 'I now know the Christian name of the woman concerned. She was called Rosalind. But I have no surname. Would you, by any chance, have a letter written by Montague? A signature perhaps? An example of his handwriting would be very helpful.'

Sir Frederick looked closely at Powerscourt. He looked as though he might be about to ask how the handwriting could help. But he didn't. He rummaged about in the drawers of his enormous desk.

'This should serve, I think.' He handed over an envelope addressed to himself. 'That,' he said, 'is Montague's hand. I presume you would like to keep it.'

Suddenly Powerscourt felt absolutely certain that Sir Frederick Lambert knew the full name of the mysterious Rosalind. But, for reasons of honour or personal loyalty, he was not prepared to say.

'Sir Frederick,' said Powerscourt, 'forgive me if I sound arrogant when I say that it should only take me a couple of days to discover the surname of this unfortunate lady. I know that you feel bound by honour and human decency to guard the secrets of your colleagues. I respect you for that.' Powerscourt was trying to cut off Lambert's escape routes. 'But we are dealing with murder here. Garrotting may be the work of a professional assassin, hired by a person or persons unknown. The killer or killers may strike again. If, by any chance, you know the surname of this Rosalind, I beg you to tell me. I know it may have unfortunate consequences for the lady in question, but there are more important considerations than the manners and conventions of society. It may save lives.'

Powerscourt stopped. Then he went on quite suddenly, 'I do not need to tell you, Sir Frederick, that the name would be treated with the utmost discretion.'

Sir Frederick Lambert looked sadly at Dido's palace, shortly to be engulfed by the flames. He did not look Powerscourt in the eye but stared at his painting, as if he wanted to improve it.

'Mrs Rosalind Buckley,' he said very quietly. Powerscourt had to strain to catch the address. '64 Flood Street, Chelsea.'

William Alaric Piper was waiting for the American millionaire William P. McCracken in his office in Old Bond Street. Piper was wearing a dark blue pinstripe today over a cream silk shirt with a single rose in his buttonhole. The black shoes were polished to perfection. Eight days had passed since McCracken had offered him eighty thousand pounds for the Raphael Madonna. Piper had told McCracken that he had another buyer with the first refusal on the painting, that McCracken would have to wait.

And what a wait it had been. The American had grown increasingly impatient. At first the letters to Piper from the Piccadilly Hotel had come only twice a day. Then they turned into a flood, four, five, six, or even seven. Piper did not reply to any of them. McCracken began to call at the gallery in person. Mr Piper was not available. Mr Piper was at a meeting on the other side of town. Mr Piper was in the country. Mr Piper was at the National Gallery.

William Alaric Piper had indeed been to the National Gallery, in his brown check suit, three days before. The gallery were most flattered that de Courcy and Piper were prepared to give them the first refusal on Raphael's *Holy Family*. They regretted that they were unable to offer more than seventy thousand pounds. The claims on the public purse, Mr Piper must understand, were many and various. The gallery director did not mention that an election was in the offing. Politicians were always reluctant to spend large sums on paintings before the voters went to the polls. It left them open to charges of extravagance, of wasting taxpayers' money on foreign fripperies, sometimes scantily clad. The director wondered if the dealers would ever work out that the best time to tempt the National Gallery was in the period immediately following an election. Any purchases then would be forgotten by the time of the next one.

So Piper had resolved to put McCracken out of his misery. He knew the American was hooked. Once McCracken felt this overwhelming need, this passion for purchasing the Raphael, he could be lured into other purchases in years to come. McCracken looked perfectly healthy to Piper. Suppose he sold him two or three paintings a year at these sort of prices. A quarter of a million pounds a year. Two and a half million over ten. Five million pounds over twenty years. Piper would have to get hold of the paintings, of course, but two and a half million pounds profit out of one client over twenty years sounded rather good to Piper. And McCracken must have friends. Rich friends whose social jealousy might be aroused by the beautiful paintings on McCracken's walls. Maybe McCracken would build a little gallery as an extension to his vast mansion.

Now William Alaric Piper faced a dilemma. McCracken had offered him eighty thousand pounds, cash, not stock, he remembered. Piper was always doubtful about American stock. Cash was safer. He felt sure that McCracken would go to a hundred thousand, maybe even a hundred and twenty, to secure the *Holy Family*. He could say his other potential client had raised his offer. Tempting, very tempting.

There was a knock on the door. William P. McCracken, in a blue check suit, shook Piper warmly by the hand. 'Why, Mr Piper,' he said, 'I reckon it would be easier to get to see the President of the United States than it is to see you!'

'Do you see your President often, Mr McCracken?' said Piper with a smile.

'Sometimes I have to see him when I feel my competitors are being unreasonable, Mr Piper,' said McCracken, taking out a gigantic cigar. 'And I usually see him six months before an election in case he needs any help with his campaign funds. But what of the Raphael, Mr Piper? I don't mind telling you that I've lost more sleep about that painting than I ever did over the purchase of the Boston to Hartford railroad three years ago. And that could have left me a broken man!'

'The Raphael is yours, Mr McCracken. I managed, not without some difficulty, to persuade my other client to withdraw. I have had to promise him something very special in return. And I had to agree a slight increase in the purchase price, unlikely to trouble a serious collector like yourself. For eighty-five thousand pounds in cash, Mr McCracken, one of the world's most beautiful paintings is yours. I must say I envy you. The thought of being able to look at that Raphael every day for the rest of my life, in the morning sunlight, in the heat of the day, in the afternoon shadows, would fill me with such joy.'

William P. McCracken pumped Piper's hand in a vigorous embrace. 'From the bottom of my heart I thank you, Mr Piper,' he said. 'Why, we should celebrate. Let me take you out for a bottle of champagne!'

Piper pleaded the press of business. But he did agree to dinner at the Beaufort Club that evening. 'Looking to the future,' said Piper, 'I cannot promise, Mr McCracken. But I believe I may shortly have something which would interest you. It may come to nothing, but the work is divine.'

'I'd be very interested in any future propositions, Mr Piper.'

William Alaric Piper leaned back in his chair. 'Let me offer a word of advice, now you have joined the ranks of the great collectors, Mr McCracken. As you know, there is no possible parallel between the world of business and the world of art. But a great businessman, a great industrialist such as yourself, will have a balanced portfolio of investments, not only railroads but steel, not only steel but mining and exploration, not only mining and exploration but banking and property and so on. When one goes down, the other goes up. In the same way the great collectors hold a wide variety of the great Masters in their portfolios. Not only Raphaels but perhaps Giovanni Bellinis from the great days of Venice, Gainsboroughs maybe, Holbeins, Van Dycks, some of the great Rembrandts.'

Piper did not mention that he had two Rembrandts in his basement which Mr McCracken's compatriots refused to buy because they were too dark.

'What might you get your hands on soon?' asked McCracken.

'It is a Gainsborough, Mr McCracken. A Gainsborough of the very highest quality.'

McCracken searched his memory. He found it hard to remember the names of the painters. 'Gainsborough the guy who did all those aristocrats in their country parks? Lots of real estate behind them?'

'How right you are, Mr McCracken,' Piper smiled. 'Absolutely correct.' And, he said to himself, I shall certainly drink a glass of champagne with you this evening. The Gainsborough, after all, was something very special.

Lady Lucy intercepted her husband as he was hanging up his coat in Markham Square. 'Francis,' she whispered, 'that young man from the gallery is here. He's waiting for you upstairs.'

'Is he a nice young man, Lucy?' asked Powerscourt with a smile. 'Why are you whispering?' Powerscourt was at the bottom of the stairs now. Lady Lucy put her hand on his arm.

'It's Christopher Montague, Francis.'

'What about him?' said her husband, his mind already engaged with Jason Lockhart of Clarke's Gallery, presumably sitting peacefully in the Powerscourt drawing room.

'It's this.' Lady Lucy's whisper was even quieter now. 'Somebody left Christopher Montague a great deal of money about six months before he died.'

'Did they indeed?' said Powerscourt, fresh avenues of investigation opening up before him. 'How do you know?'

'I bumped into a cousin of mine coming out of the shops in Sloane Square. I'd been buying clothes for the children. Sarah, you know Sarah, Francis, you met her at Jonathan's wedding a couple of years ago, she said everybody in the family knew about it.'

Jason Lockhart of Clarke's Gallery was sitting nervously on the sofa. He was about thirty-five years old, wearing a dark blue suit with a white shirt and a discreet tie. 'Lord Powerscourt,' he said, 'I came as soon as I could when I received your note. My apologies to your wife for arriving before you had returned. How can I help you in your inquiries?'

'You were going to start a magazine, I believe,' said Powerscourt, thinking about Lockhart's voice. He sounded very like most of the other inhabitants of Old Bond Street but there was something wrong about the vowels. 'With Christopher Montague. What can you tell me about it?'

'It was going to be called *The Rembrandt*,' said Lockhart, 'a magazine for the art connoisseur.'

'And what about the article by Christopher Montague, Mr Lockhart? Did you read it?'

'I did not,' said Jason Lockhart, 'but I knew what it was going to say.' Powerscourt waited. 'The article was going to be called "Fakes and Forgeries in Venetian

106

Painting". It was based on the exhibition that recently opened at the de Courcy and Piper Gallery. There are something like thirty-two paintings supposed to be by Titian. Christopher thought only two, maybe three, were genuine. Fifteen Giorgiones, only four by the master. Twelve Giovanni Bellinis, only one by the hand of Bellini himself.'

Master, thought Powerscourt, returning to Lockhart's voice, master spoken with a very short a. Somewhere in the north of England? Yorkshire perhaps?

'Forgive me,' said Powerscourt with a smile, 'forgive me for asking such a stupid question. But how does a gallery like yours or de Courcy and Piper know whether a painting is genuine or not?'

Jason Lockhart laughed. 'That's just the point, Lord Powerscourt. The gallery finds as many works of Titian or Giorgione as it can. It arranges with the owners to lend them to the exhibition, to be returned or sold afterwards. The gallery always accepts the attribution of the lenders. If the Duke of Tewkesbury says his Titian is a Titian, then the gallery accepts that it is, indeed, a Titian. There's always a clause in the small print of the catalogue that all attributions are the owners' not the gallery's. That lets the gallery off the hook.'

Powerscourt had decided that the original accent, now heavily overladen with the upper crust of Mayfair, was definitely Yorkshire. 'I see,' he said. 'So the Christopher Montague article would have been a bombshell. It would have offended everybody, the owners, the galleries, the dealers, the purchasers who would not have known whether they had bought the real thing or a fake.'

'Exactly,' said Lockhart. 'There was absolutely nothing else that could have offended so many people so deeply.'

'Would de Courcy and Piper have been hardest hit,' asked Powerscourt, 'seeing that it was their exhibition that was being torn to pieces?'

'Initially, yes,' admitted Lockhart. 'They would have been very hard hit. But it wouldn't have taken long for it to emerge that every other gallery behaved in exactly the same way.'

'And what of your position in your own gallery?' said Powerscourt, his mind racing. 'Would your employers have been pleased that you were associated with such a venture?'

'They knew all about it,' said Lockhart. 'I suspect they thought it might be enough to force de Courcy and Piper out of business altogether. All's fair in love and war in Old Bond Street, Lord Powerscourt, believe me.'

Powerscourt remembered the Italian books Christopher Montague had taken out of the London Library or ordered from elsewhere. 'What did the article say about the false Titians, Mr Lockhart? That they were bought on the Grand Tour, and the buyers were deceived by unscrupulous dealers?'

Lockhart looked at a painting of the lower Himalayas on Powerscourt's wall, purchased since his return from India. Powerscourt wondered if he was going to pronounce it a forgery.

'Christopher thought that was where most of them had come from,' he said. 'But there was something else. Christopher intended to say that at least three, if not four, of the paintings on display were very recent forgeries. That would have caused a sensation.'

'And what of these Americans, the very rich ones who have been buying works of art at a fairly rapid rate lately? Have they all been taken in? Have they spent their thousands of dollars on junk?'

'God knows, Lord Powerscourt, God only knows.'

One thing struck Powerscourt with absolute certainty as he showed Jason Lockhart out of his house. The real beneficiary, the absolute winner out of the whole affair would have been Christopher Montague himself. His second book was about to come out. His article destroyed the provenance of most of the Venetian masterpieces in England. Who could a poor purchaser turn to in order to be sure that his Veronese was genuine? That his Tintoretto wasn't a forgery? That his Giorgione wasn't a fake? Why, the expert was at hand. Christopher Montague is your man. Powerscourt wondered how much he would charge for verifying the attribution of the masterpieces. Ten per cent? Fifteen? Twenty-five? He might have inherited a large sum in the past six months, but he was about to become richer yet. Much richer. Was there somebody else in the London art world who enjoyed this position of Attributer in Chief at present? Would such a somebody want Montague dead?

Part Two

Gainsborough

9

The rats. They would have to do something about the rats. They had become quite shameless, no longer bothering to scuttle away into the wainscoting or disappear through the holes in the floorboards. Soon they would be sitting up in rows and demanding food, or eating away at the paintings. Orlando Blane walked up the length of the Long Gallery, hoping against hope that the sound of his footsteps would drive them away.

As he reached the end of the room he stared sadly out of one of the five great windows. Outside it was a blustery autumn day. Chaos was continuing its relentless advance across the gardens. The roses had run wild, threatening to strangle the other flowers that had once lain beside them in neat ordered beds. The fountain in the centre of the garden had long ceased to flow. The cheeky statue of Eros on the top was turning a dark metallic green. Way over to his left he could still see the edge of the lake, the water dark and forbidding. In the summer evenings Orlando had been allowed to wander round its rim, the watchful guard the regulation twenty steps behind.

Orlando Blane was a prisoner. He was still not absolutely sure where he was. Occasionally he thought he could smell the sea. The vast house, unoccupied now except for himself and his jailers, sat alone in its thousands of acres, the long drive to the nearest road blocked by a rough barricade of trees. There were four of them, watching round the clock to make sure he did not escape. He was forbidden alcohol, even weak or watered beer, for alcohol had played its part in his downfall. His function was to paint to order, for Orlando Blane was a very talented artist. In better times, with a less chequered past, he might have had a prosperous career in London or Paris.

He stared down the Long Gallery at his work for the day. On his stretcher a painting was beginning to take shape, a painting that bore a remarkable similarity to a Gainsborough.

Orlando looked out at the dark clouds swirling across a stormy sky. He thought about Imogen, the great love of his life, now hundreds of miles away. No, he would not think about Imogen. His mind went off, entirely of its own accord, to the French Riviera five months before. He saw again the mesmerizing turn of the roulette wheel, he heard the tiny click as the ball dropped into its slot. He heard again the measured voice of the croupier, *rien ne va plus*, no more bets, the gamblers waiting, watching for the little ball to fall into its slot once more. He remembered five days of triumph at the tables. Even now, he still shook slightly as he thought of the sixth day when everything went wrong and his world changed for ever.

The colours. Maybe it was his training that made him remember things so vividly, the dark grey, almost black, of the sea as he walked the mile and a half from the casino in Monte Carlo back to his cheap lodgings along the coast at three or four o'clock in the morning. The first faint lines of yellow on the horizon as the sun came up to bring in a new dawn, the pale blue water that had deepened to azure by the time he woke up, the delicate pinks of the setting sun as he set out once more for the gambling tables. The green of the roulette table. The bright red on which he staked so much. The shiny polished black that eventually claimed his fortune.

Orlando remembered the private language of the roulette wheel, spoken in the soft but authoritative voice of the croupier. *Pair* meant betting on an even number, *impair* on an odd one. *Passe* for a winning number between nineteen and thirty-six, *impasse* for one between nought and eighteen. *Rouge* for red, *noir* for black, *le rouge et le noir* that had dominated all his thoughts during his sojourn at the wheel. Nought for the casino, the one factor that gave the proprietors a slight mathematical edge over the gamblers who had come to break the bank.

He had been playing on a system all his own. On his very first visit to the casino, Orlando had merely watched. A very fat Frenchman had won a great deal of money. A slim blond Englishman had lost a great deal. A beautifully dressed Italian had made a small amount. For three nights Orlando watched one table. He placed the odd bet to pay his rent at the casino. He noted the fall of every ball in a red notebook. He saw one of the supervisors whispering something to one of his companions – here was a man developing a system all his own. The casinos loved people with systems. They welcomed them with open arms and vintage champagne once they were established players. Generous credit was offered to those with the right connections. For the casinos knew that all systems were doomed to fail. Even with the one European zero as against the American two or even three, Orlando had heard, in the wilder gambling saloons of the Midwest, the odds were always stacked in favour of the bank.

Orlando Blane had gone to Monte Carlo to seek financial salvation, to make a fortune. He had no money of his own, only debts. He was wildly, hopelessly in love with

Imogen Jeffries, only daughter of a rich London lawyer. Orlando would see her in his daytime dreams in his little cot in the back room of his *auberge*, looking out over the train tracks and the wild countryside behind the sea. She was tall and dark, with teasing grey-blue eyes. She moved with a sinuous grace that took his breath away and she held him very close in her arms when she kissed him goodbye at the railway station on his journey to the south of France. Imogen's father, a man obsessed with his property, its size, its prospects, its ability to support generations of unborn Jeffries far into the future, absolutely refused to agree to his daughter marrying a penniless man. Most girls, Orlando thought, would have tried to deter their beloved from staking their joint futures on the spin of a small wheel in Monte Carlo. Imogen had been entranced. Danger called her like a drug.

'Come back rich, my darling,' she had said to him. 'Then I can hold you in my arms all night long. Come back ever so rich.'

As he studied his red book Orlando came to an interesting conclusion. The table he had watched showed a very slight tendency to produce reds rather than blacks. Many people, he remembered, played a variety of a system called Martingale, made famous by Sir Francis Clavering in Thackeray's *Pendennis*, who lost enormous sums through his blind belief in its efficiency. The system depended on waiting for a run of five successive blacks. Then, on the sixth spin, a bet was placed on red. If the winning number was black again, the bet was doubled. And so on through a vast variety of permutations. But Orlando knew there was a fault at the heart of the Martingale system. Its adherents believed that after five blacks in a row the odds must be in favour of a red next time. They were not. They were exactly the same each time. The wheel has no memory of where the ball landed

116

last time round. Each time there was a fifty-fifty chance of red or black turning up. He resolved to bet in moderate amounts on red. Red after all was Imogen's favourite colour. Nothing else. No almighty chance on a single number with odds of thirty-six to one against. No combinations of numbers, no *pair*, no *impair*, no *passe*. Just red. *Mesdames et messieurs, je vous en prie. Faites vos jeux.*

Orlando remembered being very nervous the first night he gambled seriously. The minimum stake was one thousand francs, just under ten pounds in English money. Orlando had one thousand pounds working capital, handed over to him out of Imogen's bank accounts. He gambled the minimum stake which paid out the same amount if you won. One thousand francs would bring you another thousand. He brought a sketch-book with him. Sometimes while he watched he would dash off lightning drawings, character sketches of the croupiers or his fellow gamblers. He backed red eighteen times in all. If the law of averages had been perfect he would have won nine and lost nine. The law of averages was not perfect that first night. He won twelve times and lost six. The croupiers smiled at him as he left to collect his winnings. Gambling with such small stakes was never going to be a problem for the Société des Jeux de Monte Carlo. On his trial run Orlando had made sixty pounds.

On the following two nights he increased his stakes very gradually. By day three he was five thousand pounds ahead. Five thousand pounds, he said sadly to himself, would never satisfy Imogen's father. Twenty-five would do. Better thirty. Forty would be perfect.

On days four and five the casino had increased the size of the maximum permitted bet to one hundred thousand francs, roughly one thousand pounds in English money. Orlando's system held. Behind his chair each night a small clean-shaven Frenchman with black eyes was watching. He was not watching the progress of the game. He watched the lightning sketches that Orlando threw off in his notebook.

'Forgive me. Your drawings, monsieur,' the Frenchman had said, 'tonight they are in the style of Toulouse Lautrec, so good they could pass for the real thing. Can you draw in anybody else's style, monsieur?'

Orlando Blane hardly heard him. He was counting his winnings. 'Tomorrow night, monsieur,' Orlando said very quietly, 'I shall draw in the style of Degas.'

Now he was eighteen thousand pounds ahead. Was that enough? Would eighteen thousand be enough to marry his Imogen? Should he pay his bill, check out of his miserable *auberge*, head for the railway station and take the train home to London? Orlando did not. He did check out of his *auberge*. He booked himself into the grandest hotel in Monte Carlo and prepared himself for one final apocalyptic night of glory.

The doors of the casino closed at four o'clock that morning. At five minutes past the manager convened an emergency meeting in his room.

'We cannot go on like this,' he said. 'Soon we may be in severe financial difficulties. This Englishman is winning too much. The other players too, they are putting their money on the red. They are winning too. What, in God's name, is happening?'

The senior croupier shook his head. 'I do not know, sir,' he said. 'He is not cheating. He is not interfering with the play in any way. It's just red, red, red.'

'Where is that damned Professor?' said the manager angrily. The casino had summoned a Professor of Mathematics from the University of Nice, an expert in chance and probability, in the theory of patterns and numbers.

'He was wandering round the gaming rooms the last

118

time I saw him,' said the casino security manager. 'In fact he wasn't actually upright, he was lying on the floor, checking that the table was perfectly level. Which it is, apparently.'

'He was what?' shouted the manager. 'We are in danger of losing everything and this fool is crawling about on the floor! Is he drunk?'

'No, I am not drunk,' said the Professor of Mathematics. The Professor was in his middle fifties, with receding hair and thick glasses and a worried air. His hobby was collecting notes on the weather. He believed that if he kept his records long enough the day would come when he could predict with almost total certainty, ninety-three per cent probability in his private estimation, what the weather would be the following day. So far he had thirty years of weather records, originally kept in the back room of his house, now stored in a very large shed in his garden.

'It is a most interesting phenomenon,' the Professor began, looking at the casino staff as if they were a particularly dense collection of first year mathematics students, 'this run of numbers should not have happened. But it has. For a student of probabilities, it could become a classic case. It will feature in the textbooks for years.'

'Never mind your bloody textbooks, Professor,' said the casino manager angrily. 'This run has been going on for five days. Will it continue? Or will it stop?'

The Professor of Mathematics looked back in the notebook where the numbers were stored. He filled three pages with calculations written in a small spidery hand.

'I am seventy-five per cent sure that the run on red will stop tomorrow. But it might not. It could, logically, carry on for ever, but I do not think it will.' He smiled at the casino staff.

The manager stared at the Professor of Mathematics.

He was used to these probabilities by now. He had yet to hear the man from the University of Nice get as far as a hundred per cent sure. Ninety-eight per cent was as good as it got.

'But what do we do?' said the manager. 'We can't close the casino down. They are a very superstitious lot, these winning gamblers. If we moved the table with a different wheel to a different room, what would you say the chances were of the Englishman continuing to play?'

The Professor leant back in his chair and closed his eyes. The three other men watched while the calculations whizzed round in his head.

'Based on the studies of Professor Kuntzbuhl in Vienna, and Professor Spinetti of Rome, on the psychology of gamblers, based admittedly on work with prisoners in jail for non-payment of gambling debts in their respective cities, I should say the chances are between twenty-five and thirty per cent. They are very superstitious, these gamblers. Change the table, change anything at all and they feel their luck has gone. They stop playing.'

'No more bets? None at all?' said the manager sadly.

'No more bets,' said the Professor, firmly.

'What else do you suggest, Professor?' the casino manager felt sure the balding academic would have some suggestion. The casino didn't pay him five thousand a year as a consultant for nothing.

'For the moment, I regret to say, I have nothing to suggest. Chance follows its own logic, however irrational it may seem to the uninitiated. Chance's logic says the table must return to normal.'

'There is one other question,' said the croupier. 'I have been watching this young man very carefully. I think he has a figure in his mind for his winnings. I suspect he may be quite close to it. He may, of course, keep on gambling after he has passed it and throw it all away.

Gamblers on a run tend to think they are immortal. Should we increase the size of the maximum stake? It is the most likely way to recoup the money, is it not, Professor?'

'Seventy-eight per cent probability, I should say,' the Professor replied. 'Probably. Assuming he comes, that is. I cannot put a figure on that though I should say it is over sixty-three per cent.'

'He'll come,' said the manager firmly. 'I feel it in my bones. Ninety-nine per cent probability. And when he comes, the table, gentlemen, will carry double the size of the maximum stake. On reflection, don't double it. Make it two hundred and fifty thousand francs, two thousand five hundred pounds. The largest stakes ever seen in this casino, maybe in the whole of France. Come, Englishman, come, we shall be ready for you. *Mesdames et messieurs, je vous en prie. Faites vos jeux.*'

The hotel had cleaned Orlando's clothes. As he made his way to the casino shortly after eleven o'clock he wondered if that would bring him bad luck. The sea was very calm, a crescent moon shining on the water. Carriages were bringing the night's gamblers to the tables. Orlando changed all his money at the *caisse*. He considered playing with only half of his winnings until he reflected that his system depended on a long run of play. He slid quietly into his normal place at the table, to the left of the croupier. Two of the other players were known by sight. They had followed him on his last two visits to the roulette wheel, copying his bets, although with smaller stakes. One was a little old lady with white hair who Orlando privately referred to as Grandma. The other was dressed in military uniform. He had a very long face with a deep scar running down his cheek and a black eye patch over his left eye. He was Pirate. On the other side of the table was an erect old gentleman, accompanied by a remarkably pretty girl. Orlando

121

suspected that the casino employed a cluster of female beauties to make friends with the male customers and ensure that they spent the maximum amount on the cards or at the wheel. She became Grandad's Little Friend. The final player was an officious-looking middle-aged man, permanently checking his watch, as if time gave clues to the final destination of the roulette ball. He became Bank Manager. Behind him his artistic friend whispered into his ear as he sat down. 'Good evening, my friend. You still have the sketchbook, I see. Degas tonight, did you say?'

Behind an enormous mirror across the Salon Vert from Orlando's position the manager of the casino and the Professor of Mathematics were seated at a little table, opera glasses in their hands. The mirror was two-way. The casino men had a perfect view.

'Well,' said the manager to the Professor. 'Are you confident?'

'I think so,' he said. 'But we shouldn't expect it to become apparent immediately.'

The manager worried about the lack of a percentage. He worried if he had been right to raise the stakes to this incredibly high level. He took a deep pull on his cigar and settled down to wait.

Orlando did not place any bets for twenty minutes. He watched the play. Pirate had lit a foul-smelling cigar, the smoke rising in planes towards the ceiling. He opened his sketchbook and did a rapid drawing of Grandad's Little Friend. She turned into a Degas ballerina, very scantily clad. Orlando stared in astonishment at the ceiling. He hadn't looked closely at it before. Up there, gazing happily at the gamblers below were three naked women, who might have been the Three Graces. All were smoking cigars.

Bank Manager had been placing a series of small bets, mostly on the odd numbers. His pile of chips was diminishing rapidly. At seven minutes to twelve Orlando made his first move. He placed his largest chip, a bright pink one, on red. He was betting two and a half thousand pounds. Grandma and Pirate followed suit. The croupier spun the wheel and flipped the ball around the bowl. *Rien ne va plus*, no more bets. The wheel slowed down, the ball hovered agonizingly between the black 33 and the red 16. Orlando held his breath. Pirate, he noticed, had closed his one good eye. Grandma was clutching at a crucifix round her neck.

'*Seize*,' said the croupier impassively. '*Rouge*.'

Orlando now had a fortune of just over twenty thousand pounds, the minimum he thought necessary to marry his Imogen. Damn it, they might become poor after a while. He resolved to press on.

'*Merde!*' said the manager in his hidden box. '*Merde!*'

'Do not upset yourself,' said the Professor. 'The night is yet young.'

From outside came the faint rumble of the last train to Nice. The moon had gone in and the sea front was dark, some rich men's yachts bobbing rhythmically up and down in the harbour.

Orlando was unruffled. He backed red for the next four spins of the wheel. Each time it was black. Grandma looked at him sadly as if she thought his magic powers had deserted him. Pirate had pulled out after three losses. A crowd had gathered round the table to watch the handsome young Englishman lose a fortune.

'I believe he has ten thousand pounds left,' said the manager to the Professor. 'What will he do?'

'Continue,' said the Professor, who had grown rather fond of Orlando. 'I am eighty-five per cent certain he will continue. I fear he may go on even when he has lost all his money.'

The great clock in the main hall of the casino struck one. Three times in succession the *noir* triumphed over the *rouge*. Orlando was down to his last two and a half thousand pounds. He couldn't work out what had happened. The tendency to red seemed to have been replaced by a tendency to a malignant black.

He placed his last chip on the red. '*Faites vos jeux,*' said the croupier, preparing to spin the wheel. Grandma suddenly decided to re-enter the fray. But this time she was betting against Orlando. She put her money on black. '*Rien ne va plus,* no more bets,' said the croupier, as the ball slowed down. It settled noisily in its compartment.

'*Vingt-quatre. Noir,*' said the voice of doom.

'Congratulations, Professor,' said the manager, clapping him on the back. 'Some champagne for you, perhaps? A cognac?'

'No, thank you,' said the Professor. 'Are you going to give the young man any credit at the *caisse*? I do hope not.'

'We have to live, Professor,' said the manager cheerfully. 'I told them to let him have another ten thousand English pounds. No more.'

Orlando waited. He took out his sketchbook and turned Pirate into an El Greco face, the eyepatch replaced. He did another Degas impersonation of Little Friend. He walked slowly through the crowd to the cashier's. The crowd dissolved before him as if Moses was repeating the parting of the Red Sea in the casino at Monte Carlo. He is the young milord, they whispered to one another. He has lost everything. He is a professional gambler. He has come from America to break the bank. He will win again. Never have I seen such skill at the table. Such nerve.

The cashier advanced him ten thousand pounds without a question. The manager's compliments, monsieur. *Bonne chance, monsieur.*

The croupier was sweating slightly as Orlando

returned. He wiped his brow with a white handkerchief. The smoke was very thick. The crowd around the table had increased. From the ceiling the Three Graces with their cigars looked down. Their faces said they had seen it all before. The manager and the Professor leant forward in their seats. The smoke was obscuring the view.

Rouge, said Orlando. *Noir,* said the croupier. *Rouge,* said Orlando. *Noir,* said the croupier. Five thousand pounds down. This incredible run of blacks could not continue. It was mathematically impossible.

Rouge, said Orlando.

Noir, said the croupier as the ball came to rest.

Seven and a half thousand pounds down. One last throw would begin the revival of his fortunes. *Rouge,* said Orlando. The ball clattered round the bowl. Pirate was staring intently at the wheel. '*Courage,*' murmured his French friend behind him. The little old lady made the sign of the cross. She had placed her last chips on the red along with Orlando.

The ball was slowing now. 'Which colour, Professor?' whispered the manager. The Professor looked at pages and pages of equations beside him. 'Black,' he said sorrowfully.

There was a murmur in the crowd as the ball hovered over the wheel. The Englishman is broken. He is finished. Can he pay? It seemed to be a choice between a black 2 and a red 25. Orlando looked at his last chip, sitting on the table. Grandad's Little Friend had her two hands on the old man's shoulders, straining for a better view.

The last rattle. The ball settled into its compartment.

'*Deux,*' said the croupier. '*Noir.*'

Orlando waited for half an hour at the table. He noticed bitterly that the next four rotations all ended in reds. He wondered about Imogen, their dreams of happiness lost in the spin of a wheel. He wondered what he was going to say to the cashier. He wondered if he would be sent to prison, left to rot like the Count of Monte Cristo in a miserable cell deep inside the Chateau d'If. He wondered how he could tell Imogen. He knew she wouldn't be angry, only sad that their plan had failed.

At a quarter past two he left the table. His French friend followed him. The little old lady embraced him. 'My poor boy, ' she said, 'my poor boy.' The Pirate saluted him. 'What courage,' he said. 'What bravery.' The croupier shook his hand. '*Au revoir, monsieur*. I hope we shall have the pleasure of seeing you again.'

Orlando's friend led him to a quiet alcove off the main reception. Three Greek philosophers seemed to be having an argument on the walls behind them.

'Mr Blane,' said the Frenchman, 'my name is Arnaud, Raymond Arnaud. Before we come to the business, let me ask you one question. Can you paint as well as you can draw?'

Orlando stared at the man. Paint? Paint? What on earth was he talking about? 'Of course I can paint,' he said, 'I paint better than I can draw. I was trained at the Royal Academy and in Rome. But what of it? It does not matter now. I owe this casino ten thousand pounds. I do not have ten thousand pounds.'

Raymond Arnaud put his arm across his shoulders. 'Mr Blane, my friends and I, we have been looking for a man like you. We will pay your debt. It does not go well with those who do not pay here. In France they are more lenient. But in Monte Carlo the authorities feel they have to make examples of those who gamble and cannot pay. Otherwise their casino would sink under a mountain of unpaid debts.'

Orlando could hardly believe his ears. Escape was being offered by this improbable Frenchman. 'What do I have to do in return?' he said.

'You paint,' said the Frenchman 'you come and work for us in the world of painting. When you have earned enough to pay off your debt, we let you go!'

Raymond Arnaud did not say that he was the French associate of a firm of London art dealers, based in Old Bond Street. He did not say that they had been looking for somebody like Orlando Blane for eighteen months.

Orlando came back from his reverie. A flock of starlings was flying past the house, heading for the lake. He walked back down the Long Gallery to his stretcher and looked at his Gainsborough. He took the illustration from the American magazine out of its folder. Just the children, his instructions said. Don't worry about a likeness for the parents, it might seem too much of a coincidence. Just the children, not too perfect a likeness. He reached for his brushes and began to work.

Orlando had never discovered where the instructions came from, or who sent them. He presumed they came from London. All he had to do was to work every day in the Long Gallery. In the evening he played cards with his jailers.

They played for matchsticks.

10

Lord Francis Powerscourt was having trouble with a letter. He stared gloomily at the full extent of his composition so far.

1st November 1899.
Mrs Rosalind Buckley,
64 Flood Street,
Chelsea.
Dear Madam,

Powerscourt was writing to the lover of the late Christopher Montague, one-time art critic, recent inheritor of a very large sum of money. He stared out at the trees in Markham Square.

'Please forgive this intrusion on your privacy,' he began.

I have been asked by his family to investigate the death of the late art critic Christopher Montague. I have been given to understand that you were a friend of his. I would be most grateful if you could spare me the time for a brief conversation about Christopher. Any such conversation would, of course, be entirely confidential. I would be happy to call on you in Flood Street at a time of your own choosing. Alternatively, should business take you in the direction of Markham Square, my wife and I would be pleased to receive you here. Yours, Powerscourt.

He read it through again. Was it too cold? Did he sound like a solicitor about to impart bad tidings? Should he have said more than he had? Should he have mentioned the possibility of further deaths? No, he would leave it as it was, he decided.

But one fact worried him more than anything else. Lady Lucy's intelligence system had revealed that Mr Buckley was a solicitor, partner in the well-known firm of Buckley, Brigstock and Brightwell. And that Mr Buckley was at least twenty years older than his wife. And that Mr Horace Aloysius Buckley had not been seen in his office for over three weeks. He had not been seen there since the day following the murder of Christopher Montague.

Johnny Fitzgerald decided he was going to enjoy his outing to Old Bond Street. He had a large parcel under his arm. He peered enthusiastically into the windows of the galleries, paintings for sale on offer, further exhibitions due to open shortly promising a cornucopia of artistic treasures.

He entered the offices of Clarke and Sons. The reception looked like a London club, he thought, portraits of previous Clarkes, drenched in respectability and sombre colours, hanging proudly on the walls.

'Good morning,' Johnny said cheerfully to the young man behind the desk.

'Good morning, sir,' said the young man. 'How can we help you?'

'It's this Leonardo here,' Fitzgerald said, 'it belongs to my aunt. She's thinking of selling it. I wonder if you could tell me what it's worth?'

The young man had sprung to attention at the mention of the word Leonardo. He had only been with the firm a few weeks but even he had absorbed enough to realize that a Leonardo was the ultimate prize. He would be remembered as the man who secured the da Vinci for Clarke's. He would become famous. Other, better paid jobs would surely follow.

'Very good, sir. How wise of you to bring it to us.' The young man pressed a small bell on his desk. 'If you would like to come with me, sir, one of our experts will talk to you and examine the painting.'

Fitzgerald was escorted up a half flight of stairs and shown into a small room looking out on to the back of Old Bond Street. There was an easel by the window and a couple of rather battered chairs. A bowl of fading flowers sat sadly on a side table.

'Mr Prendergast will be with you in a moment, sir.' The young man bowed slightly and made his way back down to reception, thinking about the tale he would tell his friends later that evening. 'Just walked in off the street, calm as you please, a Leonardo under his arm.'

Johnny Fitzgerald wondered how old you had to be before you became an art expert. The answer was not long in coming. Another young man announced himself as James Prendergast and shook Fitzgerald warmly by the hand. Fitzgerald thought he must have been in his late twenties. 'Good morning, sir. Perhaps we could have a look at the painting?'

Fitzgerald unwrapped his parcel and placed it on the easel. 'Fitzgerald's the name, Lord Fitzgerald of the Irish peerage, to be precise,' he said. 'Here you are, Leonardo's *Annunciation*.'

Most Italian Annunciations took place in broad

daylight. The Leonardo happened at first light. A beam of strong sunlight came through a window and lit up the face of the Virgin. Her green robe fell in shadowy folds towards the floor. Just inside the window, leaning on a table, was the angel of the Lord, dressed in light blue. Careful examination showed the rest of the contents of the room, a humble single bed, a washing table with a bowl. The scene was mysterious, the expression on the Virgin's face apprehensive, as if she could not quite believe what was happening to her.

'The shadows, Lord Fitzgerald, the shadows,' said Prendergast reverentially, 'how beautifully he handles the shadows.' He paused, trying to imagine the price if the thing was genuine. It certainly looked genuine. A faint note of greed came into his voice with his next question.

'How long has it been in your possession, might I ask? How was it obtained?'

'It's not mine, actually,' said Johnny. 'It belongs to my aunt. Some distant relation of hers bought it in Milan on the Grand Tour years and years ago. She's got lots of this kind of stuff lying about the place.'

The young man's face lit up at the prospect of further treasures. He was not an expert on Leonardo, in truth he might have had difficulty telling a Corregio from a Caravaggio, but he did know that Leonardo had lived in Milan. He was fairly certain about that. Or had that been Titian who lived in Milan?

'It is a most excellent work, sir. Perhaps you could come with me to one of our senior partners on the first floor. I'm sure he would love to see it.'

They get older as you go up the stairs, Johnny said to himself, as he followed young Prendergast to the next floor. It seemed to be the wrong way round. They should make the young ones walk up all the stairs. Maybe the views were better higher up.

'Mr Robert Martyn, Lord Fitzgerald. Lord Fitzgerald's Leonardo.' Prendergast made the introductions. Johnny felt pleased that the Virgin had attained human status in Clarke's Gallery. Robert Martyn was a small man in his forties, with a prosperous paunch and very powerful glasses.

'Delighted to make your acquaintance, Lord Fitzgerald,' he said. 'And so this is the Leonardo.' The same reverential tone, Johnny noticed. It's as if the entire staff of Clarke and Sons, art dealers, think they're in church when they look at an Old Master. Martyn took out a magnifying glass and examined the painting carefully. 'The handling of the paint is very similar to that in Leonardo's *Virgin of the Rocks* in the National Gallery,' he said. 'And the green is very similar. And look at the bottom left-hand corner. Everything is very vague down there, as if the painter hadn't quite finished it.'

'What does that mean?' asked Fitzgerald in a loud voice, determined not to ape the customs of the art dealers.

'Why, my lord,' said Martyn, 'it makes it even more likely that it is a Leonardo. He was notorious for never finishing his paintings. He got bored, perhaps. Or another idea sprang into his mind. Very fertile brain, Leonardo, quite remarkable.' Martyn made it sound as though he had dinner with Leonardo every other Tuesday at his Pall Mall club.

'But come, Lord Fitzgerald, I fear that we must trespass further on your patience. Our managing director would love to see it. It is not every day that we are privileged to see such a great work, is it, Prendergast?' He nodded at his younger colleague. 'Perhaps you could accompany us to the next floor where our managing director's office is. Our Mr Clarke, Mr Jeremiah Clarke, is the fourth member of his family to hold the position. We are fortunate to have such continuity in a changing world.'

Johnny guessed that Mr Jeremiah Clarke would be in his sixties if age followed the levels of the building. He was wrong. Jeremiah Clarke was in his mid-seventies, a sprightly old man with very red cheeks and a shock of white hair.

'Well,' he said, looking closely at the painting, 'it is most remarkable.' He walked to the far side of his enormous office and looked at it from a distance. He advanced to a mid-point, half-way across the room. Finally he placed himself a foot or two away and looked closely at the angel for a couple of minutes. Martyn and Prendergast stood solemnly on either side, as if they were two sidesmen bringing the collection to the front of the church for the presentation.

'Remarkable,' said Clarke. 'Mr Martyn, what is your opinion?'

Martyn spoke in hushed tones. 'It seems to me, sir, that there is a very strong possibility that this is indeed a lost Leonardo. But I would have to consult the documents. I think we should call in the experts.'

'We could make you an offer for the painting now, if you would be prepared to consider that option.' Jeremiah Clarke had seen so many people who brought valuable works to his firm in need of ready cash. Johnny Fitzgerald was having none of that.

'What would you be offering now?' he said with a smile. 'I'm sure it's a lot less than it would fetch once the world knows it is genuine.'

'I'm sure we could run to four or five thousand pounds. Cash,' said Clarke. Johnny had been told that if the painting was genuine the initial bidding would probably start at one hundred thousand pounds, with American millionaires to the fore. There were so few Leonardos left anywhere in the world, the thing was virtually priceless.

133

Clarke sensed that his visitor was not impressed. 'However, Lord Fitzgerald,' he purred on, 'we would much prefer to wait. But it would help if you could leave the painting with us for a week, maybe longer, so that our experts can have a proper look at it.'

'No,' said Johnny Fitzgerald. The three men looked at each other in astonishment. This had never happened before in the one-hundred-and-seventy-year history of Clarke's. A client refusing to leave his painting on the premises! It was impossible!

'Why ever not?' said Martyn sharply.

'It's not that I don't mind the experts looking at it and doing whatever they do,' said Fitzgerald. 'But I'm going to take the painting away with me. When you have made the appointments for the experts, you let me know and I'll bring it back. I'll bring it back as many times as you like.'

'But why? Don't you trust us?' said Jeremiah Clarke.

'It's my aunt,' said Johnny, 'the lady who owns the painting, you see. Five years ago she decided to sell a Van Dyck. She took it to one of your competitors around here – she was a lot more mobile in those days. The gallery said it was worthless and sent it back. Three years later her Van Dyck was sold for a very large sum of money. You see, the gallery hadn't sent her back the original at all. They sent her back a copy. They kept the original and then sold it after a period of time. It's as well my auntie reads all the papers and the magazines or she'd have never found out what happened.'

Clarke and his colleagues made sad and comforting noises. 'What a breach of trust!' 'Abuse of clients!' 'Disgraceful behaviour!' But they looked ever so slightly guilty. Johnny took up his picture, wrapped it in its thick brown paper, and made his farewells.

'Just let me know when your experts want to see it, then,' he said cheerfully, as he headed for the door. 'I'll bring it back myself, I promise you. I look forward to hearing from you, gentlemen. A very good day to you all.'

Out on the pavement Johnny Fitzgerald laughed loudly. The looks on their faces had been most enjoyable. He peered around the shopfronts of Old Bond Street. His eye fell on the offices of de Courcy and Piper, 'art dealers of quality', said the legend on the door.

'Good morning,' Fitzgerald said cheerfully to the young man behind the desk.

'Good morning, sir,' said the young man. 'How can we help you?'

'It's this Leonardo here,' Fitzgerald said. 'It belongs to my aunt . . .'

'What do you think she'll wear, Lucy?' said Lord Francis Powerscourt to his wife.

'That's a most unusual question for a man to ask,' said Lady Lucy.

'Well, she can hardly turn out in black, can she?' said Powerscourt. 'But then again, she wouldn't feel happy in pink or something like that, would she?'

Lady Lucy laughed. 'I'm sure you'd get it right, if you had time to think about it, Francis. Even you. I bet you anything you like she'll be in grey. Probably in dark grey. Sad, but not actually mourning. Maybe a black hat.'

Mrs Rosalind Buckley had replied remarkably promptly to Powerscourt's note inviting her to Markham Square. She was due in five minutes' time. He had asked Lady Lucy if the conversation would be easier with another woman present. Lady Lucy had thought about it for some time.

'I think she might say more about her private life to a woman on her own than she would to a man. In fact I'm sure of it. But talking to a man and a woman would be difficult for her. I think she would be more reluctant to speak in those circumstances. I think you need to speak to her on your own, Francis. Good luck!'

Mrs Rosalind Buckley was indeed wearing grey, dark grey, when she was shown into the drawing room on the first floor. She was tall and slim, an inch or two taller than Christopher Montague, Powerscourt thought, with curly brown hair, full lips and very sad big brown eyes. She looked about thirty years old, but it was hard to tell. Powerscourt thought that men of all ages could easily have fallen in love with her.

'Mrs Buckley,' he said, rising from his chair, dropping *The Times* on to the floor, 'how very kind of you to come. Please sit down.' He ushered her into the armchair opposite his own. She began to take off her gloves. The gloves, he noticed, were black.

'Lord Powerscourt,' she said, trying vainly to manage a smile, 'it was the least I could do after what happened to Mr Montague. Please feel free to ask whatever you wish. I shall try to bear it.'

Christ, thought Powerscourt, she's not going to start crying already, is she? Weeping women always upset him.

'Perhaps I could begin with the simplest question of all, Mrs Buckley,' he said. 'How long have you been friendly with Mr Montague?'

They both knew what friendly meant.

'About a year and a half,' she said.

'Really? As long as that?' said Powerscourt. 'How did you meet him, may I ask?'

'We met at the preview of an exhibition of Spanish paintings in Old Bond Street. I'd gone with one of my sisters. Christopher, Mr Montague I mean, was entrancing about the paintings.'

'And did you know about the article he was working on at the time of his death?' asked Powerscourt.

'I knew about it,' said Mrs Buckley proudly. 'I had a

key to that flat in Brompton Square. I used to go and see Christopher when it was dark.'

Powerscourt could see her now, hurrying along in the shadows, keeping out of the light, racing towards the sanctuary of her lover hidden away behind the Brompton Oratory.

'Can you remember what it said?' asked Powerscourt. 'Forgive me if these questions are painful.'

Mrs Rosalind Buckley looked hard at Powerscourt. 'I can't remember the arguments,' she began. 'They were very learned with lots of references to Italian and German professors in Rome and Berlin. But basically he said that most of the paintings on show in the exhibition of Venetian Paintings at the de Courcy and Piper Gallery weren't genuine. Some of them were copies and some were recent forgeries.'

Powerscourt had been reading Christopher Montague's first book about the birth of the Renaissance. An idea suddenly struck him. For the one thing that rang out from the Montague writings about Italian paintings was that he loved Italy, he loved the art, he loved the light, he loved the countryside, he loved the cities, he loved the food, he even loved the wine.

'You know that Mr Montague inherited a very large sum of money abut six months before he died,' he said quietly. 'Do you know what he intended to do with it?'

There was a long pause. Powerscourt noticed that Rosalind Buckley's hands were gripping the sides of her chair very tightly. Lady Lucy's granddaughter clock was ticking softly in the background. There was a sudden sound of crying as if Thomas or Olivia had fallen down the stairs.

'I do,' she said. She said no more. Powerscourt waited. The crying was dying down as the child was carried up to the nurseries on the top floor. Still Powerscourt waited. Then he could bear it no longer.

'Let me try to help you, Mrs Buckley, if I may.' He was looking directly into the large brown eyes. 'Please correct me if I'm wrong. I think Mr Montague was intending to buy a house or a villa in Italy. Maybe he had already bought it. Somewhere in Tuscany, I would imagine, would have been his favourite. He wrote beautifully about Tuscany, and about Florence in particular. Somewhere between Florence and Siena perhaps?'

There was another of those pauses. Rosalind Buckley looked as if she might cry.

'You're absolutely right, Lord Powerscourt,' she said sadly. 'Christopher, Mr Montague I mean, bought a villa near Fiesole up in the hills two months ago. He was going to write his books there.'

Powerscourt felt the questions were getting more difficult.

'And were you going to join him there, Mrs Buckley?' he asked quietly. 'Up there in the hills with those wonderful views across the mountains?'

This time there was no pause.

'I was,' she said defiantly. 'Of course I was going to join him.'

Powerscourt thought they would have been very happy, Montague writing his articles under the shade of a tree perhaps, Mrs Buckley keeping house in the sunshine, tending the flowers in the garden. But the worst part had now arrived.

'I'm afraid,' he said, 'I have to ask you about your husband now, Mrs Buckley. It won't take long.'

Rosalind Buckley bowed her head. Powerscourt couldn't tell if it was shame or an invitation to proceed.

'Did Mr Buckley know about your friendship with Mr Montague?'

Mrs Buckley kept her head bowed, staring at the patterns in the Powerscourt carpet.

'He did,' she said.

'How long ago did he find out?'

'About four or five weeks ago.'

That would be about a week before Montague's death, Powerscourt reminded himself. Just a week. Long enough to make a plan.

'Do you know how he found out?' asked Powerscourt softly.

'I think he found a letter from Christopher in my writing desk,' she said sadly, her eyes now looking up at Powerscourt. 'He had no business to do such a thing.'

'Indeed not.' Powerscourt was quick to sympathize. 'May I ask what his reaction was?' he said in his gentlest voice.

Rosalind Buckley replied in even quieter tones. Powerscourt had to lean forward to catch the words. 'He said he was going to horsewhip the two of us,' she whispered. 'My husband may be a lawyer but he can be very violent.' Rosalind Buckley shuddered. 'He said Christopher's behaviour was unworthy of a gentleman.'

Powerscourt wondered whether he should ask the next question. He felt he had no choice. 'Do you know where your husband was,' he asked, 'round about the time when Christopher was killed?'

'I wish I could help you there, Lord Powerscourt,' she said, 'but I can't. You see, since the day when he found out about my friendship with Christopher, my husband hasn't been in the house. I haven't seen him at all since then.'

After she had gone Powerscourt stretched out on the sofa. Damn, he said to himself, damn. I forgot to ask her about Christopher Montague's will. Had she inherited all the money? The house in the Tuscan hills? And he wondered about her phrase towards the end when he asked about her husband's whereabouts at the time of the murder. I wish I could help you there, she had said. Was that simply what it appeared? Or did she wish that she could implicate her husband in Montague's death, and be rid of him once and for all?

I wish I could help you there.

11

Orlando Blane pulled two paintings away from the wall and into the light by the window in his Long Gallery. On the left was the *Portrait of a Venetian Gentleman* by Zorzi da Castelfranco, better known as Giorgione. On the right was the *Portrait of a Venetian Gentleman*, by Orlando Blane in the manner of Zorzi da Castelfranco, better known as Giorgione. Through a window in the top left-hand corner was a hazy outline of Venice's Doge's Palace, with the prisons to the right. Inside the room a man in dark clothes stood with a counter in front of him. On the counter there rested a book, maybe an account book. The man's right hand rested on the book, holding a blue package, possibly containing money. The man was looking sideways at the painter, as if Giorgione, or Orlando Blane, owed the Venetian gentleman a substantial sum, late in repayment.

The two paintings were identical, except in one regard. Orlando pressed his thumb very gently into the paint on the left-hand portrait. It was hard, dried out over four hundred years. Then he repeated the process with the painting on his right. It was soft. The hardening process would have to be speeded up. Tomorrow he would put the fake Giorgione in a specially adapted oven in the stables.

Then he would apply a coat of size, and later, when

the size was properly dry, he would put on a coat of varnish. By that time he hoped the two pictures would be indistinguishable. Orlando had only used paints that would have been available in Giorgione's time. He had consulted a number of volumes in his library from Vasari *On Technique* to *Methods and Materials of Painting of the Great Schools and Masters* by Charles Eastlake. He felt sure that none of the so-called experts could tell which one was a fake. In three days the fake would be despatched he knew not where by his jailers downstairs.

The original would stay in the Long Gallery for a week or two to make sure there was no possibility of the original and the forgery being swapped over accidentally. Then it too would be despatched to an unknown destination from Orlando's prison. Orlando suspected, but he did not know for sure, that the original had been sold. The unfortunate purchaser would eventually carry away not a Giorgione but a Blane. Of what his masters intended to do with the original he had no idea.

'Let's just run through the possibilities,' said Powerscourt. 'There seem to me to be a number of people, far too many people, in fact, who might have wanted to kill Christopher Montague.' Johnny Fitzgerald and Lady Lucy were sitting on the sofa, Powerscourt on the chair by the fireplace. Dusk was falling over Markham Square.

'Right,' said Fitzgerald cheerfully. 'Let's begin with the most obvious candidate, Horace Aloysius Buckley, solicitor of Buckley, Brigstock and Brightwell, cuckolded husband of Rosalind. Consumed by jealousy, he decides to kill Christopher, the younger man. He must have felt ever so proud, Horace Aloysius, when he led his beautiful bride to the altar, an older man making off with one of the most attractive women in London. Then she betrays him. Think of the shame. Think of the gossip. Think of the sniggers behind his back. Think of his embarrassment when people begin to whisper about how she has deceived him. So he pinches the key from his wife's dressing table, maybe he made her tell him where it was, he goes round to Brompton Square, out with the garrotte, end of Montague. How about that?'

Lady Lucy frowned. Even after years of living with her husband and Johnny Fitzgerald and their murders and their murderers she found the way they talked about the victims rather too flippant for her taste.

'But why would he remove some of the books, Johnny?' she said. 'What was the point?'

'Easy,' said Johnny Fitzgerald, 'all the books were about art. Art was what brought them together. Art made them fall in love. Art destroyed the husband's married bliss, if bliss it was. Horace Aloysius decides to destroy some of the art, and the article, as he has destroyed Montague. Maybe the books are even now locked up in some storeroom at Buckley, Brigstock and Brightwell. Maybe he arranged for them to be dumped in the Thames, or taken away as rubbish. And, to cap it all, he hasn't been at his offices since the day after Montague's death.'

Lady Lucy got up to draw the curtains. Powerscourt watched her do it, admiring the grace of her movements over there by the windows. He smiled at her as she returned to the sofa. Lady Lucy could read his thoughts sometimes. She blushed slightly.

'I'm not convinced,' said Powerscourt. 'It might be true. But it looks too plausible to me. What about this?'

He stared briefly at the Moghul chessmen on their table by the window, standing to attention, waiting for another battle.

'Christopher Montague was about to become a very famous man in the world of art. Two books, the second due out very soon, on Northern Italian paintings. One article which demolishes most of the pictures in the de Courcy and Piper Gallery as copies, forgeries or fakes. So who would you turn to now to know if your Italian Old Master is genuine? Why, to Christopher Montague. He would have made a fortune charging for the correct attributions, maybe a percentage of the sale price every time a painting changes hands. Think of it! An income guaranteed for life! And if these Americans start buying up Old Masters in huge numbers, the prices will go up. Ten per cent of fifty thousand pounds could go a long way.'

Powerscourt paused and looked at Johnny Fitzgerald's glass. It was, unusually, empty. 'So this is the question, Lucy and Johnny. Who held that position before? Who was Christopher Montague going to depose, to displace? Who saw their livelihood, maybe not their livelihood, but their prospects for great wealth, suddenly removed from under their noses? Jealousy, professional not personal, and greed are a formidable cocktail.'

Lady Lucy looked at her husband again. 'So, Francis,' she said, 'according to your theory, somewhere in London is an art expert who was going to be toppled from his throne. And he killed Christopher Montague?'

'Correct. And that explains why the magazine article disappeared and some of the books were taken away. The murderer couldn't leave anything behind which might allow somebody else to finish the article and ruin his own position.'

Johnny Fitzgerald helped himself to another bottle of claret from the sideboard. 'I'm not convinced by that theory, Francis,' he said, wrestling with the corkscrew. 'Let's try another one to do with the art world,' he went on with a smile as the cork popped out of the bottle. 'Let's just think about that exhibition he was writing about. Suppose you were in charge of that. Suppose you hoped to sell lots and lots of lovely Venetian paintings. You hear on the grapevine that somebody is going to denounce most of them as fakes or forgeries. You are going to lose a great deal of money. Twenty Titians, was it, or something like that, they thought they had? Now down to three? Seventeen Titians would have made you pots of money. Now it's all gone. So they trot round to Brompton Square with a piece of picture cord, ideal for garrotting, and wring Montague's neck. And, for good measure, they destroy the article and get rid of the compromising books.'

'That's not bad, Johnny, not bad at all,' said Powerscourt. Fitzgerald happily refilled his glass. 'But there's one more possibility we shouldn't discount,' Powerscourt went on. 'The only problem is that it has to do with Montague's will, and we don't know what that contains. But it could work something like this. Let's think about Christopher Montague. He has bought his villa near Florence. He has part of one fortune still intact and stands to make many more by attributing works of art for a fee. But somebody couldn't wait for that to happen. Maybe the somebody was deep in debt and needed money in a hurry. The somebody was going to inherit all he had, including the Italian property. Christopher Montague's heir was also his murderer.'

'Have you two quite finished?' said Lady Lucy. 'I think all of your theories are perfectly plausible and I am more confused than I was when we started.'

'I'm sure we could produce some more potential murderers, Lady Lucy,' said Johnny Fitzgerald cheerfully. 'Maybe four's quite enough for now.'

Powerscourt had wandered over to the chessboard. He lifted the Moghul King from its position in the back row and placed it carefully in the centre of the board.

'Christopher Montague was going to be a King,' he

said sadly, 'in his own world.' Powerscourt looked carefully at the chessboard. 'Maybe his Italian villa was actually a castle. The bishops of the Church would have come to him to know about the authenticity of the pictures on their walls. The art dealers and the art experts would have been the knights, darting in unexpected directions around the black and white squares of his life. Maybe Rosalind Buckley was the Queen. The serried ranks of pawns are the books and the articles Christopher Montague had yet to write.' Powerscourt picked up a knight and fingered it delicately.

'For God's sake,' he was almost whispering, his mind far away.

'. . . let us sit upon the ground
And tell sad stories of the death of kings:
How some have been deposed, some slain in war,
Some haunted by the ghosts they have deposed,
Some poisoned by their wives, some sleeping
   killed . . .'

Powerscourt picked up the King again and returned it gently to the back row.

'All murdered.'

William Alaric Piper stared in amazement at the front of Truscott Park, home of the Hammond-Burkes. There were builders everywhere, repairing windows, men on the roof taking out the broken tiles, gardeners beginning the long task of restoring the grounds.

'It does your heart good to see it,' he said cheerfully to his companion. 'The healing benison of the Old Masters comes to Warwickshire in the heart of the English Midlands!'

146

'It does indeed,' said Roderick Johnston, senior curator of Renaissance paintings in the National Gallery. Privately Johnston thought with even greater gratitude of the benison of his percentage in the final sale of Raphael's *Holy Family*, purchased from Truscott Park for the princely sum of forty-five thousand pounds and sold on for a prince's ransom, eighty-five thousand pounds, to Mr William P. McCracken, American railroad tycoon and senior elder of the Third Presbyterian Church at Lincoln Street, Concord, Massachusetts. Twelve and a half per cent of eighty-five thousand – he had made the calculation at least a hundred times – was ten thousand, six hundred and twenty-five. Pounds. Roderick Johnston could buy a new house. He could buy a place in the sun large enough to hide from the nagging of his wife.

'Come,' said Piper, alighting from the carriage, 'we must find our host.' Johnston struggled towards the house with a number of heavy bags, including a number of long metal tubes.

James Hammond-Burke too seemed to have been touched by the benison of the Old Masters. He greeted them warmly in his hall. He smiled. He offered them tea in the morning room, their conversation broken occasionally by the shouts of the builders.

'Mr Hammond-Burke, good morning to you,' said William Alaric Piper, in fulsome mood. 'Allow me to introduce Mr Roderick Johnston, the art expert of whom we spoke earlier. Mr Hammond-Burke. Mr Johnston.'

Piper beamed happily round the room in proprietorial mood. 'Work has already commenced, I see,' he said. 'How proud I am to think that the beautiful Raphael has enabled you, Mr Hammond-Burke, to beautify your own surroundings in this way.'

James Hammond-Burke might have been feeling more cheerful. But he was as keen on money as before. 'You said that Mr Johnston was going to make a proper inventory of the pictures here,' he said. 'What do you think the chances are of finding some more Old Masters?'

Piper looked serious. 'The quest for beauty is admirable indeed,' he said, 'but it will not be rushed.' Don't let them raise their hopes too high before we start, he said to himself. 'Mr Johnston will look at the pictures on display. Then he will search the rest of the house to see if there may be some hidden away in the servants' bedrooms or piled up at the back of an attic. Then Mr Johnston will work on his inventory. It may not be completed for some time. I see you have already looked out some of the papers and other documents relating to the purchase of the works.'

Piper jumped slightly as a loud crash from outside echoed round the room. It sounded as though an entire section of bricks from the roof had all come down at once. The dust was rising half-way up the windows.

'My goodness me,' he said, 'the price of restoration may be temporary inconvenience, but it will pass. Is everything clear, Mr Hammond-Burke? My carriage is waiting and I propose to leave you in the tender care of Mr Johnston here. You could not be in better hands!'

As his carriage rolled through the countryside back to the railway station, Piper thought again of the asterisk system developed by his partner Edmund de Courcy. These told the initiated how severe were the financial problems of the owners of the paintings. One asterisk meant major trouble, might be persuaded to sell. Two asterisks meant technically insolvent, desperate to raise money. And three asterisks meant that financial Armageddon was imminent and might only be averted by the judicious sale of some of the family heirlooms. The fourth asterisk meant a house where rather newer Old Masters could be planted to provide a history and a provenance that would convince unwary buyers. Creating a legend for the painting was how Piper put it to himself. For concealed in Johnston's luggage was a remarkable Gainsborough, and an eighteenth-century frame, broken down into sections. Johnston was to leave the Gainsborough in an attic for a few days while he worked on the main body of the pictures on the walls of the house. Then it would be discovered. Johnston also had in his possession a couple of documents written on eighteenth-century paper with eighteenth-century ink. These concerned the commission and receipt of a full-length portrait of Mr and Mrs Burke of Truscott Park, Warwickshire, and their two children. The correspondence came from Bath. The signature at the bottom of the documents was of one Thomas Gainsborough, painter and Royal Academician.

Four asterisks, in the Piper code, meant that the owner was not to know that the painting had been planted on him, rediscovered, as Piper preferred to put it. He felt sure that Hammond-Burke would be perfectly convincing in defence of the picture, particularly when he had been shown the papers. The alternative, the fifth asterisk, was to pay the alleged owner a large sum of money to pretend the painting had been in his family for generations. William Alaric Piper didn't like the option of the fifth asterisk. Think how much money he was paying out already. He had paid for the painting to come into existence. He might have to pay more for a correct attribution. He had to pay for his gallery. It was hardly worth the enormous amount of time and thought and trouble he took to bring new Old Masters into the world as it was.

As his train pulled out of Stratford station he thought again of Mr William P. McCracken. Piper had already promised him the possibility of a tasty morsel. How delighted, how generous McCracken would be when it was dangled in front of his nose!

Lord Francis Powerscourt was back in the Royal Academy offices in Burlington House. Sir Frederick Lambert, President of the Academy, was looking slightly better than on the last occasion, although the flesh was still sagging round his eyes. Powerscourt noticed that Dido preparing her pyre, one of Lambert's own works, on view the previous visit, had been removed from the walls. Perhaps the pyre had consumed her. In her place was a rather plaintive canvas, of Ariadne standing on the beach at Naxos, surrounded by her handmaidens. All bore the marks of a night of debauchery, leaves and sections of bushes attached to their scanty robes, marks of wine, or perhaps blood, turning from purple into dark black. Just visible in the trees was Dionysus, a cluster of grapes in his hair, a stick in his hand, grinning salaciously at his new initiates. On the hill behind the god, a solitary bull stood, pawing the ground, a reminder perhaps of the Bull Ring and the Minotaur Ariadne had left behind in Crete. Higher up the hill a flock of sheep were grazing peacefully. Ariadne was staring sadly out to sea, one bloody hand raised to her forehead. Making good speed across the dark blue waters of the Aegean, a ship with black sails was heading for Athens. Ariadne had been abandoned by her paramour. Theseus had deserted her on the island.

'Sir Frederick,' said Powerscourt, 'I have been thinking a lot about the late Christopher Montague.'

Sir Frederick bowed his head as if they were both attending a memorial service.

'How damaging would his article have been to the firm of de Courcy and Piper? Could it have brought them down?'

'Well . . .' said Sir Frederick, pausing while a coughing fit racked his body. 'Forgive me. The article would have caused a sensation. It might have brought them down – all would depend on the strength of their financial position, their reserves and so on. It is certainly likely that they would have lost a lot of sales. But they could have survived.'

'And what of Montague's own position?' Powerscourt went on. 'Would he have become the foremost authority on Venetian paintings, whether they were genuine or not, I mean?'

Another coughing fit reduced Lambert to silence. He took a clean handkerchief out of his drawer and wiped his lips. Powerscourt saw that the handkerchief was now flecked with blood. Was time running out for the President of the Royal Academy?

'He would have become the leading expert on that period, yes.'

'So how much would he have been able to charge for these attributions, Sir Frederick? Presumably they could have added tens of thousands of pounds to the value of the painting? And, equally pertinent,' Powerscourt was trying to make the interview as short as possible, 'who would he have replaced as the main authenticator of such pictures?'

Sir Frederick looked at him sadly. A minor coughing fit gave rise to another handkerchief, produced as if by magic, from the drawer. Powerscourt wondered how many he had to bring with him each day. Ten? Twenty?

'When I became President of this institution, Lord Powerscourt, I tried to introduce a code of conduct for the attribution of paintings. I was trying to take it out of the shadows of greed and secrecy where it has dwelt for so long. I failed. None of the participants would agree to it.'

Sir Frederick gazed sadly at his painting of the

abandoned Ariadne. There had been no code of conduct for the behaviour of heroes, breaking all the rules as they swaggered across the ancient world.

'The real problem, Powerscourt, is with what you might call the sleepers. Suppose you are the resident expert on Italian paintings at the Louvre. People come to you for attribution of the painting they have bought. You are a recognized authority on the subject. So far, so good. But what happens if the expert is also on the payroll of the dealer who is selling the painting? Then you are no longer impartial. You have a financial interest in the sale of the painting. You will receive a percentage of the final sale price. You are no longer impartial, you are a secret beneficiary of the sale. And a secret it had to be since your attribution would be worthless if the purchaser knew you were on the payroll of the dealer. The highest percentage I have heard of – rumour, alas, only rumour – was twenty-five per cent of the final sale of the painting. That may seem rather a lot, but, remember, the dealer still receives three-quarters of the money. I'm sure it has led to a general rise in prices in the art market.'

Sir Frederick paused again. Powerscourt felt that the proud old man would not welcome sympathy. 'There must be a number of people who would have lost money if Christopher Montague had lived. He would have become the foremost authority on Italian paintings in Britain. Some people would have lost. A couple of the people at the National Gallery are said to go in for it. Or you can go to Germany. For some reason, Lord Powerscourt, people feel that German authentications are the last word, that they are bound to be right. If only they knew.'

A pale ghost of a smile passed across the sunken features.

'There's an elderly professor in Berlin,' he began. Powerscourt remembered from his first visit how much the old man enjoyed telling his stories. 'Wife dead, that sort of thing. Professor's word is at least as good as the Pope's in saying what's true and what's not true. A leading firm of art dealers in Berlin, no, *the* leading firm of art dealers in Berlin, employ two very pretty girls for one purpose only. Girls can hardly spell, let alone write, let alone compile a catalogue. They are sent, one at a time, with the attribution neatly written out, only waiting for a signature. God knows what they do with the old professor when they see him, but it always works. If the blonde doesn't get it, the brunette will. Sort of Scylla and Charybdis of the Prussian art world. The dealers, Powerscourt, whether in Germany or here, will do anything to get what they want.'

The old man smiled as he thought of the irresistible fräuleins on the Unter den Linden. Powerscourt wondered if the same tricks were current in London.

'But in fact, Sir Frederick, as we both know, the article never appeared. The exhibition goes on. Those paintings may yet sell. Somebody has got what they wanted from the death of Christopher Montague, is that not so?'

'Of course you are right, Lord Powerscourt. I suspect that may be very important for you in your investigation.'

'Just one last question. We have talked about these Americans, flocking here like the sheep in your painting on the wall, to be fleeced by the greedy and the unscrupulous. Should they be warned? That they might be buying rubbish?'

Another coughing fit paralysed Sir Frederick Lambert. 'Damned doctors,' he muttered, 'they said that new medicine would stop these fits. Doesn't bloody well work. Forgive me.' Another handkerchief appeared. More blood than last time, Powerscourt noticed as it vanished from sight.

'I have written to my counterpart in New York, Lord

Powerscourt, warning him of the possible dangers to his compatriots. He has not seen fit to reply. I do not know whether it would be wise to warn them from another quarter, business, perhaps, or politics. You may know those worlds better than I do.'

Sir Frederick looked very pale and frail all of a sudden. Powerscourt thought he should have been at home in bed. 'Please believe me, Lord Powerscourt, when I say this. I know I am ill. I apologize to you for my spasms. But I would not want you to stop coming here with your questions. I am as anxious as you are that the murderer of Christopher Montague should be brought to justice. Even if we have to hold our last conversation on my death-bed, I still want you to come.'

Over a hundred miles away to the north-west the senior curator of Renaissance paintings at the National Gallery decided the hour had come. It was just after three o'clock in the afternoon. Roderick Johnston had spent three days in the house and in the company of James Hammond-Burke at Truscott Park in Warwickshire. He had completed his catalogue of the pictures in the main body of the house the day before. The previous day he had spent in the outhouses and the attics, climbing through dusty trapdoors into even dustier lofts in search of forgotten paintings. He had assembled them all in rows in a top-floor room, looking out over the river and the deer park. He could hear the shouts of the workmen above him, repairing the roof of Truscott Park.

Had Mr James Hammond-Burke been a more agreeable man Johnston might have stayed for a day or two longer. But he was not a good companion. His conversation was limited to complaints about the costs of the restoration work and the possible value of any paintings Johnston might discover in the bowels of his mansion.

Roderick Johnston placed one picture against a Regency chair where it would catch the afternoon light. The subject matter of the painting was slightly obscured by a thin film of dust it had accumulated over the recent days, resting paint side upwards in the dustiest attic Johnston could discover. It showed a man and a woman with their two daughters seated on a bench in the English countryside, a dog at their feet. Ordered fields stretched all around them. To their left a long avenue, flanked by trees, disappeared towards the horizon, and, presumably, towards the large house that lay at the end of the drive, property of the family in the foreground. Johnston knew the picture well. He had brought it with him in one of his long tubes.

The curator set off at a rapid pace down the stairs, through the drawing room with its fake Van Dycks, through the dining room with the Knellers. He was almost out of breath when he found James Hammond-Burke staring ruefully at one of the new windows in the morning room.

'Bloody thing's not straight,' he said bitterly, his dark eyes flashing. 'You'd think those bloody builders could manage to put a bloody window in straight, wouldn't you?' He stared accusingly at Johnston as if he were the foreman responsible. 'Whole damned thing will have to come out again. Damned if I'm going to pay for that.' He paused as if he had just realized who Johnston was.

'What do you want?' he said roughly. 'Have you finished your damned catalogue or whatever it is?'

Johnston remembered the advice of William Alaric Piper. Don't tell him all at once. Draw it out as long as you can. Make him wait before you tell him it might be a Gainsborough. Only might. Suspense makes them keener.

'I think you should come with me, Mr Hammond-Burke,' said Johnston firmly. 'I've got something I want to show you.'

'What?' said Hammond-Burke. 'What the devil is it? Is it worth anything?'

'I think you should see for yourself, Mr Hammond-Burke,' said Johnston, leading the muttering owner back through the house and up to the room on the top floor.

'There!' said Johnston at the doorway, pointing dramatically towards the painting by the chair.

James Hammond-Burke walked across the room and peered at the painting.

'What do you think it is? Where did you find it?'

Roderick Johnston took a feather duster from a table and began to brush very lightly at the surface of the picture. He thought the dust should come off quite easily. It had only been in the attic for a few days.

'I found it in an attic,' he said. 'Looks as if it has been there for some time. It might, it just might, be a Gainsborough.' The duster had reached half-way down the painting by now. The four figures were clearly visible, and the avenue behind them. 'I shall have to take it away, of course. And I shall have to look at this bundle of documents I found beside it.' Johnston pointed to a pile of papers on the chair, mostly written with eighteenth-century ink on eighteenth-century paper. 'These may give us some more information. It is too soon to say for now.'

'A Gainsborough,' said Hammond-Burke, rubbing his hand through his black hair.

'A Gainsborough, by God. How much is that worth?'

12

Powerscourt found his brother-in-law William Burke sitting in his study with the floor covered in sheet after sheet of paper, a snowstorm of paper. A curly-haired nephew greeted his uncle with delight.

'Good evening, Uncle Francis, have you come to see Papa?' asked nine-year-old Edward Burke with an air of innocence. Powerscourt looked quickly at the childish scribblings on the carpet. All of them seemed to contain versions and variants of the seven times table. Not all of them were as Powerscourt remembered. Surely seven times eight wasn't sixty-three? Was seven times nine really one hundred and seventy-four?

He smiled happily at his nephew. 'Good evening to you, Edward,' he said. 'You've been helping your father with his arithmetic, I see. Very kind of you.' There was a loud grunt from Edward's father in his chair by the fire.

Edward Burke picked up his best pencil from the floor. 'I expect you'll want to talk business,' he said with a worldly air that belied his years but promised well for his future. 'May I go now, Papa?'

Powerscourt realized that his arrival had been a gift from the gods for Master Edward, now released from the torture of tables and arithmetical calculations.

'Yes, Edward, you may go,' said his father wearily,

going down on his knees to collect the pieces of paper and throw them vigorously on to the fire.

'Honestly, Francis.' William Burke was married to Powerscourt's second sister, Mary, and was becoming a mighty force in the City of London. Multiplication and division on an enormous scale were his daily bread and butter. 'It's hopeless. Completely hopeless. Edward has no more idea of the seven times table than I have of Sanskrit,' he said. 'What's going to become of him? When I was that age I knew all those damned tables, right up to twelve times twelve. They're not very difficult, are they?'

'I'm sure it will come good in time,' said Powerscourt diplomatically.

'I wish I shared your confidence,' said the anxious father. 'Even when you explain to him that you can keep adding sevens, it's no good. Three times seven is just seven plus seven plus seven. And so on. Total waste of time.'

Powerscourt felt that he too might become confused if confronted by seven plus seven plus seven. Better change the subject.

'William,' he said, 'I need your advice. It's about American millionaires.'

Burke cheered up and lit a large cigar to erase the memory of his son's arithmetical failings. 'Fire ahead, Francis,' he said happily. This was safer ground.

'I'm investigating the death of an art critic called Christopher Montague,' Powerscourt began, knowing that his brother-in-law was as discreet as he was rich. 'He was writing an article about that exhibition of Venetian paintings that has opened recently in London. He was going to say that most of them were fakes or recent forgeries. Ninety per cent or so.' Powerscourt thought the percentage figure would appeal to Burke's brain.

'My goodness me,' said Burke. 'Is that the thing at the

de Courcy and Piper place in Old Bond Street? Mary dragged me round it the other day. Can't say I enjoyed it very much. All look the same to me, cheerful Virgins for the Annunciation, holy-looking Madonnas with their infants, sad Christs on the Cross. Always some bloody Italian landscape in the background, full of horseflies and mosquitoes, no doubt. What have the Americans got to do with it?'

'The Americans, as you well know, William,' said Powerscourt, 'are just beginning to buy this sort of stuff. Montague's article was never published. Nobody knows most of the things are fakes or forgeries. Should somebody warn them?'

Burke found a final piece of paper by the side of his chair. Seven times four, said the childish hand, forty-seven. Seven times seven, seventy-seven. He took another draw on his cigar.

'Very public-spirited of you, Francis, I should say. I think, however, that unless Anglo-American relations are at a very low ebb, possibly on the verge of armed conflict, that the answer is no.'

'Why do you say that?' said Powerscourt.

'If everybody in London and New York spent their time warning the other side of the Atlantic about fakes and doubtful products, Francis, the telegraph lines would be permanently jammed.'

Powerscourt looked confused.

'Sorry, let me explain.' William Burke leant forward in his chair and stared into his fire. The last relics of the mental arithmetic were curling into ashes.

'Think of the two great stock markets in London and New York,' he went on. 'Each one is permanently trying to interest the other in its latest products. It's like a game of tennis, except the balls are liable to explode when they hit the ground. We try to interest them in some doubtful loan to Latin America, unlikely to be repaid. They send back share offerings in Rhode Island Steel, unlikely to pay any dividends. We hit back with an unrepeatable offer in a mining company in some remote part of Borneo most of the promoters couldn't even find on the map. They reply with watered stock in American railroads. None of those would be a safe home for anybody's savings, but they're traded just the same.'

'Watered stock?' asked Powerscourt. 'How on earth do you dilute a share?'

'I had a beautiful example only yesterday. This is how it works. As an example of becoming even richer than you already are, it's almost perfect. Say you buy the New York central railroad for ten million dollars. You stop all the stealing that went on under the previous man. You improve it, newer, faster engines, that sort of thing. Then you buy the Hudson railroad for another ten million dollars, which complements the New York Central in its freight transport and its passenger lines. Now, wait for it, Francis, here comes the masterstroke. You form a new company to amalgamate the two lines. You call it the New York, Hudson and Central Railroad. You float it on the New York Stock Exchange. You say this new line is worth fifty million dollars. You've spent twenty million on the original two. Now you award yourself thirty million dollars of new stock. You make sure the thing pays a high dividend, think how many shares you have in it, after all. Sit back and count the money. That's watered stock, Francis. These millionaires have been at it for years, coal, steel, railroads, banks. And they have the nerve to offer the stock over here as well as in New York.'

Powerscourt smiled. 'What you're saying, William, is that there isn't much difference between dubious stocks and fake paintings?'

'Exactly,' said William Burke. 'In the City the doubtful stock is all dressed up in fancy language, open markets, free flow of goods and capital across international boundaries, the right of individuals and companies to make free choices. I'm sure it's the same in the art world. There was a right load of rubbish in the catalogue of those Venetian paintings, delicate brushwork, sfumato, whatever the hell that is, sounds like something you might keep your cigars in, tonal balance. What, in God's name, is tonal balance? Looked like a lot of hot air to me.'

'Thank you very much, William. I shall take your advice. I shall not tell the Americans about the forgeries. And now, if you will forgive me, I must go home and make plans about Thomas's mental arithmetic.'

Orlando Blane was looking very closely at the reproduction of Mr and Mrs Lewis B. Black in an American magazine. Orlando had no idea who Mr Black was or why he had been sent this page from the publication. All he knew was that he had to produce a painting of the Blacks, singular or plural, in the manner of a great English portrait painter. Orlando wished he knew what colour Mrs Black's dress was – it swept round her slim figure in a beguiling fashion. On her head was a small hat composed almost entirely of feathers. Orlando liked the hat. Especially he liked the feathers. Plenty of people had appeared with vaguely similar hats in the past.

He was walking slowly up his Long Gallery. The rain was beating on the windows. Orlando noticed that the plaster was beginning to rot away underneath the pane. He kicked it gently with his right boot. There was a small white cloud and tiny fragments of plaster, dirty white and grey, settled slowly on the floor. Maybe the rats would like to have them for their afternoon tea.

Gainsborough? he said to himself. No, he'd just delivered one of those. Sir Thomas Lawrence? Orlando always felt close to Lawrence – the man had earned many fortunes and never managed to hold on to any of them. Hoppner, bit further away in time? The splendidly named Zoffany who Orlando felt should have been a Greek philosopher, forever arguing with Socrates in the public squares of Athens? None of those, he decided. Sir Joshua Reynolds was the man, grander than Gainsborough, the man who brought Italian techniques back into English painting. Mr and Mrs Black? Double or single? He wondered briefly if the price would be less today for a single portrait as it was when Reynolds was in his pomp. Probably not.

Orlando turned and looked at one of the messages on his wall. He had dozens of these, pinned all around the Long Gallery, extracts from works of art history or quotations about Old Masters. This was one of his favourites:

> On the lowest tier were arranged false beards, masks and carnival disguises; above came volumes of the Latin and Italian poets, among others Boccaccio, the Morgante of Pulci, and Petrarch, partly in the form of valuable printed parchments and illuminated manuscripts; then women's ornaments and toilet articles, scents, mirrors, veils and false hair; higher up, lutes, harps, chessboards, playing cards; and finally, on the two uppermost tiers, paintings only, especially of female beauties . . .

The words came from Jacob Burckhardt's book on *The Civilisation of the Renaissance in Italy*, published some forty years before, sitting happily in a first edition on Orlando's bookshelves. It described the precise order in which objects were placed on the Bonfire of the Vanities in Florence in 1497, the Dominican friar Savonarola no doubt supervising the arrangements in person. Orlando always felt proud of his profession. Above, and therefore more important than the books, above the masks, above the devices to enhance women's beauty, above the musical instruments, came the paintings, especially of female beauties. Orlando would make Mrs Lewis B. Black a beauty, fit for any bonfire.

He thought of his own beauty, cast into a different sort of bonfire, a bonfire of a marriage to a man she did not love. Orlando suddenly remembered the night he had fallen in love with Imogen, three weeks after he met her. He let the memories wash over him as he walked back to one of the great windows and stared out at the rain falling on the ruined gardens. It had been at a ball, a ball in one of the most romantic houses in England. The house itself was quite small, surrounded by a moat, and boasting three priest's holes inside where the persecuted Jesuits were said to have hidden from the agents of the Elizabethan state. Imogen had been very excited by those, climbing into one and demanding that Orlando close the secret door for at least ten minutes so she could understand what it must have been like.

It had been early summer, Orlando recalled. There was a great marquee round two sides of the house, open to the water. Imogen and he had danced for most of the night. They dined on lobsters, washed down with pink champagne, and strawberries, sitting at the very edge of the marquee, their feet almost touching the green water of the moat. Orlando remembered that a drop or two of strawberry juice had fallen on to his sleeve. When it dried it looked like blood on his cuff.

As the dawn came Orlando and Imogen were so passionately in love with each other that the other dancers moved away to make room for them. It was as if they were in the centre of an enchanted circle, a circle of love so bright that it dazzled their neighbours on the wooden floor. Orlando remembered it as a feeling of *ekstasis*, ecstasy, standing almost outside yourself to worship the grace and the beauty of the girl you held in your arms. He looked again at his quotation. Perhaps the flames of their love had been too bright. Perhaps the two of them had been consumed like the vanities in Savonarola's bonfire.

When the music stopped they had gone for a walk in the soft morning light. The birds had been up for hours to welcome another dawn. Dew glistened off the fields. He told Imogen he loved her under a great sycamore tree that had stood for hundreds of years. Maybe the tree had sheltered other lovers in the past.

In the days that followed – why were his memories always of bright sunshine, Orlando wondered, had it never rained? – they would meet for walks across Hyde Park, past the gleaming horses on Rotten Row, past Prince Albert's statue to look at a different circle, the Round Pond in Kensington Gardens. Once he had taken Imogen to Windsor and he had rowed her up the Thames in a boat. She had a broad-brimmed hat to keep the sun off and she leaned back on her cushions in the stern of the boat, her face in shadow, her hand trailing in the water, her eyes fixed on her boatman. As they went upriver the noise of the town died away. The mighty castle, grey and forbidding even in the sunlight, seemed to shrink in size. The only noise was the singing of the birds and the soft plops of Orlando's oars.

' "Shall I compare thee to a summer's day?" ' Orlando whispered.

' "Thou art more lovely and more temperate:
Rough winds do shake the darling buds of May,
And summer's lease hath all too short a date." '

Imogen had laughed. 'Two people can play Shakespeare sonnets, you know,' she said, 'the nuns were very keen on Shakespeare sonnets. Well, most of them.

' "Love's not Time's fool, though rosy lips and cheeks
Within his bending sickle's compass come:
Love alters not with his brief hours and weeks
But bears it out even to the edge of doom." '

They pulled the boat into the side of the river and tied
it up under a pair of weeping willows, the water dark
and cool in the shade. They set out for a short walk
across the empty fields.

Imogen had her arm wrapped round Orlando's waist.
She stopped suddenly and looked straight into his blue
eyes. 'We're not doomed, are we, Orlando?' she said.
'We're not going to the edge?'

Imogen had met him off the train when he came back
from Monte Carlo. She laughed that reckless laugh of
hers when he told her about his failure, that there was no
fortune to secure their future.

'It's fate,' she said. Orlando often wondered if the fate
of doomed love had some secret appeal for Imogen. 'Fate
is now calling me to a different future,' she said, nestling
closely to him as the crowds streamed down the
platform. She took him for tea in the great hotel at the
side of the station. There, amidst the potted palms and
the trays of sandwiches and the distant music of the
orchestra, she told him the terrible tidings.

'In three weeks' time, at St James's Piccadilly, I am to
be married. I do not love him. I will never love him. I will
not bear his children. But my father insists.' She paused
while the waiter brought the tea. He smiled at them. The
circle of love was still wrapped around the pair in spite
of the terrible news.

'I shall not give you up, Orlando,' she said defiantly. 'I
shall never give you up. Whatever happens.'

That was when he had started drinking again, Orlando
remembered. When he was with Imogen he didn't need to
drink at all. It was intoxicating enough just to be with her.

165

His new captors from the tables of Monte Carlo had installed him in a sad little flat near Victoria station until they worked out where to send him. Orlando didn't remember much about that time. He remembered starting one marathon drinking session three days before the wedding was due to take place. He started with wine, then brandy, then armagnac. Armagnac could make you forget, he decided. He did remember falling asleep on the steps outside St James's, Piccadilly the night before Imogen's wedding, an armagnac bottle half full inside his coat. A policeman had escorted him away. Orlando thought he had been sick through the railings of Green Park as he staggered back to his sordid quarters. Two days later, his captors had come for him – he was still drunk – and taken him away.

Ever since the start of his incarceration he had pleaded with his captors to let him write to Imogen. He could send a letter to her father's house for forwarding to the new address. For weeks they had refused. And then, three days before, his chief captor, known to Orlando as the Sergeant Major, a great pirate of a man with an enormous brown beard, had brought him the news.

'My masters,' he always referred to them as 'my masters', 'have agreed that you may write to the lady. They are pleased with you. And you may have drink this week-end. Only on Friday or Saturday, mind you. No more after that.'

Lord Francis Powerscourt was in a train, returning to Oxford. The note that summoned him had been cryptic. It asked him to meet Chief Inspector Wilson at an address on the Banbury Road in that city at twelve noon. Nothing more. Powerscourt wondered if this was the same Wilson he had met in an earlier investigation, a death by fire at Blackwater House. He smiled as he remembered the young fire investigator Joseph Hardy who had played such a prominent role in rescuing Lady Lucy from a Brighton hotel near the end of the inquiry.

Then he started thinking seriously about forgers. He hadn't given the forger much consideration before. As his train pulled out of Didcot station, Powerscourt was joined by a very old lady, who refused all offers of assistance and eventually settled herself down in a corner of his compartment. The old lady took out a copy of *An Outcast of the Islands* and began to read, muttering to herself sometimes as if she was reading aloud. Conrad's characters are a long way from Didcot, even from cosmopolitan Oxford, Powerscourt thought, returning to his forger. He realized suddenly, as he stared blankly at the passing countryside, that it would be easier, much easier, to find the needle in the proverbial haystack. Where was the forger? Was he in London? Was he somewhere in Europe, only coming to England to deposit his counterfeit goods? Was he attached to some great house with a history of paintings, increasing their holdings of Old Masters with forged art and forged terms of reference? Was he in the employ of one of the dealers, forging, as it were, to order? Was he forging purely for money, to become as rich as some of his subjects? Was he a frustrated contemporary artist, who turned to fakery as revenge on a hostile art market? Whoever he was, wherever he was, he realized as the train pulled into Oxford station, the man must have been trained somewhere. And that probably meant, if he were a home-grown forger, the Royal Academy. He would write to Sir Frederick immediately he returned to London.

There were a couple of policemen on guard outside the house in the Banbury Road when he arrived. The building was of recent construction, a solid red-brick edifice with a decent garden at the back.

'Good morning, Lord Powerscourt. Very kind of you to come. You haven't changed a bit, my lord.'

Chief Inspector Wilson was plumper now, the waist slightly larger, the hair considerably less. But his honest, worried face was still the same.

'Chief Inspector,' said Powerscourt, 'how very good to see you again. You are well, I trust?'

Wilson led Powerscourt into the ground floor of the building. 'I am well, my lord, but all is not well here at 55 Banbury Road. A young man has been murdered. Name of Jenkins, Thomas Jenkins, former fellow of Emmanuel College. He was garrotted, my lord. The same method of killing as in the murder of that man Montague in London. I read about that in the papers. I got in touch with Inspector Maxwell down there and he told me you were investigating the Montague murder, my lord.'

Powerscourt turned pale. Jenkins, who had been the closest friend of the late Christopher Montague, Jenkins who had walked him across Port Meadow for lunch at the Trout Inn, refusing to answer his questions.

'Was he killed here, in this house?' asked Powerscourt.

'He was. Let me explain the layout here first of all, my lord.' Chief Inspector Wilson advanced along the hallway. 'This house belongs to the college. Three of its younger fellows live here. They take all their meals except breakfast at Emmanuel and do their teaching in rooms up there. This room here,' Wilson opened a door to the left, 'was Jenkins' bedroom.'

The room was of a good size, windows opening out on to the Banbury Road, quite tidy. Powerscourt supposed that somebody must come to clear up.

'This little room here,' Wilson went on, 'was a simple kitchen where the gentlemen could make tea and toast for themselves.' Two cleaned cups were standing on the draining board.

'Does the college servant remember washing these cups up, Chief Inspector?'

Powerscourt was back in Christopher Montague's flat in Brompton Square with the clean wine glasses.

'The servant, my lord, is emphatic that he did not wash up those cups. And he says that Mr Jenkins never washed up anything at all in his life. He just placed his dirty things in the kitchen.'

Powerscourt was wondering about a tidy murderer, a murderer who took the trouble to clean up wine glasses or teacups even after he had killed somebody. Did he have something to hide?

'This room here,' Wilson opened another door on to a large room with an ornate ceiling, looking out over the gardens at the back, 'was his living room and his study combined.'

There was a large desk by the window, a wall full of bookshelves, a leather sofa and a couple of brown armchairs. Powerscourt noticed that the bookshelves, unlike those of Christopher Montague, were still full.

'Thomas Jenkins was found by the desk here,' the Chief Inspector went on, 'sitting in his normal swivel chair. As I said, he'd been garrotted, my lord. There were great purple and black marks around his neck. The doctors think he must have been killed between four and seven o'clock yesterday afternoon.'

'Who found him? Was anything found in the room?' asked Powerscourt.

'A college servant found him, round about nine o'clock yesterday evening. He was worried that Mr Jenkins hadn't been down to evening hall at the college. He thought he might have been ill, so he looked in. And there he was, stone cold.'

Powerscourt walked over to the window and looked out into the garden. A couple of squirrels were climbing up a tree. A garden bench sat empty in a corner of the lawn. He pulled at the window frame. It shot up easily as if it were opened often.

'Any evidence of how the murderer got into the house, Chief Inspector?' asked Powerscourt. 'Do either of the other two remember letting him in at all? Could he have climbed in through this window?'

'The other two gentlemen are not here at present, my lord,' said Chief Inspector Wilson wearily. 'They are out of Oxford altogether, one in London, one in Germany, looking at medieval manuscripts, they say.'

'God help him,' said Powerscourt, peering down at the grass underneath the window. There was no sign of any footprints but the rain could have washed them away.

'It's the garrotting that troubles me,' said Wilson. 'Never come across it before. Not in these parts anyway.' Powerscourt told Wilson about the article Christopher Montague was writing on fake paintings, about the gaps in the bookshelves, about his friendship with Mrs Rosalind Buckley.

'Did the servant say anything about the man's papers, Chief Inspector?' asked Powerscourt. He opened the desk and pulled open all the drawers. As in Brompton Square, they were completely empty.

'Was Jenkins in the habit of moving his papers up and down between here and the college?' Powerscourt asked.

'I asked the man about that,' said Wilson. 'He said that Mr Jenkins never moved his papers away from that desk. Not for as long as he'd been here. He might take a few bits and pieces up to the college but he always brought them back.'

'There was a reason why someone might want to remove the papers from Christopher Montague's desk. Lots of reasons, in fact. But why take Jenkins' papers too? He was a historian, wasn't he, Chief Inspector?'

'He was, my lord. An expert in the Tudors, so his man said. Couple of Henrys and an Elizabeth if my memory serves me.'

'I can't see,' said Powerscourt, staring into the garden, 'how detailed knowledge of the religious questions at the time of the Reformation could make you a target for a murderer.'

'Two murders, Lord Powerscourt. Maybe only one murderer. Do you think they are connected?' Wilson went on, more confused than ever.

'Yes, I do,' replied Powerscourt, 'I'm sure they are connected, though for the moment I am damned if I know how. Could I make a suggestion, Chief Inspector?'

'Of course you can, my lord, your suggestions are always helpful.'

'It would be most interesting to discover if this person had been in Oxford recently. It's a lawyer who has vanished from his offices in London, a Horace Aloysius Buckley, of the firm Buckley, Brigstock and Brightwell, husband of Montague's lover Mrs Rosalind Buckley. You might inquire about the wife as well, while you're about it. I think she was a friend of Jenkins.'

The Inspector was writing the name in a small brown notebook. Powerscourt had pulled the desk out from the wall and looked down the back. There was nothing there, only the dust of Oxford.

'Lord Powerscourt,' Wilson was putting his notebook back in the breast pocket of his uniform. 'I almost forgot. You asked if the college servant found anything in the room. He found this under the chair.'

He picked up a tie that had been carefully placed on the bottom tier of Thomas Jenkins' bookshelf. 'According to the servant, this is not one of Thomas Jenkins' ties,' said the Chief Inspector. 'It looks as if the murderer may have left it here by mistake.'

Powerscourt wondered briefly why a man would want to take off his tie before committing murder. Or after he'd done it. It didn't make sense.

'I know where that tie comes from,' he said. 'It's not an

Oxford tie at all. It comes from Cambridge, Trinity College, Cambridge, to be precise.'

And where, he wondered, as the two squirrels performed some daring acrobatics in their North Oxford garden, had Horace Aloysius Buckley gone to university?

13

'Now then, Edmund,' said William Alaric Piper, 'it's time to begin planning the next exhibition. Our Venetians are going to New York in six months' time, as you know. What next?'

Piper checked the red rose in his buttonhole. He was in his light brown suit today with a cream silk shirt and pale brown brogues. Edmund de Courcy was in conservative tweeds, peering down at the notebooks in front of him, the records of his travels round the country in search of art that might sell.

'What about portraits, English portraits?' he said at last. 'Lots and lots of those about.'

'Excellent,' said Piper, rubbing his hands together, 'but not English Portraits. The English Portrait.' Suddenly Piper could see the publicity material, the appeal to the Americans as tens or even hundreds of English aristocrats and gentry lined the walls of his gallery upstairs, resplendent Reynoldses, glorious Gainsboroughs, Romneys and Lawrences by the dozen.

'How many do you think you could get, Edmund?' he said.

De Courcy flicked through the pages of his notebooks, scribbling hard as he went.

'Nearly a hundred, I should think,' he replied finally. 'Maybe more.'

'And how many do you think would be genuine?' said Piper.

'Maybe a quarter?' replied de Courcy.

'Never mind,' said Piper with a grin, 'that's better than these damned Venetians upstairs. Go to it, Edmund. Call the masterpieces home to the de Courcy and Piper Gallery. We shall give them a good show. And,' he laughed, 'good prices too, real or fake.'

There was a knock at the door. 'Mr Piper,' said the footman, 'Mr McCracken to see you.'

Two weeks had passed since Mr William P. McCracken, railroad millionaire from Massachusetts, had taken possession of his Raphael. Had William Alaric Piper been able to see what had happened to *The Holy Family* since it passed into American ownership, his heart would have been filled with joy. Most sensible people would have locked it away in the hotel safe. After all, it had cost eighty-five thousand pounds. Not William P. McCracken. He had bought an easel of the right size and placed it in the centre of his suite in Room 347 of the Piccadilly Hotel. When he retired for the night he took the painting with him, not literally, but he placed the easel at the end of the bed so he could see it first thing in the morning. On one occasion he even arranged his Raphael just outside the door of the bathroom so he could view it from his bathtub.

As Piper led him upstairs to the special viewing chamber above the main gallery, William P. McCracken was excited about this new offering from de Courcy and Piper.

'You said I could see it at the end of last week, Mr Piper. Why, I guess we Americans just aren't very good at waiting. I've gotten to be very eager to see this picture. Gainsborough you said.'

174

Piper made soothing noises as if he were talking to a child. 'It's waiting for you, Mr McCracken,' he said, 'right here.' Piper did not disclose that he had travelled down to Truscott Park the day before and handed over a cheque to James Hammond-Burke for eight thousand pounds for his Gainsborough. 'There may be more masterpieces here, Mr Hammond-Burke,' Piper had said in his most expansive mood. 'We must wait till our man has completed his work on the catalogue.'

Once again the viewing room had been specially prepared. The windows were open this time. The painting sat on an easel, shrouded by a pair of curtains. Piper pressed a switch to bring on the illuminations. Then he pulled slowly on the cord. The curtains fell away.

There, seated on a bench in the middle of an enormous park, sat Mr and Mrs Burke, of Truscott Park in the county of Warwickshire. Standing behind them were their two children, a dog lying at their feet. It was the beginning of autumn, the leaves on the trees beginning to change colour.

'God bless my soul!' said William P. McCracken, staring very hard at the children. 'It's a miracle, it really is.'

William Alaric Piper said nothing. It was, he reflected to himself, indeed a miracle that two children should have arrived in London on the pages of an American magazine, and been turned into a new Old Master by Orlando Blane in his Long Gallery.

'Mr Piper, sir,' said McCracken, taking off his hat, 'let me tell you something. I really can't believe this. Those two girls look almost the same as my own two dear children back home. My Daisy has brown eyes, and this little girl has blue, and Dorothy's hair is a little darker than this one here, but otherwise, it's uncanny.'

McCracken walked to the back of the room and looked

at the painting again. 'I must have it, Mr Piper,' he said fervently, 'I must have it. Think of what Maisie, that's Mrs McCracken, will say when she sees it! Think what the girls will say! I can see it now, Mr Piper, on the wall in the living room back home in Concord, Massachusetts. There's some vulgar religious picture my wife picked up hanging above the fireplace at present, Moses leading the children of Israel out of Egypt. Well, Moses can just lead them all someplace else now. This Gainsborough will sit there perfectly. Imagine what the neighbours and the elders of the Third Presbyterian will say when they come to see it! My entire trip to Europe will have been worthwhile if I can carry it back across the Atlantic.'

William Alaric Piper coughed slightly. 'Mr McCracken,' he said in mournful tones. 'We have a problem.'

'Problem, what problem?' said McCracken, standing defiantly by the picture as if he would fight anybody who tried to take it away from him, 'I thought you said this thing was for sale?'

Piper nodded. 'It was for sale, Mr McCracken. When I spoke to you of the Gainsborough, it was for sale. Not any more. The owner has changed his mind.'

McCracken put his arm around the frame. 'You can't do this to me, Mr Piper. Not now when I've had the chance to see it. Please, not now.'

'I'm afraid it happens more often than you would think, Mr McCracken,' said Piper mournfully. 'The owner decides to sell. He is quite determined. The painting comes down to be sent away. There is a gap on the wall. I'm sure a man like yourself with such sensitivity to the beauty of paintings, can understand what it feels like. After a day or two the owner feels sad. Then it gets worse, Mr McCracken. After a week or two it becomes like a bereavement, a death in the family, gone from the walls of the family drawing room.

176

Eventually it becomes unbearable. The owner has to have the painting back.' William Alaric Piper fiddled briefly with the rose in his buttonhole as if he were going to cast it over a coffin making its last journey down into the grave. 'Can you see that, Mr McCracken?'

'Sure I can see that, Mr Piper. It's how I felt some years back when I thought I'd lost the deal to buy one of my Boston railroads. But I came through it. Yes, sir. We Americans like to get what we want, Mr Piper. What do I have to do to buy the painting?'

Piper shrugged his shoulders. Impossible, said the gesture.

'Let's try talking dollars here, Mr Piper. What sort of price did the owner think he would get for this Gainsborough?'

'I fear it is not a question of money,' said Piper, 'it is a question of loss. Beautiful things bring their own special powers. The owners get addicted to them, as if they were some terrible drug.'

William P. McCracken thought of the Raphael in Room 347 of the Piccadilly Hotel and his worship of it. 'I can see that,' he said. 'But I'm not going to give up. What price did the owner want?'

Piper decided it was time to give in. 'Twelve thousand pounds was his asking price,' he said, 'maybe a bit high for a Gainsborough, but the thing will always keep its value.'

'Double it,' said McCracken decisively. Piper could suddenly see what had made him such a power in the railroads of America. 'Just double it. But please, Mr Piper, can you get me an answer in the next twenty-four hours? Throw some more money at it if you have to. I had to wait a long time for the Raphael. I couldn't bear to have to wait as long again.'

William Alaric Piper drew the curtains back over the

painting. 'Leave it with me, Mr McCracken. I will see what I can do. But I am not hopeful of success.'

Lord Francis Powerscourt was looking at a map of South Africa and shaking his head sadly. Powerscourt had marked on his map the three railway towns of Ladysmith, Mafeking and Kimberley now under siege in the war with the Boers half a world away. The greatest Empire the world had ever seen was being humiliated by a couple of tiny Republics in the vast expanse of Southern Africa. His thoughts on military strategy were rudely interrupted as Johnny Fitzgerald burst into the room.

'What news from Old Bond Street, Johnny?' said Powerscourt, closing his atlas with a thud.

'I'm glad I don't really have to sell anything, Francis. That's a very strange world. I've been back to all three of them, Clarke's, Capaldi's and de Courcy and Piper, while their experts looked at the picture. Actually it was the same expert all three times. And the odd thing was, he never let on in the other two places that he'd seen the Leonardo before.'

'Do you think he was being paid three times for the same attribution, Johnny? Did he say it was a Leonardo?' asked Powerscourt.

'I'm sure he was paid three times. Twice he said it wasn't a real Leonardo. He always took a very long time peering at the picture. So after the first time I pretended to fall asleep.'

'And what did you discover during your slumbers, Johnny?'

'Well,' said Fitzgerald, moving by force of habit towards the sideboard, 'thirsty work, Francis. I think I'll try a little of this white Beaune, if I may.'

Powerscourt was always fascinated by the speed of

his friend in the complicated business of finding corkscrew, opening bottle, pouring liquid into a glass. On this occasion it took less than ten seconds.

'I think,' Fitzgerald settled back into his chair, Beaune in hand, 'I think I discovered two things. The man's name was Johnston, I'm pretty sure of that. Big fellow, looked like a prize fighter. Didn't catch the Christian name. On one occasion at Clarke's I heard a bit of the conversation between the Clarke people after Johnston had left and before I'd woken up. They said they wished Montague was still alive, as if they thought he was better than Johnston.'

'And the other thing?' said Powerscourt, wondering if Johnston was the expert who would have been supplanted by Montague, a man who might lose enough to turn him into a killer.

'The other thing was at de Courcy and Piper's. Johnston seemed to know them very well, as if this was regular work. Piper asked him if he would attribute it to the school of Leonardo. That would make it worth quite a lot. Not as much as a real Leonardo, of course.'

Days awake and asleep in Old Bond Street had given Johnny Fitzgerald an easy familiarity with this strange new world. 'They'd moved away to the other side of the room by this point, Francis, as if they didn't want anything overheard, so I didn't catch it all. There was a lot about percentages, about normal terms. Piper was very excited about some American called Black who's arriving in London shortly. He seemed to think he could sell it to him for thousands and thousands of pounds.'

Johnny Fitzgerald stared into his glass. 'Another thing, Francis, I don't suppose it means much. The last time I was at de Courcy and Piper's the porters were carrying in an enormous package. It looked like it contained three or four large paintings. And it said on the front that it came from Calvi or Galvi, somewhere like that.'

There was a knock on the door and the footman handed Powerscourt a letter. It was from Chief Inspector Wilson. And it contained the remarkable news that not only had Mrs Rosalind Buckley been seen in Oxford shortly before the murder of Thomas Jenkins, but that Horace Aloysius Buckley, her estranged husband, had been seen in that city on the very day of the murder.

'What do you make of that, Johnny?' said Powerscourt, handing the letter to his friend.

'Looks perfectly straightforward to me,' said Johnny. 'Of course it may not be. But if you were a betting man, Francis, you would surely say that our Horace Aloysius is now the hot favourite in the Montague Jenkins Memorial Handicap. Almost impossible to get any decent odds on him at all at present. Christ, look at it. He finds out Montague has been carrying on with his wife. End of Montague. Then, maybe he's employing private detectives, he finds out that she's also carrying on with this Jenkins person. End of Jenkins. I should say Horace Aloysius is three to one on, myself. What say you, Francis?'

Powerscourt stared at the floor. 'I'm not placing any bets, Johnny. It's too plausible. It's too obvious. For the moment, I think Horace Aloysius is probably in the clear. Deranged, possibly. Overwrought, probably. Unstable, certainly. But a murderer? I'm not sure. I'm really not sure.'

Two foxes were standing very still on the upper terrace of Orlando Blane's ruined garden. They were so still that Orlando wondered if they might be statues. Then, very slowly and with a total disdain for their surroundings, they trotted down the terraces until they came to rest right underneath the windows of the Long Gallery. Perhaps the rats send them messages, Orlando thought to himself, secret despatches in animal language under the ground to the foxes' den. Come along! Nobody here! Rich pickings for all!

Orlando looked at his easel. It had a large blank canvas waiting for him. The ground had been carefully filled in on the Friday before. His head was still hurting from a weekend of drinking that ended with him being carried to bed at three o'clock on Sunday morning. He had lost all his money, had been his first thought on waking. He groaned slightly as he remembered that he had only lost the contents of three matchboxes, playing cards with his jailers.

Sir Joshua Reynolds was waiting for him. So was the wife of Lewis B. Black, American millionaire, with the feathers in her hat. Orlando tried a preliminary drawing of the hat on his sketchpad. He noticed that his hand was shaking slightly. Damn, he said to himself. If that doesn't improve I won't achieve much at all today. He looked up at the quotation, pinned on his wall behind the empty canvas. It was the great Italian historian Vasari, on his friend Michelangelo:

> He also copied drawings of the old masters so perfectly that his copies could not be distinguished from the originals, since he smoked and tinted the paper to give it an appearance of age. He was often able to keep the originals and return his copies in their stead.

Orlando smiled. He walked very fast up and down the Long Gallery three times. He checked his hand. It was better now. Very slowly an elaborate hat, composed almost entirely of feathers, began to appear on his pad.

The offices of Buckley, Brigstock and Brightwell were on the basement and the ground floor of an old house just off the Strand. Legal country, Powerscourt noted, as clerks old and young, bearded and clean-shaven, erect and stooping, hurried to their destinations, bundles of files and legal documents clutched tightly in their hands. People's lives are crossing the road here every day, he thought, wills, marriage settlements, fathers trying to disinherit unruly sons, new companies being born, old ones laid to rest, all wrapped round with lawyers' string.

He asked to see the senior partner. A nervous young man, fresh from university perhaps, showed him into the office of Mr George Brigstock. Mr Brigstock looked exactly what a family solicitor ought to look like, Powerscourt felt. He was about fifty, in a rather old-fashioned suit, his grey hair receding up his temples.

'Good morning, Lord Powerscourt. How can we be of assistance?' said Brigstock.

He thinks I've come to make my will, Powerscourt thought. Complicated estate perhaps, complicated dispositions, enough to keep the solicitors busy for at least a year and a half.

'Forgive me,' said Powerscourt with a smile, 'I haven't come here on legal business. I've come to talk to you about your senior partner, Mr Horace Aloysius Buckley. I am an investigator, Mr Brigstock, and . . .' Powerscourt paused slightly to let the effect of what he was about to say sink in, 'I am currently investigating two cases of murder. I have reasons to believe that he may be able to help me in my inquiries.'

Mr George Brigstock did not flinch at all at the mention of murder. 'Mr Buckley is out of town at present,' he said. 'I am sure he will return shortly.'

'But that's just the point, Mr Buckley.' Powerscourt was leaning forward now. 'You say you are sure he will return shortly. But you don't know when, do you? He could walk in right now, or he could not walk in for the next three months. Is that not so?'

Brigstock did not reply.

'Mr Brigstock, I am most anxious to speak to Mr Buckley. I have reason to believe that the police may issue a warrant for his arrest very soon.'

'On what charge?' said the solicitor.

'Murder,' said Powerscourt. 'In the course of my work I do a lot of business with the police. I am shortly on my way to Oxford to see the Chief Inspector in charge of the inquiry into the second murder, a young man called Thomas Jenkins. The circumstantial evidence against your colleague is strong. As yet there is no direct proof. But the longer Mr Buckley remains away, the more suspicious the police will become. If the man has nothing to hide, they will say to themselves, why does he not come forward? So, Mr Brigstock, have you any idea where he might be? Mr Buckley has not been home for a considerable period, owing to difficult domestic circumstances. He was in Oxford the day of the murder. He could have been there at the time the deed was committed. Where is he now?'

'I do not know,' said Brigstock sadly. 'Let me ask you a question, Lord Powerscourt. Do you believe he is responsible for these terrible murders?'

Powerscourt wondered if the lawyer saw a tide of scandal sweeping over Buckley, Brigstock and Brightwell as the senior partner was arrested for murder. A soldier or a seaman committing murder in drink or passion only rated a few lines in the newspapers. Doctors or solicitors or, even better, bishops charged with murder had the newspapermen in a frenzy of speculation and the reading public thirsty for more. Maybe the clients would disappear, maybe the whole firm would go under, a lifetime's careful work lost in a day of headlines.

Powerscourt was quick to reply. 'No, I do not believe he is guilty,' he said. 'I am not sure why I think that, but

I do. Tell me, Mr Brigstock, when people are in great strain they sometimes have a place of refuge they go to, maybe somewhere they knew as a child, a place where they can sort out their lives, or let time show them what to do. Did Mr Buckley have such a place?'

George Brigstock shook his head. 'Not that I know of,' he said.

Powerscourt pressed on. 'He didn't have a family place in the country, did he? A place of his own? Or brothers or sisters he could have gone to stay with?'

'There was only one brother, and he is in Australia. Melbourne, I believe.'

'Mr Buckley was under considerable strain, I am sure,' said Powerscourt, wondering if his mission was a waste of time. 'Did he have any hobby or pastime he always wanted to indulge? I have heard of people who want to ride to hounds with every hunt in England, or visit every railway station in Britain. Did he have something like that?'

'I don't think so,' said Brigstock. He looked closely at the files on his desk. 'There is just one thing, now I come to think about it. He mentioned it to me once, maybe twice in the last fifteen years. But I do not see how it could possibly help you, Lord Powerscourt.'

'What is it, man?' asked Powerscourt, growing impatient.

'Well, I'm sure it can't be what you want. But he did say that one day, when he had the time, he was going to attend Evensong in every cathedral in England.'

'What? All of them?' asked Powerscourt.

'All of them,' said Brigstock, 'from Canterbury to Ripon, from Exeter to Durham.'

'God bless my soul,' said Powerscourt. 'I suppose there are worse things a man could do. One thing before I go, Mr Brigstock. Do you by any chance have a photograph of Mr Buckley anywhere in your offices?'

The young man was despatched on a mission to the basement and returned with a small dusty photograph. It showed Horace Aloysius Buckley in cricket flannels and a white sweater, bat in his hand. He was scowling at the camera.

'It was taken at a lawyers' cricket match a couple of summers ago,' said George Brigstock. 'He'd just been given out to a dodgy bit of umpiring. I'm afraid Buckley doesn't look like that most of the time. He had a splendid collection of very conservative suits.'

However eccentric you were, Powerscourt reflected, as he stared at the man in the photograph, the grey hair, the small moustache, the angry eyes, you wouldn't be attending Evensong in your cricket flannels. Some people went on pub crawls, Powerscourt thought. Maybe Horace Aloysius Buckley is now on a cathedral crawl, his anxious spirit eased every afternoon by the singing of the choir, the slow processions up the nave, the regular beat of the collects and the hymns. It would explain why he was in Oxford. Christ Church had a cathedral, he remembered. But where on earth had he gone now on his pilgrimage? Gloucester? Hereford? Lichfield? It was almost as difficult as finding the bloody forger, he said to himself as he left the offices of Buckley, Brigstock and Brightwell, the nervous young man escorting him right on to the street outside. Lord now lettest thou thy servant depart in peace.

Sir Frederick Lambert of the Royal Academy had gone very pale, almost grey. The coughing fits still racked his body from time to time, the bloodstained handkerchiefs departing from his lips to a place of concealment in the enormous desk. Ariadne was still abandoned on her island, the black sails carrying Theseus away. Powerscourt felt slightly disappointed that the painting

185

had not been changed. He was growing rather fond of the mythological scenes. He wondered if they had Evensong on Naxos, Ariadne's island, peasants in smocks, Dionysus himself in the front pew, a patriarch with a vast beard leading the islanders in prayer.

'Johnston,' Powerscourt began, 'big man. Attributes paintings. Where does he come from, Sir Frederick?'

'If he's the Johnston I think he is,' said Sir Frederick, 'he's the senior curator of Renaissance paintings at the National Gallery. They say he's got a very ambitious wife.'

'Would that pay well? The National Gallery, I mean, rather than the wife?' asked Powerscourt.

Sir Frederick laughed. 'Nowhere in the art world pays well, Lord Powerscourt. It's as if they expect people to have a private income or make money from their own work.'

'So Johnston might have a motive for wishing Christopher Montague out of the way?'

'Yes, he might have such a motive. Montague would probably have become the leading expert, the one everybody wanted to consult.'

An enormous fit of coughing overtook Sir Frederick. He got up from his chair, clutching a couple of handkerchiefs, and staggered around the room, bent almost double from his spasms. Powerscourt waited.

'There's something else I've got to tell you, Powerscourt,' he went on, as he finally regained his desk. 'I only heard this the other day. In the weeks before Montague's death there was a rumour going round the auctioneers and the art dealers that his article was going to denounce most of the paintings in that exhibition as fakes. Nobody knows where the rumour came from, but it circulated widely.'

A whole circle of suspects floated past Powerscourt's brain. Horace Aloysius Buckley, on his knees at

186

Evensong. He remembered Inspector Maxwell telling him that a man called Johnston from the National Gallery had been the last person to see Christopher Montague alive. He could see Roderick Johnston, a great bear of a man, turning over a length of picture cord in his hands. Someone from Clarke's or Capaldi's or de Courcy and Piper, peering intently at a scene from one of their paintings, a Cain and Abel maybe, David and Goliath. Ever present in his mind were the terrible marks on Christopher Montague's neck.

Part Three

Reynolds

14

Mrs Imogen Foxe was sitting in the morning room of her great house in Dorset. The wind was swirling round the terrace outside the tall windows, blowing the leaves away. Beyond it lawns and gravel stretched for a hundred and fifty yards to a small lake with an island in the centre. In her left hand she held a bundle of letters. The top one was from her mother – how well she knew that handwriting – probably another missive telling her to be a proper wife. The next one was from her sister, and probably carried the same message. The third was from a cousin in America, the fourth was in an unknown hand, almost certainly male. As she opened it, two letters fell on to her lap. She almost stopped breathing. Then her heart was beating very fast. She looked around to make sure she was alone and hurried out into the garden, clutching the letters in her hand.

The first was a very formal note, indicating that if she wished to reply to the other letter, she could do so to the above address. The correspondence would be sent on. The second was from her former lover, Orlando Blane.

'My darling Imogen,' it began, in Orlando's rather flowery hand,

I cannot say what I feel because others are going to

read this letter. I cannot say where I am. I cannot say what I am doing. But I am well and I long to see you. The people here say they will consider allowing you to come and stay here or nearby. I do hope you will say yes. I am not allowed to write any more. Remember the sonnets. Orlando.

Imogen felt her emotions running away with her. She read the letter again. It was all very mysterious, very romantic. Sonnets. She remembered the trip up the Thames from Windsor, Orlando rowing away, looking impossibly beautiful with those blue eyes sparkling against the water. When she was twelve years old she had decided that she could only ever fall in love with a man with blue eyes. She hadn't broken her vows yet. Sonnets, Shakespeare sonnets, whispered under the leaves of a weeping willow on the bank, her hand trailing in the cool water.

Love's not Time's fool, though rosy lips and cheeks
Within his bending sickle's compass come:
Love alters not with his brief hours and weeks
But bears it out even to the edge of doom.

It sounds as if Orlando is a prisoner somewhere, she said to herself. He cannot say where he is or what he is doing. Why would anybody want to kidnap Orlando and lock him up in a dark tower? She remembered the man who had paid his debts in the casino. Maybe he had Orlando under lock and key. Imogen peered closely at the letter to see if there were any clues as to its origins. There were not. She set off to walk to the lake, holding the letters very tightly in case the wind blew them away. She shivered slightly, not only from the cold.

We're both prisoners, she thought. Orlando is locked up somewhere unknown, I am locked up inside a marriage to a man my parents forced me to marry. She had resigned herself to her fate. She went to the local dinner parties, full of hearty squires and their buxom wives, talking endlessly of hunting and the threat of higher taxes under a Liberal government. She received her husband's guests, drifting through the evenings as if she were in a dream, her mind far away. She knew that most of the neighbouring families thought Granville Foxe had married a mad woman, seduced by her beauty into forgetting the vagaries of her temperament, the odd silences, the lack of attention she paid to local affairs. And, they said, she reads poetry, sometimes in foreign languages like French. No greater proof of insanity or mental decay could have been produced in hunting country than that. But on one point Imogen had remained absolutely firm since the wedding night. She locked her bedroom door.

When she reached the lake, the surface was choppy, a couple of ducks bobbing up and down by the water's edge. She began composing her reply to the letter. She would make it very formal, she decided. Mrs Imogen Foxe thanks Mr Peters for his invitation to visit Mr Orlando Blane and has great pleasure in accepting.

Powerscourt found Chief Inspector Wilson pacing up and down the late Thomas Jenkins' room in the Banbury Road. Wilson was looking perplexed.

'There's not a lot of progress, my lord,' he said, 'apart from a couple of people who remember seeing Buckley in Oxford on the day of the murder. We have talked to everybody who lives round about, all the streets for a hundred yards or so from here, and nobody saw anything unusual on the day the unfortunate Jenkins was killed. No strangers. Nobody out of the ordinary at all.'

Powerscourt produced his photograph of Horace Aloysius Buckley in his cricket flannels. He told him of his conversation with Buckley's partner and the secret passion for Evensong.

'All the cathedrals in England, did you say?' Chief Inspector Wilson's reaction was the same as Powerscourt's own. 'How many are there altogether, for God's sake?'

'I was trying to count them on my way here on the train,' said Powerscourt. He fixed his mind on an imaginary rail map of England. 'St Paul's and Southwark in London wouldn't be much of a problem. Rochester, Canterbury, Chichester, Winchester, Salisbury, Exeter, Gloucester, Worcester, Hereford, Coventry, Peterborough, Ely, Norwich, Lincoln, York Minster must count as a cathedral as it's got an Archbishop, Ripon, Durham, Carlisle, Christ Church here in Oxford. That's nearly twenty-one of them, probably some more I've forgotten.' Did Bury St Edmunds have one? Did Manchester? Did Birmingham? It seemed a bit unfair for the west of England to have three close together at Worcester, Gloucester and Hereford when the north was scarcely supplied. Were the people more pagan north of the Wash?

Chief Inspector Wilson rubbed his hand across his forehead. 'Evensong or no Evensong,' he said, 'I don't mind telling you, my lord, that my superiors think we should issue a warrant for Buckley's arrest. It's the tie, my lord. Mrs Buckley told us that the Trinity College, Cambridge tie we found on the floor in Jenkins' room belonged to her husband. She recognized a dark stain near the bottom.'

'But you can't arrest a man because of a tie, Chief Inspector. Hundreds of people must have those ties and some of them will have stains near the bottom,' said Powerscourt.

'I know that as well as you do, my lord,' said Chief

Inspector Wilson. Powerscourt suspected Wilson might often have trouble with his superiors. Wilson would never become a professor in his native city but he could be obstinate, stubborn, reluctant to admit he was in the wrong.

'They say, my superiors,' he went on – was that a faint note of sarcasm in the way he said superiors, Powerscourt wondered? – 'that it all has to do with motive. This Buckley man finds out that his wife has been carrying on with the first corpse, the man Montague.' Powerscourt shuddered slightly at the thought of carrying on with a corpse. 'So he kills him. Then he discovers that she's been coming to Oxford to see this man Jenkins. Maybe she was carrying on with him as well. So Buckley kills him too. You have to admit the motive looks pretty strong.'

'But you don't believe it, Chief Inspector, do you?' said Powerscourt.

'I do and I don't, if you see what I mean, my lord. There is absolutely no evidence, no witnesses, nothing. The Oxford killer seems to have been an invisible man, if you follow me. You don't believe it, do you, my lord?'

Powerscourt paused for a moment. There were three squirrels chasing each other up and down the trees in the garden. Far off faint cheers could be heard from a college football field.

'It's the garrotting,' he said finally. 'It's so very un-English, if you follow me. Bandits in Sardinia or Corsica or Sicily go round garrotting their enemies, and their friends too if the newspaper reports are to be believed. But I can't see Mr Buckley doing it.'

'I'm not sure I can hold them off for much longer,' said Wilson rather miserably. 'And this Evensong business, they're just going to laugh at that.'

Small drops of plaster were falling from the ceiling, breaking into fragments on the floor. Orlando Blane stared moodily at the latest evidence of decay in his Long Gallery, the dust threatening to spoil his paintings. Rats, he decided, he could cope with. The rotting walls he could cope with. But this latest cascade of dust, small bomblets falling at the upper end of the vast room, threatened his very existence. There would have to be some kind of screen, he decided, staring helplessly at the beginnings of his Sir Joshua Reynolds of Mrs Lewis B. Black, wife of an American millionaire. He had finished his drawing for the painting two days before.

Orlando glanced briefly at another of the notes pinned round the walls of his prison. Seven people were released when the Bastille was stormed at the start of the French Revolution on the 14th July 1789, he read. Four of them were forgers.

His Reynolds was progressing well, a volume of Reynolds' own writing acting as midwife to the birth from beyond the grave. Orlando had placed Mrs Black on a seat in an imaginary landscape. A delicious sunset, all soft pinks and scarlets, lay behind her, the dying light illuminating her hair and her hat. Orlando was pleased with the hat, the ostrich feathers shimmering above her golden curls. Now he had to improve the sweep of the long cream dress that flowed down to the ground. And the gloves lying in her lap. There was something wrong with the gloves.

Then he thought of Imogen. He had heard nothing since his letter some days past. Suddenly Orlando reached for his sketchpad and filled a page not with hats or gloves or sunsets but with figures. Orlando had tried not to think about money since he had lost so much of it at Monte Carlo. But now he tried to work out how much he had earned for his keepers. Four copies, two Titians, one Giovanni Bellini, one Giorgione had left his prison.

Orlando suspected that they were going to be sold to unsuspecting Americans who would keep them in their homes or in their private museums, away from the inspection of the experts. They could be worth anything from five to thirty thousand. One fake Fragonard, probably about five thousand. One fake Gainsborough, say seven to ten thousand pounds. One fake Sir Joshua Reynolds, nearing completion, probably destined for another American millionaire, five thousand pounds minimum. Whichever way you looked at it, Orlando thought, he had easily repaid the ten thousand pounds he had lost.

He stared at the horizon beyond the rain falling on the ruined gardens. Where was he? When Imogen comes, he said to himself, it's time to think about escaping.

Lord Francis Powerscourt was lying face down on his drawing-room carpet, peering at a large map of England. He had borrowed a red pencil from the children's quarters and had drawn a series of lines connecting the cathedral cities of England to each other and to London. His map now looked like a diagram of the flow of the human blood round the body, red lines criss-crossing each other in regular patterns. Now then, he said to himself, if you were planning to attend Evensong in every single one, how would you do it? You can only take in one cathedral per day. Horace Aloysius Buckley had been in Oxford on a Thursday, five days before. The sensible thing to do would to be to carry on to Hereford, Worcester and Gloucester. That would take you up to Sunday. Assuming you went to Gloucester last, and Powerscourt was only too aware that his assumptions could all be wrong, you could attend Evensong in Bristol on Monday and Wells on Tuesday. Maybe even now Horace Aloysius Buckley was staring at the extraordinary carvings on the front of Wells Cathedral, preparing himself for another helping of Evensong. Then he would, presumably, return to London. Norwich beckoned. So did Ely and Peterborough in the Fens. Powerscourt knew that it would be hopeless to hop from one cathedral to another, trying to catch up with the wandering pilgrim. He would have to place himself across the route, waiting for three or four days perhaps for Buckley. Lincoln, he decided, staring gloomily at Lincoln on his map, that was where he would prepare his ambush.

'Francis, whatever are you doing?' Lady Lucy had entered the room without his knowledge and was standing by his side. She knew her husband was capable of eccentric behaviour from time to time, but this seemed a little excessive, even for Francis.

'I am planning a journey, an interception, Lucy,' said Powerscourt, rising to his feet and smiling apologetically at his wife.

'Can I come too?' said Lady Lucy practically.

'Of course you can,' said Powerscourt, 'but it might be rather boring. Unless you like Evensong, that is.'

'I'm very fond of Evensong, as a matter of fact, but I have something rather important to tell you. I've been talking to my relations.'

Powerscourt groaned inwardly. That could take weeks, months, even years. The main phalanx of his wife's relations, the brothers, sisters, uncles, aunts and their varied progeny, would have constituted a reasonable congregation for Evensong in any cathedral in Britain. Add in the auxiliaries and the outriders of Lady Lucy's family diaspora, the first cousins, the second cousins and their appendages, and there would be standing room only at the back of the nave.

'There's no need to make that face, Francis.' Lady Lucy was smiling now. 'I've been trying to help you in your investigation.'

'I'm very grateful to you, Lucy,' said Powerscourt, cheered by the thought that he didn't have to make contact in person with the entire tribe, 'and what have you discovered?'

'Well,' said Lucy, sitting in a chair by the fire, 'I thought I'd ask around about these art dealers. The Clarkes have been there for years and years, no skeletons in their family cupboards apart from one earlier proprietor who ran away with his neighbour's wife.'

'What happened to him?' asked Powerscourt. 'How far did he get?'

'He only got as far as Dover, I'm afraid. His sons went after him and persuaded him to come back just as he was about to board the packet to Calais.'

'They must have been very persuasive, the sons, I mean,' said Powerscourt, looking keenly at Lady Lucy's eyes.

'Pistols, not words, apparently, were the order of the day. They say the father never forgave them. However, that's not important. Then there are the Capaldis, originally from Italy. Very devout Catholics, apparently, friendly with all those people at the Brompton Oratory.'

Powerscourt had a sudden vision of Christopher Montague, the empty bookshelves, the empty cupboards, the great wounds on his neck, just one hundred yards from the Oratory in Brompton Square.

Lady Lucy paused. 'That leaves de Courcy and Piper,' said Powerscourt, suspecting that some crucial piece of evidence was about to be revealed. 'Which one of those two has the interesting past?'

'It's de Courcy, Francis, Edmund de Courcy.'

Powerscourt suddenly remembered Lucy telling him a story during one of his earlier investigations into the death of Prince Eddy, Duke of Clarence and Avondale. That had been a fairy story with a young man and his mother, a young man in love, a dead wife at the bottom of the steps leading down to her garden.

'There are three branches of the de Courcys, Francis, as I'm sure you know.'

Powerscourt didn't but he nodded vigorously all the same.

'One lot are in Cumbria,' Lady Lucy went on, 'enormous estates, lots of money, all they do is hunt and fish, that sort of thing. Then there are the Nottinghamshire de Courcys, pots and pots of money from coal. Now, this is the interesting part, Francis, Edmund de Courcy says he comes from the Nottinghamshire de Courcys. But he doesn't. He comes from another branch altogether.'

Powerscourt thought of the de Courcy family as a train line, branching out all over England, red lines on his map connecting Nottinghamshire to Cumbria. Change at York, probably.

'So where does he come from?' he said. 'And why should he lie about his origins?'

'I can only guess about why he should lie,' said Lady Lucy, trying to stick to the facts in the manner approved by her husband. 'But he comes from Norfolk. The Norfolk de Courcys have lived for centuries in a huge house near the sea, not far from Cromer. But the family fortunes have collapsed. Edmund de Courcy's father, Charles Windham de Courcy, ran away to the south of France to live with some Frenchwoman. He left three children behind in Norfolk, Edmund, who was the eldest, and his two sisters. Then this Charles de Courcy had another two children with the Frenchwoman. When he died they discovered that he had spent most of the family fortune. What was left was divided between the English branch, including Edmund's mother, and the French family. But there wasn't enough money to go round. The great house is closed up. Nobody lives there now. Edmund has entered the art world.'

Lady Lucy looked sad, the bald facts of her narrative hiding so much private pain, a family torn apart.

'And where are the mother and the two sisters now, Lucy?'

'They're living abroad. It's so much cheaper over there.'

Powerscourt asked the obvious question. 'But why should Edmund lie about his family? There's no shame attached to going to live abroad. People go to the south of France or Italy all the time. And would you suppose that the mother would be happy in France, fearing she might bump into her husband's mistress at the bakery or the hairdresser's or somewhere like that?'

'It's a pretty big place, the south of France,' said Lady Lucy defensively. 'I'm sure there are plenty of hairdressers, more than enough to go round.'

'Suppose the family had plenty of pictures up there in Norfolk, Lucy,' said Powerscourt. 'Edmund could have gone into the art world to get the best prices for them. When he's got enough money, he'll bring the rest of his family home.'

'That still doesn't explain why he lied about them,' Lady Lucy replied.

'Or,' Powerscourt rushed on, his mind racing through the facts of his investigation since the death of Christopher Montague, 'suppose the opposite. There are no pictures in the house in Norfolk. De Courcy employs a forger. Maybe the forger is in the same place as his family. Maybe one of his sisters is rather a star with the brushes and the impasto. Maybe it's some embittered local artist, desperate for money. Every time de Courcy crosses the Channel to see his family he brings a lot of forgeries back with him, hidden in the bottom of a suitcase, wrapped up inside his fishing gear, God knows. Did nobody know exactly where they had gone, the mother and the sisters de Courcy?'

201

Lady Lucy paused. She knew somebody had mentioned somewhere unusual to her.

'Corsica,' she said at last. 'Northern Corsica. Place called Calvi, I think.'

'Calvi?' said Powerscourt, suddenly remembering Johnny Fitzgerald telling him about a great bundle of paintings arriving at the de Courcy and Piper Gallery. What were Johnny's words? 'It said on the front that it came from Calvi or Galvi, somewhere like that.'

He picked up the atlas on the floor and began turning the pages furiously. Ireland, no. Scotland, no. Germany no. France, yes. Off the southern coast, its northern section pointing like a finger at the Italian Riviera, was Corsica. And in a bay at the northern end of the island sat Calvi.

He showed Lady Lucy the map and smiled at her. 'We're going on a journey,' he said. 'What do you know of Corsica, Lucy?'

Lady Lucy paused. 'Mountains,' she said, 'huge mountains. Wild coastline, I think. And,' she shuddered slightly as she thought of going to the granite island, 'feuds, bandits, vendettas, murderers.'

15

'Premises secured,' said the telegraph message. 'Corner of Fifth Avenue and Fifty-Sixth Street. Ample space for display of treasure.'

William Alaric Piper rubbed his hands together with delight. At last, his agent in New York had secured a base for him, a base that would be converted into a gallery for the display of his paintings. The Venetians, currently on display on the floors above him to the ungrateful Londoners, who had bought in insufficient quantities in Piper's view, the Venetians would cross the Atlantic. Surely, he reflected, America must have been discovered in Titian's lifetime, if not that of Giorgione. Perhaps they had met Amerigo Vespucci on their travels. Now they could all be reunited in the plutocratic magnificence of Fifth Avenue. He read on.

> Another millionaire en route. Arrives tomorrow. Piccadilly Hotel. Name of Cornelius P. Stockman. Dime store money. Single. Not fond of religion. No Crucifixions. No Madonnas. No Annunciations. No dark pictures. No Rembrandts. No Caravaggios. Suggest women, possibly without clothes. Regards. Kempinski.

William Alaric Piper was having trouble with his latest millionaire. He had taken Lewis B. Black on his normal introductory tour, the National Gallery, the weekend at a grand house in the country, the reverential tour round his own exhibition. William P. McCracken, Piper reflected bitterly, may have been overly susceptible to the views of the elders of the Third Presbyterian in Lincoln Street in his home town of Concord, Massachusetts. His wife might have had strong views about pictorial propriety. But at least he had talked. Lewis B. Black scarcely spoke at all. In the National Gallery on a visit lasting almost three hours he had uttered precisely two words in front of a Turner. 'Nice sunset.'

In Piper's own gallery he had hummed and erred in front of various paintings. He seemed to be pregnant with speech. But no words came out. For a man of Piper's temperament, volatile, mercurial, this was maddening. He wanted to pick up Mr Black, not a very large man, and shake him. After two or three hours in his company Piper would feel exhausted, emotionally worn out. He wondered if it was damaging his health. He would have to go to his doctor. Maybe there would be some pills he could prescribe.

When William Alaric Piper tried to work out why Black spoke so little he could only guess. Maybe words were like money. The less you talked the richer you would become. After ten or fifteen years you would become a word millionaire, you would have a hoard, a treasure trove of unspoken thoughts. Maybe Black spent his life surrounded by people who wanted him to make decisions. Close down that factory. Invest in these bonds. Buy this mansion in Newport Rhode Island. Silence would torture his staff as surely as it tortured Piper. Surely, he felt, Cornelius P. Stockman could not be another of the silent plutocrats.

Lord Francis Powerscourt felt like a pygmy, a dwarf, a midget. He was surrounded by other pygmies, dwarves and midgets, humans ranged in front of the west front of Lincoln Cathedral, a vast structure like a fortress guarding the glories of God within. Powerscourt had been in the city for two days now in search of the elusive Horace Aloysius Buckley and the sheer size, the weight, the massiveness of the ancient building still overpowered him. It makes Stonehenge look like something a group of children might put together if they were left with a heap of bricks in a garden, he thought. Maybe God had prefabricated it in heaven and dropped the whole edifice down on to this unlikely Lincolnshire hill. The later bits, he reminded himself, dated from somewhere about 1265, over six hundred years before.

In the mornings Powerscourt waited in attendance at the railway station, looking at the passengers who decamped off the services from London or Peterborough or Ely. In his pocket he had the likeness of a scowling Horace Aloysius Buckley in cricket flannels and a white sweater, bat in his hand. No Buckley had appeared so far. Powerscourt carried his likeness from the lower section of the town up the aptly named Steep Hill. He carried Mr Buckley round the glories of the cathedral, the friezes showing Adam and Eve being expelled from the Garden of Eden, little stone people with little stone animals in a little stone boat leaving Noah's Ark, the Harrowing of Hell where the monstrous jaws of hell itself are stuffed with the souls of tiny naked sinners, Lust, with a man and a woman having their private parts gnawed at by serpents. He took him along the nave, drenched with space and light, the stone vaults reaching up to heaven. He showed the likeness of Horace Aloysius Buckley the Lincoln Imp, frozen in stone up a pillar, a little devil complete with horns and claws, covered in feathers, unable to prey on humankind any more.

Powerscourt would always remember the moment he found the living Horace Aloysius Buckley. Faintly from somewhere outside the cathedral, a house in the close perhaps, a choir was practising. And his name shall be called Wonderful, Counsellor, the Everlasting Father, the Prince of Peace. The voices soared upwards, the strings chasing them through the octaves to rise above the choir, knitting the sound together, driving it forwards, higher and higher. Hallelujah, Hallelujah, Hall-el-uj-ah. The word echoed in Powerscourt's brain all through his first conversation with the London lawyer, husband of the beautiful and enigmatic Rosalind Buckley, former lover of the late Christopher Montague.

Buckley was sitting on a stone bench in front of the Angel Choir, messengers of God dispensing the justice of the Lord. He was wearing, not cricket flannels, but a nondescript suit of pale blue with a dark shirt and an undistinguished tie. His shoes were scuffed as if he had been walking a great deal.

'Are you Mr Horace Buckley?' said Powerscourt in his gentlest voice.

Buckley stared at him in terror, his eyes bulging, his hands clutching at his watch chain as if it would deliver him from evil. 'I am,' he stammered, 'and who on earth are you?'

Powerscourt felt he could have announced himself as the Angel Gabriel or Moses recently returned from the mountain top and been believed.

'My name is Powerscourt,' he said softly. 'I am investigating the deaths of Christopher Montague, art critic, and Thomas Jenkins, late of Emmanuel College, Oxford.'

Buckley looked paler yet. His hands began a series of convulsive movements round the watch chain, like a nun with her rosary. 'I see,' he said finally, with the air of a man whose past has finally caught up with him, 'I see.'

'I don't think we should talk in here,' said

Powerscourt, looking apprehensively at the various representatives of God's purpose on the surrounding walls of the Angel Choir. 'Come with me.'

Powerscourt led him past the north choir aisle and along the north-east transept into the cloister. There was a feeble sun here, casting faint shadows across the cloisters. Hallelujah, Powerscourt heard in his head again, Hall-el-uj-ah. He realized suddenly that he had Buckley's movements the wrong way round. He couldn't have come from the south at all. He must be on his way back from the north, from Durham perhaps, last resting place of the Venerable Bede. Maybe Carlisle, though Powerscourt remembered from his train map with the red lines that connections were difficult.

'How many cathedrals have you visited now? For Evensong, I mean?'

Buckley looked at him in confusion. How on earth did the man know what he had been doing? 'Eighteen, I think,' he said finally, talking like a man in a dream. 'I've got to go to Ely and Peterborough on the way back.'

'I must ask you about the murder of Christopher Montague, Mr Buckley,' said Powerscourt, passing, he noticed, the carving of The Man with the Toothache on the cloister wall. Poor fellow, Powerscourt thought, how long has the unfortunate man been suffering? Seven centuries of toothache? God in heaven.

Buckley twitched at his tie. He pulled his jacket straight. He's returning to being a lawyer, Powerscourt said to himself.

'Yes, of course,' said Horace Aloysius Buckley firmly. 'It was terrible. The poor man looked so distraught, sitting in his chair with his neck that purple colour.'

'God bless my soul, Mr Buckley! Did you see him when he was dead? In that flat in Brompton Square?' asked an astonished Powerscourt.

'Let me explain to you,' said Buckley, looking furtively

about him. Only the cold stones of Lincoln's cloister were listening. 'I had known about Rosalind's friendship with Montague for some time. She's very proficient at archery, you know. She used to tell me she was going to meetings all over the place. I suspect she was really going to see Montague.' Powerscourt had a sudden vision of a Diana with her bow, clad in a skimpy pale pink shift, one breast exposed, a quiver full of arrows at her back, cursing the hunter Actaeon who is turned into a stag and torn into pieces by his own dogs. Was it Titian? Perhaps he could check with the President of the Royal Academy.

'She used to go out at all kinds of strange times in the evenings,' Buckley went on. 'I followed her. She always went to the same place, to that flat in Brompton Square. I saw him come down one evening to say goodbye. They embraced on the doorstep. I was only twenty feet away, hiding behind a tree. It was terrible.'

Buckley paused. Powerscourt waited. He said nothing. He observed that Buckley had stopped under the head of a lion, a rather fierce lion. 'Forgive me, Powerscourt, for burdening you with my domestic troubles,' Buckley went on, his fingers still describing strange arabesques around the watch chain, 'it is strange if you marry late. I do not think I was ever very attractive to women. So, as the years pass, you think you may end your days as a bachelor, happy enough perhaps, but without the consolations of wife and children.'

Powerscourt suddenly thought of Lucy standing beside him with his map on the floor, of Thomas rushing around the house, of Olivia snuggled up on the sofa next to her mother. Hall-el-uj-ah.

'Then I met Rosalind,' Buckley went on. 'I lost my head over her. I could not believe it when she agreed to become my wife. I had to ask her to say yes three times when I proposed to her.' He paused again and looked down at the worn stones at his feet. 'I knew where she kept the keys to Montague's flat. I had them copied. Four days before he died I went to see him. I offered him twenty thousand pounds to leave England, to go and live abroad, never to see Rosalind again.'

'What did he say?' said Powerscourt, suddenly very afraid. Once the police knew what Buckley had just told him they would have to arrest him. They would have no choice. He could see Buckley in the witness box, a hostile jury before him, a sombre judge fingering his black cap as Buckley fingered his watch chain.

'He was very polite. He asked for four days to think about it. No doubt he talked to Rosalind about it. I was on my way to talk to him that night. Only he was dead when I got there.'

'Did you notice anything unusual about his flat?' asked Powerscourt.

'Some of the books had gone,' said Buckley. 'The desk was empty. I couldn't help myself. I thought there might be letters in there, you see, from Rosalind. But it was completely empty. It must have been about eight o'clock.'

A bell tolled very loudly somewhere above their heads. It went on tolling. Powerscourt thought you must be able to hear it ten miles away across the bleak Lincolnshire countryside. He looked at his watch.

'Mr Buckley,' he said quietly. 'I find your story fascinating. But it would be a great pity if we both came all this way and missed Evensong.' He led the way past a wooden Virgin and Child on the wall into the main body of the cathedral. They took their seats at the back of St Hugh's Choir. A small congregation, the old and the mad of Lincoln, Powerscourt thought, were sitting upright in their pews.

The choir was oval in shape, the stalls of dark brown wood. On the back of some of them were inscribed the names of the local livings attached to the holder of that particular office of the cathedral. The precentor, Powerscourt noticed, seemed to have had about eight livings attached to his position. Seated angels carved on the choir desks were playing a portable organ, harps, pipes, drums. And his name shall be called Wonderful, Counsellor, the Everlasting Father, the Prince of Peace.

The footsteps of the choir and the clergy echoed around the cathedral as they processed up the nave towards the high altar and turned to take up their positions. The senior choristers wore black capes edged with blue. The others wore blue cassocks with white surplices on top. A verger with a staff preceded the Dean.

'When the wicked man turneth away from his wickedness that he hath committed,' the Dean's voice was a rich bass, sounding as though it was regularly lubricated with fine port, 'and doeth that which is lawful and right, he shall save his soul alive.'

The congregation knelt for the prayers. Powerscourt could feel Buckley whispering the words to himself as they proceeded. Man must be word perfect by now, said Powerscourt to himself, he's on his nineteenth Evensong in as many days.

They rose to their feet. The choir were singing now, faces solemn as they looked down at their music sheets or watched the conducting hands of the choirmaster.

'My soul doth magnify the Lord: and my spirit hath rejoiced in God my saviour.' The treble voices were rising towards the vaults above. The great organ looked on. The wider congregation of saints and sinners, bishops and precentors interred beneath the floor listened too as the Magnificat went on.

'He hath put down the mighty from their seat, and he hath exalted the humble and meek.' Buckley's eyes were closed. Powerscourt wondered what happened to those treble voices when they had broken. Did they turn into fine tenors or altos, still able to sing on into their adult years? Or did the glory of their youth simply vanish for ever, replaced by a perfectly normal adult voice with no distinction at all? It seemed rather unfair.

More prayers. Then, as prescribed in the order of service in the Book of Common Prayer, in Quires and Places where they sing, here followeth the Anthem, composed, the Dean's fruity voice informed his worshippers, by the former master of the choir of this cathedral, William Byrd.

That was when Powerscourt noticed another procession. Not a procession of men and boys in cassocks and surplices, but men in a different uniform, the dark blue of the Constabulary of Lincolnshire. They were trying to walk softly to avoid interrupting Evensong but their boots sounded like a posse come to arrest a murderer in the night. Three of them remained by the door of the west wing. Powerscourt thought he recognized the balding head of Chief Inspector Wilson, a determined expression fixed on his face as if he were a gargoyle from the walls outside. The rest fanned out to guard the various exits. There must have been a dozen of them.

Powerscourt wondered if he should tell Buckley, still listening raptly as the last notes of the anthem died away, his hands still now, eased perhaps by the beauty of the music to desist from the frantic scrabbling at the watch chain. He did not.

'Lighten our darkness, we beseech thee, O Lord, and by thy great mercy defend us from all perils and dangers of this night.' The Dean was on the final prayers now, the choir still standing, Buckley on his knees, Powerscourt peering through the tracery at the positions of the policemen. The perils and dangers of this night have certainly arrived for Horace Aloysius Buckley, Powerscourt thought, and they may last for more than forty days and nights. They might last for ever. Or a

211

noose and a drop might put an end to them for the rest of time.

The blue cassocks and the white surplices made their way out of St Hugh's Choir. The old and the mad of Lincoln shuffled out slowly, gossiping quietly with their neighbours. Powerscourt put a restraining hand on Buckley's shoulder.

'Don't go yet,' he whispered quietly. 'There are policemen everywhere. I fear they may have come for you.'

The hands started their desperate motions with the watch chain.

'I don't think they will arrest you in the cathedral itself,' said Powerscourt to his companion. 'I think it counts as a place of sanctuary.' But not for long, he said to himself, as Buckley's eyes started round the building.

'Is there anything more you want to tell me?' said Powerscourt. How had they found Buckley, he wondered? Had the Lincoln Imp escaped from the walls and flown to Chief Inspector Wilson's dreary office in the Oxford police headquarters? Had one of the angels floated through the flying buttresses with the same message of doom? 'Why were you in Oxford the day Thomas Jenkins was killed?'

'Powerscourt . . .' Buckley had become quite calm. 'Please believe me. I did not kill Christopher Montague. I did not kill the man Jenkins. I had gone to Oxford to attend Evensong at Christ Church. I took tea with my godson at Keble beforehand. It was a coincidence that I was there at the same time as the murder.'

'Do you need a lawyer, if they do arrest you?' said Powerscourt. He saw two of the policemen had arrived at the north end of the choir and were waiting for them to leave. A guard of honour to take Horace Aloysius Buckley from the house of God to the police cells of Lincoln.

'I am a lawyer,' Buckley replied with a bitter smile. 'Let me ask you one question. Do you think I am guilty?'

Powerscourt paused. The policemen were shuffling anxiously from foot to foot. The bell was tolling again.

'No, Mr Buckley,' he said at last, 'I do not think you are guilty.'

One of the policemen coughed, loudly, as if ordering them out of the sanctuary of the choir. Horace Aloysius Buckley rose from his seat. Powerscourt accompanied him to the door. Buckley went with courage, Powerscourt felt, his head held high for the ordeal that was to come.

Chief Inspector Wilson waited until they were just outside the west front, pygmies once more in front of the great building.

'Horace Aloysius Buckley,' he said in his official voice, 'I am arresting you in connection with the murders of Christopher Montague and Thomas Jenkins. I must warn you that anything you say may be taken down and used in evidence.'

They bundled Buckley into a waiting carriage and rattled off over the cobblestones. The choir were practising again, the sound louder outside the great walls. They must have gone straight from Evensong back to the rehearsal. This time the words were bitter to a listening Powerscourt.

'I know that my Redeemer liveth,' the beautiful treble voice soared above the towers and the statues of Lincoln Minster, 'and that he shall stand at the latter day upon the earth.'

16

A familiar voice greeted Powerscourt on his return to Markham Square. The voice was accompanied by heavy footsteps across the first floor landing.

'Is little Olivia hiding in this room?' There was a sound of chairs being moved. 'No, she's not,' said the voice. More footsteps. The voice was in the drawing room now, Powerscourt himself half-way up the stairs.

'Maybe she's in this room instead,' said the voice. 'I'm not sure I'll ever be able to find her, I shall have to look for her until midnight at least.'

There was a very faint squeak as if Olivia Eleanor Hamilton Powerscourt, now five years old, might indeed be in that room. Hide and seek, Powerscourt thought, Olivia's favourite game. He had once lost her for an entire afternoon playing hide and seek at his country house in Northamptonshire when Olivia had hidden so successfully in the branches of a tree that she was virtually invisible from ground level. Hide and seek, it must be hereditary, he had been playing hide and seek with murderers for years.

'Is she behind this chair? That would be a very good place to hide. No, she's not.' Johnny Fitzgerald grinned at Powerscourt and put his index finger to his lips, requesting silence.

'There's a great big sort of trunk thing over here. I wonder if she's inside there. Let me see if I can get the lid off. My word, it's very heavy.' Johnny Fitzgerald made heaving and groaning noises as if he was pulling a carriage and four up the King's Road single-handed.

'No, she's not. She's lost. I shall never find her at all.' Johnny's voice sounded sad now.

'Ah ha,' he said more cheerfully, 'I know where she must be. She's underneath this little table with the big cloth over it that reaches right down to the floor. I'll just bend down now, I'm going to lift this cloth up and then Olivia will be found. Here we go. Up it comes. This is where she must be . . . But she's not there!'

A note of astonishment brought out another faint squeak from over by the windows. Powerscourt made a sign to his friend. He pointed first to the double doors that divided the drawing room in two. They were not wide open, but not completely closed. There was just enough room behind the door for a little person to hide. Then he pointed to the window.

'How silly of me,' said Johnny Fitzgerald, who never tired of playing games with the Powerscourt children, 'of course I know where she is. I should have thought of it before. She's hiding behind those doors over there.' He made especially noisy footsteps as he crossed the room. 'It's no good, Olivia,' he said cheerfully. 'Time's up. Going to get you now. This is where you are.'

Johnny opened the doors with a great flourish. 'Goodness me,' he said, 'she's not here either. I shall have to give up.' Powerscourt by now had tiptoed over to the curtains. He made another sign to Johnny, pointing first to himself, then to a space behind the rocking chair in the corner.

Fitzgerald winked at his friend. 'How could I be so stupid?' he said loudly. 'I know where she is. I know exactly where she is. She's over here, hiding behind the curtains. I'm just going to run my hands down them and see what I can find. Here I come.'

With that Fitzgerald himself hid behind the rocking chair. Powerscourt's hands began to run down the curtains. He felt the top of a head. He knew exactly where she was ticklish. He wondered if it would work through the heavy material of Lucy's new curtains. There was a stream of giggles. A small girl, with the same blonde hair as her mother, sprang from behind the curtains. 'Papa!' she said. 'Papa!' and she jumped into his arms. 'I thought you were Johnny Fitzgerald. He was here a minute ago. Have you magicked him away?'

'Boo!' said Fitzgerald leaping up from behind his hiding place. 'Boo!'

All three dissolved into laughter, Olivia eventually trotting off downstairs for a cold drink. She said she got very hot and a bit frightened behind the curtains.

'I often wish,' said her father, sinking into a chair by the fireplace, 'that finding murderers was as easy as finding Olivia playing hide and seek.'

He told Johnny about his trip to Lincoln, about the arrest of Horace Aloysius Buckley. He told him about Lucy's discovery that de Courcy's mother and sisters were in Corsica.

'Are you going to go, Francis? To Corsica, I mean.'

'I think so,' said Powerscourt, 'Lucy's very excited about it. She's got hold of some book which is full of spine-chilling stories about blood feuds that can go on for generations, families murdering each other over trivial things like who owns an olive tree, for heaven's sake.'

'De Courcy and Piper have a porter who comes from Corsica,' said Johnny Fitzgerald. 'Little swarthy fellow but strong as a goat. All roads lead to Corsica all of a sudden. I think I should come with you, Francis. I think it might be very dangerous. But let me tell you what I have discovered about our mutual friend Johnston, the man who works at the National Gallery.'

Nathaniel Roderick Johnston, senior curator in Renaissance paintings at the National Gallery, known to work in secret for the art dealers of Old Bond Street as an authenticator of Old Masters, a man who could well have lost those valuable commissions if Christopher Montague had lived. A suspect for the murders, believed to be the last man to see Montague alive.

'I followed him home one day, Francis, just to see the kind of house he lived in. And the funny thing was this. I waited for a long time for him to come out of the National Gallery one evening. And who do you think I saw him come out with, virtually arm in arm, practically embracing each other at the top of those steps?'

Powerscourt looked at his friend. 'Piper?' he said with a smile. 'William Alaric Piper?'

'Well done, Francis, absolutely correct. Rather impressive, I may say. Anyway, I followed our Roderick back to his house in Barnes, or maybe Mortlake. I'm not sure where one stops and the other begins. Now then, what sort of house do you think our friend lives in? A little cottage by the river perhaps?'

Powerscourt remembered visiting the French Ambassador at his home in Barnes some years before. The place was full of great big modern houses with rather superior lions guarding the front gates.

'Not a little cottage, I think, Johnny,' he said. 'Big modern place perhaps? Lions on guard outside?'

'Big, yes. Modern, no. Lions, no,' said Fitzgerald, searching eagerly in the Powerscourt drinks cabinet. 'What have we here, Francis? St Aubin? Excellent. May I?'

A glass of white burgundy accompanied Fitzgerald back to his chair.

'Right on the river it is, that house,' he said. 'Middle of

217

the eighteenth century, I should think. Front door's by the water for the days when the Thames was the main road. Place must be worth a fortune. You couldn't possibly afford it on his salary. There's another thing, Francis. Mr and Mrs Johnston only moved there from some little house in North London a couple of years ago. And there's more.'

'How did you come by this information, Johnny?' said Powerscourt.

Johnny Fitzgerald looked appreciatively at his glass. 'Drink, Francis. Beer rather than wine. The local pubs to be precise. There's a whole lot of them down there by the river. Boating people, some City men, a few lawyers, the local shopkeepers. Mrs Roderick told the fishmonger the other day that they've just come into some more money, left them by a relative. This, Francis,' Fitzgerald refilled his glass happily, 'is what she said: "We'll always be grateful to Mr Raphael for leaving us the money. We might buy a house in the Cotswolds, maybe in Italy."'

'Mr Raphael,' said Powerscourt thoughtfully. 'I like that. Oh yes, I like that very much. Has Mr Raphael been in London lately, Johnny?'

'As a matter of fact, he has,' said Fitzgerald, 'I've been doing a lot of drinking in this investigation. I got friendly with some of the porters at the art dealers when I was carting my auntie's Leonardo around. I go and see them on Fridays sometimes, they always drink a lot at the end of the week. *The Holy Family*, by our friend Mr Raphael, was recently sold to an American millionaire for eighty-five thousand pounds. The porters didn't know what the commission would have been for authenticating it, but they reckoned it would have been between twelve and a half and fifteen per cent. Sometimes more.'

Powerscourt looked thoughtful, his mind busy with mental arithmetic. He hoped he could manage it more successfully than William Burke's son.

'Would you kill somebody to keep those commissions, Johnny? Ten and a half thousand pounds or so at the bottom end of that scale, maybe thirteen thousand seven hundred and fifty at the top?'

Johnny Fitzgerald peered into his glass. 'Think of it like a vineyard, Francis,' he said at last. 'You might not kill for one year's supply of superb white burgundy. But if you thought the murder might guarantee you a lifetime's supply of the stuff, or the commissions if you like, year after year after year . . .' Fitzgerald polished off his glass once more and helped himself to a refill. '. . . then you might just do it. Particularly if you had an ambitious wife, who likes dropping names in the fishmonger's.'

Visibility was down to about a hundred yards. A mist had fallen over the waters that separated the port of Calvi, on the north-western side of the island of Corsica, from mainland France. Powerscourt and Lady Lucy were standing on the deck of the steamer peering into the void. Powerscourt was thinking about Corsica's most famous son, native not of Calvi but of Ajaccio further to the south. Napoleon must have sailed down these passages on his way to Egypt, a disastrous expedition which ended with the future Emperor abandoning his armies in the shadows of the Pyramids and fleeing back to France in case he lost power. Napoleon must have seen his native island looming out of the sea on his left when he made his escape from Elba, the hundred days of glory that ended in the charnel fields of Waterloo, and another sea voyage to the yet more remote island of St Helena.

Gradually the mist began to clear and a watery sun crept out of hiding to light their passage. Very faintly, to the starboard side, he could see the outline of a long strip of land, Cap Corse, the northernmost tip of the island. Then, as the sun broke through, he saw the island clear for the first time.

'My God, Lucy, it's very beautiful. Look at the coastline.' A curling succession of beaches lay peacefully on the shore, small breakers climbing lazily up the sand. Between them were rocky bays where the sea crashed against the rocks, faint lines of spray easily seen from their boat.

'Look at the mountains, Francis, just look at them.' Lady Lucy was shivering softly as she spoke. 'They're much bigger than anything in Wales or Scotland.'

Ahead of them at the end of a long semicircular bay fringed with pines lay the port of Calvi, its improbable citadel standing guard over the little town. Behind it, behind the beaches, behind the rocky promontories where the spray shot upwards in the late afternoon sun, behind everything were the mountains. Great jagged peaks lay in enfiladed rows behind the plain, bare rocky slopes rising towards the sky. They brooded over the island. We have been here long before the various humans came, they said, before the Greeks, before the Romans, before the Saracens, the Pisans, the Genoese, the French. We shall be here long after you have all gone. Dotted about on the slopes minute villages could be seen, lofty campaniles a place of lookout against invaders from the sea.

They dined on kid and roast potatoes, washed down with the fierce local wine. Powerscourt thought Johnny Fitzgerald would have found it interesting, a word he frequently used when confronted with crude and uncivilized vintages. They walked around the streets of Calvi as the wind rose and brought great breakers hammering on to the sands of Calvi's beach. Behind the sand the mountains, almost black now, brooded over the Gulf of Calvi.

'Do you have a plan for tomorrow, Francis?' said Lady Lucy, walking along the little quayside dotted with fishing boats and a few cafés where the native Calvais were settling down to an evening of cards and wine.

'I am going to see the police chief in the morning, Lucy. The Commissioner of the Metropolitan Police gave me an introduction. He has the most magnificent name. He's called Antonio Imperiali. What do you think of that?'

'Do you think he's descended from the Emperor himself?' said Lady Lucy, drawing her shawl tight around her neck as the cold wind whipped in from the sea.

'He may be,' said Powerscourt, watching a fishing boat cast off its moorings and set out to sea, a villainous crew working busily on deck. 'I think the Corsicans did pretty well out of Napoleon's Empire. They fought all over the place, all the way from Austerlitz to Moscow, I think. Seventeen of them became generals in the Grande Armée. Wouldn't be surprising if some of the natives ended up being called Imperiali.'

The real Captain Imperiali was a swarthy pirate of a man, with a greasy moustache and a self-satisfied manner. He looked carefully at Powerscourt's introduction.

'How is it with my colleagues in London?' he asked. 'They do not yet catch the Ripper, I think.' Powerscourt was amazed at how the fame of the Whitechapel murderer had reached the Corsicans and lived on for years after the event. Murders, he thought, had always been a staple of Corsican life if Lady Lucy's book was to be believed. Maybe they thought there was a vendetta, a blood feud, running through the streets of the East End. Later, not very much later, he was to regret his frankness with Captain Imperiali.

'I am looking for an English family who live in the area,' he said. 'I think they are called de Courcy, although they may be living under a false name. I have reason to believe that they are resident in the neighbourhood of Calvi. There is no suspicion of any crime having being committed by them. And I am looking for a forger, a man who may operate out of the same area, maybe even the same house, I do not know. If there is a forger here, there would be a lot of traffic in canvases and paintings being shipped back to England.'

Captain Imperiali smiled a conspiratorial smile. Powerscourt noticed that his teeth were terrible. There were great gaps in his mouth, like the gaps in the mountains behind his office.

'See how you come to the right place for your information, Lord Powerscourt,' he said. 'I take a look at these papers here.' He waved at a mountain of apparently unsorted material on the table next to his desk. Outside a police seagull perched cheekily on the window sill. 'Now then . . .' Captain Imperiali began a hunt through his documents. 'My colleagues in the French police, when they come here, always they talk to us about the filing systems, the order, the routines of the police work. But we Corsicans do not like the filing systems, the routine, the order of the police work. I do not even think my countrymen like the police work very much either. Here it is! This is what you need.'

He pulled a large sheet of paper from the surrounding chaos. 'When they come here to live, the foreigners, they have to register with the authorities. I think I have seen this family in Calvi sometimes. A mother and two daughters, one very pretty, perhaps you will like her, Lord Powerscourt. They are indeed called de Courcy. And they live in a big house called La Giocanda at the back of the main square in Aregno, the Aregno on the hill, not the one on the shore. Oh yes,' Captain Imperiali leaned back in his chair and took another puff on his cheroot, 'I think this young milady would certainly like me. Most of the foreign women fall for the charms of the Captain Imperiali!'

A wolfish look crossed his face. Powerscourt wondered if his ancestors had been pirates, carrying protesting maidens away in their marauding expeditions across the Mediterranean.

'I am most grateful, Captain,' said Powerscourt, trying to remain charming. 'And what of the forger? Or paintings sent abroad from here?'

'I do not know about any forgers operating in the Balagne, our part of Corsica,' said the Captain. 'We do not have,' he began to laugh at his own witticism, 'we do not have the registration forms for the forgers, you understand! Registration forms for forgers, that would excite the policemen from France, I am sure!'

Powerscourt laughed at the Captain's little joke. He began thinking it was time to leave. Except for the canvases. Did the man know anything about the canvases?

He did. 'Paintings being sent away?' Imperiali said, the gaps between his teeth clearly visible again. 'There are always paintings being sent away. This English family, I think, they have been sending old canvases with old paintings to London for some time. But what of it? The people in London must have something to hang on their walls. No great artist has yet come forward with the scenes from the life of Jack the Ripper, I think. They would be very popular here in Corsica.'

Two days later Powerscourt and Lady Lucy were trotting along the main road from Calvi to Ile Rousse. The turn-off, a track rather than a road, Powerscourt suspected, would be about half-way along. A card had been despatched to the de Courcy family in their hilltop mansion, saying that Lord and Lady Powerscourt were visiting the area and would like to consult Mrs de Courcy about the problems of living here as an expatriate. Their coachman, a short swarthy man who did not smile or speak, concentrated on steering his horses round the potholes in the road.

The day before Powerscourt had taken Lady Lucy on a pilgrimage. A couple of miles to the south of Calvi a long thin rocky promontory stretched out into the waters of the Mediterranean. The land was rough, the sea crashing in on all sides, adventurous seagulls flying low beneath the cliffs. 'They call this place La Revellata, Lucy,' said Powerscourt, 'I want you to imagine you are a British sailor about a hundred years ago. Britain is at war with revolutionary France. Corsica is a place of supreme strategic importance in the Mediterranean. Whoever controls it can control the sea lanes, the traffic, not just of men of war and ships of the line, but the ordinary produce of the neighbouring areas. No olive oil, no timber for export. So, the British need to capture the rocky outpost. They need to control Calvi.'

Powerscourt paused and waved at the vast expanse of grey sea stretching out to a distant horizon. 'You are the captain of an English ship, Lucy. Your admiral tells you to make a landing on this patch of coast. And to bring some of the ships' guns with you. Where would you bring them ashore?'

'I don't think I'd be very good as a sailor, Francis,' said Lady Lucy. 'My family have always suffered from seasickness. That's why they all joined the army.'

'Pretend you're a good sailor, Lucy. Where would you land?'

'There's only one place where you could bring things ashore without being crushed to pieces on the rocks,' Lady Lucy said sensibly, pointing to a tiny beach a hundred yards away. 'There. On that little patch of sand.'

'Very good, Lucy,' said Powerscourt, pulling her down towards the inlet. 'So, maybe in the daytime, maybe in the dark when the Corsicans aren't looking, you bring your men and your guns ashore. You haul the guns up this terrible slope – think how long that must have taken, the sailors pulling at the ropes, swearing viciously as they lost their foothold, sometimes perhaps the guns too heavy to move at all. You reach the top. You move them along the coast until they overlook the town of Calvi on that hill over there.' Powerscourt pointed upwards to a rise in the ground which looked down at the citadel on the other side.

'Come, Lucy,' he said, a wave covering his boots as he stood on the tiny beach, 'we must gain the rise over there. Maybe it was dark.' Powerscourt was panting slightly now as he hastened up the track back the way they had come, holding firmly on to Lady Lucy's hand, warm and soft to his touch. 'Maybe the orders said the guns had to be in position by dawn. Somewhere over there,' he pointed at a towering flotilla of mountains, staring imperturbably down on to their island, 'somewhere behind the highest peak, you see streaks of faint green or blue. As the sun comes up the battery is in position, staring down at the unsuspecting inhabitants of Calvi, soon to huddle together inside their citadel. You fire two shots to tell the fleet out there in the bay,' he pointed to an empty sea, 'that you have arrived. The sailors build a tower so the signal midshipman can send his messages to the admiral. Then you start the bombardment.'

'How long did it last?' said Lady Lucy, suddenly deciding to sit down on a convenient lump of granite. Hot work pulling all those guns up the hill. Powerscourt was lying on the ground, inspecting the seagulls who whirled in the clouds above him.

'It lasted four weeks. The English poured eleven thousand shot and three thousand shells down into the tiny town. But that's not the important bit.' He rose and pulled Lady Lucy to her feet.

'You, as I said, are the captain in charge. One day you are bending to your work again, aligning the guns perhaps, or inspecting the mountings to see they haven't fallen out of true. There is a terrible accident. You, the captain, are hit in the face by an explosion of stones. The surgeon, a man more used to sawing limbs off in the heat of battle than tending people's faces, is summoned from the fleet. Grave doubts are expressed as to whether you will ever see again. You may be blind for life, that impossible person, a sightless sailor, doomed to eke out your days on half-pay in some forgotten village or begging for your daily bread on the streets of Portsmouth.'

'So what happened, Francis?' Lady Lucy looked concerned at the prospect of life as a blinded sea captain.

'He only lost his right eye,' said Powerscourt, smiling.

'And who was this sea captain, Francis?'

'I've always thought it remarkable that he was nearly put out of action here on the island of his greatest enemy,' said Powerscourt. 'Down there,' he gestured vaguely to the south, 'was Napoleon's birthplace. Here Horatio Nelson, the man who stopped him invading England at Trafalgar, nearly lost his sight.'

226

17

The road from Calvi to Ile Rousse skirted the shore. Sometimes Powerscourt and Lady Lucy could look back on the bay of Calvi with its semicircular bay and its pines, sometimes all they could see was the unforgiving land, dotted with stones and the occasional sheep, olive trees bent into strange twisted shapes by the force of the Corsican wind. As they came down a hill they could see another perfect beach, half a mile or more of sand with a fortress at one end and rough rocks marking its limit at the other. The coachman pointed his whip upwards to the hills and the mountains. 'Aregno up there,' he said, flicking a fly from his face.

Perched at the top of the hill, in a perfect circle on its crest, was the mountain village of San Antonino. It looked like a jewel in the weak afternoon sunlight. Only close up could the visitor have seen the crumbling masonry, the holes in the roofs, the vanished windows that bore witness to Corsican poverty. Aregno was half-way up the hill. They stopped briefly to let a flock of sheep go by, the shepherd staring at them angrily as if they had trespassed on his land. Powerscourt patted his pocket for reassurance. Lady Lucy held very tightly on to her bag.

'What do you think we should say to the family, Francis? We can hardly ask them if they think their son

227

killed Christopher Montague, can we?' Lady Lucy had to speak quite loudly against the noise of the wheels as they struggled up the track.

'We said we have friends who are thinking of coming to live here. And we could mention the Venetian exhibition – was that their son who had organized it? And,' Powerscourt added darkly, 'surely some of your relations must have known these people in England.'

'Even here, Francis, half-way up a Corsican mountain,' said Lady Lucy, 'you can still manage to reproach me about my family. I can't help it if there are so many, can I?'

'Of course not,' said Powerscourt loyally. 'Look, I think we've arrived.'

The coach had stopped in front of a very handsome house behind the main square of Aregno, a quarter dominated by mangy dogs and a quartet of gnarled old men gossiping in a dingy café. A cracked bell in the tower of the church was trying to toll the hour of three.

La Giocanda was a mansion on four floors, built in the finest style of the French eighteenth century. It would not have looked out of place on the mainland, on the outskirts of a provincial town perhaps, or nestling on a hilltop surrounded by its thousands of acres and rich fields. Powerscourt wondered how anybody could have had the money to build or maintain it in this island of rock and granite. A limping footman showed them to the drawing room on the first floor, with magnificent views ranging down to the coast and the distant blue of the Mediterranean.

Mrs Alice de Courcy was surrounded by her two daughters, Julia and Sarah. Lady Lucy wondered how long it had been since they had entertained English visitors in this beautiful room. The girls' clothes were impeccable, but in a style that had gone out of fashion in London three years before.

228

'Good afternoon, Lord Powerscourt, Lady Powerscourt, welcome to Aregno. May I introduce my daughters Julia and Sarah?' Mrs de Courcy was behaving exactly as she would have done at home in Norfolk. 'Some tea, perhaps,' she went on, casting a meaningful glance at the servant, who hobbled off towards the lower floors, uneven noises coming from his boots as he limped down the stairs.

'How very good of you to receive us at such short notice,' said Powerscourt gallantly, noting how little furniture there was in the room, apart from a couple of sofas and some small tables.

'Do you find Corsica a pleasant place to live, Mrs de Courcy?' asked Lady Lucy, 'I think we mentioned that we have some friends who are thinking of coming to live here.'

Alice de Courcy smiled. 'Well, it's certainly cheap,' she said, 'much cheaper than the south of France.'

The two girls looked shocked. Surely Mama should not have mentioned such a thing just a few minutes into their acquaintance. They had no idea of the trouble their mother took to save money, economizing on food, on clothes for herself, on furniture for the house, on travel. They could not have known how much of her day was spent thinking about money, or the lack of money. Only on the girls did she willingly spend it. She told her daughters after the visitors had gone that she had been thinking about the lack of money that morning, she had been thinking about the lack of money that afternoon, she had been thinking about the lack of money even as the visitors were shown into the room. It had, she said, just slipped out. She was so sorry if she had embarrassed them.

Lady Lucy was quick to spot the blushes spreading up the girls' cheeks, their looks away to hide their shame.

'Why, Mrs de Courcy,' she said brightly, 'that is the

229

single most useful thing you could have told us! Our friends, the ones we mentioned in our note, are indeed most concerned about money. They lost all their fortune in some imprudent investments. Now they are waiting for an inheritance but the rich uncle is in no hurry to die.'

'And there must be other advantages,' Powerscourt chipped in to join the rescue party. 'The countryside is very beautiful.'

Alice de Courcy smiled at them both. 'I think the girls find the countryside more appealing than I do. They walk for miles up into the mountains and along the coast. I'm afraid that after a time I found the mountains oppressive. It's as if they're watching you, judging you all the time. Now I find myself longing for somewhere flat. When we get back to East Anglia I shall be able to breathe freely again.'

'And is there much in the district in the way of society?' said Lady Lucy, suddenly aware that she sounded like a new arrival in the flat lands of the Home Counties. 'Are you able to mingle freely with the local people?'

The two girls laughed bitterly. Outside the windows Powerscourt noticed two huge mountain birds, kites or buzzards he thought, circling slowly above the house. Three times he saw them pass, their wings scarcely moving at all, before they vanished from sight to scour the valley below.

'Julia, Sarah,' said their mother, 'perhaps you'd better speak about that.'

'Well,' said Julia, 'we've hardly got to know any Corsicans at all, apart from the servants and the shopkeepers in Calvi and Ile Rousse. There aren't any gentry left here at all. Only poor people. And most of the Corsicans are very poor. I don't think they like having strangers living with them at all.'

'There are a few English people living round here,'

230

said Sarah, 'but they're either very old or very eccentric. One man has come to live here until he's climbed every mountain in the island. A brave prospect, no doubt, but it makes for limited opportunities for conversation once you've heard of his latest conquest, the mountain I mean, and the high cost of hiring local guides.'

The limping servant returned with a tray of tea. Mrs de Courcy did the honours.

'I think we've been to two balls and three afternoon parties in the three years we've been here,' said Julia bitterly. 'Sometimes they have a dance when the French ships call into the port, that's all. Once we went to a celebration of New Year where all the dishes were made with chestnuts, chestnut bread made with chestnut flour, chestnut purée, chestnut sorbets. It was terrible.'

Lady Lucy felt it was time to move on from the social isolation of the girls, perched up here part-way into the mountains with the kites circling round them. Maybe they had eagles higher up. Or vultures.

'Tell me, Mrs de Courcy,' she said brightly, 'is the Edmund de Courcy who runs the de Courcy and Piper Gallery in London any relation of yours by any chance?'

Alice de Courcy suddenly came alive, thoughts of the lack of money banished by the mention of her son.

'Edmund,' she said proudly, 'is my son. How is the gallery doing? Is it prospering?'

'They have just had a most successful exhibition of Venetian paintings, Mrs de Courcy,' said Powerscourt, his brain shifting suddenly into a different gear. 'I believe there is talk of the firm opening in New York.'

'New York?' said the girls in unison, social isolation suddenly at an end in a glittering succession of soirées on Fifth Avenue and boxes at the Metropolitan Opera House.

'Well,' said Powerscourt, smiling at their enthusiasm, 'I don't think it's opened quite yet.' That did not

231

diminish the eagerness of the girls. Lady Lucy saw them both sink into a kind of reverie, a dream of escape.

'Does Edmund manage to find the time to visit you and the family here?' asked Powerscourt in his most innocent voice.

'He is very busy with his work, you understand, Lord Powerscourt,' said Mrs de Courcy, pouring Lady Lucy another cup of tea, 'but he has been to see us twice. He stayed for four days and a morning the first time, the second time he could only manage three nights and an afternoon before he had to go home.' Powerscourt could imagine how every detail of the visit would have been discussed time after time by the three women after Edmund had left, a piece of treasure to last them into their lonely future.

'We are able to help him in his work,' said Sarah. 'We collect old pictures and old picture frames for him and send them over to London.'

Old pictures, old frames, thought Powerscourt. Did forgers need old frames, old canvases on which they could produce fresh works in the manner of the past?

'But tell me, Lady Powerscourt,' said Julia, 'did you attend the exhibition yourself? Did you see Edmund? Was he with anybody special?'

'And what about his great friend,' said Sarah, 'George Carrington, the one who was going to marry that Emily Morgan? Has he married her yet?'

'And his other friend, the one Mama always liked,' Julia carried on the interrogation, 'Robert Packard, is he married yet?'

'And,' said Sarah, carried away on the flood, 'our own dear friend Harriet Ward. Has she married that army officer of hers?'

'Philip Massie?' said Julia, blushing slightly. 'Any news of him?'

'Ladies, ladies,' said Lady Lucy, banging her spoon against the side of her cup to plead for silence, 'please, please. Let me try to answer your questions where I can. I did indeed see your brother at the Venetian exhibition, but he was talking to a huge man, well over six feet, who looked like a prize fighter.' Roderick Johnston, thought Powerscourt, he of the National Gallery, the large house on the river in Mortlake, recent inheritor from the munificence of Mr Raphael. He suddenly wondered about Mr Raphael's picture frame. 'As to the rest of your queries,' Lady Lucy went on, 'I can only help you with one of them. George Carrington did marry Emily Morgan, last year I think. The daughter of one of my second cousins was a bridesmaid, I seem to recall. As for the rest I cannot help you now. But if you would like to give me a list of your questions I shall see what I can do and I shall write to you from London. I don't suppose your brother is of much assistance in such matters. Men usually aren't.' She smiled ambiguously at her husband, who nodded sadly in agreement.

'May we go and write our list, Mama?' said Julia, as she and Sarah prepared to depart.

'Of course,' said Mrs de Courcy, 'how very kind of Lady Powerscourt to take the trouble to assist you.'

Powerscourt had walked over to the window. Below him in the untidy yard was a miscellaneous collection of old cartwheels, bits of broken furniture, dead sofas whose springs were hanging out in the afternoon sun. He raised his eyes.

'The view is magnificent, Mrs de Courcy. Mountains and sea, the perfect romantic cocktail. Do you tire of it?'

Alice de Courcy winced. 'You may call me unromantic, if you wish, Lord Powerscourt, but I tired of it very quickly. It leaves me cold now. I think the girls like it, however.'

'And are there any plans,' Powerscourt turned to face

his hostess, 'forgive me if this sounds a rude question, but do you have any plans to come back to England?'

'I'm sure the girls could come and stay with us during the season, if they would like that,' said Lady Lucy, offering support and the prospect of unlimited supplies of young men to aid her consort.

'You have both been very kind,' said Alice de Courcy. 'I will tell you, but I would ask you not to pass it on to anybody else.' The surest way, in normal circumstances, thought Powerscourt, for a piece of news to be disseminated as widely as possible inside a week. But he and Lady Lucy would be true.

'Edmund has always said,' the pride in her son rang through Alice de Courcy's words, 'that when he has made enough money from the gallery to repair our house in Norfolk and for us all to live comfortably, then he would bring us back. He thought it would be two years from now. But he wrote last week to say that things had gone better than expected with the gallery.' She paused. They could hear a pair of horses' hooves fading away down the hill.

'We could be home for Christmas,' she said. Lady Lucy could see tears of happiness forming in her eyes. 'But please don't tell the girls. I want it to be a surprise.'

Powerscourt was wondering how much money it would take to repair a house near the Norfolk coast left empty for three or four years as they set out down the stairs of the eighteenth-century house in Aregno. Maybe the estate needed improvement as well. Thirty thousand? Forty thousand? He thought of the eighty-five thousand paid for the Raphael. Suppose it was a forgery. Suppose a number of other forgeries had been sold by the outwardly respectable firm of de Courcy and Piper, art dealers of Old Bond Street. Suppose de Courcy took half the proceeds. Surely he could bring his family home now? And suppose some of the forgeries might have been exposed by the late Christopher Montague? Much better to have him out of the way.

His thoughts were interrupted at the front door.

'Wake up, Francis,' said Lady Lucy. 'The carriage has gone. It's simply disappeared.'

'Oh dear,' said Mrs de Courcy anxiously, 'that does happen sometimes with the local coachmen. They forget they're meant to wait, or they have to be somewhere else. One of ours ran off one day because he had to go to his cousins' hunting party on the other side of the island.'

'Damn,' said Powerscourt, striding to the front of the little drive to see if the coachman had joined the drinkers in the café in what passed for Aregno's main square. He hadn't.

'How long would it take to walk down the hill?' he asked the girls.

'Much better to be going down the hill than up it,' said Sarah, handing over their letter to a better world. 'We've done it in just over half an hour. You should be able to catch the train back to Calvi in Algajola down at the bottom. There's one in about an hour and a half.'

They set off down the slope, a pealing campanile at the edge of Aregno's main square observing their passage down the hill. Ahead of them, sometimes hidden by the folds in the track, lay the pale sands of Aregno beach. To their right the scrub stretched out across the valley to another campanile in the village of Corbara, staring out towards the red rocks of Ile Rousse. Calvi was, for the moment, invisible. Behind them the mountains, cast in deep shadow, watched over their island.

'I don't like it,' said Powerscourt, slipping slightly on a hairpin bend. 'Why should that fellow have gone off like that? We paid him well enough, heaven knows.'

'Had you given him the money for the whole day, Francis?' said Lady Lucy practically.

'Well, I had, as a matter of fact,' replied Powerscourt. 'I thought it was the decent thing to do.'

'Well, there you are,' said Lady Lucy. 'He's probably gone off to drink it all away in some bar with his friends.'

Powerscourt muttered inaudibly to himself. All Lady Lucy could catch was the word savages, repeated several times.

They had gone about a third of the way, walking in the shade where they could, when it started. From somewhere higher up on the hill, a shot rang out. Powerscourt's instant reaction was that it was Corsicans hunting, a chase for wild boar or the wild goats that sometimes came down from the mountains. Then there was another shot. Powerscourt pulled Lady Lucy to the ground at the side of the path. The bullet had ricocheted off a rock in front of them and shot off down the valley. It had been only feet away.

'Christ, Lucy, this is getting dangerous. These people are firing at us, for God's sake.'

'Should we run for it? Maybe they think we're a couple of wild boar.'

'We'll run for it in a moment,' said Powerscourt, pulling something from his pocket. 'When we do, keep to the right side of the track. Below those rocks, they may not be able to see us clearly. After I've taken a shot at them, we'll go.'

Powerscourt climbed very gingerly up the rocks and peered out over a boulder. He fired one shot up the hill and then they fled down the mountainside. The path was never straight. Sometimes there were more hairpins, then they would climb for a hundred yards or so before the track dropped down again towards the sea. Powerscourt was thinking desperately about everything they had done since they arrived in Corsica. What had placed their lives in danger? Why hadn't he left Lady Lucy behind? Why hadn't he brought Johnny Fitzgerald instead? Johnny was a much better shot than he was. And what had he said to place them in such peril? Lady Lucy was panting slightly now. They paused just in front of a stretch of open ground. There were no rocks here to give them cover. Only an ancient olive tree guarded the route for the next hundred yards. Powerscourt grabbed a stout stick lying at the side of the road. He took off his jacket and placed it carefully at the end of his makeshift pole. He shoved it forwards at the height he would have been had he been taking the next part of the route at a running crouch. He waited for about five seconds. Somewhere over to the right, another shot rang out. A bullet went neatly through the left-hand shoulder.

'Christ,' said Powerscourt. 'I think we may have to crawl this bit. Do you think you're up to crawling along this filthy road, Lucy?'

Lady Lucy grinned at him. 'I always used to beat Thomas and Olivia in the crawling races when they were little, Francis,' she said. 'I think I beat you once in a race across the drawing-room floor.'

Powerscourt remembered the game of hide and seek just a few days before, Olivia giggling behind the curtains.

'All right, Lucy. One shot at them. Then we'll go.'

Powerscourt fired again across the slopes. Then he set off, crawling as fast as he could go. When he had gone a few paces, he heard another shot, fired up the hill not ten feet away from him. He looked back briefly to see Lady Lucy putting his other pistol back into her bag. Then she too shot off at full speed on all fours, the rocks bumping into her arms.

There was no answering fire from the hills. Lucy and Powerscourt were reunited under a clump of trees.

'Christ, Lucy,' said Powerscourt, 'I didn't know you

had my other gun. I didn't know you could shoot like that. Are you all right?'

'I'm fine. I'll tell you all about it later,' said Lady Lucy, 'we still need to get out of here. Should we abandon this path and run for it across the open country?'

'I thought of that,' said her husband, 'but there's no cover at all over there. We'd be sitting ducks, visible for miles around. I think we need to run as fast as we can. It's always harder to hit a moving target. If we sit still in any one place, we're for it. Have you enough strength for a long run, a couple of hundred yards, Lucy? You're not too tired? God, I wish I hadn't brought you here.'

'I'm fine, Francis, I wouldn't have missed this for the world. I'd rather not die in Corsica, though, if that's all right with you.'

Powerscourt took her hand. There were faint trickles of blood near her left wrist where she had collided with a rock. Somehow that made Powerscourt angrier than ever.

They set off at a trot that turned into a gallop and then back into a trot. It was easier on this rocky terrain to run at medium pace rather than at full speed. Powerscourt wondered if anything they had said at the de Courcy house in Aregno could have led to this declaration of war. No, it could not, he decided. And even if they had become suspicious, it was unlikely that the de Courcy family could have organized a shooting party in this amount of time. Hold on a minute, he said to himself, they knew we were coming. They had known at least a day before with the delivery of the card. But somehow he still couldn't see Alice de Courcy or her daughters hiring a couple of Corsican bandits. The coach driver? He was in the shade of some very large boulders now, the kites, scenting possible human prey perhaps, circling ominously overhead. Lady Lucy was looking pale, but she kept up a good pace. Powerscourt motioned to stop. Ahead was the longest straight stretch of track they had encountered so far. A couple of derelict farmhouses stood on their right, the glass long gone from the windows, a battered door swinging from one hinge.

As if to greet them, a couple of shots pinged off the rocks twenty yards ahead. This little bit here, Powerscourt felt, this could be what their enemies had decided on as the killing field. Well, he bloody well wasn't going to let them. The trick with the jacket was unlikely to work again. He wondered about Lucy's hat. He tried to remember what the army instructors in India had told them about ambushes in broken country.

'Are you all right, Lucy? You've done magnificently so far. There's only one thing for it now. Whatever we do, we can't stay in the same place. I want you to run for those trees at the end of this straight bit. Run in a zigzag. Vary your pace if you can. While you're on your way I'm going to take a shot at these characters. They must come out into the open if they're to get a decent aim. When you've got to the far side, do the same for me. See if you can hit one of these bastards. Don't fire from the same place, dodge about as much as you can.'

Powerscourt didn't say the chances of hitting somebody armed with a rifle with a pistol at a couple of hundred yards distance were extremely remote. He kissed Lady Lucy briefly on the cheek.

'Run, my love, run! Run like hell!'

Lady Lucy took two deep breaths and shot out from beneath the trees. She gathered pace. Powerscourt was half-way up a tree, scouring the landscape for the hidden rifles. Lady Lucy was back in her childhood, following the hunting of the stags in her native Scotland with her grandfather. Only this afternoon she was the stag. She made a dramatic stop three-quarters of the way across. Still no shots. With a final burst of speed she disappeared into the shadows. She was panting deeply. She was through. She had made it. Still no shots.

Powerscourt came down from his tree. Maybe they didn't want the woman. Maybe they had no quarrel with her. Maybe they wanted the man. A faint reminder of the smell from Captain Antonio Imperiali's cheroot came back to him as he took several deep breaths. Something was nagging at his brain. Now was not the time to think of it. Lady Lucy had found an overturned cart at the side of the road. She climbed half-way up. There was a good view of the mountainside behind Francis through the broken wood.

Powerscourt set off at a gentle pace. Lady Lucy peered through her makeshift stockade. What had her grand-father told about shooting pistols? She saw a shape coming out from behind a clump of trees two hundred yards up the hill. Powerscourt had suddenly accelerated. He was running very fast now. The man on the mountain drew his rifle up to his shoulder. Just before he settled it, Lady Lucy fired. She thought the bullet went into the trees to his left. The man ducked down. Powerscourt was three-quarters of the way across. The man rose again a couple of yards to the right from where he had been before. He must have been crawling on all fours. Lady Lucy fired again. She didn't see where the bullet went. She only knew that her husband was pulling her off the cart and behind a clump of trees.

'They'll think we're going to take a rest now. Run, my love, let's keep going.'

Their strength was beginning to run out. Sometimes Lady Lucy stumbled. Powerscourt stopped briefly several times to hold on to his side. 'Stitch,' he said ruefully to Lady Lucy. Powerscourt was wondering again about the police chief. He had mentioned that he was looking for the de Courcy family. He had mentioned that he was looking for a forger. He had, he thought,

240

implied that the two might be linked in some way. Surely that must be the cause of this Corsican violence. But had the policeman himself ordered it? Was he part of the conspiracy with the forger? Had the policeman told somebody else? Had the policeman telegraphed to brother Edmund in London, keeper perhaps of the forger and his secrets? Was that what caused the assassination attempt, here on the slopes beneath Aregno with the impossible blues of the Corsican sea washing away at the beach? Somebody could have killed Christopher Montague in his flat behind the Brompton Oratory because he was about to reveal the existence of the forger. Were Powerscourt and Lady Lucy to be further victims? Nobody, absolutely nobody, Powerscourt felt certain, would investigate closely the deaths of two strangers on this island. Shooting accident. Very regrettable. The man must have had the sun in his eyes. Very regrettable. Soon forgotten. Maybe the de Courcy women would put flowers on their graves.

Lady Lucy was praying for her children. Then they could see salvation. A couple of hundred yards ahead, on the far side of a group of comforting trees, was the railway line, the beach and, on their left, the little town of Algajola with its train station. Powerscourt outlined the final plan of campaign under the trees.

'We'll do it as we did before,' he said. 'You go first. Lie low in those bamboos on the far side of the railway line. I'll keep you covered. Then you do the same for me.'

Lady Lucy seemed to have acquired a last reserve of strength. She shot over the railway line and zigzagged her way into the bamboo. No shots ran out from the mountainside. In the distance she heard a siren. Maybe a rescue party was on the way. Powerscourt took a long series of deep breaths. He could see Lady Lucy standing on something to get a better view. There was another hoot from the siren. Three hundred yards away he could

241

just see the little Corsican train approaching before it vanished behind a headland. He started running. Lady Lucy could see a man and a rifle peeping out from an abandoned farmhouse up the hillside. She took very careful aim at the farmhouse. The man disappeared. Powerscourt was fifty yards short of the railway line. Lady Lucy saw a glint from the late afternoon sun on the rifle, now peeping out from the other side of the farmhouse. The train was at the end of the beach now, chugging sedately towards its next stop.

There was a shout from Powerscourt. His boot was caught in one of the sleepers on the railway line. He waved helplessly at Lady Lucy. The train was now a hundred yards away, tons and tons of doom heading unstoppably towards Powerscourt. Lady Lucy shot out from her bamboos, firing one desperate shot at the farmhouse up the hill. She reached Powerscourt in what seemed like seconds. She could see a terrified train driver, his brakes now full on, staring helplessly at the disaster ahead. Lady Lucy reached down in the middle of the line. She pulled Powerscourt's boot off. She saw from out of the corner of her eye that the train driver had closed his eyes. He was praying out loud.

'Jump, Francis, jump!' Powerscourt dived full length to the side of the driver's cab, only a few feet away. Lady Lucy sprang back the other way. One further shot came down from the mountain slopes. It passed over the train and made a slight plop as it fell into the peaceful waters of Algajola Bay. Fifty yards on the train stopped. Lady Lucy ran in front of it and held Francis in her arms. 'Thank you, Lucy,' he said. 'You've saved my life. Again.' He held her very tight.

Less than a minute later they were inside the train. Powerscourt went to thank the driver, still shaking at his controls. Lady Lucy sank back on to a hard wooden seat on the side furthest away from the mountains.

Powerscourt flopped down beside her. He looked at the ruins of Lady Lucy's clothes, her dress badly torn, a hole where one of her knees had been. The blood by her wrist had dried now, a dark stain running up her left arm. There was a scratch mark on her face, where one of the bamboos had caught her on the desperate dash to the railway line. Powerscourt was still clutching his left boot, miraculously undamaged by the passage of the Bastia to Calvi rail service above it. His clothes, so immaculate in Mrs de Courcy's drawing room an hour before, were almost rags. His right trouser leg had a hole in the middle, a trickle of blood still running down it from a cut on the granite rocks. His left hand was dark, bruised from his fall in front of the train.

They smiled at each other. Powerscourt thought how beautiful Lucy looked, her blue eyes sparkling in the light off the sea.

'I think I found an omen, Francis.' She smiled across at him, Powerscourt shifting uncomfortably on his wooden billet. 'I saw it in one of the shops in Calvi yesterday and I forgot to tell you.'

'What is this omen, Lucy?' said Powerscourt, scowling at the blood on his knee.

'It's the motto of Calvi. Do you know what it is?'

'I'm afraid to say, Lucy, that up until now it has passed me by.'

Lady Lucy paused for the memories.

'It's Semper Fidelis, Francis. Forever Faithful.'

Forever Faithful, Semper Fidelis, last words in a letter to Powerscourt from a young man who committed suicide in Sandringham Woods in one of his earlier investigations into the strange death of Prince Eddy, eldest son of the Prince of Wales. Forever Faithful, Semper Fidelis, words Powerscourt had used to express his own loyalty to the dead man's memory as he searched for the truth. Forever Faithful, Semper Fidelis, words spoken by Francis and Lucy to each other on the deck of a great liner as they sailed to their honeymoon in America.

Powerscourt smiled. He took Lady Lucy's blood-stained hand into his own and pressed it very tight.

'Forever faithful, Lucy. Semper Fidelis.'

Lady Lucy had tears in her eyes.

'Semper Fidelis, Francis. Forever faithful.'

18

Lord Francis Powerscourt and Lady Lucy were sitting in a corner of their hotel bar, Powerscourt facing the entrance, his right hand never straying far from his pocket. They were in clean clothes after an alarming encounter with the local plumbing. The bathroom was a few feet away down the corridor, an enormous bath in dark wood panelling, rusty pipes running up the wall. When the hot tap was turned on, there was at first a distant rumble, like thunder in the mountains. Then the rumble faded to be replaced by a ferocious rattling of machinery. The pipes began to tremble, then to dance to some strange Corsican rhythm, shuddering against the wall, beating against each other. The performance was accompanied by a barrage of steam so great that it was almost impossible to see across the room. But the water was hot, the metal symphony gradually subsided, their aching limbs were soothed by the heat.

'I never knew you could shoot like that, Lucy,' said Powerscourt, sipping very slowly at a glass of local white wine.

'My grandfather taught me,' said Lady Lucy, remembering a day long ago in the hills behind her grandfather's house. 'It was in Scotland. Everybody else had gone on a fishing expedition. The two of us were alone in the house.

'"I've taught all my male grandchildren to shoot," my grandfather said suddenly after lunch. "Think I'd better teach you as well." So he took me into the hills with some kind of ancient archery board and a couple of pistols. I had to keep on trying until I could hit the centre of the board. "If you end up in India," my grandfather said, "married to an army colonel or the Viceroy or somebody like that, you never know when you mightn't need to shoot straight."'

'Did you intend, at that point, to marry a future Viceroy, Lucy? Supper dances at Simla in the Viceregal lodge, that sort of thing?' said Powerscourt in his most serious voice.

'I don't think a future Viceroy was much in my thoughts at that point, Francis. Rather a dashing young Captain in the Black Watch.'

'And was your grandfather pleased with your efforts?' asked Powerscourt, rubbing slowly at the bruise on his knee.

'He was,' said Lady Lucy happily. 'He said he wouldn't like to be a tiger or a rebellious native trying to take me by surprise.'

There was a sudden rush of footsteps to their table.

'Lord Powerscourt, Lady Powerscourt.' Captain Imperiali cast his eyes up and down Lady Lucy. 'I have just heard the terrible news about what happened this afternoon. It was all a terrible mistake. I have come to apologize for the behaviour of my fellow Corsicans.'

The Captain pulled a chair from the neighbouring table and deposited his ample frame upon it.

'In what way was it a mistake?' said Powerscourt. Some mistake indeed, shots pursuing them down the mountainside, rifles waiting for them in the open stretches of the road. He felt sure that Imperiali knew more than he would say. Perhaps he had instigated it himself.

246

'It is a tradition,' said Imperiali, smiling at Lady Lucy as he spoke, 'a tradition in the village of San Antonino. Perhaps we have too many traditions here in Corsica. They call it the Traitor's Run. Over a hundred and fifty years ago, Lady Powerscourt, there was war in the Balagne, the French against the Genovese. San Antonino and the other places up there were with the Genovese. Calvi was always loyal to Genoa. But up in San Antonino a young man betrayed the village to the French. For money, you understand. So the people of San Antonino take him and his fiancée out on to the road down to the coast. 'Go and find your French friends down there,' they say, kicking them both on the start of their journey. Then they followed them down the mountain. The young men of San Antonino let the traitors almost reach the bottom so they think they are safe. Then they kill them. Their bodies are cut up into pieces and left for the wolves.'

'What a horrible story,' said Lady Lucy, avoiding Captain Imperiali's eye.

'This is what is important, Lord Powerscourt.' Imperiali was leaning forward, his hand fingering his unlit cheroot. 'Every year since then, the young men of San Antonino replay this event. That is why it is called the Traitor's Run. A young man is drawn by lot from the people of the village. He has to persuade a young woman to accompany him. The anniversary is today, my lord. Today is the day for the Traitor's Run. You were not the only people running down the mountainside. Perluigi Cassani and Maria Cosenza from San Antonino were also running down. The young men think you are the traitors. So they shoot. But they never intend to kill. Always they shoot at the running persons on the day of Traitor's Run. But in over a hundred years nobody has been hit or killed. It is like a game, even though it is more serious than a game. Nobody intended to kill you this afternoon. It was a case of the mistaken identity. You were quite safe.'

Captain Imperiali paused to light his cheroot. 'On behalf of the people of Calvi, on behalf of the people of Corsica, may I apologize most seriously,' he said.

'We are most grateful for your apology,' said Powerscourt. He wondered if Lady Lucy's book on Corsica made any mention of a Traitor's Run. It was certainly a good story. He wasn't yet sure if he believed it.

'May I have the pleasure of taking you both to dinner in Calvi's finest restaurant?' the Captain went on. 'The lobster there is superb. And they specialize in wild boar, a great delicacy in these parts.'

Powerscourt thanked him for his offer, but said they were both tired and would prefer to remain in their hotel. Maybe another day.

'Do you know when you are going to leave the island, Lord Powerscourt?'

Powerscourt said they had no plans to leave for the present. Captain Imperiali bowed to them both and departed, the smell of his cheroot still lingering in the air.

'Well, Lucy,' said Powerscourt, 'did you believe a word of it?'

'What a revolting man he is,' said Lady Lucy firmly, 'the way he looks at you is quite appalling. Did I believe it? I think I probably did – I'm sure anybody we ask here in the next few days will all swear it's true. It's not the sort of thing that would be in the guidebooks. It might put people off.'

'There is a boat to Marseilles first thing in the morning,' said Powerscourt. 'I've booked two passages in the name of Fitzgerald. Do you like the thought of becoming Lady Fitzgerald, Lucy?'

'Very much,' Lady Lucy replied. 'But I must ask you one question. When you aimed at those people on the hill this afternoon, were you intending to hit them?'

'Of course I was,' said Powerscourt, 'weren't you?'

'I most certainly was not,' said Lady Lucy, 'I was aiming about ten feet away from them and praying that I wouldn't hit anyone at all.'

'Why ever not?' said Powerscourt, draining his glass of Corsican white wine.

'Oh Francis, can't you see? Suppose we had killed one of them. That would have been the start of a vendetta. Our lives, the children's lives, would all be at risk to the Corsicans' terrible passion for revenge. I don't think I could have slept safely ever again. They'd have followed us all the way to London.'

Powerscourt was lost in thought. Corsicans in London. Corsican killers in London. Corsicans who garrotted their enemies.

William Alaric Piper was pacing nervously up and down the street outside his gallery. He was waiting for Lewis B. Black, the taciturn American millionaire whose silences unnerved him to the point of illness. Piper resolved to say as little as possible, though he doubted if he could bear a prolonged period of silence.

'Good morning to you, Mr Piper,' said Lewis B. Black, shaking him by the hand, 'fine weather we are having this morning.'

This was the longest single speech Piper had ever heard from the taciturn millionaire. Maybe London was beginning to have an effect on him.

'If you would like to come with me, Mr Black,' said Piper, leading the way up the stairs past his gallery to the holy of holies on the second floor, 'I think I have a painting that might interest you.'

Piper opened the door and turned on the lights. There on the easel sat a Joshua Reynolds, Clarissa, Lady

Lanchester, perched on a seat in an imaginary land-scape with a glorious sunset behind her. She was wearing a cream dress. Her small hands were folded in her lap. And on her head was a hat of the most expensive and exquisite feathers the London milliners of the late eighteenth century could provide. But the face was not from the eighteenth century. Of course it had been painted to look like an eighteenth-century face. But the face that stared back at Lewis B. Black bore an uncanny resemblance to Mildred, also known as Mrs Lewis B. Black of New York City. It had been copied from the page of the magazine Edmund de Courcy had stolen from the Beaufort Club.

Lewis B. Black rubbed his eyes as if he couldn't quite believe what he was looking at. He took three paces to the left, then three paces to the right. He went so close that his nose was almost touching the canvas.

'This for sale?' he said finally.

'Yes,' said Piper. He didn't think the delaying tactics he had used on McCracken would work with Black. The man might simply disappear.

'Fifteen thousand,' said Black, putting his hand in his pocket as if to check he had that much cash about his person.

'Pounds or dollars?' said Piper.

'Dollars,' said Lewis B. Black.

'Pounds,' said Piper. His mental arithmetic was not strong – de Courcy looked after the accounts – but he knew that a pound was worth a lot more than a dollar.

'Dollars,' said Black again.

'Pounds,' repeated Piper.

'Dollars,' repeated Black. Piper thought Black might go on like this all day.

'Fourteen,' said Piper.

'Fourteen what?'

'Sorry, fourteen thousand pounds. That's a whole thousand off for you, Mr Black.'

'Ten,' said Black.

'Ten what?'

'Ten thousand pounds, sorry,' said Lewis B. Black.

Piper rejoiced that they had finally settled into pounds. He felt the Bank of England would have been proud of him.

'Fourteen thousand pounds.' He stuck to his guns.

'Eleven,' said Black.

'Thirteen,' said Piper.

'Twelve,' said Black.

'Split the difference,' said Piper, who would have settled for ten if he had to. Almost all of that was clear profit after all. 'Twelve and a half thousand pounds.'

'Done,' said Lewis B. Black. But what he said next was music to Piper's ears.

'This Lady Lanchester woman in the picture,' he said, nodding at his wife on the easel, 'did this Reynolds guy do any more paintings of her? Or did anybody else at the time?'

Piper felt like an early prospector who has just discovered a rich seam of gold. This was the California gold rush come to Old Bond Street.

'I will have to check in our library,' he assured Lewis B. Black, 'but I think from memory that there are two other portraits of Lady Lanchester in existence, another one by Reynolds, the other, I think, by Gainsborough. Would you like me to see if I can find them for you?'

The interview room was very small. There were no windows. A bare light bulb cast a miserable light over the occupants. Horace Aloysius Buckley had lost weight in prison. His face was drawn. The drab grey of the prison uniform did not suit him. The clothes were several sizes too big for him, hanging loosely off his shoulders, the trousers sagging at the waist.

'Horace,' said his partner, George Brigstock, 'your case may come up for trial sooner than we thought. Two cases scheduled for the Central Criminal Court have had to be postponed. We must instruct a barrister at once.'

Buckley shuddered slightly at the news that his trial might be sooner than expected. Sometimes at night, tossing on the worn-out mattress in his cell, he dreamed of judges with black caps chasing him down the nave of a cathedral, shouting at him to keep still so they could pass sentence.

'Do you have any suggestions, George?' said Buckley. The firm of Buckley, Brigstock and Brightwell, solicitors, did not deal in criminal cases, but the world of the law in London is a very small one.

'Sir Rufus Fitch will be taking the prosecution case. Do you know Sir Rufus, Horace?'

Outside the footsteps of the warder sounded loud on the stone floor as he paced up and down in the corridor outside.

'I have met Sir Rufus, George, I thought he was rather pompous.'

'What do you say,' said Brigstock, consulting a sheet of paper in front of him, 'to Sir Idwal Grimble? They say he's very good in cases of this kind.'

Horace Buckley looked unblinking at the face of the warder, peering in through the glass slit. Sometimes he still couldn't believe all this was happening to him.

'Sir Idwal?' he said. 'He's another pompous fellow. He and Fitch would be like a pair of battleships that take a couple of hours to change course. Too heavy. Can't manoeuvre.'

'A number of people spoke very highly of Pemberton, Miles Pemberton.' Brigstock tried another name. 'Nobody thought he could get that fellow who was accused of murdering his mother-in-law off last year, but he did.'

'I think he was lucky,' said Horace Aloysius Buckley. 'The prosecution's man hadn't done his homework properly. And he's pretty pompous too.'

'My own personal choice,' said Brigstock, beginning to despair of ever coming up with a barrister acceptable to his partner, 'is for a younger man, a coming man.'

'Do you have somebody in mind?' asked Buckley, suddenly aware that his time in the interview room was nearly over.

'Pugh,' said Buckley, 'Charles Augustus Pugh. He's young, he's quick, his brain probably works faster than Sir Rufus Fitch's. They say he's very good with juries too.'

'I have heard of this Pugh,' said Buckley as the warder began the slow process of opening the door. 'Instruct him, if you please. And tell him,' the warder was repeating Time's Up as if it were some kind of mantra as he ushered George Brigstock towards the daylight, 'tell him, for God's sake, to get in touch with Lord Francis Powerscourt.'

Mrs Imogen Foxe had taken her correspondence down to the lake again. Well, not the entire correspondence, just one letter, another missive from the mysterious Mr Peters in London. It began with instructions for a meeting in five days' time at the Bristol Hotel near Waterloo station in London. She was to present herself at the reception desk between one and two o'clock and ask for Mr Peters. She had to understand that from that moment on, a number of unpleasant things were going to happen to her. Her eyes and the upper part of her face would be wrapped in bandages. She would be given a stick to help her walk. She would have to rely on Mr Peters or one of his assistants to guide her on her journey.

If she disclosed any of these details to a single living soul, she would not meet Mr Orlando Blane on this occasion. She would never see him again. Her family – Imogen winced at this point – and her husband would also be informed about what she proposed to do.

Imogen read the letter three times and resolved to burn it when she returned to the house. She walked slowly round the lake, a light breeze rippling across the surface. She thought she saw a kingfisher shooting across the opposite side of the water. She couldn't be sure. She hugged herself as she thought of Orlando. Another sonnet of Shakespeare's came back to her, learnt by heart under the unforgiving eyes of the nuns and the battered reproduction of the *Assumption of the Virgin* on the convent wall,

> O! Never say that I was false of heart,
> Though absence seemed my flame to qualify.
> As easy might I from myself depart
> As from my soul, which in thy breast doth lie:
> That is my home of love; if I have ranged,
> Like him that travels, I return again.

Thoughts of travel sent her into Blandford, the nearest town. She presented herself at the counter of Barnard and Baines, the best, the most expensive outfitters in the place. She ordered six of their finest shirts.

'Will those be for Mr Granville, madam?' said the old assistant. Barnard and Baines had been clothing the Foxe family for generations. They had records of the neck sizes of all of them for the past hundred and twenty years.

'No, it's for my brother,' Imogen blushed slightly, 'a size smaller than Mr Granville, I should say.'

She also purchased two pairs of dark gentleman's trousers and a jacket. Then she went to the local bank where she withdrew two hundred pounds in cash. The cashier looked round as if to ask for his superior, but Imogen's most charming smile brought forth the money.

I can hide all these things in my luggage, she said to herself. Orlando may not have any decent clothes at all. And with two hundred pounds, we could go anywhere in the kingdom.

Lord Francis Powerscourt was dreading this interview. He knew he had put it off for far too long. He paused at the edge of Rotten Row in Hyde Park, the horses and their perfectly groomed riders trotting sedately along. He could still go home. He could be back in Markham Square in ten minutes or so. Then he remembered his last conversation with Lady Lucy the night before.

'You must see him, Francis, you know that as well as I do,' Lady Lucy had said.

'What can I say to him?' her husband pleaded. 'Did you kill Christopher Montague? Did you also kill Thomas Jenkins? What did you do with the books?'

'You're being silly, Francis. And, what's even more uncharacteristic, you're trying to run away from something. Think of poor Mr Buckley, in his cell or wherever he is these days. Surely you owe it to him.'

Powerscourt sighed and proceeded on his way to Old Bond Street where he had an appointment with the firm of de Courcy and Piper, art dealers. To be precise, with Edmund de Courcy, son and brother of the de Courcys of Aregno, Corsica. And the second last person to see Christopher Montague alive.

De Courcy was surrounded by pieces of paper when Powerscourt was shown in.

'Sorry for all this mess,' he waved at his desk, 'it's our next big exhibition, The English Portrait. I've been making lists of all the places where the paintings might come from.'

Powerscourt removed a couple of books from a chair and sat down. 'I met your family recently,' he said, 'over there in Corsica. Your mother was well. Your sisters . . .' He paused briefly. 'How could I put it, I think they are a little starved of company.'

Edmund de Courcy laughed. 'Starved of the company of young men,' he said, with an elder brother's cruel accuracy, 'but I understand that you had a rather unpleasant experience during your stay. I was in Aregno myself two years ago on the day of the Traitor's Run. Guns going off all afternoon, people shouting at each other. We wondered at first if a revolution had broken out.'

That was very neat, Powerscourt thought. Edmund de Courcy himself a witness at the Traitor's Run. Yet again he wondered if the annual ritual was real or lies, genuine or fake. Rather like the paintings in de Courcy's gallery, he said to himself. It all came down to a matter of attribution in the end.

'Well, it was certainly an exciting afternoon,' Powerscourt said with a smile. Then he moved on to more dangerous ground.

'Tell me, Mr de Courcy,' he asked, 'how well did you know Christopher Montague?'

De Courcy shook his head sadly. 'Of course I knew him,' he said, 'what a terrible business. I saw him in the street on the afternoon he died. And that other poor man in Oxford too. Quite terrible.'

'Did he come to the opening of your current exhibition here, Venetian Paintings?'

De Courcy blinked several times. 'I'm trying to remember if he did,' he said slowly. 'I'm sure he must have been here. Yes, I do remember him on that occasion. He came with a very pretty young woman.'

Powerscourt summoned up his mental image of Mrs Rosalind Buckley, estranged wife of a man incarcerated for murder in Newgate Prison.

'Quite tall?' he said. 'Curly brown hair, big brown eyes?'

De Courcy looked confused. 'No,' he replied, 'she was quite small. She didn't have brown hair, it was almost black. And the eyes were blue, I think, rather striking.'

'Did you catch her name, by any chance?' said Powerscourt.

'No, I don't think I did.'

Outside they could hear the voice of William Alaric Piper telling the porters to be careful with a picture, apparently being moved down to the basement.

'Tell me about forgers, Mr de Courcy.' Powerscourt seemed to have lost interest in Christopher Montague's companion. 'I understand Mr Montague was going to say that most of these Venetian paintings were not original, that some were old fakes and some very recent fakes. Did you know about the article?'

De Courcy blinked again. It seemed to be a mannerism of his, Powerscourt thought. 'Oh, yes, everybody knew about that article before it was due to appear,' de Courcy said. 'Indeed, it was being produced with the help of one of our competitors along the street here.' He nodded out of the window towards Old Bond Street.

'But forgery is nothing new in the art business, Lord Powerscourt. The Greeks did a very profitable trade selling fake antique statues to the Romans, for heaven's sake. Most of the rich English who went on the Grand Tour brought back forgeries with them, thinking they were genuine, hanging them happily on the walls of their homes. Believe me, Lord Powerscourt, I visit a lot of the great houses full of paintings. I've lost count of the fake Titians. There must be more Giorgiones in the Home Counties than the man ever painted in his lifetime. Velasquez is rife in Hampshire, there's a house I know of in Dorset which claims to have six Rembrandts in their drawing room. I doubt if a single one of them was painted in Holland. Florence today could field a couple of rugby teams of forgers, Forgers United and Forgers Athletic perhaps. You can't stop it.'

Powerscourt smiled. Somebody on the floor above was hammering something into the wall, nails or picture hooks perhaps, to bear the weight of yet another painting, real or fake.

'Would it have made any difference to the success of your exhibition,' he said, 'if the article had appeared just after it opened?'

De Courcy shook his head. 'I don't think so,' he said firmly, 'I think the exhibition was always going to be a success. We're taking it to New York, you know.'

Rich pickings over there, Powerscourt thought. Some of the European buyers might be able to tell a forgery from the real thing. But he was doubtful about the buyers of Fifth Avenue.

'Your house in Norfolk,' he said, changing the direction of his attack. De Courcy sounded pretty impregnable on the subject of forgery. 'Do you think you will be able to open it up again? I understand it is abandoned at present.'

'Oh yes, it is,' said de Courcy, 'abandoned, I mean. There's nobody there at all. The place is completely empty. There's nobody there. I do hope to be able to bring my family back from Corsica, though. If things continue to go well with the business I might be able to do it quite soon.'

'I'm sure your mother would like that,' said Powerscourt diplomatically. 'Do you have any Corsican links here, any Corsicans working as porters in the gallery or anything like that?'

'We did have one Corsican here,' said de Courcy, 'but he had to go home only the other day. His mother died.'

'Poor man,' said Powerscourt, getting up from his chair. 'Just one last thing, Mr de Courcy. The young woman who came to the opening night of the exhibition with Christopher Montague. Did you have a Visitors Book on that occasion? Might she have left a name in there?'

De Courcy said he would fetch the Visitors Book from the other office. Powerscourt stared idly at some of the pieces of paper on de Courcy's desk. There seemed to be some form of private code on them. Some had no stars, some had one, some had three.

'Here it is,' said de Courcy. 'We'll have to go right back to the beginning.' He turned back the pages of the thick leather-bound book.

'Here we are,' he said, 'half way down the page. That's Christopher Montague's signature. And underneath it, written with the same pen I should say, Alice Bridge. No address, I'm afraid.'

19

Imogen Foxe was thinking of all the words she knew that meant black. Jet-black, inky black, Stygian gloom, dark as pitch, darker than the gates of hell. She could not see. She had travelled to London and made her rendezvous with the mysterious Mr Peters in the hotel near Waterloo station. There she was taken to a bedroom on the second floor where her eyes were covered with a black mask, and then so tightly bandaged that she could see nothing at all. A different man, she thought from the smell, had brought her to a different railway station and helped her to her seat in what she suspected was a first class carriage.

The man watched her all the time, especially her hands. If she moved a hand to her face he leant forward as if to restrain her. 'Terrible accident, terrible,' he had said to the guard on the train. 'The doctors think she will recover her sight in the end. It's rest in the country she needs now.'

Imogen's world may have been black but her heart was dancing with joy. At the end of this mysterious journey, there was Orlando, Orlando she had not seen for months. She tried desperately to catch the announcements at the stations where they stopped. Maybe they could give some clue to their destination. But just as the announcer reached the words, 'This train is calling at,' her companion coughed loudly or began talking to her so she missed the names of the stations.

Her other senses, she noticed, seemed to have improved. She could smell the tobacco smoke in her companion's clothes even though he wasn't smoking. She heard the rumble of the wheels on the rails in a way she had never heard it before. Occasionally she heard the sound of footsteps in the corridor outside, crisp and precise. She wished those feet would stop and talk outside her door, then she might catch a clue about where they were going.

But in spite of the bandages over her eyes and the mask which made her feel like a circus performer or a harlequin in a parade, Imogen was happy. She might have been in the darkness. But she was travelling towards Orlando.

Johnny Fitzgerald, never an early riser, was having a late breakfast in Markham Square the day after the Powerscourts' return and the Powerscourt interview with Edmund de Courcy. Johnny devoured a couple of eggs, embellished with bacon and a squadron of mushrooms, while he listened to the Powerscourts' Corsican adventure.

'Did you believe that story, about the Traitor's Run?' he asked Lady Lucy.

'I don't know if I believe it or not,' said Lady Lucy, consuming a small piece of buttered toast, 'I just don't know.'

'Suppose it's not true,' said Johnny, between mouthfuls, 'that can only mean one thing.'

'What's that?' said Powerscourt looking gloomily at more bad news from South Africa in his newspaper.

'It must mean that Edmund de Courcy, or persons working for him, are the killers. They have this forger,

261

hidden away somewhere, producing fake Titians or Giorgiones for that exhibition in Old Bond Street. They hear a whisper on the street that Christopher Montague is about to produce an article denouncing the things as fakes. They get rid of Montague. Then they hear that his friend up in Oxford may have known what was in the article. He is sent off to meet his Maker too. Then, out of the blue, the two of you turn up in Corsica, asking questions about forgers of all things. The one place they could kill you both off with no questions asked is on that bloody island. So out come the guns. It's a miracle you survived. Maybe they're so used to taking pot shots at the wild boar they aren't so good with humans. But it's obvious, surely. De Courcy must have had a wire from that man Lady Lucy liked so much, the policeman in Calvi. Wire goes back from Old Bond Street. Exterminate Powerscourts. Coast now clear for further forgeries and further fleecing of American millionaires.'

Johnny leaned back in his chair with a triumphant smile. 'I think I could manage a little more bacon,' he said, reaching forward to refill his plate. 'Hungry work solving mysteries at breakfast time.'

Powerscourt glanced up from a dramatic account of the siege of Kimberley, Cecil Rhodes and his diamonds locked up together by the Boers. He wondered what the Boers would do if they captured Rhodes. Ransom him? For diamonds?

'I wish I could agree with you, Johnny,' he said. 'I just don't know if that story about the Traitor's Run is true or not. But the whole thing looks too bloody obvious to me. We go and see Mrs de Courcy and the pining daughters. The coachman disappears. Happens all the time, they say. Scarcely are we out of the front door than the bullets start pinging off the rocks. Whoever killed Montague was pretty smart about it. We're still not sure who did it. Same thing with Thomas Jenkins. The murderer is almost an invisible man. If we'd have been killed on the Aregno road, it would have been too obvious for words.'

'You don't think you're being too clever, Francis?' said Lady Lucy. 'Just because it looks obvious doesn't mean it's not right.'

Powerscourt laughed. 'Maybe,' he said. 'There is one thing we must do,' he went on, folding the newspaper into a neat square, 'we must find this young woman, Alice Bridge, who accompanied Christopher Montague to the Venetian exhibition. Do you have any ideas about her, Lucy?'

Lady Lucy smiled an enormous smile. 'I shall ask around my relations, Francis. All of them, if necessary. They do have their uses, you see.'

Powerscourt laughed. 'A hit, Lucy, a very palpable hit.' He stopped suddenly. There was something at the back of his mind. He felt it might be important. His eyes drifted off to rest on the curtains where he had found Olivia in hiding. Hiding, that had something to do with it. Johnny Fitzgerald and Lady Lucy stared at him, wondering where his mind had gone to now. Perhaps he had travelled to South Africa or gone back to Corsica.

'That's it,' said Powerscourt suddenly, returning from his reverie. He hadn't been abroad at all, merely half a mile or so away in the offices of de Courcy and Piper in Old Bond Street. 'It's something de Courcy said to me yesterday,' he went on, pausing while he remembered the exact words.

'Out with it, man,' said Fitzgerald, well used to these leaves of absence. Sometimes it took an irritatingly long time for his friend to return.

'It was when I asked him about his house in Norfolk,' Powerscourt went on, ignoring the interruption. 'I said I understood it was abandoned at present. This, I think, is what he said. 'Oh yes, it is, abandoned, I mean. There's nobody there at all. The place is completely empty. There's nobody there.'

'What of it?' asked Lady Lucy.

'Well,' said Powerscourt, surprised that it wasn't totally obvious to his listeners, 'he says the same thing four times. Abandoned. Nobody there. Place completely empty. Nobody there. Why should he say it four times? As if he was trying to convince me.'

'I see,' said Johnny Fitzgerald. 'You think that the place may not be empty?'

'And that inside,' Lady Lucy carried on, 'there might be somebody with a lot of old canvases sent from Corsica, forging away in the middle of nowhere in North Norfolk. That's where the forger is.'

'Well, he might be,' said Powerscourt. 'I think you ought to take a trip to de Courcy Hall, Johnny. Discreetly, of course, very discreetly. Have a look around. I shall be too busy here, analysing the replies of Lucy's relations about the whereabouts of Alice Bridge. I expect there will be hundreds of them. But if you find anything of interest let me know at once and I will come and join you.'

'Please check in the local guidebooks before you go, Johnny,' said Lady Lucy. 'Make sure there aren't strange local customs up there at this time of year. Shooting strangers, for instance. I'd hate to think of an East Anglian version of the Traitor's Run.'

The Committal Hearing for Horace Aloysius Buckley at Bow Street Magistrates Court was very brief. The magistrate was an elderly man, completely bald, with a disconcerting habit of taking his spectacles off and replacing them almost instantaneously. Sir Rufus Fitch was in ponderous mood, presenting his witnesses and taking them through the evidence very slowly and very carefully. Chief Inspector Wilson provided much of it, principally an account of his various interviews with the defendant in which Horace Buckley confessed to being in Montague's room on the night of the murder. Edmund de Courcy and Roderick Johnston testified to seeing Montague on the day of his death. Mrs Buckley gave her deadly evidence about the tie. There was a witness who had seen him in Brompton Square round about the time of death. Other witnesses, a college porter and a delivery man, attested to Buckley's presence in Oxford on the day of Jenkins' death.

Charles Augustus Pugh had decided to present no witnesses at all at the hearing. He read through all he knew about the case for the third time the night before. He had no idea what sort of defence to offer. Rather than show any of his hand, he had resolved to keep quiet until the real trial. But as he listened to the evidence, he knew how poor his hand really was. I certainly don't have any aces at this stage, he said to himself. I don't have any Kings or Queens. I don't even have a jack. The best I can do, for now, is something like the three of clubs. He resolved to call on Lord Francis Powerscourt at the earliest possible opportunity

Cornelius P. Stockman was the tallest man William Alaric Piper had ever seen. He was about six feet nine inches tall, probably even taller than Captain Ames of the Horse Guards, the tallest man in the British Army, who had led the procession on Queen Victoria's Diamond Jubilee Parade two years before. Piper wondered if they put something in the water supply to produce this race of giants. The man looked as though he would have to bend down to pass through most English domestic doors.

'Stockman's my name,' he said to Piper, stooping slightly to shake Piper's hand as they met in the reception of the Old Bond Street gallery. 'Been hearing you've got some pretty fine pictures here, Mr Piper. My friend Bill McCracken gave me good reports of you.'

Piper smiled to himself as he remembered his last meeting with the railroad millionaire. He had handed over the Gainsborough in his own little office, McCracken towering above him.

'Fifteen thousand pounds, I'm afraid, Mr McCracken,' he had said. 'The previous owner took a lot of convincing, I'm afraid. But the Gainsborough is yours.'

William Alaric Piper firmly believed that the higher the prices the more genuine the paintings appeared to their new owners. He remembered the story of the American millionaire who had refused to buy a Velasquez because it was on offer for only five hundred pounds. If the dealer had doubled or trebled the price, Piper was certain it would have been sold.

McCracken had picked him up in an American bear hug and danced around the room.

'Mr Piper, how can I ever thank you? Perhaps when you come to Boston you will be our guest in our house in Concord! Mrs McCracken and the Misses McCracken will be so delighted with this here Gainsborough!' With that he wrote out a cheque and departed back to his hotel where the McCracken Gainsborough could join the McCracken Raphael to delight and enchant their new owner on their easels in room 347 of the Piccadilly Hotel.

Stockman was dressed rather like a cowboy going to church on Sunday, with great boots and a wide-brimmed hat.

'What sort of pictures do you like, Mr Stockman?' said Piper hesitantly. 'Our gallery is full of these Venetian pictures at present, but we do have other things stored elsewhere.'

'Let me be frank with you, Mr Piper. Stockman's my name, Cornelius P. Stockman. My grandfather came from someplace out in the Ukraine – the family's name

266

was Rostowskowski or some damned thing like that. People out Kansas way couldn't be pronouncing that. Grandpa Rostowskowski worked with cattle so they changed the name to Stockman and that's what we've been ever since. We're simple people in Kansas, Mr Piper. I tell you what I don't like. I don't care for any of those religious pictures. No, sir.'

Piper reckoned that a quarter or more of the paintings in his exhibition were no use on this occasion.

'Those holy women give me the creeps, Mr Piper, I don't mind telling you. And those damned portraits of all those noblemen all dressed up in their finery.' Piper had a sudden vision of a Venetian Doge in cowboy boots, guns strapped to the leather trousers at his side, striding across the Piazza San Marco for a final shoot-out at the Bridge of Sighs. 'They give me the creeps too. My grandfather left the Ukraine because of the tyranny of all those damned nobles. Our country fought with yours long ago to get rid of a King, why, I don't think nobles and counts and marquises have any place in a democratic society like America.' Piper thought about suggesting that an aristocracy of wealth might have replaced one based on birth, but felt the moment was inopportune. He also felt there might be only half a dozen pictures on the walls that would appeal to his transatlantic visitor.

Certainly Cornelius P. Stockman was moving round the exhibits at considerable speed. Five Titians, three Giorgiones and a host of works by lesser masters were circumnavigated in less than two minutes. A quartet of nobles were dismissed in about fifteen seconds flat. Piper was on the point of asking precisely what sort of pictures Stockman did like when the Kansas giant stopped. He stopped at precisely the same point as William P. McCracken some weeks before when the sight in front of him summoned up the memories of the elders of the Third Presbyterian in Lincoln Street in Concord,

Massachusetts. Piper wondered wearily which of the innumerable varieties of American religion was about to be invoked now. Fifteenth Methodist on Washington Boulevard perhaps? Kansas First Baptist? Lutheran Memorial on Jefferson Drive? Maybe Mormons. Was Kansas anywhere near Salt Lake City? He didn't think so but he wasn't sure.

But Cornelius P. Stockman seemed to have different beliefs. He stared reverently at the painting in front of him. The background was an idyllic landscape in the Veneto, a plain in the centre with some distant mountains. On the right a small town in brown climbed lazily up a hill. Lying across the centre of the picture on a satin sheet with a dark red pillow was a young woman. She was completely naked. Sensuous and sensual, the sleeping Venus looked as though she had dropped down from heaven for a peaceful afternoon nap in the Italian countryside.

'My word, Mr Piper, my word. That's so beautiful. This Giorgione fellow, did he paint any more of these women?'

Piper was desperately trying to remember if the painting was real or a forgery. If it was forgery, he could take a lower price.

'I think there is one other painting called *Leda and the Swan*,' Piper said, 'but Leda is not as prominent as the sleeping Venus. She occupies a much smaller space in the painting if you follow me. And I think it's in an Italian museum, very hard to get things out of Italian museums, Mr Stockman. But,' Piper brightened up as he thought of it, 'Titian, another of the great masters, painted a number of women *au naturel*, as we say.'

'*Au naturel*, did you say? In Kansas, Mr Piper, we call them nudes. Tell me, did these pictures go on display in Venice or wherever it was? I reckon the locals must have been queuing round the block to get a sight of them.'

Piper smiled. 'I don't think they went on display. They were painted for the private quarters of the rich where the nobility and the wealthy merchants could enjoy them in private.'

Stockman bent down at least a foot and a half to take a closer look at the *Sleeping Venus*. 'Why, Mr Piper,' he said, 'that's just what I propose to do. I live alone, apart from the staff, and I've got one huge room where I hang my pictures. I can enjoy them in peace there.'

Piper had a sudden inspiration. 'Could I make a suggestion, Mr Stockman? I always think of these paintings as being like a person, you see, an old friend perhaps, that you enjoy having in your house. Maybe this *Sleeping Venus* would look and feel rather lonely on your walls. Maybe I could collect some more nudes, of the highest quality, of course. A group of them would surely look better in your private gallery than a single Giorgione?'

Cornelius P. Stockman was still peering intently at the Venus. 'It's a long way from Venice, Italy, to Kansas City, Kansas,' he said. 'I tell you what, Mr Piper, you get me as many of these as you can. I'll take a bundle of them. I've got some rather dreary pictures of French peasants somebody advised me to buy in Paris a couple of years ago. Man called Tryon, I think, somebody called Rosa Bonheur. Reckon they could move house to make room for the ladies.'

'What sort of numbers were you thinking of?' asked Piper, angry with himself once more that his mental arithmetic wasn't as good as it should have been. 'Three? Four?'

'Four?' said Cornelius P. Stockman derisively. 'Don't think four would make much of an impact.' Piper suddenly remembered a terrible American painting he had refused to buy some years before. It showed some everlasting plain in the American Midwest, the entire surface covered with cattle moving stupidly but purposefully towards what might have been a railway depot in the distance. Men on horseback patrolled the outer reaches of the herds. Clouds of dust covered the plain. If you dealt in that number of cattle, four Venetian women, naked or not, might seem a trifle.

'Get me a dozen,' Stockman said decisively. 'I'll buy the lot.'

'I am dying,' the letter had said. 'I mean we are all dying all the time, but my portion of days is now very short. Very soon I may have to go into hospital. Please come and see me at my home before it is too late. I have some information for you about forgers.'

Sir Frederick Lambert's handwriting was very shaky. On some of the letters, the 'y's and the 'p's, the down-strokes hurtled unstoppably down the page. Powerscourt, hurrying towards Lambert's house in South Kensington, hoped he wasn't too late. There was a slight drizzle falling on the pavements, glistening off the backs of the horses as they pulled their masters through the squares of Chelsea.

A middle-aged nurse in crisp white uniform showed Powerscourt into the study. This was a small room, entirely lined with books and tapestries. Powerscourt was slightly disappointed there were none of Sir Frederick's own paintings on the walls.

Sir Frederick had looked unwell every time Powerscourt had seen him in his offices in the Royal Academy, coughing blood into an endless supply of clean white handkerchiefs, hiding them in a secret cache behind his desk. Now his body seemed to have collapsed completely. The flesh on his face had been sucked inwards, his cheeks hollow with the disease. The skin on his wrists and hands looked like dirty parchment scarcely able to cover the bones below. His eyes, which had been so full of life, were glazed.

Powerscourt wondered if he was full of drugs to ease the pain.

'Powerscourt,' said Sir Frederick, just able to raise himself from his chair and shake Powerscourt's hand, 'how good of you to come.'

'You are looking well, Sir Frederick,' lied Powerscourt. 'No doubt you will be up and about again soon.'

'Nonsense, man,' said Lambert, just able to raise a smile. His face looked even more gaunt. 'The doctors tell me I have less than a month to go. I get frightened, you know.' He looked down at the wrecks that had been his hands, the hands that had made all his paintings with such touch and delicacy, the hands that had brought him fame and fortune. 'When I look at myself in the mirror, I don't recognize myself at all. I doubt if the Good Lord would admit anybody who looks as wasted as I do. The other inmates might not like it.'

'You never know who you might meet up there,' said Powerscourt, 'maybe Michelangelo is doing them another ceiling.'

'We do not have much time, my friend,' said Lambert. 'That nurse is such a bully, I wonder she doesn't go and work in a prison. I am only allowed fifteen minutes with you.'

The President of the Royal Academy produced a package from his pocket. 'Look at all these stamps,' he said. Powerscourt looked down at them, wondering if the old man had lost his mind as well as his body. French stamps, Italian stamps, Russian stamps, German stamps. There must have been more than fifty of them.

'Ever since you first came to see me,' the old man said, 'I've been inquiring about forgers. I've now had over sixty replies from all the leading museums and authorities in Europe.'

Powerscourt remembered that the old man was still President of the Royal Academy. Even now the vultures would be circling round his job, lobbying here, promising favours there in order to take over the most prestigious post in British art.

'I've narrowed it down to two,' Lambert went on, shuffling his stamps into neat piles. 'The first one is a Frenchman called Jean Pierre Boileau. He's about fifty years old. They say he tried to make a career in Paris as a painter but he never sold anything at all. Then he disappeared somewhere in the Auvergne and wasn't heard of for years. It transpired that he had an arrangement with a gallery in Florence for old paintings he could pick up on the trips he took around the south of France. The point was there weren't any trips. There was only a trip to the barn beside his little house which he had converted into a studio. He specialized in Italian paintings.'

'What happened to his arrangement with the gallery in Florence?' asked Powerscourt.

'Somebody smelt a rat, somebody from one of the big galleries in Rome. It was all hushed up. There was no publicity about the fact that the gallery had sold a heap of fakes.' Sir Frederick was arranging his stamps into piles from their country of origin. About fifteen French ones were mustered on the left-hand side of the little table in front of him.

'It's a curious thing, Powerscourt,' he went on, 'whenever there is a forgery or a fake is discovered, everybody in the art world closes ranks. Thing gets hushed up as quickly as possible. The victims of the fraud get their money back. Very quickly, sometimes with the proviso that they keep their mouths shut.'

'Do you think Monsieur Boileau is back in business now?' asked Powerscourt, watching with fascination as a small regiment of German stamps took up their position before him.

'I do not,' said Lambert, shuffling slowly with the Russians, all adorned with the head of the Tsar, 'I think he would be too old. I think his nerve might have gone if he'd been caught once.'

'And the other forger? Is he French too?'

Only the Italian stamps remained. 'The other one,' Lambert spoke slowly, as if talking was becoming difficult, 'is English. Quite young. Extraordinarily talented. He studied here at the Royal Academy not so long ago. Then he went to study in Rome. I think he worked for a time for the leading picture restorers in Paris – restoration, some say, is a cousin, if not a brother or a sister, to forgery. Then he disappeared. There were stories about gambling debts, about an unhappy love affair, about drinking to excess. But he has simply disappeared off the face of the earth. He may be dead, of course, but I doubt it.'

Maybe he's hidden away somewhere in *la France profonde* or some remote mountainous area in the Apennines, Powerscourt said to himself. Maybe he's in Corsica. Maybe he's locked up on the wild coast of Norfolk, in the crumbling splendour of de Courcy Hall. Abandoned. Nobody there. Place completely empty. Nobody there at all.

The four great powers of Europe were now assembled in neat piles on Lambert's table. Powerscourt wondered briefly about alliances, Triple Ententes between Rome, Paris and St Petersburg perhaps, as Lambert swept them all into the jumbled heap they had been a few minutes before. Powerscourt thought he must repeat this process over and over again. Rather like the diplomats of Europe.

'Do you know his name?' said Powerscourt, mesmerized by the new kaleidoscope of stamps.

As Sir Frederick smiled his cheeks became almost completely hollow. He might have been a ghost. 'He is called Orlando Blane,' he said, 'and a very charming young man he was. I met him, you know, when he was studying at the Academy. Very quick, but not quite stable. Always liable to go off the rails.'

'And none of your informants have any idea where he is at present?' asked Powerscourt.

'Nobody has any idea at all. But if you can find him, you may have solved the mystery, or part of the mystery. I think I have told you before that I was very fond of Christopher Montague. His death is such a loss to the art world. May I ask you a question, Powerscourt?' The voice was beginning to fade. 'Do you know who killed him?'

Powerscourt thought briefly about lying, about saying that he was on the very edge of a great discovery. But he knew Sir Frederick deserved better than that.

'No, I do not, Sir Frederick,' he said sadly, 'it is a very difficult case.'

'Can I ask you one favour, Powerscourt? Can you find the answer before I go? I'm not sure I could find out once I'm dead, if you see what I mean. And I'd hate to pass on without knowing the answer.'

Sir Frederick's eyes were pleading with him, a last plea from a man who thought he had less than a month to live.

'I shall do my best, Sir Frederick.' Powerscourt suddenly got up and took the old man's two hands in his own. They were very cold. The surface felt like marble. 'I shall do more than my best to find the answer for you. The next time I come, I pray you will be better than you are today. And I shall tell you who killed Christopher Montague.'

As he walked home through the wet squares of South Kensington, the light fading fast from the streets of London, Powerscourt thought he now had two deadlines. One was to find the murderer before Horace Aloysius Buckley was wrongly convicted of the crime and hanged by the neck until he was dead. The other was to find the murderer before death came to call for the President of the Royal Academy, Sir Frederick Lambert, arranging the stamps of the Great Powers of Europe into neat piles on his table.

Part Four

Titian

20

The carriage stopped. A harsh wind hit Imogen Foxe full in the face as she was ushered towards a house she could not see. They took her to a darkened room, where the shutters were drawn and no lights were lit. Very gently her escort removed all the bandages and the wrapping from her eyes.

'You may find the light difficult at first,' he said. 'I suggest you wait here for about five minutes. It should seem easier then.'

Orlando Blane was peering out of one of the windows of the Long Gallery. A full moon had come out from behind the clouds. The wind was rustling through the trees, blowing the leaves across the unkempt lawns. To his left the surface of the lake was uneven, small waves driven in towards the shore.

Imogen winced as the man opened the door and shafts of light fell across the room. It was, she saw, a small sitting room with pictures lining the walls and a great globe standing inscrutably by the window. Gradually her eyes became accustomed to the light. She stepped into the hall, a huge high chamber with a great staircase leading to the upper floors.

'May I go to him now?' she asked meekly. Great humility, she had decided, must be her watchword at the beginning with these guards, the keepers of Orlando. When she knew them better, other policies might prove more fruitful.

'Up the stairs and turn left,' the man said, 'keep going to the end of the corridor. Then it's the door in front of you.'

Orlando was wondering how he could escape from his prison. His recent letters requesting release, pointing out how much money he must have earned from his captors, had gone unanswered. He wished he knew where he was – after a couple of weeks he had been so absorbed in his work that he hadn't bothered to notice anything else.

Imogen passed a couple of stags' heads, dust lying across the antlers, at the top of the stairs. She checked the doors on her way down the corridor. They were all locked. She could see a little beam of light coming under the door at the end.

Orlando moved away from his window and began walking the hundred and forty feet towards the far end of the Long Gallery. His footsteps echoed off the floorboards, small pieces of plaster still lying on the ground. He didn't hear the first knock. The second was louder.

'Come in,' said Orlando, not bothering to turn round. He presumed it was one of the guards making sure he was still here. They usually checked every hour.

The footsteps kept coming, very quiet footsteps now as if their owner was crossing the floor on tiptoes. Should she speak? Imogen saw that Orlando would reach the end and turn about in less than a minute. She stopped by the fireplace half-way up the Long Gallery. She was breathing very fast. Now, surely he must turn now. But he didn't. Orlando stopped at the far window, gazing out at the bent trees around the lake, the dark water glistening in the moonlight.

Imogen could bear it no longer. 'Orlando,' she called out very quietly. 'Orlando.'

278

Orlando Blane turned. He couldn't believe what he saw, an Imogen in dark grey travelling clothes, an Imogen with red eyes, a weary Imogen after her long journey, but Imogen. His Imogen.

'Imogen, is this really you?' He walked very slowly down the room to take her in his arms, fearful that the wraith by the fireside might suddenly disappear into the night.

'It is, my love,' she said. 'Oh yes, it is.' She broke the spell. She ran as fast as she could and fell into his arms. They remained wrapped around each other for over a minute, neither daring to speak. Then it came in a great rush.

'Imogen, did they wrap your eyes up . . .'

'Orlando, what are you doing here . . .'

'You must be tired after your journey . . .'

'Are you a prisoner here . . .'

Orlando laughed and clapped his hands together. 'Stop, stop,' he said, trailing his fingers through Imogen's left hand. 'Let's do it like this. You can ask me three questions. Then I can ask you three questions. All right?'

Imogen nodded. She wondered briefly what she should ask first. Then it came to her.

'Orlando, do you still love me?'

Orlando Blane laughed again. 'Of course I do,' he said. 'You didn't need to ask that one. You know it already.' He kissed her very gently on the lips.

'Second question then,' said Imogen, drawing Orlando over to a small sofa by the fireplace. They heard a sudden scurrying across the ceiling.

'Don't worry about that,' said Orlando, pointing above his head, 'that's only the rats taking their evening exercise. They usually run about at this time of day. They're quite harmless.'

'Second question, then,' said Imogen. 'What are you

279

doing here? Are you a prisoner or something like that?'

'That's two questions.'

'No it's not.'

'Yes it is.'

'No it's not.'

'Very well,' said Orlando, 'I'll let you off just this once. One question. What am I doing here? I'll show you.'

He walked down the gallery and pulled a selection of canvases from the wall. '*Portrait of a Man* by Titian,' he said. He pulled another one into the light. '*Portrait of a Man* by Titian. You don't have to be the director of the National Gallery to see that they're the same. Which one is the real one, Imogen?'

Imogen looked at them carefully. The same Venetian nobleman, his body at right angles to the artist, the same blue doublet, the same dark blue cloak thrown across the shoulders.

'That one is the real one, Orlando,' Imogen said, pointing at the one furthest away.

'Wrong,' said Orlando triumphantly. 'That one is a Blane. This one is a Titian. This is what I do. I'm a prisoner here. One Sergeant Major and three of his men guard me round the clock. If I go for a walk one of them comes with me. I don't know where I am – they brought me here with my eyes wrapped up so I was as blind as a bat. It all has to do with that ten thousand pounds I lost in Monte Carlo. When I've paid that back, I will be set free on certain conditions. I don't know what they are. But I am certain they have made much more than ten thousand pounds out of me by now.'

Orlando paused and pointed his hand up and down the Long Gallery. 'This is my prison cell. It must be the finest cell in the whole of Europe – maybe they imported the rats to remind me that it is only a prison cell after all. This is where I do my work. I fake to order. I forge what others tell me. I do not know where the instructions come from, somewhere in London, I suppose. Sometimes they send paintings up here for me to copy. Recently they have been sending me illustrations of various American families. I have to turn them into Gainsboroughs or Reynoldses, people like that. I mean, I take the modern face and drop it into my version of a Gainsborough.'

'What happens to them, Orlando? Is there something very wicked going on here?'

'That was your third question, my love,' said Orlando, giving her three rapid kisses. 'It'll be my turn in a minute. I can only guess what happens to them, but I think it must go something like this. Somebody goes to an exhibition where this Titian is for sale. A price is agreed, quite a steep price, I should think. The dealer tells the purchaser he must clean the picture and make sure the frame is in good condition. The picture comes up here. I make a copy. Both go back to London. The purchaser takes away, not the real thing, but my copy. The dealer hides the real one away for a couple of years. Then he brings it on to the market.

'As for the Gainsboroughs, I think that is rather cunning. The reason for sending me the illustrations from the American magazines must be that the father, with or without his family, is coming to London. The dealer shows him my Gainsborough. The American is astonished by the likeness to his wife or daughter, all dressed out in eighteenth-century finery. So he buys it.'

The storm was getting up outside. Orlando took Imogen over to the middle window of the five. The tops of the trees were bending in a hideous nocturnal ballet. Here and there in the remains of the garden branches had been wrenched away from their trees and were being blown towards the broken fountain in the centre.

'You see that first window, Imogen?' Orlando pointed

down towards the door she had come in by. 'That is where I think about the day's work, the right brushes, mixing the right paint in the right fashion. The second window is where I think how to finish the paintings, the glazes, the varnish, the final touches. This window,' he drew her to him very closely, 'this is where I think about you.'

The rain was lashing against the window. Orlando noticed that two further cracks had appeared in the upper pane. He closed all the shutters except the middle one, Imogen's window, Imogen who was now right beside him in his prison.

'My turn to ask the questions now,' he said, leading her back to the sofa. 'What's been happening to you, my love?'

Imogen told him about the terrible wedding, the reception where she had refused to smile, the honeymoon where she had first locked her door. She told him about her life in the country, the boring neighbours, the incessant talk of hunting, the lack of civilized conversation, the endless letters from her mother and her sisters exhorting her to be a good wife. She told him about how she felt cold inside all the time, down there in Dorset surrounded by the deer and the lake, how she knew her life was not meant to be like this, about how time and boredom numbed the senses until she felt she was only half alive. Maybe everybody else felt like that all the time, she didn't know.

'I feel more alive here with you, Orlando, than I have felt for months and months.'

Orlando took her in his arms again.

'Where do you sleep, Orlando? Surely not in here? If your bedroom is as grand as this Long Gallery, you should have a four poster bed at least.'

Orlando pulled Imogen to her feet and led her towards the door at the far end.

'Four poster bed?' he laughed, putting his arm around her waist. 'That's precisely what I do have.'

'Francis, Francis, I think I've found her.'

Lady Lucy had rushed into the drawing room at Markham Square, not stopping to leave her hat and gloves in the hall down below. Her husband was sprawled full length on the sofa, staring up at the ceiling.

'Found who, Lucy?' He rose to his feet and gave his wife a quick kiss on the cheek. Lady Lucy's face and eyes were very bright from walking through the cold London afternoon.

'You should be very pleased with me,' she said, drawing off her gloves. 'You said it might be very important.'

'I'm sure I'll be very pleased, Lucy,' said Powerscourt, 'but only if I knew who it was you have found.'

'You even made disparaging remarks about my relations at the time, Francis.' Powerscourt groaned inwardly, checking outside in the hall that none of the army of relations had come to invade the house. 'Well, without them, we might never have found her. For heaven's sake, Francis, where have you gone to, lying on that sofa over there? Have you forgotten this investigation completely and gone to fight the Boers or something like that?'

'I was thinking about Horace Aloysius Buckley, the man who went to Evensong. Shouldn't think there's much in the way of Evensong where he is now. But please, tell me, who have you found?'

Lady Lucy completed the business with her gloves and laid her hat down on a side table. She stared at her husband with some exasperation.

'Honestly, Francis,' she said, 'I thought you would have known by now.'

Powerscourt had known for some time. 'Let me hazard a guess, Lucy. You have found Alice Bridge, the young woman who went to the Venetian exhibition with Christopher Montague. I suspect the reports from your intelligence operatives, also known as your relations, may have told you that she has been rather under the weather recently.'

'It is,' said Lady Lucy, 'I mean it is Alice Bridge. And people do say that she has not been herself recently. How do you know that?'

'It was a guess. Now then, do you know where she lives, what manner of person she is?'

'Her father is a successful financier in the City of London. They live about a mile away from here in Upper Grosvenor Street, Number 16. She's twenty-two years old and, my third cousin tells me, remarkably pretty.'

'And why,' said Powerscourt, moving slowly towards a writing table in the corner of the room, 'does the third cousin say she has not been herself?'

Lady Lucy watched as Powerscourt began writing his letter, those long thin fingers wrapped round his pen. 'The official story, Francis, you know what families are like for putting out information that may or may not be accurate to cover over some family problem, is that she was upset because her sister has left London and gone to live in the country.'

Powerscourt was writing furiously now. Alice Bridge was unhappy. Could her unhappiness have anything to do with the death of Christopher Montague, strangled by the neck until he was dead?

'I think we have to be as good as gold, Orlando,' said Imogen Foxe. The pair were sitting in the Long Gallery after breakfast. Normally Orlando ate with his jailers in the kitchen, but they had turned the room where Imogen

284

took off her bandages the night before into a small dining room and let the young lovers eat alone.

'If we look as if butter wouldn't melt in our mouths they may lose interest,' she went on. 'And I intend to flirt outrageously with the two younger men down there. That redhead can't be more than twenty-four or twenty-five.'

Orlando Blane winced at the thought of the flirting.

'It's no good looking like that, Orlando, it's got to be done if we're going to get you out of here.'

'Not too much flirting, please.'

Imogen was not to be put off. 'The one thing that must not happen, Orlando,' she seemed to have taken charge of the situation, 'is that you get behind with your work. So I'm going to sit up at the other end there and keep out of your way.'

Orlando smiled. 'You don't suppose, that you might find it necessary to say something from time to time, just a few words now and then to let me know what the weather's like at the far end of the room, that sort of thing?'

Imogen laughed. She said she would take a walk for a while to ensure Orlando was left in peace. 'What are you forging now?' she asked as she set off. 'I'd like to know.'

Orlando explained that he was working on a lost Giovanni Bellini. It had adorned the walls of a church in Venice until the building was ravaged by fire about twenty-five years before. Everybody assumed the painting of Christ with a couple of saints had been destroyed. But the canvas was about to be rediscovered, having left Venice with the family who rescued it. First, the lost masterpiece had to be born. In Orlando Blane's Long Gallery.

'These people know their business,' said Orlando. 'A picture known to have existed is much more likely to be believed in than one that turns up out of the blue. It has a history already.'

The wind had dropped from the night before as Imogen stepped out of the front door, the redhead a respectable few paces behind her. Rain was falling steadily across the countryside. A tattered group of crows was flying across the fields. She walked away from the house to a path that led on to the main drive. She wondered how far down the drive she would be allowed to go. To her right the fields stretched out for a couple of miles before they stopped at a wood. Ahead, set back from the path, was a little church. Even at a hundred yards Imogen could see the holes in the roof, tiles blown away by the wind. To her left a red-brick stable block where she presumed there must be horses. Horses. She wondered if she and Orlando could creep down in the night and ride away. Steady, she said to herself, steady. We don't even know where we are yet. The great Jacobean house, the derelict fields, she could be anywhere. She set off down the drive, remembering that she must have come this way the day before. Ten paces behind her, like a faithful guard dog, the redhead maintained his vigil. She was passing a pond and another group of abandoned buildings. Perhaps this had been the home farm in better days. As the path rose up a little hill Imogen wondered if it was time to talk to the redhead. What was his name? Where did he come from? Did he like it here? She rehearsed the opening moves in her mind and decided against it. Too soon.

Six hundred yards away a man was fiddling with the aperture on his binoculars. It was as though he couldn't believe what he was seeing. The man was lying in a circle of trees to the right of the drive and was virtually invisible from all directions. Yes, it was. It was definitely a woman, young and very attractive if these German glasses were to be believed.

Johnny Fitzgerald had seen the redhead before. He had seen all the guards. He had heard the carriage coming to the house the previous evening but he could see nothing at all. This girl must have been inside, Johnny decided. Was she a prisoner? Was the redhead a warder? Or a nurse in some form of mental asylum? Were these people guarding some dangerous lunatic in there? Was the girl the lunatic? Was the girl deranged?

Johnny Fitzgerald had based himself in one of the few hotels left open on the sea front of Cromer. The main rooms looked out over the grey sea, occasional fishermen venturing out for crab or lobsters. The waiters were bored, serving bored food in a bored dining room where only one other couple came to dine. They were so bored that they scarcely spoke to each other. Even Johnny's bottle of Beaune, a cheerful draught in happier places, seemed bored. It tasted flat as if it had had enough of Cromer and its beach.

He watched as the little drama continued on the drive. When the girl was about three hundred yards away from Johnny's hiding place, the redhead came up to her. They spoke a few words. The girl turned round. Johnny could not hear what was said. He watched as the slim figure walked slowly back to the house, possibly deep in thought, or lunacy. This afternoon, Fitzgerald said to himself, I'm going to work my way round to the other side of the house. I'll go to those woods at the back and see how close I can get.

Imogen thought later that she could so easily have missed it. A grey stone blended into a grey wall between the house and the stable block. The stone made her heart beat faster and the blood rush to her face. It was a milestone, aged and worn now but with the legend still faintly legible through the green lichen. She pretended to retie her boot as she bent down and tried to read the words. The redhead was about twenty paces behind her, approaching fast. She peered desperately at the milestone. One arrow pointed in a southerly direction.

Norwich, twenty miles, it said. Another arrow pointed north over the woods. Cromer, three miles.

Imogen and Orlando were on the north coast of Norfolk.

Alice Bridge had declined Powerscourt's invitation to Markham Square. Instead he was making his way to 16 Upper Grosvenor Street on one of those rare winter days when the sun shone on London for tea at four o'clock. He wondered how Johnny Fitzgerald was faring up in Norfolk.

The drawing room in Upper Grosvenor Street was formal. Portraits lined the walls. A fire burned brightly in the grate. Cucumber sandwiches and a fruit cake were already in position. Powerscourt thought the house was probably run like a military operation.

Alice Bridge was not alone. The room was dominated by her mother, Mrs Agatha Bridge, who sat very erect in her chair, her hair tied in a formidable bun, her ample bosom jutting forward like the prow of a ship. Her daughter sat nervously by her side, looking as if she were in protective custody. Powerscourt felt the interview might prove difficult.

'Lord Powerscourt,' Mrs Bridge boomed out to him as he faced her on the sofa, 'I understand you want to ask my daughter some questions.'

Powerscourt put on his most deferential manner. 'Yes, I do, Mrs Bridge,' he said, 'just a few simple questions. It shouldn't take long. And thank you so much for inviting me here to tea.'

'Do you make it a habit, Lord Powerscourt, to go about London making inquiries about people's private lives?'

'I am an investigator, Mrs Bridge. It is my profession.'

'A profession?' Mrs Bridge was peering at him as if he

were some lowly form of pond life. 'A profession of prying and peeping into respectable citizens' privacy? Surely this great city of ours has other professions which might occupy your time more properly?'

'In my time,' said Powerscourt, determined not to be engulfed by this wave of hostility, 'I have been an officer of Her Majesty's armed forces. I have letters from the Prime Minister thanking me for services rendered to the Government and the country. Please, Mrs Bridge, I am sure it would be better if I asked my questions and troubled you no more.'

Tea arrived, an enormous silver teapot polished to perfection. 'Tea, Lord Powerscourt?' Powerscourt wondered if it was a peace offering, or merely a truce before hostilities were recommenced.

'Thank you very much,' he said, watching Alice Bridge carefully out of the corner of his eye. She looked very uncomfortable, but whether that was caused by her mother's manners or the delicacy of her own position he could not tell.

'Tell me, Miss Bridge,' Powerscourt moved to take the initiative, 'how well did you know Mr Christopher Montague?'

Alice Bridge blushed bright red. She glanced quickly at her mother before she replied.

'I knew him quite well.'

'Did you go with him to the opening of the Venetian exhibition at the de Courcy and Piper Gallery in Old Bond Street?' asked Powerscourt.

'I did,' said Alice Bridge, avoiding her mother's gaze and looking down at the carpet.

'I was not cognisant of the fact that you had accompanied him to that exhibition,' said Mrs Bridge, looking at her daughter sternly. 'And how did you come by this information, Lord Powerscourt? More snooping about, I presume, more impertinent questions?'

Mrs Bridge was beginning to irritate Powerscourt considerably.

'I would remind you, Mrs Bridge,' he said firmly, 'that Christopher Montague is dead. So is his greatest friend, a man called Thomas Jenkins of Emmanuel College, Oxford. They will, unfortunately, be in no position to attend any more exhibitions in future. Tell me, Miss Bridge,' he turned to look at Alice, still staring sullenly at the carpet, 'when was the last time you saw Mr Montague?'

Alice Bridge took a deep breath. 'Mama says I'm not to answer any more questions.'

Her mother drew herself up to her full height. Some mighty broadside was about to be delivered into the centre of HMS *Powerscourt*. He just managed to get in first.

'I put it to you, Miss Bridge, that you were perhaps very close to Christopher Montague in the last months of his life. I put it to you that you had kept your family in the dark about the affair. I put it to you also that refusing to answer any perfectly innocent questions may make people suspicious, more suspicious than they would have been if they knew the true story.'

'Mama says that I'm not to answer any more questions.' Powerscourt wondered if the answers would have been forthcoming if her mother wasn't there. He felt sure that Christopher Montague would not have seemed a very desirable catch to the mistress of 16 Upper Grosvenor Street. Powerscourt heard a sort of blowing sound from Alice's right. The broadside was coming.

'Suspicions? Suspicions, Lord Powerscourt?' Mrs Agatha Bridge was in full cry. 'Are you saying that you suspect my daughter of being involved in some way in this murder? I tell you, Lord Powerscourt, I never met the young man. I would not have considered him a suitable escort for Alice, or indeed any other respectable young woman. People like Montague are a danger to the nation's morals. Look at that terrible man Wilde. They should all be sent to prison.'

'Nobody is suggesting that your daughter is involved with the murder,' said Powerscourt. 'That is why I find this refusal to answer any questions so very strange. Miss Bridge, I am asking you for the last time, how close were you to Christopher Montague?'

Powerscourt thought later that she might have been on the edge of tears. Perhaps it was Montague's name that did it. But the answer was the same.

'Mama says I'm not to answer any more questions.'

As he made his way back to Markham Square, Powerscourt wondered just how close Alice Bridge had been to the dead art critic. He thought again about the clues and the suspects in this case. He thought about de Courcy and Piper and the benefit their gallery had derived from the death of Christopher Montague. He thought about Roderick Johnston, a man who might have lost most of his considerable income if Montague had lived. He thought about the wine glasses and the tea the murderer must have washed up each time he struck. He thought about the tie in Thomas Jenkins' rooms on the Banbury Road in Oxford. He resolved to summon reinforcements of a sort in the person of William McKenzie, a tracker who had worked with Powerscourt and Fitzgerald in India and on several other cases since.

Afternoon rain had replaced morning rain in the bleak countryside of North Norfolk. Orlando was staring at his preliminary drawing for the Bellini on his easel. Imogen, still exultant from her morning discovery, was staring out at the woods behind the house.

'I've been here for months,' had been Orlando's verdict on his past record, 'and I never saw that milestone. You come here and find it on your first morning in the place. I'm ashamed of myself.'

'Never mind, darling,' Imogen had whispered back, fearful of being overheard by their captors. 'At least we know where we are.'

Later that afternoon, when Orlando had finished his work, they were to go on a reconnaissance mission up into the woods at the back.

Inching his way forward through the same woods, Johnny Fitzgerald was beginning to wish that Norfolk could be moved somewhere else, somewhere drier, the south of Spain perhaps, maybe even the Sahara, where the damp wouldn't work its way through the toughest clothes he possessed. He could see the back of the house now. If he moved another thirty feet to his left he would be able to see if any of that part of the house was inhabited. He dare not go any closer in case one of the guards came out on afternoon patrol.

Now he could see clearly through his glasses the Long Gallery on the first floor, the five great windows, some with their shutters half open, looking out on the sad remains of the garden and the lake to his right. He worked his way slowly across the windows. There, at the end furthest away from him, was the girl he had seen that morning. Next window, nothing, only a dark interior. Third window, he thought he made out a small sofa, by an enormous fireplace. Fourth window, he could see a door in the far corner. Fifth window . . . Johnny took his glasses off and wiped the lens with the only dry cloth he still possessed, tucked in under his shirt. The cloth felt warm against the surrounding damp. He put the binoculars back to his eyes and squinted through.

There was a man and an easel. Johnny was sure it was an easel. Making a minute adjustment to the aperture he thought he saw a line of paintings stacked up against the wall next to the door. The man was now working at his easel with a pencil or a brush, Johnny couldn't tell. But he felt strangely exultant up there in the squelchy mud of the de Courcy woods, rain dripping down his forehead, finding its own way into his boots. Had Powerscourt known all along? Had he divined somehow that here, in this remote spot, guarded by an unbroken length of red-brick wall and a couple of unfriendly lodges, was the man who might hold the key to the whole investigation? Johnny Fitzgerald put the glasses back in their case and began to crawl up the hill towards safer ground. Johnny didn't think any strangers found in the de Courcy woods would be invited in for a comforting glass of sherry.

Ten minutes later he was lying in a clump of trees at the top of the hill. The house was only just visible through the trees. It was the voices he heard first, the girl's voice asking the man if he had walked up this way before. Then he heard the man reply, saying something about not having gone very far up this path as it was so damp. The wind was carrying their voices up the hill. Johnny peeped out. On his left he saw the long red-brick walls of the home garden, unpruned fruit trees and untended vegetable patches no doubt concealed within. Christ, they were coming straight for him. If they kept walking for another ten minutes they would virtually fall over his feet.

Run or stay? Johnny wormed his way deeper and deeper into the sodden earth. He heard the girl wondering what they would see when they reached the top. Five minutes now. Johnny wondered if he should write a quick message and hand it over to them as they passed, his hand rising out of the undergrowth like the hand that came to take King Arthur's sword in the lake at Avalon. He wondered what it should say. Hello Forger perhaps. Hello Mrs Forger. Do you want to get out of here?

Three minutes. Johnny Fitzgerald was wriggling

deeper into the earth. Then he heard the voice of salvation.

'I'm afraid that's as far as we can go today.' The redhead was twenty paces behind them. The walking party turned round, reluctantly Johnny thought, and headed back towards the house.

Johnny waited another fifteen minutes before he extricated himself from his earth. He noticed he had been sweating profusely in spite of the rain and the sodden ground. He patrolled the grounds at very long range for the rest of the afternoon. No one, prisoner or captor, ventured out of the house.

Back in the hotel of the bored, looking out at the grey waves rolling up the beach, the seagulls squawking in unison fifty feet above the water, he composed his message to Powerscourt.

De Courcy Hall seems empty. But not. Party of four guards, possibly ex-army. Two prisoners. Forger, young man mid to late twenties. Mrs Forger, beautiful girl, possibly younger. Easel and numerous paintings spotted in forger's quarters. Suggest you abandon fleshpots of London. Incomparable welcome here in this hotel. Norfolk weather magnificent. Fitzgerald.

21

Charles Augustus Pugh's office was a temple to the existence of files. Files single, files in bundles, files with red ribbon, files with black marched in perfect order along a series of shelves that stretched up to the ceiling along three sides of the room. Two large windows looked out on to the perfectly manicured lawn of Gray's Inn. At a large desk in the centre, also festooned with files, Pugh sat with his feet up on the desk, puffing happily at a small cheroot. His exquisite dark blue jacket was hanging languidly from the back of the chair. Across an equally exquisite waistcoat was a watch chain in very thin gold which he would finger from time to time. Pugh was about six feet tall with a Roman profile and a Roman nose that gave him a powerful air in court.

'What have we got then,' he asked cheerfully, 'to smite the Philistines with? They didn't say very much at the committal hearing, lot of stuff about motive, couple of witnesses who had seen him on the way to Montague's flat and up the Banbury Road in Oxford. Can't decide whether to call Buckley as a witness or not.'

'There are any number of people who could have killed Montague,' said Powerscourt. 'My problem is that at the moment I don't know which one of them did it. How long have we got before the trial?'

'Bloody postponements,' said Pugh. 'You'd think when people get sent up to the Central Criminal Court, the prosecution would have sorted things out properly. But no. Two postponements in the past few days. Could be up there by the end of next week.'

'Christ,' said Powerscourt. 'Right, Mr Pugh, here goes.'

'List of suspects, then. Nothing like throwing mud in their eyes. Confuse the jury. Leave them thinking any conviction would be unsound.'

'Number one,' said Powerscourt, staring in amazement at the sheer number of the files. He wondered briefly if somewhere in a hot corner of the Egyptian temples some scribes had lived, surrounded with roll upon roll of papyrus, details of the construction of pyramids perhaps, carefully drawn up lists of what the current ruler wanted to take with them before they were incarcerated in their mausoleums in the sand.

'Edmund de Courcy,' he came back to the present, 'possibly with the support of his partner William Alaric Piper, art dealers. Montague's article was going to say that most of the works in their exhibition of Venetian Paintings were fakes, and some were recent forgeries. That would have been very bad for business. De Courcy may have also tried to kill me.'

He told Pugh the details of the flight down the hill from Aregno, the story of the Traitor's Run. Pugh was writing with deceptive speed in a notebook in front of him.

'Must be an interesting life, being an investigator, Powerscourt. Bloody sight more interesting than a monk's life here with all these damned files, punctuated by occasional outings in front of the judge.'

'Number two,' Powerscourt went on.

'Pardon me a moment, pray,' said Pugh. 'You don't know if there is any evidence that de Courcy or Piper was seen in Brompton Square?'

'No,' said Powerscourt sadly, 'but de Courcy did employ a Corsican at his gallery. You'll be amazed to hear that the man has recently gone home. Family bereavement, I think. Corsicans go in for garrotting, as you know.'

Powerscourt noticed that Charles Augustus Pugh had just drawn the outline of the mountainous island on the page in front of him.

'Pity he's gone home,' he said. 'Don't suppose the Corsican authorities would be very keen on sending him back to us. Tighter than those criminal families in the East End, I shouldn't wonder.'

'Number two,' Powerscourt went on, 'Roderick Johnston, senior curator of Renaissance paintings at the National Gallery. There is a growing demand for people to authenticate paintings, Americans wanting to be certain they're taking a genuine Corregio back to Cincinnati, that sort of thing. Montague's article would have confirmed that he, Montague, was now the leading authority in Britain, if not in Europe, on the attribution of Italian paintings. End of the line for Johnston. The man's been living above his means for years. Harridan of a wife, keen to acquire pretty houses in the Cotswolds or grand villas in the hills above Florence. Johnston had a very strong motive for wanting Montague out of the way.'

'What sorts of sums are we talking about?' asked Pugh. 'Quick fifty pounds in notes? Envelopes stuffed with five hundred in cash?'

Pugh's voice was a rich deep bass. It sounded very quiet, here in his chambers. Powerscourt imagined it could be a potent weapon in the courtroom, rising to intimidate the opposition witnesses, rising and falling as he made his final appeal to the jury.

'Think thousands, Mr Pugh, maybe tens of thousands.'

Pugh whistled at the size of the sums.

'Suppose you have an artist of the highest class,' said Powerscourt, 'a Derby winner of an artist. Let's take Raphael. You are a dealer, Mr Pugh. This Raphael comes into your possession. You have a rich American client, keen on building up the best collection in the United States. He has a very suspicious mind – he didn't get all his millions in steel or railroads by believing everything he's told. You prove to me that it really is a Raphael, he says. If it's real, remember, it might be worth seventy or eighty thousand pounds. If it's not real, it's virtually worthless. Enter Roderick Johnston. Or enter Christopher Montague. You, the dealer, are at their mercy, unless you already have them on the payroll. Even then, they can name their percentage of the final price. Could be ten or fifteen. I believe it has been known to go up to twenty-five for the authentication. But once you, the dealer, have it, you have the sale.'

'And they say,' said Pugh, 'that lawyers are overpaid. Perish the thought. And, presumably, once you are accepted as the best authenticator around, dealers will be queuing up for your services? The money will just keep on rolling in?'

'Exactly so,' said Powerscourt.

Charles Augustus Pugh took his perfectly polished black boots off his desk.

'Any more?' he said. 'I think we could make quite a lot of mud with those two. I just don't know if it's enough to get him off.'

'There is,' said Powerscourt. 'There is one other candidate but I do not feel sufficiently confident to give you the details at this stage. It's only a hunch.'

'Would you be able to tell me in confidence? No notes in my book, no mention of it anywhere.'

Powerscourt told him. Pugh leaned back in his chair and put his hands behind his head. 'God in heaven,

Powerscourt, 'he said. 'I can see perfectly clearly why you might think that. God knows how you prove it.'

Orlando Blane and Imogen Foxe were eating their last supper. Orlando was so nervous that his hand shook as he tried to cut into the thick sausages their captors had provided. Imogen kicked him under the table. First of all they talked about horses, horses that had won the Oaks or the Derby in happier times gone by. Imogen found the potato frightfully hard to swallow – it was as if her body was refusing to do what she told it.

Imogen told him about the terrible war in South Africa, the endless sieges, beleaguered little communities of soldiers and civilians trying to eke out their rations before starvation finished them off, the British relief expeditions forever delayed by the skill of the elusive Boers who never lost a battle. They simply got back on their horses and rode away into the veldt.

Tonight Orlando and Imogen were going to escape. For days now they had never altered their routine, Imogen walking in the morning while Orlando worked at his easel, the two of them walking in the late afternoon, supper watched by their captors, then early to bed. That was particularly important in their minds. For four successive nights they had retired just as the guard came on his final patrol shortly after nine o'clock.

Their plan was to wait a couple of hours after that until the guards too had gone to sleep. Then they were going to swing themselves out of the window on a rope improvised from the stout sheets on the bed, and head for where they thought Cromer was. There must be trains, Imogen had said, early morning trains going south to Norwich. Once they reached Norwich they could head for London. Then they would be safe. So intent were they on the immediate details of their flight that they had given no thought at all to what they would do when they arrived in the capital.

Back in the Long Gallery Orlando changed into the fresh clothes Imogen had brought him from Blandford. Imogen noted with pride that they fitted him like a glove. They packed one bag between them. They peered anxiously into the wild night outside. Imogen began to make the rope of sheets that would lead them to freedom.

Johnny Fitzgerald had brought Powerscourt on a great loop of a ride that took them on to the long drive that led up to de Courcy Hall. 'God help sailors on a night like this,' Johnny muttered to himself as the wind rose and turned into a storm. It was whistling through the trees, their upper branches bent into fantastic arabesques by the speed of its passing. Ahead of them in the great woods at the back of the house they could hear cracks like pistol shots as branches were severed from the trunks that bore them.

'Look, Francis,' whispered Fitzgerald, 'two hundred yards away you can see the stable block. I think we should leave the horses here in case they make a noise.'

They abandoned the horses and tiptoed forward, bent almost double into the wind. Snow was falling fast now, the stable block and house scarcely visible. Then they froze in their tracks. A bell was ringing, not from the church two hundred yards to their left, but from inside the ghostly features of de Courcy Hall itself. They pressed forward.

'What, in God's name, is that bell for, Francis? It's well after eleven at night,' muttered Johnny, taking shelter behind a tree.

'I doubt very much if it's for evening prayers in this place, Johnny. Let's get further forward. Sounds like a general alert to me. Place isn't on fire, is it?' whispered Powerscourt.

Fitzgerald led them forward at a rush to the walled garden. They could just see the side of the house. Lights had been turned on. There was a lot of confused shouting of orders. Then they saw a party of four men, some with rifles, come running at the double from the front of the house and then turn left towards the woods that led to Cromer.

'Where are the forger's quarters, Johnny?' whispered Powerscourt. 'I think they must have tried to escape.' He wondered suddenly what instructions the jailers had in case of flight. Recapture, certainly. But an escaped forger might be able to tell the tale of his endeavours with brush and glaze, locked away in de Courcy Hall. That could be very embarrassing for somebody in London. Would they rather he was dead? Like Christopher Montague? Powerscourt wondered macabrely if they had brought the garrotting wire with them, those men who had just rushed up the hill, tucked into an inside pocket. Or would they shoot the forger dead, another shooting accident in Norfolk? So unfortunate, officer, he should never have been wandering about in the field of fire.

Johnny Fitzgerald led him round to the back of the house. There were no lights on in the Long Gallery, only the snow driven in against the windows. Powerscourt thought you could see ten yards in front of your face, no more.

'Look, Francis.' Fitzgerald was pointing to the end window. It was still half open. An improvised rope could just be seen, dangling to the ground, the white of the sheets almost invisible in the swirling snow.

'My God, Johnny,' said Powerscourt. 'The birds have flown. But what a night to choose. We'd better get after them.'

Powerscourt and Fitzgerald set off up the hill. Neither had any clear idea what to do if they encountered the guards. Powerscourt suddenly remembered what Lady Lucy had said to Fitzgerald before he left for Norfolk: 'Please check in the local guidebooks before you go, Johnny,' she had said. 'Make sure there aren't strange local customs up there at this time of year. Shooting strangers for instance. I'd hate to think there's an East Anglian version of the Traitor's Run.'

Now they were right in the middle of it.

The first stages of the escape had gone very well. Orlando shinned down the improvised rope and laughed when his feet touched the ground. Imogen had thrown down their bag and shot down the sheets to join him. She put her finger to her lips. Hand in hand they set off up the hill, their bodies swaying together sometimes in the wind.

The snow exhilarated them at first. Imogen darted off and threw a couple of crisp snowballs at Orlando. Then they realized they couldn't see very far. Then they felt they might be lost. The route had seemed very clear when surveyed in the daylight on afternoon walks or from the windows of the Long Gallery. Up the hill, following the line of the path. If they kept going straight after that they should reach a boundary wall. As long as they continued in the same direction they should come to the sea, they should come to Cromer, they should reach freedom. But you couldn't see where you were going in the blizzard. They might be going back to the house itself for all they knew.

Then they heard the bell. 'My God,' whispered Orlando, 'that can only mean one thing. They're coming after us. Let's hurry.'

Imogen wondered if their pursuers would be able to navigate any better than they could. They had reached the top of the hill. The woods were less dense on the far side. She held Orlando's hand very tight and pressed forward into the snowstorm.

Powerscourt noticed that the four men in front had spread out in a V formation, each man no more than fifteen paces from his neighbour. He pointed it out to Fitzgerald who raised his hand in a mock salute. 'Sergeant Major,' muttered Johnny, 'advance according to the drill book.' They were deep in the woods now, the snow covering the tracks behind them. The mud rose up their boots. The snow got into their eyes, making visibility yet more difficult.

'What's ahead, Johnny?' whispered Powerscourt, fearful of the fate of the escapees.

'More woods,' replied Fitzgerald, 'then a wall. Trees stop just past the wall. Open country for a bit. Then over a hill and Cromer's on the far side.'

Then the whirling of the gale was interrupted. Two shots rang out into the night. They were immediately followed by a parade ground bellow. 'Cease firing! Bloody fool!'

One bullet caught Orlando in the thigh. It was only a flesh wound but the blood poured out of it, lying in scarlet drops that turned dark against the snow. He limped into the shelter of the last clump of trees before the open ground.

'My love,' whispered Imogen, 'how bad is it? Can you walk?'

Orlando had turned as pale as the falling snow. Instinctively he held on to his wounded leg.

'I think we should tie something round it,' said Imogen, remembering an article she had read recently on good nursing practice. She tore one of Orlando's new shirts into strips, as she had torn the sheet into strips a few happier hours before. They huddled together into the trees scarce daring to breathe. Thirty feet away they could hear a man floundering towards them.

Powerscourt and Fitzgerald had flung themselves to the ground when they heard the shot. Years of military training made it instinctive. They heard the order to cease fire.

Then they rose very slowly to their feet and set off up the hill. Powerscourt felt in his pocket.

'Do you have a gun, Johnny?' he whispered. Fitzgerald nodded. Even at six feet away he had to squint to see the nod. The snow was now lying nearly an inch thick on the ground. Some of the trees, not in direct line of the blast, were covered in snow from head to toe. Then they heard the Sergeant Major once more.

'Twenty paces to the right,' he shouted. 'Twenty paces to the right. Now!'

Imogen held Orlando's hand very tight as the man stumbled away from them towards the boundary wall. The snow was easing now, but the wind kept up its ferocious battering against the woods of de Courcy Hall.

'They're ahead of us now, Orlando,' Imogen whispered into her lover's ear, 'they're heading for Cromer. Can you walk?'

Orlando managed a brief hobble out of their clump of trees. He nearly fell over. He reached out for Imogen's shoulder. The flow of blood had eased. It was now seeping slowly out of his thigh and dripping down his new trousers.

'Christ,' said Orlando. 'It's bloody painful. Maybe you

could rub some snow into it. That might ease it. But I don't think I could get as far as Cromer, not with our four friends up ahead.' He staggered a few paces more. Imogen bent down to rub snow on to his leg. The babes in the wood were wounded now, the prospect of escape lost to a rifle shot in the dark.

'What do you think we should do?' asked Imogen, struck by the terrible thought that Orlando might bleed to death up here in the woods, and she would be left to drag his corpse back to the house for ignominious burial.

'I know it's hard, my love,' said Orlando, wincing with the pain. 'I think we've got to go back. If I can get that far.'

Limping, hobbling, tottering, staggering, occasionally falling, Orlando and Imogen set off on their return journey to de Courcy Hall.

Powerscourt and Fitzgerald halted at the boundary wall. The snow had almost stopped. The surrounding carpet of white meant you could see much further once you were out of the woods. Against this ghostly landscape they watched as the four guards made their way in regular order across the fields. They waited for about five minutes. There was no sound from up ahead, only the relentless lashing of the wind.

'What do you think, Johnny? Should we go after them?' said Powerscourt.

'Why not?' replied Fitzgerald, always eager for the chase.

'It's only this. If the forger and his lady had been crossing this field, we would have seen them. Or we would have heard shouts of capture.'

'Do you think they're dead, Francis? One bullet each?' said Fitzgerald.

'I don't think so. It would be fantastic shooting to hit

two people in this light. Look, why don't we do it like this. You carry on following our four friends up there. I'll go back to the house and get the horses. If I find the forger, well and good.'

'Fine,' said Fitzgerald.

Powerscourt watched his friend jump over the boundary wall and set off across the open country. He turned and began to make his way back through the woods. When he came out he noticed that he must have gone way over to the right as he was at the edge of the lake. Then he started running at full speed towards the front door. For in the snow there were footprints, two sets of them incredibly close together. The footprints made an irregular path, reeling like a pair of drunks going home, across the garden towards the main entrance. There were dark marks beside and between them. Powerscourt followed the trail that led past the Long Gallery and into the front of the house.

A trail of blood.

22

Orlando Blane was lying on the sofa in the Long Gallery. Imogen knelt beside him, washing the blood from his leg, a new bandage ready to wrap round his thigh. On the easel behind him, the outlines of his Giovanni Bellini stood perfectly still. There was a pale light, reflected from the snow outside.

'Imogen, I'm so sorry,' said Orlando. 'If I hadn't got shot we might have made it to Cromer.'

'Don't worry about that.' Imogen stopped work on his leg to wipe the sweat from Orlando's brow. The tottering journey down from the woods had left him exhausted. His face was pale, his skin totally white.

'The worst thing is this,' he said, 'you were only allowed to come because they were pleased with me. Now they won't be pleased with me at all. They'll send you away first thing in the morning.' Tears began rolling slowly down the pallor of his face.

'Don't cry, my love, please don't cry.' Imogen stroked his hand, wondering what would happen to him if he didn't see a doctor very soon.

'I wonder what they'll do to me,' said Orlando very quietly, taking Imogen's hand into his own, 'what the punishment will be for trying to escape. Maybe I'll be locked up here for years and years. Maybe I'll never see you again.'

This was more than Imogen could bear. She busied herself with the new bandage on Orlando's thigh, her tears dropping softly on the floorboards. Overhead they could hear the rats on night patrol, scurrying round on the floor above.

Then they heard footsteps coming along the corridor.

'Maybe we have to say goodbye now,' said Orlando. He leant forward, grimacing with the pain, and kissed Imogen on the lips. The footsteps were half-way along the corridor.

'I shall always love you, Imogen,' said Orlando.

The door was flung open. A tall man with curly brown hair and deep blue eyes stood in front of them. They had never seen him before.

'Good morning to you both. You,' the figure strode over to inspect Orlando's wound, 'must be Orlando Blane. And you,' he smiled at Imogen, 'must be his friend. We must get out of here at once. I have a couple of horses up by the stable block. My name is Powerscourt.'

Johnny Fitzgerald watched the four men disappear over the brow of the hill. He had served for years with Powerscourt as intelligence officers of the Crown. They had saved each other's lives in battle. One of the main jobs of intelligence, Powerscourt had often said, was to try to anticipate not only what the enemy were going to do next, but what they were going to do after that. Johnny could go back to de Courcy Hall and help Powerscourt with whatever was happening there. Or he could move ahead and find out what the Sergeant Major and his three friends would do once they reached Cromer. At least one, Johnny suspected, would be sent to watch the railway station. But the others? The wind was still howling through the trees behind him as Johnny made his decision. He set off at a loping run across the snow-covered fields. It was twenty minutes after midnight.

Powerscourt took in the easel, the canvases stacked up by the door, the art books lining the walls. Now is not the time to ask questions, he said to himself. Later, later.

'Can you walk?' he said to Orlando Blane. 'Perhaps if you lean on me it would be easier.'

Orlando struggled to his feet and put his arm around Powerscourt's shoulder. 'I can manage,' he said. 'I'm not sure how long I can hold out. Imogen, do you remember seeing a stick by that little table in the hall?'

Imogen shot off down the corridor, past the stags' heads with the dusty antlers, and returned with a stout walking stick. The journey was very difficult. Twice Orlando fell, dragging Powerscourt down with him into the snow. The blood had started flowing from his wound again, Imogen dabbing at it with the remains of the sheets from the bed. On their left the storm still rampaged through the woods, leaves and small branches occasionally flying through the air. When they reached the walled garden Powerscourt leant Orlando Blane against the gate and ran to find the horses. Could Orlando manage on a horse? Should they just throw him across it like a wounded man being brought back from battle?

Imogen had the answer. 'I have some experience with horses,' she said to Powerscourt. 'Put him across the saddle and I will ride behind him. I've done it before.'

Powerscourt was on the verge of asking where she had learnt this technique, now proving invaluable in a snowstorm in the middle of a Norfolk night, when she told him.

'My sister fell off once miles from anywhere and injured her back. I had to bring her home.'

'I wish it would start to snow again,' said Powerscourt, staring up at what he could see of the sky. 'Then it would cover our tracks. If it doesn't we're going to leave a route map behind us for any of our friends to follow.'

Very slowly the tiny cavalcade set off from de Courcy Hall. Imogen had the reins in one hand, the other trying to anchor Orlando in his position. She wondered if they should have tied him on. Powerscourt brought up the rear, casting nervous glances behind. Fifteen minutes later they reached the main lodge, twin cottages on either side of the road. Both were empty, broken panes of glass and swinging doors bearing witness to the desolation of the estate.

'Left here,' whispered Powerscourt. 'We turn right in a hundred yards or so, then right again. That's the main road to Cromer. God knows what we'll find when we get there.'

Five minutes later a man materialized out of a line of trees. He held out his hand, requesting them to stop. Imogen looked round desperately at Powerscourt. Was this the end of their escape? Had they come this far only to be recaptured so near their destination? Powerscourt dismounted and shook the stranger by the hand. Bizarre introductions were made as the snow began to fall again.

'Johnny Fitzgerald, this is Imogen. And this is Orlando Blane, shot in the leg. Johnny Fitzgerald. What's the score up there, Johnny?'

'It's not good, Francis.' Fitzgerald was panting heavily. 'There's two of them watching this road about half a mile further up. Another two have gone off to the railway station.'

'Let's try putting ourselves in their shoes for a minute, Johnny.' Powerscourt was stroking his horse's head very gently, as if the animal knew the answers. 'Those four ruffians know these two have escaped. They don't know

Orlando is wounded. They don't know either of us from Adam. At some point they're going to return to the Hall to see if Orlando and Imogen have gone back there. The ruffians probably think they're hiding until the first train in the morning. They won't go back until they've seen who boards it. In a perfect world we'd just wait until the middle of the morning and go into Cromer then. But we can't. This young man needs a doctor.'

'Maybe we need a diversion, Francis.' Johnny Fitzgerald looked as though he was enjoying himself. 'Wait here for about ten minutes or so. I'm going to draw those two fellows away from the road. When you hear a scream, press on with full speed.' Johnny disappeared into the woods to their right. Imogen was stroking Orlando's head and whispering into his ear. Powerscourt watched the softly falling snow, erasing the tracks behind them.

Then there was a scream. One very loud scream. Powerscourt led the way, urging Imogen to make all speed. They heard sounds of people crashing through the bushes on their right. Then there was another scream. Powerscourt thought he could hear the two guards shouting to each other in confusion. But they were through. They had passed the point where the sentries had been on guard. Powerscourt led them on a little track which led along the sea front to the hotel. They were almost invisible from the clifftop above. Twenty minutes later Orlando was stretched out on Johnny Fitzgerald's bed. The night porter had been sent to bring the doctor.

Johnny Fitzgerald had secured a bottle of brandy and was inspecting its label with extreme scepticism. 'Don't think they'd serve this stuff in the better London clubs,' he said to Powerscourt, 'but you can't be particular after a night like that.'

'Johnny,' said Powerscourt, 'I've just had a daft idea.'

'For God's sake, Francis,' Johnny Fitzgerald was

pouring himself a giant refill already, 'it's half-past two in the morning. We've just spent an idyllic few hours wandering about in a snowstorm with Romeo next door nearly killed by one of those characters. And you start talking about daft ideas.' He took a giant's mouthful. 'What is it?'

Powerscourt smiled at his friend. 'It's those pictures, Johnny. I think they might be really useful in the court case. Do you think you could get them out of the house?'

Fitzgerald looked at him thoughtfully. 'Could one man carry them? From that big room upstairs with all those windows?'

'I think it would need two people, Johnny. I'd come with you but I want to see Romeo and Juliet safe in Rokesley. It might be too late by the time I got back.'

Johnny Fitzgerald laughed suddenly. 'Once a Sergeant Major, always a Sergeant Major, that's what I say, Francis. Where do you want the bloody things delivered to?'

'The paintings,' said Powerscourt, guessing suddenly how Johnny was going to manage it, 'should be reunited with their maker, Orlando Blane. I've always felt the need of some really first rate pictures in my country house at Rokesley.'

'Dear Lucy . . .' Powerscourt was writing again to his wife from the sitting room of his house in Northamptonshire. Rokesley Hall was host not just to its owner but to a pair of refugees, Orlando Blane, lying on a sofa by the window of the drawing room, and Imogen Foxe, currently reading aloud to Orlando from a book of romantic poetry.

I hope you and the children are well and that you received my earlier letters. This one is more prosaic, I fear, than the last two. The doctors say I will be

312

able to question Orlando the forger this afternoon. Even then I must not tire his strength. He is going to make a full recovery, but his condition was made much worse by all those hours in the snow. I hope to be home by tomorrow morning at the latest.

Lucy, I would like to ask you an enormous favour, which comes ill from one who has complained for so long about your relations! Alice Bridge. Mrs Rosalind Buckley. Could you put the tribe on full and instant alert to discover as much as they possibly can about these two young women, their families, their education, their romantic entanglements. And as quickly as possible.

Tell Thomas and Olivia that I have been riding round on a great many trains,

All love,
Semper Fidelis,
Francis.

Thirty-six hours after the lovers' flight Johnny Fitzgerald was making another visit to de Courcy Hall. He was travelling in some style, in a large enclosed carriage with an officious-looking man at the reins. Great carpets of snow covered the long drive from the main road. The roof of the little dovecot inside the walled garden had turned from red to white. The sun was shining brightly although it was bitterly cold. Johnny knew that his plan depended on two things. First, the Sergeant Major must not have reported the flight to his masters in London. Earlier that morning Johnny had checked the railway station. One of the ruffians was still watching. Another one had gone to Norwich by an earlier train. He had passed a third patrolling the road into Cromer, looking rather dejected. The Sergeant Major should be on his own in the house.

The second factor depended on the ingrained habit of obedience to superior officers drilled for years into the brains of every single Sergeant Major in Her Majesty's Army. Johnny took a quick swig from his hip flask as the coach drew up outside de Courcy Hall. He strode through the main door, shouting loudly.

'Sergeant Major! Sergeant Major!'

A bleary-eyed man approached him in the Great Hall. Fitzgerald put on his loudest voice.

'Sergeant Major!'

'Sir!' said the man, springing to attention.

So far so good, thought Johnny. 'Major Fitzgerald, Connaught Rangers. Stand at ease, Sergeant Major.'

'Sergeant Major Fitzgibbon, Royal Artillery, sir!'

Fitzgerald shook the Sergeant Major by the hand. 'I was in India most of the time,' he said, ushering Fitzgibbon to a chair. 'And yourself?'

'South Africa, sir. Zulu wars. Majuba, that sort of thing.'

'Very good, Sergeant Major. Now there seems to have been something of a cock-up with the orders here. Wouldn't be the first time, as we both know only too well. The girl was sent here to encourage him to escape. We knew the date, we knew the time, we knew the place. We've got them safe. They've been moved. Some people in London were getting suspicious. They should be in another remote location by now, somewhere in West Yorkshire, I believe. God knows why our lords and masters wanted it done like that, but they did. You can recall your men, Sergeant Major. We've taken over. Thing is, my orders are to collect the paintings and bring them too. Do you think you could give me a hand with them? I've got a carriage outside.'

'Sir!' said the Sergeant Major. Majors, even in civilian clothes, demand obedience. Ours not to reason why.

Speed, Johnny Fitzgerald knew, speed was vital. If the

man stopped to think for one minute all could be lost. The coach driver came in to give further assistance. In twenty-five minutes all of Orlando's work was safely in the back of the carriage. The delicate work of wrapping them carefully could wait until later.

'Drive like the wind,' Fitzgerald said to the coachman. 'We need to get out of here.'

As they rattled back towards the main road, the carriage swinging wildly across the rutted road, Fitzgerald could see Sergeant Major Fitzgibbon scratching his head in the doorway. The whole business had happened so fast. As they passed the church on their right, invisible in the snow, a faint cry reached them, almost lost in the wind.

'Major Fitzgerald! Come back a moment, sir. Come back!'

Powerscourt had already talked at length to Imogen about her trip to Norfolk. She told him about the meeting at the hotel in London, the trip by train and carriage with her eyes bound so tightly she could not see a thing. 'I was some kind of reward, don't you see, Lord Powerscourt? I was a prize for good behaviour. Orlando had been asking for months if he could see me or write to me. Finally they gave in. Maybe they thought I would give him a new lease of life, up there in that strange gallery with the rats prowling overhead. I don't think I'll ever forget the sound of those rats in the night.'

She had told him about the gambling at Monte Carlo, about Orlando's drinking, about the promise that he would be free once he had earned enough to pay off his debts. She told him about her loveless marriage.

'I expect Orlando and I will have to go and live abroad once all this is settled. I shouldn't mind at all.'

Powerscourt's housekeeper, Mrs Warry, had made a

great fuss of young Mr and Mrs Blane, as Powerscourt had introduced them. She had decided that what they needed was a touch of good old-fashioned English cooking, not those scraps and army rations they'd been fed up there in Norfolk. So after an enormous meal of roast beef with all the trimmings, Mrs Warry's best apple pie, and some good local cheese, Powerscourt sat down by the side of Orlando's sofa in the drawing room. Mrs Warry kept a splendid fire going. Outside more snow was falling on the Powerscourt lawns. Imogen was sitting behind Powerscourt where she could see Orlando.

'Mr Blane, there are many things I would wish to ask you. Some of them will have to wait. Let me say first of all that you are both welcome to remain here as long as you wish. Mrs Warry will be delighted to look after you. What interests me this afternoon is how the commissioning process worked, how you received your orders, if you see what I mean.'

Orlando paused for a moment before he replied. 'There were different kinds of instructions,' he began, 'but they were all delivered in the same way. Mournful – that's what I called the Sergeant Major person because he was always down in the dumps – would come and see me with a letter in his hand. He never showed me the letter – I never saw the heading on the paper, or where it came from. Tell Orlando, Mournful would say, reading it, that we wish him to do such and such.'

'You said there were different kinds of instructions,' said Powerscourt gently. 'Perhaps you could give me an indication of what they were.'

'Of course,' said Orlando. He paused again. 'Basically, there were three sorts of orders, if you like. Sometimes they would send me up an original, a Titian or a Giorgione, for me to copy.'

'Do you know,' asked Powerscourt, 'what happened to the copies?'

'I have no idea,' said Orlando. 'When they were finished, the two paintings were sent back to wherever they came from. If you pushed me, I should say that the most likely explanation is that they had sold the original at an exhibition. Then they told the new owner it had been sent away for cleaning. Then they would swap them over.'

'And the second sort of order?' Powerscourt was looking at Orlando's hands. They moved sometimes as he talked, drawing some imaginary masterpiece all on their own.

'The second sort was the smartest,' Orlando laughed suddenly. 'They would send me illustrations from the American magazines of a particular family. I was to create an English portrait, a Gainsborough or a Reynolds, with the wife or the children reproduced in my painting.'

'Would the point have been that the American father was coming to London? And that he would be bowled over by this extraordinary likeness? Bowled over to the extent of lots of dollars?'

'You have it, Lord Powerscourt. Americans often buy paintings that remind them of places or people they know. This just took it a stage further.'

'And the last sort?' Powerscourt knew Orlando would not be able to speak for very much longer. Lines of strain were beginning to appear on his forehead.

'Straight forgeries. Lost masterpieces suddenly rediscovered. It happens all the time. I was working on a lost Giovanni Bellini at the end.'

'And did they send back any comments, the people we presume were in London?'

'They did,' said Orlando. 'Mournful would appear after the post arrived and read out messages. They were very pleased with me most of the time.'

'But nobody ever came to see you in person? If you

317

met the man behind the enterprise this afternoon you would have no idea who he was?'

'Correct,' said Orlando. Imogen was beginning to move about on her chaise longue.

'I have only one more question,' said Powerscourt. 'But first I have to tell you a story.'

He told them about the murder of Christopher Montague, about the article he was writing before his death about fakes and forgeries in the exhibition of Venetian paintings at the de Courcy and Piper Gallery. He told them about the subsequent murder of Thomas Jenkins. He told them about Mrs Buckley planning to elope to Italy with Christopher Montague. He told them about Horace Aloysius Buckley, arrested after Evensong in Lincoln Cathedral. He mentioned that the trial was to start very shortly.

'You don't think this Mr Buckley is guilty, do you, Lord Powerscourt?' asked Imogen.

'No, I don't. I do not at present know exactly who the murderer is. All we can do at the trial is to point out that other people might have good reason to kill Montague. Like Messrs de Courcy and Piper, who probably employed their very own forger, hidden away in Norfolk. If that was known, it would ruin their business, destroy their livelihood. This is my last question, Orlando.' Powerscourt knew how difficult this could be. 'If I have not found the real murderer before the trial starts, would you be prepared to give evidence about what went on in Norfolk? Let me tell you what it could mean before you answer. Your name would be splashed all over the newspapers. Journalists would want to come and interview you. You would be famous or infamous for about three days, but everybody would remember that you had worked as a forger. It would mean that a future career in the world of art in England would be very difficult, if not impossible for you.'

318

Imogen had gone to sit beside Orlando on the sofa. She was stroking his hand.

'Take your time,' said Powerscourt. 'You don't have to give me a reply now if you don't want to.'

'But if I don't give evidence, Lord Powerscourt,' Orlando said, 'then this poor man may be hanged for something he didn't do?'

'That is correct,' said Powerscourt gravely.

'Let me tell you, Lord Powerscourt,' Orlando was sitting up straight now, his eyes blazing, 'we have received nothing but kindness at your hands. I might be dead if you hadn't come along. There is honour, even among forgers. The profession is as old as art itself. I could not bear to think of that poor man losing his life just because I kept quiet. If you wish me to do so, I shall gladly give evidence.'

'Well done, Orlando, well done,' said Imogen.

Then they heard a voice shouting through the house. 'Old Masters for sale!' it said. 'Buy your very own Old Master now! Titians for sale! Giorgione going cheap today! Reynolds and Gainsborough! Old Masters for sale.'

Johnny Fitzgerald walked through the door, a couple of canvases under his arm. Orlando Blane and his forgeries were reunited in Powerscourt's Rokesley Hall.

23

Rarely in its long history had Number 25 Markham Square been such a whirl of social activity. The mornings brought a constant rush of visitors, nearly always female. Streams of post, delivered by postmen, footmen or by hand of bearer, poured through the letterbox. At lunchtime Lady Lucy would go out to a rendezvous with some more of her informants. By three thirty in the afternoon she was back At Home to receive another wave. In the early evening tea sometimes turned into early evening drinks. In the evenings she and Powerscourt would dine out with yet more of her relations, Powerscourt for once not complaining about anything at all. The auxiliaries, as Powerscourt referred to the outer ring of the vast regiment of relatives, were often the most productive of all in terms of information as they moved in different circles of London society. There were now three days left before the trial.

The letters were divided into two piles, one for Bridge and one for Buckley. Lady Lucy had purchased a large black notebook, rapidly filling up with entries, the first half devoted to Bridge, the second to Buckley.

Powerscourt read all the letters. He listened gravely to his wife's account of her various conversations across the West End of London. Some of the reports came from places as far away as Hampstead or Richmond. Random pieces of information lodged themselves in Powerscourt's brain. Alice Bridge was a most accomplished pianist, he read. There was confirmation that Rosalind Buckley was noted for her skill in archery.

'What do you think, Lucy?' he said to her late one evening. They had just returned from what he thought was one of the most boring evenings he had ever spent. The obituary columns or the lists of financial prices in the newspapers, he felt, would have been more entertaining. But he had smiled, he had kept the conversational ball in play, he had done his duty. 'What do we have to show for all your magnificent efforts?' He smiled at her and kicked off his shoes to lie full length on the sofa.

'Two things, Francis. Alice Bridge has changed in the last month or two. There was definitely a romantic attachment. It seems to have ended. But nobody seems to know who it was. Nobody has heard of Christopher Montague. I think I shall be able to find out at the beginning of next week. Is that too late?'

'My learned friend Mr Pugh,' said Powerscourt, 'said he doesn't think the prosecution case will take very long. He could be on his feet for the defence as early as the second day of the trial.'

'I'll be as quick as I can,' said Lady Lucy, 'but my informant will only be back from the country late on Sunday night.'

'And the second thing, my love?' said Powerscourt, thinking that all this activity seemed to suit Lady Lucy.

'When she was much younger, Rosalind Buckley, or Rosalind Chambers as she was then, lived in Rome. There was some terrible scandal, whether it was to do with the Romans or to do with the Chambers, I do not know. But three different people have mentioned it to me.'

'Scandal in Rome,' said Powerscourt happily, his imagination drifting away. 'Poison in the College of Cardinals. Pope's mistress murdered. Swiss Guard supposed to protect the Pontiff at all times engaged in vice and drugs trade.'

'Come back, Francis,' Lady Lucy smiled at him.

'Probably all happened at one time or another, I shouldn't wonder. Should I ask Johnny Fitzgerald to go to Rome?' Johnny Fitzgerald had returned to the porters of the art world he had met earlier, buying them drinks, subtly picking their brains.

'Wouldn't the Italian Ambassador be a bit easier, Francis? He lives only a couple of streets away from here.'

'You're absolutely right, Lucy. I shall write to the fellow immediately. I'm sure Johnny would have liked Rome, you know. So very different from Norfolk.'

One resident of Markham Square was not taking part in the great round of socializing. Early every morning William McKenzie set off on private journeys of his own. Each day he was travelling further and further afield in quest of his prey. Each evening he reported another day of failure to Powerscourt. He would spread the net wider yet, he would say. Powerscourt thought he would soon end up far out of London. Maybe he would reach Guildford or even Winchester.

Charles Augustus Pugh was writing furiously at his desk in Gray's Inn very early the following morning.

'Take a seat, Powerscourt, I won't be a minute.' Pugh had been entranced by the news that the forger was prepared to give evidence. He had risen from his chair and paced round the room, addressing perhaps an imaginary jury as he went. 'A forger, a forger,' he kept muttering to himself. 'Did I hear you right, Lord

322

Powerscourt, that you also have some of his forgeries in your possession? We could have a parade of bogus Titians or whatever the damned things are called? How simply splendid! It'll be a sensation. Tell me, do you have a copy of the catalogue of the exhibition of Venetian paintings?'

Powerscourt said he was sure he could lay a hand on one. And with that news Charles Augustus Pugh had thrown back his head and laughed a laugh of pure unadulterated joy. He was still writing furiously, the courtyard outside his windows very silent. Only the birds were at their business this morning.

'Sorry about that,' he said finally, leaning back and returning his shoes to their accustomed place on top of his desk. The suit was dark blue this morning, the shirt Italian silk. 'I presume that so far you haven't managed to find the Holy Grail?'

Powerscourt shook his head.

'Never mind,' Pugh went on, 'maybe it'll turn up in time. Now this is the plan of campaign. Tell me what you think.'

Pugh paused for a moment and looked up at the ceiling. 'The weakest point in the prosecution's case is the murder in Oxford. We know that Jenkins was a friend of Montague. The prosecution will be saying that Buckley killed Montague, bloody man admits he was in the same room as the victim on the day of his death, damn it. And he had a very strong motive. He killed one, therefore he killed the other. Buckley admits to being in Oxford on the same day. Then there's that business with the tie. That's all. No real evidence that he went to the room, no witnesses apart from the man who saw him come off the train and the man who saw him at the bottom of the Banbury Road in Oxford that same day. I think we could confuse the jury about the times of Buckley's movements. And we have the godson in

Keble who gave Buckley tea. So that's the first line of attack, as it were.

'The second is the art dealer chap, Johnston. National Gallery fellow. Think we can show how much he had to lose if Montague's article came out, how many commissions would go somewhere else.

'But our best line of defence is Edmund de Courcy. Closely followed by the forger. Closely followed by the forgeries themselves. That's our strongest card. And both Johnston and de Courcy have been called as prosecution witnesses. They both saw Montague on the day he died. So I can cross examine both of them.'

Powerscourt wondered if his hunch was right. Maybe Buckley had killed them both after all. 'That sounds splendid,' he said. 'I am going to Oxford this morning to see if I can find anybody who remembers seeing Buckley at Evensong. I thought we had plenty of time before the trial starts but we've hardly got any at all. If I'd known how tight everything is, I'd have gone to Oxford weeks ago. Johnny Fitzgerald should be sending you later today the name of the Corsican previously in the employ of de Courcy and Piper.'

That faraway look came back over Pugh's Roman profile. 'What a collection of witnesses,' he said, a smile spreading slowly across his face. 'Think of it, all in the same session. A real-life forger come to the witness stand. A line of Old Masters bearing silent testament to his crimes. Edmund de Courcy, the man who almost certainly controlled the forger's activities. And to cap it all, we have the vanishing Corsican, hands stained no doubt with bloody crimes committed on his native island. The newspapers will go mad, Powerscourt, absolutely mad.'

Charles Augustus Pugh came back to earth. He stared at Powerscourt.

'Oxford, did you say? Looking for witnesses from

Christ Church? Could you do me a great favour, my friend? Could you bring me a map of the city centre? Preferably one with the railway station, the Banbury Road and Christ Church Cathedral all clearly marked? And in the biggest typeface you can find. Some of the jurors they send us nowadays are nearly blind.'

The clerk of the court had a list of names placed in his tall black hat on the table in front of him. 'Albert Warren,' he said loudly. A small nervous-looking man in a tweed suit that had seen better days came forward to take the oath. With the Bible in his right hand and a card in his left he read the juror's oath.

'I swear by Almighty God to try the case on the basis of the evidence and to find a verdict in accordance with the truth.' Albert Warren was the first man to take his place on the jurors' benches. Twelve good men and true, their names picked out of a hat in Court Number Three of the Central Criminal Court. Ratepayers, property owners, summoned for a fortnight to see justice done, maybe to deprive a fellow citizen of his life.

Charles Augustus Pugh, now resplendent in wig, gown and wing collar, watched them carefully. Only once did Sir Rufus Fitch for the prosecution rise to his feet while the man was reading the oath. George Jones was stumbling through the words. It was obvious that he couldn't read. 'Objection! Stand by for the Crown!' Sir Rufus's high-pitched voice echoed through the courtroom. Pugh noticed the objection with interest. As George Jones was led away to the back of the court to be replaced with another name from the clerk's hat, he wondered why the prosecution didn't want a man who couldn't read. Some prosecutors liked a stupid jury.

For the rest of the day Sir Rufus took the jury through the details of the prosecution case. Edmund de Courcy and

Roderick Johnston testified that they had seen Montague in the late afternoon and early evening on the day of his death. Inspector Maxwell told the court of the discovery of the body, the vanished books, the empty desk.

Sir Rufus read out the sworn statements of the people who had seen Buckley in Oxford. Chief Inspector Wilson produced as an exhibit the tie found under the chair in Jenkins' room, a tie similar to one previously in Horace Aloysius Buckley's possession. He also read out Buckley's admission that he, Buckley, had been in Montague's flat on the evening of the first murder.

Mrs Buckley, dressed in a sombre black, testified briefly to her friendship with Christopher Montague. She gave details of the tie from her husband's college, Trinity, in the University of Cambridge, that had gone missing with the stain on the bottom. Sir Rufus Fitch made it perfectly clear to the jury, without ever actually saying so, that sexual jealousy was the motive for murder.

When Sir Rufus was on his feet, he held himself absolutely still, like a human pillar. He stood in his place like some mighty Dreadnought of the law, fixing his eyes on the jury, speaking to them quite slowly. Trust in me, he seemed to be saying to them. I have been here before. I have long and distinguished experience in matters of this kind. This is all pretty straightforward. All you have to do is to bring in the guilty verdict.

Charles Augustus Pugh spent most of his time not watching the witnesses but watching the jury. Some of the time the fingers of his right hand were playing the notes of a Mozart piano concerto on his gown. He watched the ones who looked disapproving as they heard of the friendship between Montague and Mrs Buckley. He watched two middle-aged men at the back who nearly fell asleep as the waves of Sir Rufus's sonorous prose rolled across them. He watched the ones who spent their time looking at the prisoner in the dock.

Pugh was certain that many jurors reached their final verdict, not on the basis of the evidence presented to them, but according to the look of the defendant. If he looked shifty or embarrassed, if he stared down at the floor, they would decide he was guilty. Pugh had told Horace Aloysius Buckley that at all times in the court, whatever his inner feelings, he was to look like a leading London solicitor, a regular worshipper at his local church, a respected pillar of his local community. Pugh smiled quietly to himself as he checked his client's demeanour. Horace Aloysius Buckley gave his evidence clearly. He remained resolute as the evidence against him unfolded all through the afternoon. At four forty-five in the afternoon, as if Sir Rufus had to catch an early evening train, the prosecution case drew to a close.

'Not too bad,' had been Pugh's verdict as he and the Powerscourts and Johnny Fitzgerald met in his chambers at the end of the day. 'What do we have to bring to bear tomorrow?'

Johnny Fitzgerald passed him the name of the Corsican recently in the employ of de Courcy and Piper. Powerscourt said he had telegraphed to the chief of police in Calvi, the dubious Captain Imperiali, for any further details of the man. Powerscourt reported that he had had a fruitless interview with the Italian Ambassador. Scandals in Rome? the Ambassador had purred, impossible surely. Rome is the Eternal City. Scandals are simply out of the question. He had smiled pleasantly at Powerscourt throughout the exchange but said nothing. Johnny Fitzgerald was going to dinner with three Italian journalists based in London. Lady Lucy reported that she was on the verge of discovering more information about Alice Bridge's relationship with Christopher Montague.

'Will she give evidence?' asked Pugh. 'We could subpoena her tonight, if you think that would help.'

'I think a subpoena might be a bit fierce. I have lined up her two grandmothers and three aunts for a family conclave tomorrow morning,' said Lady Lucy, impressed herself by the amount of domestic firepower being brought into play. 'I'm pretty sure she will.'

'Excellent,' said Pugh. 'Tomorrow morning we begin to throw mud in their eyes.'

'Call the Dean of Christ Church!' The jury looked up with interest. Illicit love affairs, men garrotted with piano wire had been on the bill of fare yesterday. Now they were going to begin the day with a senior churchman. The Dean, the Very Reverend Oliver Morris, was an imposing figure, well over six feet tall. He was dressed in a black cassock with a silver crucifix hanging from his neck. The Dean looked as if he would have belonged to the Archdeacon Grantly party rather than the Proudie faction in the internecine doctrinal squabbles that had swirled around the Cathedral Close at Barchester. A hunting, port-drinking sort of Dean, rather than an evangelical parson, obsessed with individual sin and the need for a personal salvation. He took the oath in the confident tone of a man whose voice had filled the great cathedrals of England.

'I, Oliver Morris, do solemnly swear that the evidence I shall give shall be the truth, the whole truth and nothing but the truth.'

Pugh glanced briefly at the jury. Four of them, he thought, were impressed by this patriarch of the Church, three indifferent, the rest curious.

'Were you the minister taking the service of Evensong in Christ Church Cathedral in Oxford on 9th November this year?' said Pugh.

'I was.'

'Could you tell the court at what time the service commenced?'

'The service started at five fifteen that day. It would have lasted about forty-five minutes.'

'So it would have finished about six o'clock?'

'That is correct.'

'Dean, I would ask you to take a look at the prisoner in the dock. Please take as long as you like.' Pugh paused while the churchman looked closely at Buckley. Buckley stared impassively back.

'Do you recognize this man as a member of your congregation on that day?'

'I do.'

'Could you tell the court when you first saw him?' Pugh thought the Dean was proving an impressive witness.

'I usually take a brief look at the worshippers shortly before the service is due to begin,' said the Dean, addressing the jury as though it were attending a service in his cathedral. 'It sometimes helps to know the size of the likely congregation. I should say I first noticed him, sitting very near the choir stalls, at about five past five.'

'And was he present throughout the service?'

'He was.' The Dean stroked his crucifix.

'And did you see him afterwards?'

'I did. It is my custom at that time of year to invite those members of the congregation who wish to come back to the Deanery for tea and sandwiches, or a glass of sherry if they prefer. Some of the destitute from the city come to Evensong. It is an unobtrusive means of feeding them, getting some nourishment into their poor bodies.'

Pugh noticed the church party among the jury nodding in approval. Feed the poor. The feeding not of the five thousand but of the impoverished of Oxford.

'And did Mr Buckley attend this function?'

'He did.' Dean Morris permitted himself a slight smile. 'We had a long conversation about an expedition he was planning, to attend Evensong in all the great cathedrals of England. I gave him my blessing for the project. I should say Mr Buckley left the Deanery shortly before seven, maybe slightly later.'

'One last question, Dean,' said Pugh. 'You know Oxford well, I presume? You have lived there for some time?'

'I have lived there for ten years now.'

'Could you tell us how long it would take a man like Mr Buckley to walk from the railway station to the bottom of the Banbury Road?'

'Objection, my lord!' Sir Rufus Fitch was on his feet. 'We are here to try Mr Buckley on a charge of murder, not to recommend walking routes for tourists on their first visit to Oxford!'

'Mr Pugh?' the judge inquired politely.

'My lord, the defence intends to show serious flaws in the prosecution's account of Mr Buckley's movements while he was in Oxford. Central to that argument is the length of time it would take to walk from the railway station to the bottom of the Banbury Road, and from Keble College to Christ Church, if you will permit me, my lord. What more reliable witness could we find for such matters than the Dean himself?'

'Objection overruled, Sir Rufus. Mr Pugh.'

'Let me repeat the question,' said Charles Augustus Pugh. 'How long would it take to walk from the railway station to the bottom of the Banbury Road?'

'It would take about twenty-five minutes,' said the Dean firmly.

'It is the contention of the defence, Dean, that Mr Buckley went on his arrival in Oxford to visit his godson in Keble College. Would that route take you past the bottom of the Banbury Road, just here?' Pugh pointed to the road on his map.

330

'It could do,' said the Dean circumspectly. 'It could certainly do so.'

'And how long,' asked Charles Augustus Pugh, 'would it take you to walk from Keble to Christ Church?'

'About twenty minutes, I should think.'

'Thank you, Dean. No further questions.' Pugh returned to his desk. Sir Rufus declined to cross examine the witness, sensing perhaps that character assassination attempts on a Dean might not go down too well with the jury.

'Call Mr Paul Lucas.'

A pale, rather frail-looking young man was sworn into Court Number Three of the Central Criminal Court. Pugh rose to his feet once more, with a friendly smile to welcome his new witness.

'You are Paul Lucas, currently an undergraduate of Keble College, Oxford?'

'I am,' said the young man.

'And what are your plans,' asked Pugh in his gentlest voice, 'when your time at Oxford is completed?'

'I hope to be ordained as a priest of the Church of England, sir.' Lucas gave his future profession with pride.

'You are also, Mr Lucas,' Pugh went on, 'the godson of the defendant in this case, Mr Horace Aloysius Buckley. Perhaps you could tell the court about his visit to you on the afternoon of 9th November of this year, the day, I would just remind the members of the jury, that Thomas Jenkins was killed.'

'Yes, sir.' Paul Lucas composed himself. 'My godfather called on me in my rooms at Keble somewhere around twenty past four in the afternoon. He said that he was going to attend Evensong in Christ Church. We had tea together. He left me at a quarter to five to walk to Christ Church. I remember the precise time because Mr Buckley said something like "Quarter to five, I should be on my way."'

331

'Thank you, Mr Lucas. One final question. You are absolutely sure of those times?'

'Yes, sir, I am,' said Paul Lucas firmly.

'No further questions,' said Pugh.

Sir Rufus had decided not to cross examine the Dean. But now he could see a very plausible alibi being established in front of the jury's eyes. He rose slowly to his feet and moved into the attack.

'Mr Lucas, could you tell the court how often your godfather comes to visit you in Oxford?'

'He normally comes two or three times a term, sir.' Paul Lucas was feeling slightly overwhelmed by his surroundings.

'So what was the date when he came to see you on the previous occasion?'

Paul Lucas looked thoughtful. 'It must have been sometime in October, I think.'

'Sometime in October, but you cannot remember the precise date? Let us see what else you might be able to remember, Mr Lucas. Did your godfather send you money after his visit in November?'

'He did, sir.'

'And can you recall the date the cheque or banker's order actually arrived with you?'

'I am afraid I cannot, sir,' said Lucas after another pause, now looking rather desperately at Pugh as if he could save him from his ordeal.

'Perhaps you can help me here, Mr Lucas.' Sir Rufus was trying to kill the young man with kindness. 'You cannot remember the date when your godfather came to see you in October. You cannot remember the date when his cheque or banker's order arrived after his visit, even though that is the most recent event. But you are able to remember the precise date and time in November. Is that so?'

Paul Lucas was going quite red now. 'That is true, sir,' he said finally.

'Tell me, Mr Lucas,' another line of attack suddenly came to Sir Rufus, 'are you financially dependent on your godfather?'

'I'm not quite sure what you mean,' said the young man.

'Does he support you financially at Oxford, Mr Lucas? It takes quite a lot of money to keep an undergraduate there for three years.'

Paul Lucas looked again at Pugh. 'He does, sir. My father is dead and my mother has very little money.'

Sir Rufus had not expected to find such treasure as this. 'Do I understand you correctly, Mr Lucas? All your bills and so on are paid for by Mr Buckley? I'm sure you must be very grateful to him, is that not so?'

'I am indeed grateful to him, sir.'

'Would it be fair to say, Mr Lucas, that you would do anything you could to help Mr Buckley if he was in trouble?'

Paul Lucas may have been rattled but he could sense what might be coming.

'Of course I would help my godfather,' he said, taking his time, 'as long as it was the right and proper thing to do.'

'And would you regard it as the right and proper thing to do, Mr Lucas, to remember the precise date and time of a visit from your godfather when you cannot recall even the approximate date of his previous visit and the date his money arrived?'

'Only if it was the proper thing to do,' said Lucas.

'I put it to you, Mr Lucas, that you are only able to pursue your studies at Oxford through the generosity of Mr Buckley. I further put it to you that you were more than willing to help him by fabricating the date of his visit to you on 9th November to help your godfather be acquitted on a charge of murder. That is the case, is it not?'

'That is not true,' said Lucas, now looking rather

333

shaken. Sir Rufus sat down. Pugh rose to his feet once more.

'Let us just make sure that the jury are clear in their minds here, Mr Lucas,' he said, smiling once more at his witness. 'On 9th November of this year did Mr Buckley come to visit you in your rooms at Keble between the hours of twenty past four and a quarter to five in the afternoon?'

'He did,' said Lucas.

'Recall Chief Inspector Wilson.'

Wilson was a veteran of many trials. Indeed he was often used by the Oxfordshire Constabulary in the training of new recruits going to court and giving evidence for the first time. Always be respectful, he would tell the young men in their bright new uniforms. Don't let them rile you. Look them straight in the eye. Sound as though you believe every word you say. Think before you speak.

'Chief Inspector Wilson.' Pugh had been deferential with the Dean, gentle with the future minister of the Church. He was now charming with the Chief Inspector, but hinting ever so slightly that Wilson might not be very bright. 'I would just like to run through the prosecution account of Mr Buckley's movements in Oxford, if I may. The post-mortem said that Thomas Jenkins was probably killed between the hours of four and seven o'clock. Your first statement,' Pugh sorted through some papers in his hand, 'stated that Mr Buckley was seen at the railway station at about ten to four. There is a London train that arrives five minutes before. Is that correct?'

'That is correct,' said the Chief Inspector.

'And your second witness statement said that he was seen at the bottom end of the Banbury Road where Thomas Jenkins lived shortly before or about a quarter past four. Is that correct?'

'It is,' said the Chief Inspector, suddenly remembering Powerscourt's doubts about the second murder. He looked quickly around the court. Powerscourt was sitting directly behind Charles Augustus Pugh.

'You will forgive me, Chief Inspector, if I say that you are better acquainted with the geography of Oxford than the members of the jury. I have here a map of the relevant areas of central Oxford to assist them.'

Pugh rested a large map on the edge of the table in front of him. Powerscourt had brought it back for him on his last trip to Oxford. Pugh's junior came round to hold it steady. The map was clearly visible to the judge and jury.

'Please correct me if I make any mistakes, Chief Inspector,' said Pugh cheerfully. He took a pencil and pointed to a red line on the map that began at the railway station. 'This is the position shortly before four o'clock. Mr Buckley is at the railway station here. Then he walks along this red line,' Pugh's pencil was tracing the route on the map, 'from the station here, past the front of Worcester College here, along Walton Street, over Little Clarendon Street there and crosses the Woodstock Road. He arrives here at the bottom of the Banbury Road at about a quarter past four.'

The red line stopped. The jury stared in fascination at the map.

'Now, Chief Inspector, you, like our friend the Dean, know Oxford well. Number 55 Banbury Road is some distance up that thoroughfare.' Pugh's pencil pointed to a large circle further up the road on his map with the number 55 written inside in large letters. 'Would you say a further ten minutes away?'

'Something like that,' said the Chief Inspector, worried suddenly by the direction of the questions. Pugh's pencil was back at the end of the red line, moving slowly towards the circled 55.

'So, Chief Inspector, it would have taken Mr Buckley ten minutes to arrive at Number 55,' the pencil stopped inside the circle, 'let us say ten minutes for the despatch of Mr Jenkins, another ten minutes,' the pencil was moving quickly now, 'back to the bottom of the Banbury Road. That would make it four forty-five. Yet we know from the evidence of Mr Lucas that Mr Buckley was taking tea in Keble between the hours of four twenty and forty-five. The University of Oxford, Chief Inspector, is famed for its expertise in mathematics and metaphysics. Can you explain how the defendant could have been in two places at one time?'

Chief Inspector Wilson paused before replying. Pugh felt a momentary sense of triumph.

'It is the prosecution case that the defendant did murder Mr Jenkins on that day,' Wilson said, sensing that his face might be turning red.

'Ah, but when, Chief Inspector? When? That is the question. Let us just make the remaining journeys of Mr Buckley in Oxford on that day last month perfectly clear to the members of the jury.' Out came the pencil again. 'At a quarter to five, as Mr Lucas told us, he leaves Keble.' The second line was black. 'He comes into St Giles here, past the Ashmolean over there, past Carfax and down St Aldate's to Christ Church along this black route on the map. A journey, as Dean Morris told us, of some twenty minutes. And sure enough, he was seen in his position in the choir stalls shortly after five o'clock.'

Pugh paused. Chief Inspector Wilson looked more and more uncomfortable. Pugh's pencil was hovering over the cathedral.

'Let us just examine the final window of time in which Mr Buckley might, I stress the word might, have been able to go to 55 Banbury Road and murder Mr Jenkins. The Dean himself has just told us that the defendant left the Deanery shortly before seven. And seven is the latest time the doctors give for the time of death.' The pencil of Charles Augustus Pugh began to make darting movements between Christ Church and the Banbury Road. 'An angel of the Lord or one of the fastest runners in the University Athletics Club might have made the journey from Christ Church to Mr Jenkins' lodgings in the time available. It would take half an hour or more.' The pencil was shooting back and forth now between the two locations at a dizzying speed. 'But it was surely impossible for a man of Mr Buckley's age.' Pugh paused. Chief Inspector Wilson looked as if he was about to speak. Pugh didn't let him.

'Tell me, Chief Inspector,' he went on, 'what other evidence do you have that the defendant murdered Mr Jenkins?'

The Chief Inspector looked defiant. 'There is the tie, the tie found in his room which had gone missing from Mr Buckley's wardrobe.'

'Ah the tie, Chief Inspector.' Pugh had turned charming again. 'Have you ever lost any ties? I certainly have. There are often times when one simply cannot find them. Is that the case with you?'

'I have on occasion lost some ties,' admitted the Chief Inspector. 'My wife usually finds them later on.' There was a faint ripple of laughter around the court.

'Indeed so, Chief Inspector, indeed so. We can all lose our ties. Let me ask you a further sartorial question, Chief Inspector. Do you have any ties with stains on them?'

Chief Inspector Wilson looked quickly round the court as if checking that his wife was not there. 'I believe I may have one or two in such a condition,' he said defensively.

'Never mind,' said Charles Augustus Pugh, smiling at

the members of the jury, 'I'm sure we all have a few ties with stains on them. Could you remind the jury what sort of tie it was?'

'It was the tie belonging to Trinity College, Cambridge, Mr Buckley's old college,' Wilson replied, feeling on firmer ground.

'Trinity College, Oxford,' said Pugh, with a slightly patronizing air, 'is a very small college. But Trinity College, Cambridge is a very large college. Do you happen to know how many new undergraduates it takes in every year?'

'Objection, my lord.' Sir Rufus was on his feet once more. 'Unfair questioning of the witness.'

'Mr Pugh?' said the judge firmly.

'I was just coming to the point, my lord, before my learned friend interrupted me.'

'Objection overruled,' said the judge. 'Mr Pugh.'

'Let me tell you the answer, Chief Inspector. About one hundred and fifty undergraduates go up to Trinity College, Cambridge every year. Fifteen hundred in ten years. And assuming that a man will live for three score years and ten, that makes seven thousand five hundred people who could have been wearing that tie.' Pugh paused briefly. 'With or without a stain. Rather a lot of suspects, wouldn't you say, Chief Inspector?'

Pugh didn't wait for the answer. He sat down and began looking through his papers.

'No further questions.'

'Damned good witness, that Dean of yours, Powerscourt.' Pugh was pouring tea back in his chambers, the jacket draped once more across his chair, his own tie removed.

'Bloody well should have been,' said Powerscourt.

'The fellow was on the same staircase as me at Cambridge.'

Pugh glanced curiously at Powerscourt. He looked as if he was about to speak. But when he did it was to do with events on the following day.

'Friday tomorrow, Powerscourt. This judge likes to get away early on Fridays. He's got some huge pile in Hampshire. Needs to catch the five twenty from Waterloo. Tomorrow morning I shall recall Johnston, the National Gallery fellow, then Edmund de Courcy. I hope we can save the forger and all his works for the afternoon. I've had one of our people here speak to the newspapers, warning them that there may be a sensation in court.'

What Charles Augustus Pugh did not say was that widespread coverage in the press would publicize his name. Publicity was no bad thing for up and coming young silks.

'As yet,' said Powerscourt, 'I have had no reply from the Chief of Police in Calvi, but I sent him another wire saying that it was vital we heard any news he had as soon as possible.'

Powerscourt set off from Pugh's chambers to walk back to Markham Square. His route took him along the river, the dark waters of the Thames flowing swiftly towards the sea. Parties of gulls circled round the shipping. When he reached Piccadilly he passed the offices of the Royal Academy, all lights extinguished now, where he had first met Sir Frederick Lambert weeks before. He remembered the extraordinary classical paintings on the walls, the terrible coughing, the handkerchiefs covered with blood secreted away behind Lambert's desk. He remembered his last visit to the old man, the ruined hands forming and re-forming the stamps from his correspondence on the table in front of him, the nurse in her crisp white uniform waiting to terminate his interview. He remembered his own promise to Lambert on that occasion, that he would find out who killed Christopher Montague before Sir Frederick died. Hang on, Sir Frederick, he whispered into the London evening, hang on. We might be nearly there. Nearly, but not quite. Just hang on for a few days longer.

24

Roderick Johnston filled the witness box when Pugh recalled him on the Friday morning. He seemed to tower above the rest of the actors in the courtroom, the clerk of the court taking notes in his place beneath the judge, Mr Justice Browne himself resplendent in his dark robes, gazing now at the jury, now at this giant witness come to his court, now at Charles Augustus Pugh collecting his papers and rising to his feet.

Powerscourt was in the row behind Pugh, Pugh's young second sorting through more files in front of him. Behind him the court was packed. Word must have leaked out that there might be a sensation in court that day. At the back, pens poised over their deadly notebooks, were the gentlemen of the press, jackals come to entertain their readers with tales of vice and adultery, of murders committed by an unknown hand. Murder trials were guaranteed to cheer up the British public, battered by yet further news of British defeats in South Africa. Five days before Lord Methuen had been repulsed at Magersfontein, just a few miles from the besieged garrison at Kimberley.

'You are Roderick Johnston, senior curator of Renaissance paintings at the National Gallery, currently residing at Number 3, River Terrace, Mortlake?'

Pugh's voice was flat this morning.

'I am,' Johnston's voice boomed out round the court-room.

'Could you tell us, Mr Johnston, how much you earn from your position at the gallery?'

'Objection, my lord, objection.' Sir Rufus Fitch was at his most indignant. 'We are here trying the defendant for murder, not inquiring into the witness's financial situation.'

'Mr Pugh?' Powerscourt remembered Pugh telling him that the score so far in this case was one objection each. So far the judge was even-handed. Pugh had a bet with his junior that he would lose heavily in the final score of objections.

Pugh smiled a slight smile at the judge, but his eyes roamed around the jury. 'It is the contention of the defence, my lord, if we are allowed to present our evidence without interruption, that the financial situation of the witness is indeed germane to this case. We propose to show that if the unfortunate Mr Montague had not been murdered, Mr Johnston would have lost a very great deal of money. Mr Johnston was the last man to see Montague alive. We intend to show that he would have profited from Montague's death. It would have saved him a fortune.'

'I have to tell you, Mr Pugh,' said the judge, with a slight air of menace in his voice, 'that there had better be a sound basis for this line of questioning. For the present, Sir Rufus, objection overruled.'

'I was going to suggest, Mr Johnston,' Pugh carried on, 'that your income from the gallery alone is not enough to sustain your lifestyle, the expensive house by the river, the frequent trips abroad. Perhaps we may take that as read?'

Johnston coloured slightly. 'You may,' he said grimly.

'Please don't misunderstand me, Mr Johnston,' purred

342

Pugh, 'nobody here is suggesting that there is anything wrong with extra work giving a man a little extra income. Heaven forbid. But perhaps you could tell the court what the main source of your extra-curricular income, as it were, is?'

'I have written a couple of books,' said Johnston defensively. 'I also advise on exhibitions, that sort of thing.'

'Come, come, Mr Johnston, the gentlemen of the jury are too sophisticated to believe that such funds would be sufficient for you to move house from a humble dwelling in North London to a most desirable property in Mortlake looking out over the Thames.' Pugh could see Sir Rufus Fitch beginning to rise to his feet. He hurried on. 'But the details of your houses are not our concern today,' Pugh sensed Sir Rufus beginning to sink slowly back into his chair. 'Perhaps you could tell us what you do in the way of attributing paintings. Before you do, may I suggest to you and to the jury what is meant when we talk of the attribution of paintings?'

Sir Rufus Fitch was looking rather cross. He was telling himself that this was meant to be a murder trial not a tutorial at the National Gallery.

'Suppose you are a rich American gentleman,' said Pugh, looking carefully at the jury. 'You have made millions from steel, or railways, or coal. You have magnificent houses in Newport, Rhode Island and Fifth Avenue in New York.'

'Could I suggest, Mr Pugh, that you come to the point.' Mr Justice Browne sounded rather irritated. 'One minute you are implicitly criticizing a man for the size of his house. Now you are telling stories of American millionaires. Perhaps you could reach the point you wish to make?'

Two all, thought Powerscourt. Sir Rufus might not have intervened but that definitely counted against Pugh.

Pugh was unperturbed. 'I am coming to the point, my lord.' He smiled a deferential smile in the direction of the judge and carried on. 'Many of these rich Americans come to Europe to buy paintings. They are keen to establish their own collections of Old Masters. They go to the galleries here and in Paris and in Rome. But how do they know whether a painting is genuine or not? How do they know whether they are buying the real thing or a forgery? This is how they find out. They, or their art dealers, go to an expert. They go to a man like Mr Johnston here for what is called an attribution. If he certifies that the painting is by Titian, they are satisfied. They pay large sums of money for the Titian. Without the attribution the picture is worthless. Is that a fair description, Mr Johnston?'

And Pugh turned another smile upon his witness.

'By and large, I would say it was, yes.'

'Tell me, Mr Johnston,' Powerscourt sensed that Pugh was about to fire his heaviest artillery, 'have you recently been involved in the attribution of a Raphael?'

Johnny Fitzgerald's drinking sessions with the porters and the attendants of the galleries of Old Bond Street were now bearing fruit in the Central Criminal Court. Johnston turned pale. There was a pause before he replied.

'That is true.'

'And did you say that this picture was genuine, Mr Johnston?' Pugh was staring intently at his witness now.

'I did,' said Johnston, obviously wishing fervently that he was somewhere else.

'Perhaps you could tell the court how much the Raphael was sold for?'

'I believe the figure was eighty-five thousand pounds,' said Johnston. There was a murmur of astonishment from the spectators. The newspapermen at the back were writing furiously.

344

'And, what, Mr Johnston, was your commission for pronouncing the work genuine?'

'I am not sure of the exact figure,' Johnston began.

'I put it to you,' said Pugh, 'that your commission was twelve and a half per cent of the eighty-five thousand pounds. To translate it into hard cash, ten thousand six hundred and twenty-five pounds, for looking at a painting and saying it is genuine.'

Ten thousand six hundred and twenty-five pounds was more money than the entire jury would earn in their lifetimes. They stared in amazement at a man who could command such sums.

'I put this to you, Mr Johnston,' Pugh could sense the judge getting restless again, 'that had Christopher Montague lived, you would have lost your position as a leading attributer. He would have replaced you. Your extra-curricular earnings, these fabulous sums for inspecting a few Old Masters, would have dried up. You would have lost your main source of income, would you not?'

Pugh picked up a piece of paper from his desk. 'I have here, my lord, a statement from the President of the Royal Academy. Sir Frederick Lambert has been very unwell. He is, at present, being nursed round the clock in his home. This document only reached me very recently. I propose to see, Mr Johnston, whether you agree with it.

' "Christopher Montague was on his way to becoming the foremost expert on Italian paintings in Britain, probably in Europe." ' Pugh read the statement very slowly, as if in respect to the dying man. ' "His first book established him as a scholar of rare distinction. His second, which is about to come out, together with his article on the Venetian exhibition, would have consolidated his position. The dealers would have flocked to him for attributions of their paintings. Other practitioners in the field," ' Pugh paused to look directly at

Roderick Johnston, leaning heavily against the side of the witness box, '"would have been sidelined. That element of their income would have evaporated, more or less instantly."'

Powerscourt had drafted the statement with the President's approval two days earlier. Charles Augustus Pugh saw no reason to refer to that.

'So, Mr Johnston,' said Pugh, pausing only to hand a copy of his document to the clerk of the court, 'with Christopher Montague alive, you would have been finished. No more little extras, what did we say the figure was, ten thousand six hundred and twenty-five pounds, for the attribution of a single painting?'

Johnston spluttered. 'I cannot agree with that assessment – ' he began.

Pugh cut in. 'I would remind you, Mr Johnston,' he said, 'that we are dealing with the President of the Royal Academy here, not some twopenny ha'penny scribbler who writes for the art magazines.'

Johnston said nothing.

'I put it to you again, Mr Johnston. With Christopher Montague alive, you become poor. With Christopher Montague dead, you carry on becoming richer, year after year after year, is that not so?'

Johnston said nothing, staring unhappily at the back of the court. Small boys, employed for a few pence as runners, were crouching down beside the news-papermen, waiting to rush their copy to the presses.

Sir Rufus Fitch rose to his feet to salvage Johnston from the onslaught. 'Objection, my lord, objection. My learned friend is practically accusing the witness of murder.'

'Mr Pugh?' The judge looked up from his notebook.

'I was merely concerned with the question of motive, my lord. It is only proper that the jury should be acquainted with the facts, that there are, however unfortunate it may appear, a number of people who might have wished Montague dead.'

'Objection overruled. You may carry on, Mr Pugh, but on more orthodox lines.'

'No further questions, my lord.'

Charles Augustus Pugh sat down. Sir Rufus was on his feet again. 'Mr Johnston,' he began, 'perhaps we could clear up the main point here, without all these pieces of interesting but irrelevant detail.' Sir Rufus looked sternly at the jury as he spoke, as if he was reminding them of what their duty was. 'Did you kill Christopher Montague?'

'I did not.'

Just before the court resumed Powerscourt handed Pugh a cable from Corsica. It came from Captain Imperiali. As the jury filed in for the last session before the weekend, they were confronted by a most unusual sight. A pair of empty easels sat towards the front of the court, clearly visible to judge, jury and witnesses.

'Terrible time I had getting the judge to agree to the bloody things,' Pugh had said to Powerscourt, tucking into an enormous steak for his lunch. 'Thank God my young colleague here had found a previous trial in 1884 when an easel was permitted in court. Even then the old bugger couldn't see why we wanted two of them. I had to say that we had evidence of forgery directly pertaining to the case, that we proposed to demonstrate how one of the forgeries referred to in the Montague article was carried out. Sir Rufus was snorting like an old war horse. Didn't seem able to come up with any relevant objections for once. Only hope the old bastard isn't saving them up for the afternoon. Bloody judge made some crack about a most unorthodox defence. Well, he hasn't seen anything yet!' With that, Pugh laughed his enormous laugh and helped himself to a small glass of claret.

He began the afternoon with Jason Lockhart, the young man from Clarke's Gallery who had been going to found the new magazine with Christopher Montague. Pugh established that the main argument of the article was that a number of the paintings in the de Courcy and Piper Venetian exhibition were fakes, and that some were recent forgeries. And that news of the article was quite widely known in the little world of the art dealers and picture restorers of Old Bond Street.

Sir Rufus raised an objection, claiming the article was irrelevant. Pugh was quick on the rebuttal.

'It is our contention, my lord, that it may have been this article and the message within it that led directly to Montague's death.' Sir Rufus was overruled.

Powerscourt looked briefly behind him. Two rows to the rear, clearly placed where the judge and jury could see him, Orlando Blane was fiddling nervously with his tie. Imogen had bought him a most respectable new suit for the occasion.

Edmund de Courcy was recalled to the witness box. Charles Augustus Pugh collected a large sheaf of papers and rose to his feet.

'You are Edmund de Courcy, joint proprietor of the de Courcy and Piper Gallery in Old Bond Street?'

'I am.' De Courcy was wary, very wary. He had seen what Pugh had done to Johnston that morning.

'You are also the owner of de Courcy Hall in the county of Norfolk?'

'I am.' De Courcy was staring at the empty easels.

'Tell me, Mr de Courcy, I presume you were aware of the article Christopher Montague was writing at the time of his death, an article which was going to say that many if not most of the paintings in your exhibition were forgeries or fakes?'

348

'I was.'

Powerscourt looked at the jury. They were concentrating hard. Over to his right Horace Aloysius Buckley stood very straight in the dock.

'Perhaps you could tell the court what impact this article would have had if it appeared. I presume it would have been bad for business?'

'I fear it would have been bad,' de Courcy began.

'Worse than bad perhaps?' Pugh cut in very quickly. 'A disaster? A catastrophe?'

'It would have been very bad for business,' was as far as de Courcy would go.

'And do you regard it as significant, Mr de Courcy, that all of Montague's papers were removed from his desk so that nobody, from that day to this, has seen the actual text of the article? Would that have been good for business?'

'It certainly worked to our advantage,' admitted de Courcy. He seemed to be relying on a policy of saying as little as possible. He still stared, as if hypnotized, at the easels.

'Tell me, Mr de Courcy . . .' Pugh was at his most emollient. Powerscourt suspected he was going to bring the forgeries into play very soon. 'Were any of the paintings in your exhibition fakes or forgeries or copies? Take your time. Remember you are under oath, Mr de Courcy.'

It's like a fork with a knight in chess, Powerscourt realized. If you saved your castle, you would lose your bishop. If you saved your bishop, you would lose your castle. You were impaled. If de Courcy said yes, he would destroy his own reputation. If he said no, then the easels might do it for him. Powerscourt suddenly realized how sharp it had been of Pugh not to place the paintings on the easels immediately but to hold them up, like a time bomb, waiting to explode under the de Courcy and Piper Gallery.

'To the best of our knowledge,' de Courcy began, 'all the paintings were genuine.'

'You are sure of that? Quite sure, Mr de Courcy?' Charles Augustus Pugh looked directly into de Courcy's eyes. The court had gone very quiet. Even the newspapermen had stopped the incessant scribbling in their shorthand.

'I am,' said de Courcy, blinking rapidly.

'My lord,' said Pugh, turning to the judge, 'I propose to bring on Exhibit C.'

Two court officials hurried from the room. Exhibit A was on a little table in front of the jury. It comprised a length of piano wire similar to the one used to garrotte Christopher Montague. The prosecution believed it was important for the jury to see an approximation of the murder weapon. Exhibit B sat beside it. This was the Trinity College, Cambridge tie found in Jenkins' room on the Banbury Road in Oxford.

The porters brought in a painting about three feet high and two and a half feet wide. It sat in a gold frame. They placed it reverentially on the easel nearest to the witness box. A rather saturnine Venetian nobleman, almost four hundred years old, had come to inspect the Central Criminal Court. His body was almost at right angles to the artist, clad in a blue doublet, with a dark blue cloak thrown across his shoulders. Round his neck was a chain of very fine gold. He gazed imperturbably at the jury. The jury stared back. The judge put on a different pair of glasses and inspected the latest visitor to his courtroom. Behind Powerscourt the crowd were rising, leaning forward to find a better view.

Pugh let the excitement die down before he spoke. 'Do you recognize this painting?' he said to Edmund de Courcy.

'I do,' replied de Courcy. 'It is the *Portrait of a Man*, by Titian.'

'And,' Pugh went on, 'it appears in the catalogue of your exhibition of Venetian paintings as Item Number 34.' Pugh had pulled the catalogue out of his sheaf of papers and was helpfully showing it to the members of the jury.

'Would you be so kind,' Pugh turned to the court officials once more, 'as to bring in Exhibit D?'

There was an outbreak of whispering among the crowd. What was coming next? What rabbit was Charles Augustus Pugh about to bring forth now? The judge stared at them and raised his gavel. The whispering stopped.

Another painting about three feet high and two and a half feet wide, set in a gold frame, was placed on the next easel. The same Venetian, in the same doublet with the same cloak and the same chain around his neck stared out at the jury. He had achieved the alchemists' dream over the centuries, he had reproduced himself perfectly.

Edmund de Courcy went pale. Orlando Blane smiled quietly to himself. The public gallery made so much noise that the judge banged his gavel very loudly on his great desk.

'Silence in court! Silence, I pray you! Any more of these unseemly interruptions and I shall clear the court! Mr Pugh!'

'Do you recognize this painting?' he said to de Courcy.

'I do,' came the answer. 'It is the *Portrait of a Man*, by Titian.'

'And which of the two paintings,' said Pugh in a very firm voice, 'is the real one?'

De Courcy looked at them both very carefully. He looked at Pugh as if pleading for mercy. Not quite the Judgement of Solomon, thought Powerscourt, staring at the drama unfolding in front of him, but a terrible question all the same. He wondered if Orlando Blane knew the answer. He wondered if Pugh knew the answer, some private mark on the frame perhaps which would remind him of the difference between the true and the fake.

It was obvious that Edmund de Courcy did not know the answer. He stared at the two easels like a schoolboy looking at an exam paper for which he has done no preparation at all.

'I would not wish to hurry you, Mr de Courcy,' said Pugh, sounding faintly exasperated with his witness, 'but I repeat my question. Which is the real one?'

Still de Courcy did not speak. The two Venetian gentlemen were still inspecting the jury.

'The one on the left,' de Courcy whispered.

'I'm not sure that the jury would have heard you, Mr de Courcy. Could you speak up for the court?' said Pugh.

'The one on the left,' de Courcy replied in a louder voice. Fifty-fifty chance he's right, Powerscourt said to himself.

'Wrong,' said Pugh firmly. 'The one on the right is the original.' He turned to the court officials once more. 'Please remove the original painting and leave us with the forgery. The real Titian is far too valuable to be left here. And could you bring in Exhibit E on your way back?'

Another sea of whispers rustled across the public gallery. Was there a third Venetian gentleman waiting in the wings to destroy an art dealer's reputation? A fourth? A fifth? Powerscourt realized just how brutal a courtroom could be. It's exactly like a battle, he said to himself. Not everyone leaves the arena alive. Pugh's artillery is cutting swathes through the enemy ranks. He felt a momentary pang of sympathy for Edmund de Courcy. They might be able to save the life of Horace Aloysius Buckley, gazing open-mouthed at the drama below him. But how many others might be destroyed in the process?

This time it was a drawing that was placed on the

easel. The supply of Titians had momentarily run out. It was a society beauty who sat on the easel, perched on a seat in an imaginary landscape with a glorious sunset behind her. She was wearing a long flowing dress. Her small hands were folded in her lap. And on her head was a hat of the most expensive and exquisite feathers the London milliners of the late eighteenth century could provide.

'Do you recognize this drawing?' said Pugh.

De Courcy stared at it for some time. 'It looks like a Reynolds, a Sir Joshua Reynolds,' he said finally.

'Why do you say it looks like a Sir Joshua Reynolds, Mr de Courcy?' Pugh's interruption was lightning fast. 'Do you think it's not genuine?'

'I'm not sure. I can't be sure,' said de Courcy.

'Let me refresh your memory for you.' Pugh was burrowing among his papers once more. 'This is the final sketch for a Reynolds, called, I believe, *Clarissa, Lady Lanchester*. The painting was recently sold, Mr de Courcy, by your very own gallery, to a rich American called Lewis B. Black for a sum of over ten thousand pounds. Is that not so?'

'Yes,' mumbled de Courcy.

The newspapermen were scribbling furiously once more. One or two of the elderly ladies in the public gallery had taken their fans out and were trying to calm themselves down. God in heaven, thought Powerscourt, how many gallons of drink had Johnny Fitzgerald poured down the throats of those Old Bond Street porters? Had they opened the offices up for him at two o'clock in the morning and shown him the account books while London slept outside?

'I put this to you, Mr de Courcy. You were quite right to be suspicious of the authenticity of this Reynolds. It is a forgery, pure and simple. What is more, gentlemen of the jury,' Pugh was looking at them rather than at his witness, 'the forgery and the fraudulent copy of the Titian we have just seen were created in your own house, Mr de Courcy, in de Courcy Hall in Norfolk. You were operating a Devil's Kitchen of fakes and forgeries up there. Small wonder it was to your advantage when Christopher Montague was killed. Your own private fakery might have been exposed in the controversy. I put it to you, Mr de Courcy, that faking and forgery is a very profitable line of business. What takes the forger a few weeks or months to produce can be sold for tens of thousands of pounds. No wonder Christopher Montague's article would have been, and I quote your own words back at you, very bad for business. That is the case, is it not?'

De Courcy's reply was a mistake. 'You can't possibly prove a single word of that.'

Pugh swung round like a whiplash. He turned to face de Courcy. He stared at him. He raised his voice till it almost reached the street outside.

'I beg your pardon, Mr de Courcy. I do beg your pardon. I most certainly can prove it. The man who forged and faked on your behalf is in this very court-room this afternoon! Would you please rise, Mr Orlando Blane!'

25

Pandemonium threatened to break out. In a three hundred and sixty degree arc, about eighty pairs of eyes stared aghast at the slim handsome figure of Orlando Blane. Twelve good men and true on the jury benches, Horace Aloysius Buckley standing erect in the dock, the judge himself inspecting Orlando as if he was some outlandish specimen of foreign flower, Sir Rufus Fitch wondering what Pugh was going to hit him with next, the crowd in the public gallery, the newspapermen so astonished that they had dropped their pens.

'Silence in court! I shall not repeat myself again!'

The judge had turned red at the insult to his court.

'Your honour,' Pugh had dropped his voice again, 'with your permission I should like to ask Mr de Courcy to stand down for the moment. I should like to call Mr Blane to give evidence.'

'Sir Rufus?' The judge peered down at the prosecution counsel. There was nothing he could do in the circumstances. He nodded his assent.

Orlando made his way slowly to take the oath. Powerscourt reflected on the irony of the words. Here was a man who had cheated in the temple of art, forging and faking and copying, promising to tell the truth, the whole truth, and nothing but the truth. Would the jury believe him?

'You are Orlando Blane, until recently resident at de Courcy Hall in Norfolk?' said Pugh.

'I am.'

'Could you tell the court how you have spent the last few months?'

'I was employed to copy a number of Old Masters, and to produce, or to forge, if you like, new Old Masters for sale to rich Americans.'

'Did you know at the time who you were working for?' said Pugh.

'I did not, then,' replied Orlando, 'but I do now.'

'And who do you now believe you were working for?'

'I believe I was working for the firm of de Courcy and Piper, sir,' said Orlando Blane.

'What makes you so sure of that?' Pugh went on.

'The Titians,' said Orlando. 'The original was sent up to me in Norfolk. It was mentioned in the catalogue of the de Courcy and Piper exhibition of Venetian paintings. Therefore it could only have come from them. I created the drawing of the fake Reynolds of Clarissa, Lady Lanchester. I also created the painting of Clarissa, Lady Lanchester in the style of Reynolds which has now been sold by de Courcy and Piper to an American millionaire. They sent me an illustration of a Mr Black and his family cut from an American magazine. I was told to make a Gainsborough or a Reynolds which included a woman who looked identical to the wife of the Mr Black in the illustration. I had created, or forged, if you like,' Orlando winced as he said the word, but Powerscourt had insisted he use it liberally, 'a Gainsborough a few weeks before, so I transferred my allegiance to Sir Joshua Reynolds. I've always liked Reynolds.'

'Quite, quite,' Pugh cut in quickly, thinking that the

jury might not appreciate the finer details of Orlando Blane's preferences among the Old Masters. 'Let me recap for the gentlemen of the jury, Mr Blane. Up there in Norfolk you were a sort of mail order forger. Orders came. You delivered. You were a sort of one man manufactory of forged paintings for the firm of de Courcy and Piper. If Christopher Montague's article, of which we have heard so much, had been published, what impact would it have had on your output?'

'I am sure,' said Orlando, 'that it would have put a stop to the production of the forgeries. De Courcy and Piper would have had people crawling all over every picture they sold. They would not have dared to continue with the constant stream of fakes flowing down from Norfolk. However good they were.' He smiled apologetically at Imogen, watching pale-faced five rows away.

'So to sum up, Mr Blane,' Pugh was at his most genial now, 'with the article published, the rich seam of forgeries would have stopped. But with no article, the little gold mine you had opened up in northern Norfolk for de Courcy and Piper was free to produce as many forgeries as you could create, to be sold on for large, possibly enormous sums, if the figures we have heard for the Raphael earlier are correct, and I am sure they are, to gullible Americans. The absence of the article was guaranteed to enrich de Courcy and Piper, is that so?'

'That is correct, sir.' Orlando Blane nodded carefully.

'No further questions,' said Pugh, and sat down. He took a long drink of cold water, slightly laced with gin.

Sir Rufus rose slowly to his feet. It was time for the prosecution to throw some mud in the defence's eye.

'Mr Blane,' he said, looking at the new witness with considerable distaste, 'how much were you paid for these forgeries of yours?'

Pugh suspected this would come. He had taken

357

Orlando through the likely questions the evening before.

'I was not paid, sir,' said Orlando, 'I was discharging a debt.'

'How much was the debt for? How was it incurred?'

Powerscourt thought Pugh would rise to object. He didn't. He was holding his fire.

'The debt was for ten thousand pounds. It was incurred at the gambling tables of Monte Carlo.'

Another buzz ran round the court. The news-papermen could not believe their ears. This was almost too good to be true. One or two of them were smiling broadly at the sheer perfection of the story. It was much better than fiction.

'Have you ever been imprisoned for debt in your past life, Mr Blane?' Sir Rufus was sounding as offensive as he could.

'No,' he said. It was with great difficulty, he told Imogen later, that he did not add the words, 'Have you?'

'Did you cheat at the tables at Monte Carlo?' Sir Rufus was trying his best.

'I did not,' said Orlando, remembering Pugh's words about keeping calm at all times.

'What other crimes have you been guilty of in your time, Mr Blane?'

'Objection, your honour.' Pugh was very quick to his feet. 'My learned friend is trying to blacken the witness's character.'

'I was only trying to establish the veracity of the witness,' said Sir Rufus, looking at the jury like a pompous headmaster. 'A man who loses money he does not possess at the gaming tables, a man who cheats and deceives the public with his forgeries, cannot be regarded as a credible witness.'

'I would remind you, Sir Rufus,' said the judge, taking a surreptitious glance at his watch, 'that we are here to try Mr Buckley on a charge of murder, not to preach a morality tale to the members of the jury. Objection sustained.'

Sir Rufus Fitch sat down. Powerscourt wondered if Pugh would ask some more questions. Ship definitely hit by hostile fire, he thought. Holed but not below the water line. Pugh rose to his feet again. He had noticed the judge checking the time. About half an hour before the train from Waterloo. He wasn't finished yet. 'No more questions,' he said. 'I would like to recall Mr de Courcy, your honour.'

Edmund de Courcy returned reluctantly to the stand. He was very pale.

'Mr de Courcy,' said Pugh, taking another sip of his water, 'did you have in your employ until recently a Corsican person called Pietro Morazzini? Employed as a porter in your gallery?'

'I did,' said de Courcy, unsure where this new onslaught was going to take him.

'And was he in your employ,' Pugh went on, 'at the time of the murder of Christopher Montague?'

'I believe he was. Shortly after that he had to return home.'

'I am afraid, Mr de Courcy,' Pugh hurried on, aware that Sir Rufus might be about to mount another objection at any moment, 'that people in this country are somewhat suspicious of Corsicans. Unfortunate, no doubt, but true, nevertheless. The defence has been making inquiries about your Pietro Morazzini.' Pugh paused to search among his papers. Powerscourt felt sure that Pugh knew exactly where the message was.

'I have here,' he went on, looking carefully at the jury, 'a cable from the Chief of Police in the city of Calvi, one of the principal cities of Corsica.' He held the missive aloft. 'Pietro Morazzini had to leave Corsica because of a vendetta, a blood feud. He murdered a man in the citadel of Calvi itself. The victim's family swore vengeance on

Morazzini. He was only allowed home recently to attend his mother's funeral. They attach great importance to the last rites, these Corsicans. Then he will have to flee again. Signed Captain Antonio Imperiali, Chief of Police, Calvi.'

Pugh paused briefly. 'Did you know, Mr de Courcy, that you were employing a murderer on your staff?'

'I did not.' De Courcy was stammering now. This had been the worst afternoon of his life.

'The good Captain Imperiali does not tell us how he murdered his victim. Gun maybe. Knife possibly. Perhaps he garrotted them, Mr de Courcy. I believe there is a lot of that in Corsica.'

A silence fell briefly across the court.

'I put it to you, Mr de Courcy, that you had the motive for the murder of Christopher Montague. You had the means in the person of this disreputable Corsican you had employed, Morazzini. Did you kill Christopher Montague?'

'No, I did not,' said de Courcy.

'Did you send your very own murderer round to Brompton Square to kill him?'

'Objection, your honour,' said Sir Rufus, 'unfair and unjustified line of questioning.'

'Mr Pugh?'

'I am trying to alert the members of the jury to the fact there are other people who could have committed this terrible crime, your honour.'

'Objection sustained, Mr Pugh.'

'No further questions,' said Pugh and returned to his seat. The damage had been done before the interruption. He took another glass of his water.

As Mr Justice Browne made his way back to Hampshire, the Prime Minister was in conclave with his Private

Secretary in his study at Number 10 Downing Street.

'Look at them, McDonnell,' said the Prime Minister, pointing to a great pile of cables on his desk from South Africa. 'It's one disaster after another. These damned Boers seem able to strike at will. Our bloody generals haven't a clue what they're doing. The fools in the War Office and the Colonial Office have no idea either. We're losing this bloody war, and it's got to stop.'

'Yes, Prime Minister,' said Schomberg McDonnell.

'As a rule, as you know,' the Prime Minister went on, shaking his head at the messages in front of him, 'it is my custom to leave my ministers and my generals alone. Let them get on with the job. That day is past. I cannot let this continue. There is a complete failure of intelligence out there. Nobody knows where the bloody Boers are. Nobody knows where they may strike next. I want my own man in there, McDonnell, answerable to the generals, of course, but primarily working for me.'

The Prime Minister rose to his feet.

'Find me the best intelligence officer in Britain,' he said. 'I don't care if he is currently in uniform or not. Find him for me by Monday morning. Bring him here on Monday afternoon.'

With that the Prime Minister walked slowly from the room.

'Yes, Prime Minister,' said Schomberg McDonnell.

Opinions were divided in Charles Augustus Pugh's chambers that evening. Johnny Fitzgerald was sure the jury could no longer believe that Buckley was guilty. Lady Lucy was certain they would be forced to acquit. Powerscourt was not so sure. Neither was Pugh. He looked exhausted from his day in court.

'I wouldn't have missed it for the world,' he said to everybody, his feet in their favourite position on his desk. 'Sir Rufus looked very irritated indeed as he left. He didn't even wish me good evening as we came out of the court.'

And Pugh threw his head back and laughed his enormous laugh once more. The tension was beginning to drain out of him.

'But I don't know if it's enough. Not yet. Forty-eight hours to go, Powerscourt. Only two days left. This case will close on Monday. I have a few witnesses left to call, maybe more.' He looked meaningfully at Powerscourt. 'Then Sir Rufus will sum up for the prosecution. I shall sum up for the defence. Mr Justice Browne will deliver his closing thoughts. God only knows what they'll be like. After that . . .' He paused and looked again at Powerscourt. 'After that the jury will decide. Twelve good men and true.'

26

'Forgeries in Mayfair!' 'Fake paintings sold to US Millionaires!' 'Master Faker hidden in Norfolk Mansion!' 'London Art Dealers Employ Their Very Own Forger!' The London newspapers on Saturday morning were full of the reports of the trial. Enterprising editors sent fresh teams of reporters to de Courcy Hall itself to bring more news on the secret location of Orlando Blane. They searched in vain for Blane himself. A Mr Thomas Blane, a retired clergyman resident in Wimbledon, was disturbed several times that morning by gentlemen of the press who had discovered his name on the electoral roll. An elderly widow, Mrs Muriel Blane of Fulham, South-West London was also troubled by fruitless journalistic inquiries.

The man at the centre of the whole affair, Horace Aloysius Buckley, did not see the reports. Newspapers are not normally delivered to the cells of Her Majesty's prisons. Lord Francis Powerscourt and Lady Lucy, breakfasting with Johnny Fitzgerald in Markham Square, bought all the day's papers to read the coverage.

Charles Augustus Pugh was doing the same. He took out a small red pen and ringed the word Pugh every time he saw it. By the end of his marathon perusal – total reading time over two and a half hours – he had counted fifty-four mentions of his name against a mere sixteen for Sir Rufus Fitch.

The nurse in her crisp white uniform read the main points to Sir Frederick Lambert, President of the Royal Academy, resting in a large chair in his drawing room, a rug thrown over his knees. A faint smile crossed his lips when he heard of the diverse activities of Orlando Blane.

But one group of readers were more vigorous in their response than anybody else. Mr William P. McCracken was taking ham and eggs in the dining room of Edinburgh's finest hotel, looking out over the Royal Mile. Mr McCracken had paid fifteen thousand pounds for his Gainsborough and eighty-five thousand pounds for his Raphael. One hundred thousand pounds in total. Now he saw he could have been sold a couple of forgeries. Worthless forgeries. Mr McCracken, as he had reminded William Alaric Piper in his gallery in Old Bond Street, was a senior elder in the Third Presbyterian Church of Lincoln Street, Concord, Massachusetts. His minister and his fellow elders would not have been pleased to see him take the name of the Lord in vain that morning. 'God dammit! God dammit to hell!' he said in such a loud voice that the waitress just behind his table dropped a dish of fresh kippers on the floor. 'The bastard!' he went on, totally oblivious to his surroundings. 'The bastard! God damn him to hell!' In fifteen years of commerce nobody had outwitted William P. McCracken. 'God dammit,' he went on, 'I'll sue that man! I'll break him, if it's the last thing I do!' And with that he ordered his bill and a carriage to take him to the railway station to catch the next express to London.

Cornelius P. Stockman was not in London either. He was in Salisbury, taking a short tour of some of England's finest cathedrals, though he was not attending Evensong. His hotel room looked out over the tranquillity of the Cathedral Close. Cornelius did not swear. He did not shout. He shook with fury. He had not yet paid over any money for the *Sleeping Venus* by Giorgione and eleven other nudes from the de Courcy and Piper Gallery. But it was the fact that he, Cornelius P. Stockman, had been cheated by these treacherous Englishmen that annoyed him so much. In spite of his rage a small smile crossed his features as he thought of the *Sleeping Venus's* naked beauty. But he had ordered another eleven of them from those crooks in Old Bond Street! Twelve damned fakes to carry back across the Atlantic! The good Lord, he reflected, a thought possibly inspired by the sight of the spire of Salisbury Cathedral soaring upwards into a clear sky, the good Lord had twelve and only one a wrong un. I'm going to get twelve wrong uns in one enormous parcel. Oh no, I'm not, he said to himself. He wished he had brought his legal counsel Charleston F. Guthrie on this trip to the devious Europeans. Many times back in the States Charleston had ridden into battle in the courtrooms of New York and laid waste to Stockman's enemies. Bloody English, he said to himself, they probably have a completely different set of rules. But Stockman was not a man to take things lying down. He too set off for the railway station to return to London. He was going to find the best lawyer in the capital, whatever it cost.

Only one of the millionaires read the headlines in London. Lewis B. Black was still a resident of the Piccadilly Hotel. He had paid over ten thousand pounds for his Sir Joshua Reynolds. Black read the accounts of Orlando Blane's evidence with particular care. He checked one account with another. There was only one conclusion. The man said he had been sent the pages of an American magazine with an illustration of the Black family. His family. His wife, staring out of the portrait, so pretty in that hat with the feathers. His very own forgery. How they would laugh, back on Fifth Avenue, about how he had been deceived.

Black abandoned his breakfast and walked as fast as he could to the de Courcy and Piper offices in Old Bond Street. All the other art dealers were open, gossip swirling round about what might come next when the trial resumed on Monday. But on the offices of de Courcy and Piper there was a large sign. 'Temporarily closed due to Refurbishment' it said. Black hammered on the door in fury. Maybe the bastards were hiding inside, destroying the evidence of their crimes, burning their records. There was no reply. De Courcy and Piper had gone to ground. Black hammered even harder on the door. A couple of newspapermen came up to him.

'It's no good, mate,' they said cheerfully. 'Bugger's not there. We've been here since first thing this morning. He's gone.'

Late on Saturday afternoon an exhausted but triumphant William McKenzie found Powerscourt lying on the sofa in the drawing room of Markham Square, a mass of newspapers strewn across the floor.

'William!' Powerscourt rose and shook McKenzie by the hand. Something in the man's face suggested that he was the bearer of good tidings. 'Any news? Have you found it?'

'I believe I have, my lord, I have come to make my report.'

Powerscourt suddenly remembered that McKenzie's reports were always couched in rather lifeless prose. Names were rarely mentioned in case the report fell into the wrong hands. As a result the McKenzie accounts always required a certain amount of decoding by the recipient, unlike Johnny Fitzgerald's. These were always scrupulously accurate but read like the popular fiction of the time.

'I guessed that the party would not have made the

relevant purchase in the immediate vicinity of their house,' William McKenzie began. 'They might have been seen or recognized entering or leaving the premises. I then had to take a gamble, my lord. They could have travelled further afield by cab. But that would have been risky. The cabby might have remembered the identity of his passenger. They have, I believe, a remarkable ability to remember people's faces.'

McKenzie paused. Powerscourt said nothing.

'Or,' McKenzie went on, his features a model of concentration, 'they could have taken the underground railway, so much more anonymous. The party's nearest station is on the District Line. So I have been travelling further and further from the party's address. I drew a blank in the area around Gloucester Road. I failed in Hammersmith. I failed in Chiswick. I failed in Kew. This morning, at the very eleventh hour as you might say, my lord, I found what we sought in Richmond, the final stop on the District Line if you are travelling in a westerly direction.'

McKenzie paused again. Powerscourt was thinking of another life about to be ruined.

'The party made two trips to this particular emporium, not far from Richmond station. The first visit was two days before the murder of Christopher Montague. The second was just before the murder of Thomas Jenkins.'

'And will the owner of the emporium come to court?' asked Powerscourt. 'Will they give evidence?'

'They will, my lord. They have given me their word.'

'Did you offer any money, William?' said Powerscourt, a sudden vision of Sir Rufus Fitch moving in to discredit the witness.

'I did not, my lord. I thought the legal gentlemen might have had a field day if I did.'

Powerscourt wondered suddenly how McKenzie had

known that. Perhaps the man was a secret devotee of murder trials, a regular visitor to the courts of London and his native Scotland.

'Forgive me, William.' Powerscourt knew he should have felt triumphant, but he didn't. 'Are you certain this witness will turn up?'

'Rest assured, my lord, the witness will turn up. Why, I am going to Richmond myself on Monday morning to escort the party to the court. They start very early, those trains on the District Line.'

Early on Sunday evening Powerscourt and Pugh held a final conference in Pugh's house in Chelsea. At the same time Schomberg McDonnell was sitting in a quiet corner of the library of his club in Pall Mall. He began composing a letter to his master, the Prime Minister.

'Dear Prime Minister,' he began. 'You asked me to find the best intelligence officer in Britain.' McDonnell paused, his eye wandering over a couple of shelves filled with the complete works of Cicero. Should he tell the Prime Minister the names of the people he had consulted, the generals, the brigadiers, the majors, the staff officers? Probably not, he decided. The old man wouldn't want to waste his time with the detail. He just wanted a name.

'I believe,' he continued, 'that I have found the man you are looking for.'

27

London's finest sign writers went to work very early on the Monday morning. By a quarter to nine, a busy time in the streets of the capital, the board that previously said de Courcy and Piper had been removed from the front of the gallery of that name. The staff in the artistic world round about gazed in astonishment as a new sign was erected. The Salisbury Gallery, it announced to Old Bond Street, Art Dealers and Suppliers of Fine Pictures, London and New York.

Piper and de Courcy had spent much of the weekend in hiding at a grubby hotel near Wolverhampton. Nobody, Piper had announced gloomily, would come looking for them in Wolverhampton. Nobody did. On Sunday evening under cover of darkness they returned to London and crept down into the basement where their stock was stored. De Courcy had devised an original code to tell his partner about the pictures. Alpha meant that it was genuine. Beta meant that it was a copy of an original in the gallery's possession. Gamma meant that it was a copy of an original not in the gallery's possession. Omega meant that it was a total forgery, not based on any original, but born out of the artistic knowledge and creative energies of Orlando Blane in the Long Gallery in northern Norfolk. After that Edmund de Courcy left the gallery that had borne his name.

Piper had decided that this was the only way in which they might rescue the business. Even then, he was not sure it would work. De Courcy was to take the blame for everything. He was the sacrificial lamb, slaughtered to keep Piper afloat. 'Think of it like this, Edmund,' Piper had said to him as they stared in horror at the dinner menu in their Wolverhampton retreat on Saturday evening, 'greater love hath no man than this, that he lay down his partnership for his friend. I can keep you on as a sleeping partner. I'll pay whatever it takes to bring your mother and your sisters back from Corsica. You will still get a share of the profits if we survive. If we give in now the entire value of our stock will simply disappear. Nobody will ever buy any of it. They'll think they're all bloody fakes. It's our only chance.'

At a quarter past nine William Alaric Piper made his way slowly along Old Bond Street to his newly named gallery. He was wearing a new suit in dark grey. There was an orchid in his buttonhole. He nodded genially to his acquaintances. He was going to bluff it out. Already at the back of his mind he could feel a strategy emerging for handling his clients. He sat down at his desk and waited for the American invasion.

By the same hour a long queue had formed around the entrance to the public gallery of the Central Criminal Court. There were law students come to watch the last day of what was bound to be a famous trial in the annals of London's jurisprudence. Maybe they would read about the case in faded red leather volumes in years to come when they were senior members of their profession, Queen's Counsel at least, if not High Court Judges. Today they could see it for themselves and tell their future juniors that they had watched all the proceedings in person. There were drifters, people who always turned up to watch a great procession or a military parade because they had nothing better to do. There were phalanxes of society ladies whose loud greetings echoed up and down the streets.

'Darling, haven't seen you since Freddy's party!'

'They say that Mr Pugh is frightfully good-looking!'

'Somebody told me at the Devonshires' that the police know de Courcy did it. They're just about to arrest him.'

'Nonsense, darling. Everybody knows that poor man Buckley was the murderer. Pugh's just trying to confuse the jury.'

At twenty past nine a dishevelled-looking Johnny Fitzgerald burst into Charles Augustus Pugh's chambers. Pugh was deep in conversation with Powerscourt, fastening his gold watch chain into place, making final adjustments to his wig. Fitzgerald thrust two sheets of paper into Pugh's hand.

'That's the Italian connection,' he said, looking around desperately for coffee. 'Got some of it from Italian newspapermen here in London. Got the rest from a man who'd worked as a footman at the house in Rome. Man drinks like a fish, maybe a bloody whale. Had to keep refilling his glass, if you follow me.'

Pugh read it quickly and placed it carefully at the top of his papers. 'Thank you,' he said. 'Thank you so much.'

The judge, Mr Justice Browne, had had his hair trimmed over the weekend. He always tried to have a haircut before he gave his summing up and pronounced sentence on his victims. Powerscourt had heard somebody refer to him over the weekend as Hanging Browne. The jury looked refreshed after their two days away from court. The foreman was wearing a smart suit, as if his wife had told him he must look his best with all those press men watching. Horace Aloysius Buckley

371

looked as though he had hardly slept at all. His face was gaunt, his eyes staring from their sockets. But he held himself well on this, the last day of his trial. The area reserved for the gentlemen of the press was meant to accommodate six scribes at most. There were eleven of them there this morning, crammed tightly together like galley slaves at their oars, fresh notebooks at the ready. The judge glared at them balefully as if he was thinking of reducing their number. The journalists avoided his gaze and began scribbling on their pads. The public gallery was crammed to the rafters, a long line waiting outside in case some of those present decided to leave.

Charles Augustus Pugh, veteran of many a courtroom drama, was feeling rather nervous that morning. He looked at his tall glass and decided to wait.

'Recall Mrs Horace Buckley!'

The society ladies peered forward to see what she was wearing. The rustle of their skirts sounded like a small breeze blowing through Mr Justice Browne's courtroom.

'Mrs Buckley, forgive me if I just take you through some of the details of your friendship with Christopher Montague.'

Rosalind Buckley was wearing a long dress of very deep grey, with a small black hat. The colours suited her. She looked like a widow in mourning.

'You had known Mr Montague for some fifteen months before he died, is that correct?'

'It is,' said Rosalind Buckley in a firm voice.

'And could you remind us what plans the two of you had made for your future?' Pugh was at his silkiest, talking as if he had just met Mrs Buckley sitting next to him at a fashionable dinner party.

'We were going to live together in Italy,' she said. 'Christopher, Mr Montague I mean, was going to write there.'

'You were going to live there out of wedlock? Or out

372

of wedlock as long as your husband was alive?'

The newspapermen looked at each other in amazement. Yet another possibility crossed their minds, far faster than it struck anybody else in the public gallery.

'We were,' said Rosalind Buckley, staring at the floor beneath the witness box.

'Were you planning to have children with Mr Montague, Mrs Buckley? Bastard children born on a foreign shore?'

'Objection, my lord, objection.' Sir Rufus Fitch had been reflecting over the weekend that he had let Pugh get away with far too much. Today would be different. 'The question is purely hypothetical. It has no bearing on the case.'

'Mr Pugh?' The judge turned to the defence.

'It is our contention, my lord, that such questions may have featured more and more heavily in Mr Montague's mind in the period before his death.'

'Objection overruled. But I warn you, Mr Pugh, that I shall expect some evidence from you that this was the case.'

'Yes, my lord, I believe we shall be able to satisfy you on that score. I have no more questions for Mrs Buckley for the moment. With your permission, my lord, I would like to call Miss Alice Bridge.'

The judge grunted and fiddled with his pens.

'I, Alice Bridge, do solemnly swear that the evidence I shall give is the truth, the whole truth and nothing but the truth.'

Powerscourt looked around the visitors in the public gallery. Was the formidable Mrs Bridge in court? Pugh was several steps ahead of him. He had already spotted Mrs Bridge from Powerscourt's description, staring at the proceedings through her lorgnette, her vast bosom protruding into the courtroom. He edged a pace or two to his left, blocking out all sight of mother.

'Miss Bridge,' Pugh began, 'I believe you too were a friend of Christopher Montague?'

The girl blushed slightly. 'I was.'

'And how long had your friendship been going on?'

'A little over four months.' Alice Bridge had brought a diary to court in case she needed it, a diary that detailed every single meeting she ever had with Christopher Montague.

'Would you have described yourself as a passing acquaintance? A friend you might bump into from time to time? Or was it more substantial than that?'

Powerscourt looked round. Mrs Bridge was twisting herself into contortions as she tried to catch her daughter's eye. But Charles Augustus Pugh's broad well-tailored back stood between her and her daughter.

'It was more substantial than that, sir.' Alice Bridge was speaking quite confidently now.

'Would you have said that you were intimate with Mr Montague, that you were lovers?' Pugh was speaking very slowly, looking closely at the jury.

'I would,' said Alice Bridge proudly, now staring in triumph at the grey figure of Rosalind Buckley.

'Had Christopher Montague, and I don't need to remind you, Miss Bridge, that you are under oath here . . .' Pugh paused so the jury could appreciate what he knew was coming next. '. . . had he asked you to marry him?'

Alice Bridge did not hesitate. 'He had. We were planning to marry in St James's, Piccadilly, sir.'

There was a mighty snort at the back of the court. Mrs Bridge had risen to her feet and was trying to make her way forward to the witness box. 'What nonsense, child,' she began. The judge smashed his gavel on to his desk.

'Silence in court! Remove that woman! At once! She is interfering with the course of justice!'

Two officers of the court moved swiftly. 'I am her

mother, she's only a child . . .' Mrs Bridge's voice just reached the front of the court as she was led away.

'This is not your drawing room, madam!' Mr Justice Browne was furious. 'It is a court of law!' He paused and wiped his brow with a large blue handkerchief. 'Mr Pugh.'

'So,' said Pugh, 'you were planning to marry. Were you also planning to have children, Miss Bridge? Children who would have been legitimate rather than bastards?'

'We were.' Alice Bridge's replies were firmer with the removal of her mother.

'One final question for you, Miss Bridge.' Pugh was caressing her with his eyes, the fingers of his right hand playing another imaginary piano concerto on his gown. 'As far as you know, had Mr Montague told Mrs Buckley about your relationship?'

'He had,' said the girl.

'How can you be sure?' asked Pugh.

'Mr Montague showed me bits of the letters she wrote him. She said he'd betrayed her, that her life was ruined.'

'Thank you, Miss Bridge. No further questions.'

Sir Rufus had the sense that he was being outmanoeuvred again. He rose slowly to his feet. 'Miss Bridge,' he began, 'would you describe yourself as a truthful person?'

'Objection, my lord.' Pugh realized he might be able to throw Fitch off balance if he protested right at the beginning of the cross-examination. 'Unfair line of questioning.'

'Objection overruled. Sir Rufus.' The judge looked stern. Up in the press area one or two of the reporters were looking at the two women. Lucky Montague, they thought to themselves. Not just one beautiful woman, but two.

'I put it to you, Miss Bridge, that your entire story is

375

pure fantasy, the kind of thing young girls have daydreams about, the kind of thing they enjoy reading about in the magazines and popular fiction. Is that not so?'

The girl did not blush. She did not look down. She was, for once, her mother's daughter. She felled Fitch with six words, looking him up and down as if he had come to clean the coal cellar. 'No, Sir Rufus, it is not.'

She smiled at Pugh. Fitch felt he should beat a retreat. 'No further questions,' he said and sat down grumpily in his chair.

This, Pugh, knew, was the trickiest bit of all. Mrs Buckley was recalled to the witness stand.

'Mrs Buckley, you have heard the statement from Miss Bridge. Is it true?'

There was a long pause. A whole series of emotions, fear, doubt, anger passed across her face. Pugh hoped the jury were watching carefully. At last Rosalind Buckley spoke.

'No,' she said quietly.

'Really?' said Pugh, looking carefully at the jury. 'Are you sure?'

There was another long pause. Then the words came out in a rush.

'I mean it's true and it isn't. I did know Christopher, Mr Montague I mean, was seeing this other person.' She stopped and looked round the courtroom to stare at Alice Bridge. 'I knew it was only an infatuation, I knew it would pass. I may have written him some letters, I'm not sure. I knew he would come back to me in the end.'

'And if he didn't, Mrs Buckley?'

'I knew he would come back to me in the end.'

Pugh paused. Three of the newspapermen who worked for the evening editions crept slowly from the courtroom to file their reports.

'Mrs Buckley, I wish to ask you about the period of

376

time you spent in Rome before you were married, when you were still Miss Rosalind Chambers.'

'Objection, my lord.' Sir Rufus was up once more. 'I fail to see what relevance this period in Rome can have to the present case.'

'Mr Pugh?' said Mr Justice Browne wearily. He knew that the juniors often placed bets on the number of successful objections, keeping score as if his courtroom were a tennis court. He had done the same thing himself as a young man.

'My lord,' said Charles Augustus Pugh, 'if my learned friend would permit to me to complete the line of questioning I am more than confident that the relevance will become apparent to him. And,' he added quickly, 'to the members of the jury.'

'Objection overruled. Mr Pugh.'

'At the time of your residence in Rome, Mrs Buckley, you were between the ages of eighteen and twenty. Is that correct?'

'Yes,' said Rosalind Buckley. Suddenly she looked very very frightened.

'And for most of your nineteenth year, Mrs Buckley, Rome was convulsed with a society scandal. You will forgive me, Mrs Buckley, if I convey the briefest of summaries to the court.'

Pugh paused and took a long drink from his glass. 'A young nobleman, Antonio Vivarini, from one of the oldest families in Rome, was found dead at the bottom of the Spanish steps. It transpired that he had promised to elope with the wife of a high lay official in the Vatican. Then he broke his promise. He had laid plans to elope with another, the heiress to a great fortune. The scandal went on for a very long time because the police were unable to find the murderer. The Romans said the police had been bribed, by the heiress's father, or by the Vatican, it doesn't really matter. Can you remember who was convicted of the murder in the end, Mrs Buckley?'

Mrs Buckley looked as if she wanted to run away. 'The wife,' she said finally, 'the wife of the man in the Vatican was convicted of the murder.'

'And can you remember, Mrs Buckley, how Antonio Vivarini was killed?'

'He was garrotted,' she whispered.

Pugh had moved over to the table where the Exhibits were displayed. 'Garrotted with what?' he said in a loud voice.

The pause was almost interminable. Powerscourt and Johnny Fitzgerald both knew the answer. They knew that Rosalind Buckley must know the answer too. And they knew what the answer would mean.

'With piano wire,' she murmured.

'Did I hear you correctly, Mrs Buckley? Piano wire?' Pugh bent down and picked up the length of piano wire on the table, Exhibit A in the trial of Horace Aloysius Buckley for murder. 'Piano wire,' he was holding it up for the jury to see and twisting it slowly round his wrists, 'piano wire, rather like this?'

Rosalind Buckley nodded. Some members of the jury were staring entranced at the length of piano wire, bending its way backwards and forwards round Pugh's hands.

'No further questions for the present. Call Samuel Morton.'

Samuel Morton, although he had not realized it, had been in protective custody all morning. William McKenzie had arrived very early at his little house in Richmond. He accompanied Morton to the railway station. He brought him to the Central Criminal Court well before the queues had formed. They had one of the best views in the house until this moment when Samuel Morton took the stand. Nobody in the court knew who he was. People asked their neighbours if he had been mentioned earlier in the proceedings. Sir Rufus Fitch felt his case slipping away from him, as more and more exotic and dangerous rabbits were pulled from Pugh's hat.

'You are Samuel Morton, of Morton's Musical Supplies of George Street, Richmond?'

Morton had a clear voice. He sang in the local church choir every Sunday of the year. 'I am.'

'Perhaps you could tell the court what sort of musical instruments and other musical requirements you supply, Mr Morton?'

'Of course, sir. We sell pianos and harpsichords, a few violins, recorders, flutes, the odd viola. We also supply all the relevant accessories.'

'Do you sell piano wire, Mr Morton?'

'We do, sir. Mostly to the piano tuners, sometimes to ordinary members of the public.'

'Mr Morton, do you recognize anybody in this court to whom you have sold piano wire in the last few months? Take your time, Mr Morton.'

Powerscourt had been watching Mrs Buckley very carefully. Morton took less than a minute to reply. 'I do, sir.'

'Perhaps,' said Pugh, 'you could point the person out to us.'

Morton pointed his finger straight at Rosalind Buckley. 'That lady there,' he said, 'the one in the black hat, sir.'

'And did she come just once? Or were there several visits?'

Samuel Morton took out a notebook from his pocket. 'I always make a note of the date of the purchases, sir. It takes a long time to order piano wire from our suppliers. We have to place the order well in advance if we aren't going to run out.'

He turned over a few pages. 'Her first visit was on 4th

October, sir. Then she came back on 6th November, sir. Said she needed some more.'

'Let me remind the gentlemen of the jury, my lord,' said Pugh, speaking in his most measured tones, 'that 4th October was a day or so before the murder of Christopher Montague.' He paused briefly. 'And that 6th November was three days before the murder of Thomas Jenkins.' Pugh paused and took a sip from his glass.

'One final question, Mr Morton. Remember you are under oath here, if you will. Are you absolutely certain that the lady you have identified in this courtroom is the same lady who came to your shop in Richmond and bought two separate lengths of piano wire on the dates you have given us?'

Samuel Morton did not hesitate. 'I am certain,' he said.

'No further questions.' Charles Augustus Pugh sat down.

'Mr Morton,' Sir Rufus was on his feet once more. 'Would you say you were a successful merchant in the provision of musical services?'

'I think we do all right, sir.' Morton sounded like a very decent man. 'My family have never lacked for anything, if you understand me.'

'Quite so, Mr Morton, quite so.' Sir Rufus managed to force out one of his rare smiles. 'So how many people would you serve in your shop each day, Mr Morton? A successful man like yourself.'

'Well, it varies, sir. We always do very well in late August and September when the parents are putting their children in for music lessons. And at Christmas when people sometimes buy pianos as a family present. On average I should say I serve between thirty and forty people a day, sir.'

Pugh was scribbling a note as fast as he could. He passed it back to Powerscourt, sitting one row behind him.

'So in a week, Mr Morton,' Sir Rufus went on, 'in an average sort of week, you would serve about two hundred and fifty people or so?'

'Somewhere between two hundred and two hundred and fifty, I should say, sir.'

'Quite so,' said Sir Rufus. 'So in the ten weeks between the first alleged visit of Mrs Buckley to your store and today, you would have served between two thousand and two thousand five hundred people, Mr Morton. Is that correct?'

'Yes, sir,' Morton replied.

'I put it to you, Mr Morton, that it is absolutely impossible for anybody, however well they know their business, to remember the faces and the appearance of all their clients over such a period. Particularly two thousand five hundred clients. Is that not so?'

Powerscourt passed the note to Johnny Fitzgerald, sitting by his side.

'It's not quite like that, sir, if you'll forgive me.'

Sir Rufus's eyebrows described a quizzical upward movement.

'You see, sir,' Morton went on, 'almost all my customers are known to me by sight. Some of them have been coming to the shop for years and years. We always try to make them feel welcome, you see, sir. Nine out of ten are known to me personally, maybe more. Some of the ones I don't know I may have seen about the town, or at church, or at the children's school.'

Johnny Fitzgerald handed the note back to Powerscourt. He passed it on to Lady Lucy, sitting on his other side.

'Nevertheless, I put it to you, Mr Morton, how could you possibly remember this lady in court here today, from the vast numbers you serve, and at such a length of time?'

'Why, sir,' said Morton, as if this was perfectly

obvious. Powerscourt looked quickly at the jury. Samuel
Morton came from their world. He was one of them.
Perhaps they too were shopkeepers keeping a careful eye
on their regular customers. 'Strangers from outside are
quite rare in Richmond. It's not like the West End shops,
sir, where every customer every day is a stranger. We
don't get customers like the lady here more than once or
twice a year. She was a society lady, sir. I'm not saying
there's anything cheap or wrong about the good people
of Richmond, sir, but she was different. She was class, if
you follow me.'

Powerscourt read the note once more. 'The tide is
running very strongly in our favour. If I put Mrs Buckley
back in the witness box now, we might finish the case
before lunch. If we wait, she may compose herself or even
come back with her own bloody lawyer. Yes or No? CAP.'

Powerscourt saw that Johnny and Lady Lucy had both
put Yes at the bottom. He added a third one and passed
it back to Pugh.

'Indeed, Mr Morton,' Sir Rufus carried on. 'But I must
ask you the question once again. Are you one hundred
per cent certain – and remember that a man is on trial for
his life here – are you absolutely convinced beyond the
shadow of a doubt, that the lady here was the one who
came into your shop ten long weeks ago?'

Morton stood his ground. Sir Rufus had failed to shift
him. 'I am certain, sir,' he said, looking at the jury. 'If I
hadn't been certain, I wouldn't have identified her in the
first place, would I?'

The jury smiled. William McKenzie beamed with
delight. Horace Buckley was looking very worried indeed.
Chief Inspector Wilson was checking his notes. The bookmaker among the ranks of the press gallery was changing
his odds. After the prosecution case he had offered two to
one on for a conviction. He thought he might lose quite a lot
of money with that one. Now he offered his colleagues

even money on an acquittal. He found no takers. The gentlemen of the press did not like the odds.

Charles Augustus Pugh rose to his feet and requested the recall of Mrs Buckley. He took another long draught from his glass. Johnny Fitzgerald had been looking at the vessel with some scepticism. He sent a quick note to Powerscourt. 'Fellow's not drinking water at all. Look at the colour of the stuff. He's got bloody gin or something in there. Lucky blighter.'

'Mrs Buckley,' Pugh began with his most unusual question yet, his witness shaking slightly in the box, 'I believe that you are an expert archer and travel extensively in the pursuit of your sport. Would you say this leaves you with very strong wrists and arms, stronger wrists and arms, let us say, than those of a sedentary man like Christopher Montague?'

Mr Justice Browne looked astonished. Sir Rufus stared open-mouthed at Pugh. Pugh's junior, a bright young man called James Simpson, had wanted to bring a bow into court. 'It would be like the end of the *Odyssey* in reverse, sir,' he had said to Pugh. 'You remember the bit where none of Penelope's suitors can draw the bow. Only Odysseus disguised as a beggar can do that. Here none of the jury can pull the bow. Neither can you. But Mrs Buckley can. It would be fantastic.' Pugh doubted if he could have imported a bow into the Central Criminal Court. He saw that the scheme could backfire if Mrs Buckley either couldn't, or pretended to be unable to pull the bow either. But he wanted to convince the male jury and the male judge that a woman might be more powerful than a man.

'Archery does give you strong wrists and arms, sir,' she said demurely. 'But I fail to see what that has to do with this trial.'

Charles Augustus Pugh looked carefully at the jury. He felt he had made his point. 'I want to put a hypothesis to you, if I may, Mrs Buckley.' Pugh paused. The fingers of his right hand were back at the imaginary piano on his gown, working their way through Beethoven's Emperor Concerto. He was speaking more in sorrow than in anger, as if he sympathized with Rosalind Buckley's plight.

'I put it to you that you were furious, more than furious, with Christopher Montague for jilting you in favour of a younger woman, a woman he might have been able to marry before God, blessed in church by the Holy Sacrament, a woman with whom, forgive me, he could father legitimate children rather than bastards. I put it to you that you remembered the details of the case in Rome, not so many years before, when revenge was extracted with a piece of piano wire. I put it to you that you did indeed go to Richmond and complete your first purchase of this deadly material. On the night of the murder I suggest that you went to Christopher Montague's flat, as you had done so often in the past. I put it to you that the knowledge of what was going to happen in there only served to fuel your anger even further. For your husband was going to ask Montague for his decision about whether to give you up or not. Montague would have told him that the affair had ended some months ago. You would have been humiliated in front of your husband from whom you were already estranged. Think how he might have mocked you.

'So, I put it to you, Mrs Buckley, you entered the flat that evening with your own keys. I suggest that you took precautions to give yourself a better chance of success. The police found two wine glasses that had been washed up in Mr Montague's kitchen. His cleaning lady had not cleaned them. Mr Montague was not in the habit of washing up his glasses. I suggest you put laudanum or some similar drug into the wine to make him sleepy and less able to resist. Then you murdered Christopher Montague. You removed all the papers on his desk to confuse any investigation that might follow. You removed some of his books that might have given clues about the article he was writing on forgeries in the Venetian exhibition. The police might assume that the murder was intimately connected with what Montague was working on at the time of his death.'

Pugh paused. The jury were staring transfixed at Rosalind Buckley. So was the judge. So were the gentlemen of the press, preparing vivid descriptions in their minds of the demeanour of the witness. Only Powerscourt was not looking at Mrs Buckley. He was looking at the prisoner in the dock, Horace Aloysius Buckley opening and closing his mouth very rapidly as if he wished to speak.

'I further put it to you, Mrs Buckley,' Pugh's eloquence rolled on, 'that you also found it necessary to commit a second murder. Maybe Thomas Jenkins was in London that night and met you after the murder in Montague's flat. Maybe you thought he knew that you were the killer and could not be sure that he would keep his mouth shut. Maybe you thought he would betray you to the police. I put it to you that you took a further trip to Richmond to purchase more piano wire.'

Pugh picked up the piano wire labelled Exhibit A from its table and began twisting it slowly in front of Mrs Buckley. Powerscourt could have sworn that Pugh was bending it into the shape of a noose.

'And furthermore, Mrs Buckley, I put it to you that you brought with you to Oxford not just the wire, but also one of your husband's ties. You left it there at the scene of Thomas Jenkins' murder to incriminate your own husband. Again we find the washed-up cups at the scene of the crime, suggesting that you put laudanum or some similar substance in Mr Jenkins' tea. You removed the papers from the desk as you had removed the papers from Christopher Montague's desk in order to confuse any investigation. I put it to you, Mrs Buckley, that you committed both these murders. Is that true?'

The only sound in court was the sobbing in the witness box. Pugh pulled out a large white handkerchief and offered it to his witness. 'Compose yourself, Mrs Buckley,' he said. 'You only have to answer one question. I put it to you once more that you committed both these murders. Is that true?'

Still Rosalind Buckley gave no reply.

'I ask you once more, Mrs Buckley.' Pugh was now talking to her as he might comfort a crying child. 'Is it true?'

Rosalind Buckley looked up at the judge. 'Do I have to answer that question, my lord?'

Mr Justice Browne knew his duty. 'You need not incriminate yourself, Mrs Buckley,' he said firmly, 'you have a right to remain silent if you choose.'

Rosalind Buckley looked down at the floor. She wiped her eyes once more. Powerscourt noticed that everybody around him seemed to be holding their breath.

'Yes,' she whispered finally, 'most of it is true.'

There was a sudden shout from the prisoner in the dock. Horace Buckley might not have wanted to die, but he felt nothing but overwhelming pity for his wife at this moment.

'No! No!' he shouted. 'It's not true! It's not true! I killed them! I killed them both! Please believe me!'

'Silence in court! Take the prisoner away! Take him below!' Sir Rufus was to say afterwards that he had never seen Mr Justice Browne so angry. Horace Aloysius Buckley was weeping as they led him away. Mrs Buckley was prostrate in the witness box. The judge took up his gavel once again and banged it furiously on the desk.

'This court is adjourned until three o'clock this afternoon,' he said. 'Sir Rufus, Mr Pugh, Inspector Maxwell, Chief Inspector Wilson, I wish to see you all in my chambers at half-past one.'

28

William Alaric Piper's first American visitor arrived shortly before ten o'clock that morning. Cornelius P. Stockman stared incredulously at the new sign outside the gallery. He stared even more incredulously as Piper came out to greet him in person in the street.

'How kind of you to come and see us, Mr Stockman, at a time like this. Look,' he pointed dramatically at the words 'The Salisbury Gallery' above the door, 'a new business is going to rise, like the fabulous phoenix, from the ashes of the old. But come in, Mr Stockman, I have much to tell you, and much to show you. I have not been idle since your last visit.'

Piper sat the American down in his little office. He told him of de Courcy's treachery, how a partnership founded in trust had been broken by betrayal. He told Stockman that all communications with the forger had been conducted from de Courcy's private address; how the paintings were brought into the gallery, hidden away among the normal traffic, how de Courcy would tell him that he had discovered these paintings in country houses where the owners were so hard up for money they were willing to part with their inheritance.

'I wonder, Mr Stockman,' Piper went on, 'if even in America, that great land of freedom and opportunity, a rotten apple sometimes finds its way into the barrel and corrupts all it encounters. I hope not, I do hope not. I pray that you may never encounter such depth of treachery in your own country, that it is confined to the more decadent purlieus of Europe.'

Piper shook his head. Stockman wasn't quite sure what purlieus meant. But he couldn't give his fellow countrymen exemption from betrayal.

'I'm afraid, Mr Piper,' he said, 'that even in America we are confronted almost daily with behaviour such as this. Riches in my country are meant to be the fruit, the reward of honest endeavour and hard work. Far too many seek to attain them by fraud and deception.'

Piper looked sad at this transatlantic intelligence. 'But business must go on, Mr Stockman. A man must work. He must follow his profession. He must pursue his calling. Come, I have something to show you upstairs.'

Piper led the way to the small chamber on the top floor. He had placed six paintings on their easels, the light falling softly on the bodies of the naked women. 'See, Mr Stockman,' he said, 'this is the original of your *Sleeping Venus* by Giorgione. Without my knowledge this wretch de Courcy sent off to the forging manufactory and had a copy produced, this one opposite.'

Two naked Venuses confronted each other, both sleeping peacefully in the summer sun of an Italian afternoon. Stockman inspected them carefully.

'I shall, of course, remove the fake, Mr Stockman,' said Piper, preparing to pull a cloth over the Orlando Blane, 'and here we have the first four of the eleven other paintings you asked for.' Another four nudes, some voluptuous, some plump, some slender, all beautiful, were lying on beds and couches to titillate Cornelius P. Stockman. He could see them now, in the little gallery he had built off the main body of his mansion. He saw himself relaxing after a long day at the office, peeping in to inspect his treasures.

'Don't throw away the fake, Mr Piper,' he said, 'the lady is so beautiful I wouldn't mind having two of her.' He contemplated his future hoard. 'You carry on, Mr Piper,' he said. 'Let me know when you have reached a dozen.'

The courtroom was packed by a quarter to three, fifteen minutes before the judge was due to reopen the case after the adjournment. Powerscourt was in his place behind Charles Augustus Pugh, flanked by Johnny Fitzgerald and Lady Lucy. Two rows behind, Orlando Blane and Imogen Foxe were there to witness the final scenes. The bookmaker among the journalists, still penned in very tight together, was calculating his losses. Horace Aloysius Buckley in the dock looked as if his composure had finally deserted him. He kept staring at his wife, now flanked by two stout policemen, sitting a mere fifteen feet away from him. Neither Pugh nor Sir Rufus Fitch were in court. Chief Inspector Wilson and Inspector Maxwell were not present either. The clerk of the court under the judge's bench was looking suspiciously at the crowd, still gossiping at the back of his court as if they were in the Royal enclosure at Ascot.

At five to three the jury filed in and took their places. This would be their last afternoon in the spotlight of publicity. Two minutes later the two lawyers took their places, both looking very solemn.

'Gentlemen of the jury,' Mr Justice Browne began, looking at the twelve good men and true, 'this has been a most unusual case. I thank you for your forbearance and your patience in listening to the evidence. And the unusual features have not stopped yet.'

Mr Justice Browne paused and shuffled through the

notes in front of him. 'I was informed before luncheon today that the Crown have lost confidence in their case. There will be no final statement to you from Sir Rufus Fitch. In these circumstances it is only proper that Mr Pugh should also forgo his final statement.'

There was an uproar in court. One of the newspapermen rose to his feet and fled the court. He could just catch the late afternoon editions. Mr Justice Browne looked at the crowd sternly. He hoped he never had to try a case like this again in his entire life. It was like being the referee at a football match.

'Silence!' he said firmly. He paused until total silence returned to his courtroom. 'Any more disturbance, from any quarter,' he looked at the society ladies at the back with especial ferocity, 'and this court will be cleared until the conclusion of this case. Nobody will be allowed back.'

He turned again to the jury. 'The prosecution case may have collapsed, but we still need a verdict in this case. The prisoner has been brought here on the most serious charge a citizen of these islands can face, a charge of murder. Had the verdict been against him, it would have been my unhappy duty to pronounce sentence upon him in the manner prescribed by the law, that of being taken from this place and hung by the neck until he was dead.'

Buckley shuddered. Pugh was writing notes on his pad. Powerscourt wondered if the judge sometimes referred to as Hanging Browne regretted having to let Buckley off.

'In the different circumstances in which we find ourselves this afternoon,' the judge went on, 'it is equally important that we follow the correct procedures. Mr Buckley has had to endure a trial with the full majesty of the law. It is important that he receives a proper discharge, that he leaves the court without a stain on his character. I am therefore asking you to retire and consider your verdict. My instruction to you is that you should find for the defendant. When the prosecution have lost confidence in their own case, this means, in effect, that they too consider Mr Buckley innocent of the charges brought. You can have no doubt, after the manner in which he has conducted the defence over the past few days, that that is also the opinion of Mr Pugh. I therefore ask you to retire.'

The jury shuffled out. Normally Mr Justice Browne would have followed them out to await the verdict in his own rooms. But he stayed in his place.

Five minutes passed. Then ten. The society ladies were almost bursting with the need to talk to each other. Sir Rufus Fitch was looking at the papers in his next case. Charles Augustus Pugh sat lost in thought. This would be the most brilliant success of his career.

Fifteen minutes. Powerscourt could bear it no longer. He thought of the weeks spent looking for the evidence that could acquit Horace Buckley of murder. He remembered the fateful encounter in Lincoln Cathedral, a pale Buckley led away to the great doors to be arrested at the end of Evensong. He thought of his expedition to Corsica, himself and Lady Lucy hurtling down the Aregno road, followed by unknown gunmen. He thought of his meeting with Orlando Blane and Imogen in the snowstorm in Norfolk, Orlando's blood dripping on to the white ground. 'For God's sake, Pugh,' he scribbled, 'what are the bloody jury doing out there?' Pugh's reply was quick. 'They don't want it to seem too quick. Probably drinking the court's disgusting tea before they come back.'

Twenty minutes. At last the jury filed back into court, sighs of relief from the public gallery threatening to enrage the judge once more. The clerk read out the charge, the foreman looking nervous as he faced the judge.

'Horace Aloysius Buckley is charged with the murder of Mr Christopher Montague and with the murder of Mr Thomas Jenkins. Do you, the jury, find the defendant guilty or not guilty?'

There was a long pause before the foreman replied. Lady Lucy told Powerscourt afterwards that she was sure they were going to find him guilty after all.

'Not guilty,' said the foreman. There was pandemonium in court. The newspapermen shot for the door in one movement, running as fast as they could, elbowing the society ladies out of their way as they went. Expensive hats, valuable bags, elegant gloves were thrown to the ground as they fled Mr Justice Browne and the verdict of the jury.

'Mr Buckley,' boomed the judge, 'you are free to leave this court. You are discharged without a stain on your character.' The judge turned and departed to his private quarters. Orlando Blane was embracing Imogen Foxe with a passion rarely seen in Court Three benches away from the jury. Johnny Fitzgerald hugged Lady Lucy. Mrs Buckley, a bowed and dejected figure, was led away by the two policemen. There was an air of great happiness and rejoicing as the crowd left the court. Pugh still looked solemn. Only one person was looking miserable. The defendant, Horace Aloysius Buckley, recently acquitted on two charges of murder, should have been the happiest person in the Central Criminal Court. He was the most dejected. He looked as if victory had turned into defeat before his eyes. He sat with his head in his hands, staring at the retreating back of his wife and her police escort. When they vanished from his view, he sat down in the dock where he had been on trial for his life and began to weep.

Flushed with his success with Cornelius P. Stockman, Piper sought out Lewis B. Black in his hotel. He repeated his denunciation of Edmund de Courcy with even greater vigour than before. He protested his own ignorance of the forgeries in de Courcy's house in Norfolk. He told Black that he was trying to start again, to recover from this terrible setback to his gallery. He offered Black a cheque for fifteen thousand pounds, two and a half thousand more than he had paid for Orlando Blane's fake Sir Joshua Reynolds.

Black had consulted a leading firm of London solicitors that morning. They pointed out the length of time it would take for any case to come to court. They told him that he would, most probably, have to remain in England for the duration. They pointed out that the details of the case would be splashed all over the newspapers in Britain and America. Such publicity might be disagreeable. They pointed out, with all the delicacy they could muster, that the defence counsel would do their utmost to make Black look at best an innocent American abroad, more likely a fool.

'That's two and a half thousand more than I paid for the painting, Mr Piper,' Black said, looking at the cheque.

'I felt it was the least I could do, Mr Black, after all de Courcy put you through. Now, if you let me have the painting, I will take it away and have it destroyed.' Piper had noted that the fake Reynolds was hanging in pride of place above the mantelpiece in Black's private sitting room. Black looked up at his very own forgery.

'Do you mind, Mr Piper, if I keep the painting? I did pay for it. I've gotten rather attached to it.' Black was putting the cheque into his breast pocket.

Piper was backing away towards the door, keen to escape with so little damage.

'Tell me, Mr Piper,' asked Lewis B. Black, 'who should I say the painting is by? Back in America, I mean.'

William Alaric Piper smiled. 'Say it's of the school of Sir Joshua Reynolds, Mr Black,' he replied. 'The country houses of England are full of paintings described like that. Most of the time, they leave out "of the school of". I can't think why.'

'Congratulations, sir. Magnificent performance in court!' The clerk of Pugh's chambers was clapping him on the back. His junior was skipping up and down for joy. An impromptu celebration party was taking place in the room lined with files where Powerscourt and Pugh had first discussed the trial. Imogen was whispering to Orlando not to drink too much champagne. Johnny Fitzgerald was drinking Pugh's health perched on the side of his desk.

'Don't mind telling you, Powerscourt,' Pugh had dispensed with glasses and was quaffing deeply from a great magnum of Bollinger, 'I wasn't sure we were going to make it at the start. Not sure at all.' He laughed his enormous laugh and took another swig. Powerscourt hoped it wouldn't sit too unhappily alongside the gin and water he had consumed throughout the trial.

Two more people joined the party. Lady Lucy had taken pity on Mr Buckley, his eyes still red from weeping. She gave him a glass of champagne. He was a free man.

'Could I just have a private word, Mr Pugh?' said Buckley quietly. Pugh brought him over to the corner of the room by the window. A couple of blackbirds were hopping about on the lawn outside. 'If they bring my wife to trial, Mr Pugh, could you defend her? I would pay for it, of course.'

Charles Augustus Pugh placed his magnum on a shelf and put his arm round Buckley's shoulders. 'I don't think it would be appropriate for me to undertake the case personally,' he said. 'It might be thought that I had been instrumental in bringing her to trial in the first place after the events of the last few days. But I promise you I shall find for you the best defence lawyer in London.'

Buckley looked reassured. Lady Lucy came back to take him under her wing once more.

'I'm going to drink one more glass,' Powerscourt said to Pugh, 'and then I must go. I promised to tell the President of the Royal Academy what happened. He's at death's door, poor man.'

'Of course,' said Pugh. 'I hope you realize, Powerscourt, that the people here may be drinking my health this afternoon. But the real credit, the real congratulations should be with you. You provided the bullets. I merely fired them.'

'Nonsense,' said Powerscourt with a smile and slipped from the room. Two minutes after his departure the party was interrupted. A bulky-looking man banged his cane on the floor and asked for silence.

'I am a Government Messenger,' he announced. 'I am looking for a certain Lord Francis Powerscourt. I have reason to believe he is here. I have a letter for him from the Prime Minister.'

The curtains were tightly drawn in Sir Frederick Lambert's study. Powerscourt noticed that the piles of foreign stamps were still lined up in rows on the table in front of him. He thought the President of the Royal Academy was looking slightly better this evening. He was still deathly pale but his eyes were bright. Maybe it was the drugs.

'Only ten minutes at most,' said the nurse, 'he gets tired so quickly now.'

Powerscourt told the old man the details of the trial, the acquittal of Horace Buckley, the unmasking and discovery of Orlando Blane.

'How strange that it should have nothing to do with the art world at all. Just a jilted lover. Hell hath no fury.' Sir Frederick paused and began to cough. It had turned into a dry hacking cough now. There were no handkerchiefs stained with blood secreted down the side of his chair.

'Tell me about Orlando,' he said. 'Did you say he was married now? That might settle him down.'

Powerscourt replied that Orlando seemed to be enjoying most of the benefits of the married state without actually going through the ceremony itself. A feeble laugh came from Sir Frederick. 'Nice girl?' he said.

'Very beautiful,' said Powerscourt. 'I think her parents forced her into a marriage she did not want. Mama did not want her to marry Orlando.'

'Some mothers in the past have been very taken with young Orlando, Powerscourt,' said Sir Frederick. 'Pity he didn't find the right one.' The old man suddenly heaved himself up in his chair. He reached over to his desk and brought over a number of sheets of his headed notepaper.

'Could you write a letter for me, Powerscourt? As you did that affidavit? I might just be able to sign it.'

'Of course, Sir Frederick, I'm more than happy to do that.'

Powerscourt began taking down the old man's words. 'To Signor Pietro Rossi, Senior Director, Rossi's Picture Restoration Company, 217 Via Veneto, Rome.' The old man paused, panting slightly. 'Rossi's are the leading picture restorers in Italy,' he said, 'do a lot of work for the Vatican.' He paused again. Powerscourt thought his time must be nearly up.

'Dear Signor Rossi, I would like to recommend most highly a young Englishman of my acquaintance called Orlando Blane. He was one of the most brilliant students we ever had at the Royal Academy. I believe you would find his talents most satisfactory in your business. With best wishes to you and your family . . .'

Powerscourt passed the letter and his pen over. Sir Frederick paused before he signed it. He hoped his hands would do what they were told. In the end he took it at a gallop. Frederick Lambert, he wrote as fast as he could and sank back exhausted in his chair. The nurse was looking angrily at Powerscourt.

'And tell young Orlando,' the President of the Royal Academy said, 'that I'm going to change my will. Don't see why I should give that much money to the Society for Distressed Watercolourists. Tell him I'm going to leave him twenty thousand pounds. That should set the two of them up in Rome.'

Piper was going through his third explanation of the day to Gregory Hopkin, the director of the National Gallery, at ten to four that afternoon. William P. McCracken, purchaser of a fake Gainsborough for fifteen thousand pounds and a real Raphael for eighty-five thousand pounds, was due in ten minutes' time. Roderick Johnston, senior curator of Renaissance paintings, was sitting on the director's left, hoping that he would not be interrogated about his role in the attribution of the Raphael.

Hopkin was virtually certain that he was being told a pack of lies. He did not see how it was possible for Piper not to have known what de Courcy was doing. He did not see how the instructions for the creation of the forgeries could have been devised without the approval of both of them. In an ideal world he would have thrown William Alaric Piper out of his office and left him to the wolves. But, as Gregory Hopkin reminded himself sadly while he listened to the flow of injured innocence and personal betrayal pouring out of his visitor, it was not a perfect world. There was nothing the art circles of London or any other international centre feared more than scandal. The dealers and the galleries knew far better than their customers how fine a line divided a fake Van Dyck from the real thing, a genuine Titian from one of Orlando Blane's accomplished forgeries. The whole edifice depended on trust. It depended on the customers being reassured by the elegant offices, the fine suits, the languid tones of the English upper classes. The clients had to think they were dealing with a world with the highest possible standards, rather than one permanently on the edge of fraud.

If scandal broke, the whole London art market would be plunged into chaos. Clients would go elsewhere, to Paris or to Rome. The Americans who were reviving the market and bringing enormous prices to Old Bond Street would go elsewhere. Nobody would believe a word the London art market said. They would have the mark of Cain upon them. It could take years to recover, if they ever did. So far, Hopkin admitted to himself, Piper had extricated himself from his first two Americans rather well. But the third had paid the most money. Eighty-five thousand pounds for a Raphael was a world record at the time. Another fifteen thousand for an Orlando Blane purporting to be a Gainsborough. So, at whatever cost, William P. McCracken had to be placated.

The opening exchanges were not propitious. 'What about these bloody forgeries then?' said McCracken, no longer a rich foreign visitor in the National Gallery, but an American rail tycoon, a ruthless millionaire. He unwrapped a parcel and placed the two paintings on a chair beside him.

Piper went through his customary routine of how the rotten apple had been removed, the boils lanced, the Augean stables cleansed, how a bright new dawn had arrived for The Salisbury Gallery.

'I'm seeing my lawyers in the morning,' said McCracken. 'That thing,' he pointed to the Gainsborough, sitting innocently on their chair, 'is a fake.'

'Let me assure you, Mr McCracken,' the director of the National Gallery thought that McCracken might respond better to a man with clean hands, 'that if you wish to back out of the deal, Mr Piper here will refund you the money immediately.'

'I have a cheque here, Mr McCracken. Made out to you.' Piper fished about in his jacket pocket and produced a cheque made out to William P. McCracken for fifteen thousand pounds. He laid it on the table.

'That's peanuts,' snarled William P. McCracken. 'You took eighty-five thousand pounds of my money for this other forgery, conceived in your gallery, Mr Piper, and executed by your confederate, the forger, up there in Norfolk.'

'That's not a forgery, that Raphael, Mr McCracken, it's real,' said William Alaric Piper.

'After what we heard in court these last few days, gentlemen,' McCracken was scornful, 'no jury anywhere in the world is going to be convinced that it's real.'

'I wouldn't be sure about that,' said Piper carefully. 'In any case I have prepared a further cheque for you for eighty-five thousand pounds.' Piper laid down a second cheque beside the first as he might lay down a hand of cards.

'That is a very fair offer,' said Gregory Hopkin. 'As for the authenticity of the Raphael, Mr McCracken, I think you would have considerable difficulty in establishing it as a forgery. Mr Johnston here on my left is the foremost authority on Renaissance paintings in Britain, if not in Europe. He believes it to be genuine. So do other experts here in the National Gallery. So do I. We would all testify in court that it is a genuine Raphael. You would have to find other witnesses to attest to its false provenance. That might be difficult.'

Something snapped in William P. McCracken. He was tired of the smooth talking, the sophisticated veneer of all these wretched English people. Suddenly he wanted the clearer air of New York and Boston and the simpler certainties of the society of Concord, Massachusetts. Art was something he thought you could acquire like houses, or racehorses or yachts. Now all he could see was a kaleidoscope of mirrors with these slippery people trying to bamboozle you at every turn. No more.

'I think I'll take the cheques, gentlemen,' he said. 'I've had enough of the whole lot of you. I'm going back to the States. You can keep your lousy pictures, real or not. I couldn't give a damn.'

With that McCracken picked up his cheques and strode angrily from the room. He slammed the door behind him.

'Mr Piper?' said the Director of the National Gallery. Two terrible thoughts had just occurred to him. 'That Raphael. Real or fake?'

'It's real,' said Piper.

'And the cheque,' Gregory Hopkin went on, 'the cheque for eighty five thousand pounds. Is that real ? It's not one of your fakes or forgeries or anything like that?'

'The cheque, Mr Director,' Piper was wondering if there was any money left in his bank account, 'the cheque, like the Raphael, is genuine.'

'Don't take off your coat, Francis.' Lady Lucy was waiting for Powerscourt at the front door of Markham Square. 'This letter came for you just after you left the party in Mr Pugh's chambers. It's from the Prime Minister.'

Lady Lucy did not say how close she had come to

opening it. Powerscourt picked up a paper knife and slit the envelope open. He read it aloud.

'"My dear Powerscourt,"' he began, '"the Prime Minister is most anxious to see you, this evening if possible. He has a most important mission to discuss. I hope we shall see you very shortly, Schomberg McDonnell, Private Secretary to the Prime Minister."'

Powerscourt looked pale. He held Lady Lucy very closely for a long time. After he had gone Lady Lucy glanced absent-mindedly at the evening papers. They were full of dramatic accounts of the closing day of the trial. A headline on the opposite page caught her eye. 'Further disasters in South Africa,' it said.

Oh no, Lady Lucy said to herself. Please God, not that. Anything you like, but not that.

29

'I'll come straight to the point, Powerscourt.' The Prime Minister was sitting at an enormous desk in his study on the first floor of 10 Downing Street. Schomberg McDonnell was hovering in an easy chair by the fire.

'Damn it, man,' the Prime Minister went on, looking closely at Powerscourt, 'we've met before. In this very house, if I'm not mistaken, when you sorted out those German fellows trying to bring down the City at the time of the Jubilee.'

'I did have that pleasure, Prime Minister,' said Powerscourt, wondering if he had been called to sort out another financial scandal.

'Not bloody Germans this time, Powerscourt,' the Prime Minister went on, 'bloody Boers. Bloody Boers!' He repeated himself angrily.

'This is the problem, Powerscourt,' said the Prime Minister with real passion in his voice. 'The whole structure of military intelligence in South Africa is wrong. War Office can't sort it out. Useless bloody generals can't sort it out. They think the Boers are here. They're not. They're over there. The generals plod over there. By the time they arrive, Mr bloody Boer has disappeared again. Difficulties in the terrain, they keep telling me. Rubbish. Faulty intelligence, maybe no intelligence at all.'

Powerscourt thought he knew now what was coming.

'I've had enough, Powerscourt. If we don't sort out the intelligence, we're in danger of losing this war. Losing a war to a couple of tinpot South African Republics populated by a lot of fanatical Protestants with long beards who don't even have a regular army. For God's sake! Our international reputation is in tatters. I don't mind if the French and the Germans are jealous of this country. I don't mind if they're afraid of us. What I take exception to is that they should laugh at us, that we should become a figure of fun among the Great Powers of Europe. It's intolerable.'

The Prime Minister paused. Powerscourt saw that the portrait of Disraeli was still there on the wall, the one that had inspired him on his last visit to 10 Downing Street. Wellington was on the other side of the room. Wellington, he felt sure, would have been pretty angry abut this military and political debacle. But then Wellington had always been fanatical about the importance of intelligence.

'I asked McDonnell here,' the Prime Minister continued, 'to find me the best intelligence officer, serving or not, in the country. His inquiries led him directly to your good self, Powerscourt. Will you undertake this mission for me? Find out what's wrong with the bloody intelligence. Make a plan to get it right. Report directly to me. I want you to leave immediately. There is a fast destroyer sailing from Portsmouth this Thursday. Will you do it?'

Powerscourt paused. He didn't want to go. He didn't want to leave his family for months, maybe years. 'My service was almost entirely in India, Prime Minister. I have served only once in Africa, and then in a very different country.'

'Nonsense, man,' said the Prime Minister, 'doesn't matter where you've been. What's needed is brains, intelligence applied to the problems of intelligence. You've got all that. Why, only today, McDonnell tells me, you've solved another bloody murder mystery here in London.'

Powerscourt felt encircled. He knew he had no choice. But then, he had known that all along. 'I accept, Prime Minister. I hope I can be of service to you. Might I make one small request?'

'You may indeed,' said the Prime Minister.

'I would like to take two or three former colleagues with me, men who have served with me in India, Prime Minister.'

'Powerscourt,' the Prime Minister smiled at him, 'you can take whoever you want. Just give McDonnell the details. He'll sort everything out. You can take the bloody Landseer Lions from Trafalgar Square with you, if you think it'll help.'

Two days later Powerscourt took his children on another visit to the Royal Hospital, Chelsea. Sergeant Major Collins who had served with him in India was waiting to greet them.

'So your Papa's going off to war,' he said, crouching down to a lower level. Powerscourt had sent him a note the day before.

'Yes, he is. He's going to sort out the intelligence,' said Thomas, proud of his big new word.

'He has to write a lot of letters to the Prime Minister,' said Olivia whose knowledge of letters was largely confined to the ones she received from her grandmother.

'Did you know,' said the Sergeant Major, smiling at the children, 'that they looked all over the country to find the best man for the job? They looked everywhere.'

Thomas wasn't quite sure who 'they' would have been. Hundreds and hundreds of Sergeant Major

Collinses, he suspected, searching the country day and night.

'And they found Papa?' said Olivia. 'Mama could have told them that in the first place.'

'Look, children,' said the Sergeant Major. 'I'm going to show you something.' He took them along a corridor of rooms inhabited by the Chelsea Pensioners. Thomas and Olivia peered inside, fascinated as they had been before by the beds that folded into the wall. 'This man here, Corporal Jobbins, he went off to India where your Papa was with me. He's come back. Next room, Lance Corporal Richardson, he went away to Africa, he's come back. This man in here, Private Jenkinson, he went off to Egypt, he's come back. This one at the end, Gunner Bishop, he went off to Afghanistan, he's come back.

'And,' he went on, 'see this big room here where we're going to have our tea, all of these soldiers have been sent away. They've all come back.'

Sergeant Major Collins put Olivia on his knee and helped her to bread and butter. Over a hundred veterans looked on in envy and delight. Thomas said the bread and butter was the best he had ever tasted. They had slices of an enormous chocolate cake, Sergeant Major Collins intervening personally to secure a second helping.

'Wish I was going with you, sir,' said the Sergeant Major to Powerscourt as they left.

'I've got the next best thing, Sergeant Major,' said Powerscourt. 'William McKenzie and Johnny Fitzgerald are coming with me.'

'God help them Boers,' said the Sergeant Major. 'They should give up now if Major Fitzgerald is on his way.'

On his last night in England Lord Francis Powerscourt put his children to bed. He found Olivia in the kitchen, watching the cook preparing grown-up dinner.

He took her in his arms. She snuggled into his shoulder. Olivia said goodnight to every room in the house on her way upstairs.

'Goodnight, cook, goodnight, kitchen,' she said.

'Goodnight, Olivia love,' said the cook with a smile.

'Goodnight, dining room, goodnight, chairs,' said Olivia.

'The dining room bids you a very good night, Olivia,' said her father solemnly.

'Goodnight, drawing room, goodnight, sofa.'

'Both drawing room and the sofa wish you pleasant dreams,' said Powerscourt.

'Goodnight, stairs,' said Olivia, still clinging to her father's shoulder.

'The stairs wish you a very good night too,' said Powerscourt.

He was putting her into bed now. She was nearly asleep. 'Goodnight, Papa,' she said, almost disappearing underneath the covers.

'Goodnight, Olivia.' Powerscourt bent down and kissed her on the cheek. 'Goodnight.' He waited quietly by the side of the bed. Olivia was asleep. He waited another ten minutes, watching the innocence on the face of his daughter, praying for her future.

Thomas wanted a story. Thomas was very fond of stories. Powerscourt reached for a book on the table and began to read:

'At Flores in the Azores Sir Richard Grenville lay,
And a pinnace, like a fluttered bird, came flying from
　　far away,
Spanish ships of war at sea! We have sighted fifty-
　　three!'

406

'What's a pinnace, Papa?' asked a sleepy voice.

'It's a little ship, Thomas, a messenger ship,' Powerscourt whispered back.

'Shall we fight or shall we fly?
Good Sir Richard, tell us now,
For to fight is but to die!
And Sir Richard said again: We be all good English
   men.
Let us bang those dogs of Seville, the children of the
   devil,
For I never turned my back on Don or devil yet.'

Thomas stirred again. He was nearly off. 'The Dons are Spaniards, aren't they, Papa?'

'Yes,' whispered Powerscourt.

'And the sun went down and the stars came out
   far over the summer sea,
But never a moment ceased the fight of the one
   and the fifty-three.
Ship after ship, the whole night long, drew back
   with their dead and their shame.
For some were sunk and many were shattered and
   so could fight us no more.
God of battles, was there a battle like this in the
   world before.'

Thomas had not stayed until the end of the conflict. He was gone. Again Powerscourt watched and waited a full ten minutes by the bedside of his sleeping child. He prayed for Thomas. He prayed for his mother. Then he tiptoed slowly from the room.

'Lucy,' said Powerscourt later that evening, lying full

length on the sofa, 'I don't know what I'm going to do without you.'

'Nonsense, Francis,' she replied with a gallant smile, 'you'll be fine. You've done this sort of thing before. You've got Johnny with you.'

'I didn't know you when I was in India, Lucy.' Powerscourt remembered suddenly that her first husband had also gone off to war. He never came back. He sensed that Lucy must have been thinking the same thought.

'Promise me one thing, my love.' Lady Lucy knelt on the floor and flung her arms round her husband's neck. Powerscourt thought there were tears in her eyes. He held her very tight.

'There, Lucy, there. Please don't cry.'

'Just one thing, Francis.' She was whispering very close to his ear, her hand stroking his face. 'Please come back.'

The eight forty-five from Waterloo to Portsmouth harbour was preparing to depart. There were few coaches on the train and fewer passengers. Powerscourt thought they might have the whole train to themselves. He was leaning out of the carriage, holding Lady Lucy's hands in his. 'Lucy,' he said, 'I love you very much. I shall always love you.'

Whistles were blown. A great cloud of smoke belched out into the morning air from the engine up ahead.

'I love you very much, Francis. Come back safely. Please come back safely.'

The train had begun to move. Lady Lucy walked along with it, past a couple of porters.

'Semper Fidelis, Francis.' The train gathered speed. She had to let go of his hands.

'Semper Fidelis, Lucy,' said Powerscourt, waving

frantically as Lady Lucy's small figure began to disappear in the smoke. He could see her no longer. Lady Lucy waited until the train disappeared round a corner, heading off down the great tracks stretching out towards the south. She waited a little longer until nothing, not even the rising smoke, was visible.

She left the station and went back to her house and her children.

Sir Frederick Lambert, President of the Royal Academy, was waiting in his sitting room to dictate a new last will and testament to his lawyer.

Imogen Foxe and Orlando Blane were still asleep under the tender care of Mrs Warry at Powerscourt's house in Northamptonshire.

Alice de Courcy and her daughters Julia and Sarah were standing on the quayside in the northern Corsican port of Calvi, eagerly awaiting the boat that would take them to Nice. From there they would return to England by train.

William Alaric Piper was preparing to open his gallery in Old Bond Street for another day's business.

Mr William P. McCracken, the American millionaire, was one day out of Southampton, sailing back to New York.

There were but a few days to go before the last Christmas of the century. Colonel Francis Powerscourt and Major Johnny Fitzgerald were going to war.